Violet Evergreen

In

The Seeds of Rebellion

By: Madam Crystal Butterfly

I would like to dedicate this book to my family for always being there for me through good times and bad, and for being my number one supporters in my literary career.

Table of Contents

Chapter 0..1

Chapter 1..27

Chapter 2..52

Chapter 3..78

Chapter 4..96

Chapter 5..115

Chapter 6..129

Chapter 7..145

Chapter 8..159

Chapter 9..187

Chapter 10..198

Chapter 11..210

Chapter 12..220

Chapter 13..241

Chapter 14..260

Chapter 15..271

Chapter 16..275

Chapter 17..286

Chapter 18..295

Chapter 19..317

Chapter 20..323

Chapter 21..331

Chapter 22..342

This story is intended for older teens and adults due to mature content, including profanity

Chapter 0
The Judgment

Everyone in the Fulton County courtroom was silent. The defense attorney checked his notes for the last time before the case was to start. There was nothing special about the courtroom interior with the standard dark brown wooden judge's bench in the front, next to the witness stand. A little way from the judge's bench were two tables. One table was for the defense attorney, while the other was for the plaintiff. Several chairs were parked at each table for the attorneys and their clients. Behind the tables were dark wooden benches for the audience to watch the trial.

The defense attorney was a young elf named Bartholomew Samson. His short dark green hair complemented his peach skin and baby blue eyes. Bartholomew's face was home to a small mustache and beard. Small gold hoop earrings hung from his pointed ears. He wore a gray three-piece suit with a gray shirt and blue tie. His feet were protected by a pair of brown shoes with white socks. A woman named June Wilds, one of his clients, sat beside him.

June Wilds was a thirty-seven-year-old woman. She was blessed with unblemished rich dark brown skin. Her full lips and nails were painted in a matching shade of deep ruby red. June had on a dark green dress, her neck gently caressed by a pink pearl necklace. On her feet were a pair of black stiletto high heels.

Madam Crystal Butterfly

Mrs. Wilds's watery brown eyes were pinned on the courtroom exit. Nervously and perhaps unconsciously, she used her left hand to tap the table in a rhythmic motion. At the same time she was attempting to keep her breathing in check, June used her right arm to hold her six-year-old niece in her lap.

The little girl began to tremble, tears forming in her small eyes. In response, June quickly wiped the child's eyes. She hugged her tightly with both arms, kissing the child on the forehead.

June said, "Don't worry, Violet. This will be over soon. Afterward, we can go home and watch a fun movie."

The child had smooth chocolate brown skin and was small for her age. Her tiny round face was home to a pair of chubby chipmunk cheeks. Her head was full of thick black hair styled into several plats with tiny pink bunny hair clips at the ends. She wore a white lace dress, with lacy white socks and a pair of white shoes on her feet.

Violet looked up at her aunt with her small tearful purple eyes that glittered like sparkling amethyst. After a moment, Violet wrapped her arms tightly around June's waist and buried her tiny head in her aunt's chest. Despite June's efforts to comfort her, tears continued falling down Violet's face.

Sitting in the chair next to June was her husband Akeem. Akeem Wilds was a tall man with rich dark brown skin and friendly brown eyes. He was dressed in a black three-piece suit with a white shirt and black tie. The top of his head was home to a field of thick curly jet-black hair styled in a sponge twist. His face was also home to a small mustache and beard. A pair of black shoes adorned his feet. Seeing Violet's tears, he reached over and patted her head.

June said, "Akeem, I don't think it is good for her to be here."

2

Akeem replied, "Neither do I, but we had no choice."

Just then June's twenty-six-year-old sister May walked up to them. May's rich dark skin and eyes were complemented by the hot pink lipstick decorating her lips. The top of her round head housed a lot of thick curly dark brown hair that had been styled in several long individual braids stretching to the center of her back, where they lay tied into a ponytail with a dark green scrunchie.

May was dressed in a baby blue sundress that had a slit that started at her knees. Her throat was covered by a necklace made of gold from the mines in Ghana. Her arms were being kept warm by a white cotton sweater, and a pair of black silk stockings covered her legs. Her feet, like her sister's, were confined in a pair of red high-heeled shoes.

She asked June to let her take Violet to the bathroom so she could clean the little girl's face and get her a tissue. June agreed, and then she told Violet to go with May. Violet looked at June with tears flowing from her eyes. Slowly she climbed off of her aunt's lap. Violet using her hands wiped her face before looking up at May.

May gently took Violet's hand and they started to walk out of the room. When they were gone June leaned back in her chair and exhaled.

A voice behind her asked, "Are you ok, Mama?"

June sat up and turned around to look at her daughter, who was sitting in the audience directly behind her. Meg Wilds had the same brown skin and eyes as her parents. But unlike her parents, she was a fifteen-year-old rock and roll queen. She showed the status of her crown with her style. Her hair was dyed hot pink while styled in tight short curls. There was a black silk choker with a small diamond in the center around her neck. Her lips along with her eyes were painted with black makeup. Her nails received the same treatment with expensive black acrylics.

Meg was wearing a crimson red T-shirt which read *Donny Face was Born to Rock* in small white crystals. Her skinny legs were covered with a pair of tight leather pants being held up by a black leather belt with a buckle that contained several white diamonds. On her feet were a pair of heavy-military style black leather boots.

June told Meg, "I'm alright. I'm just a little stressed about having to deal with this trial. It's all too much since we just buried your uncle and aunt last week."

Meg replied, "Ok. Um, Mama, does Violet have to be here?"

"Unfortunately, yes. The judge was adamant about Violet being here. That way he does not have to worry about us trying to flee the country with her if we lose, which is ridiculous because we are not going to lose."

"Where would we go? The spike in demon attacks has made travel across countries impossible."

Akeem said, "It has only made travel hard for everyone except the rich. Ironically, it would have been nice if it had cut off cross-country travel altogether. Then we would be at home trying to recover from Mathew and Ivy's murders."

He then thought for a moment before asking, "June, did you make that call?"

June answered, "Yeah, I would rather be safe than sorry."

At that moment an old woman sat down next to Meg.

Meg asked, "Grandma, did you find the bathroom alright?"

Mrs. Wanda Evergreen was a very plump elderly woman. Despite her age, her rich brown skin was smooth and wrinkle-free. Her long curly gray hair was tied up into a tight bun. Wanda's normally glamorous look was nowhere to be found. Instead, her face was void of makeup and, her brown eyes shone red. From the many tears, she had recently shed.

Wanda was wearing a black dress that was covered with images of bright pink daylilies. A pair of black silk stockings covered her legs, and she had on a pair of pink pumps. Wanda was using both hands to hold the white crystal handle of her otherwise black cane.

Wanda looked at her granddaughter and said, "Those bathrooms are disgusting."

She took a breath before continuing to say, "Damn my worthless child, making us come here. I can't wait for this crap she got us involved in to be over, so I can go home and rest."

June said, "If I had known how awful the facilities were, I would have warned May. She took Violet to the bathroom to clean her face."

Wanda remarked, "It's fine. I ran into them when I was coming back. When May learned about the bathroom, she told me she was going to take Violet to the building next door."

"Is that a good idea?" June wondered aloud.

Bartholomew Samson chimed in, "We still have a good amount of time before the trial starts. Plus, the other side has not arrived yet."

Wanda asked, "You're sure that my worthless daughter and her so-called husband have no chance of winning?"

The attorney looked at Wanda and said, "It would be very unusual if they did. Your son's will states that the Wilds were to become little Violet's guardians in the event of their passing. Plus, that is barely the icing on the cake. It's amazing that the court responded so quickly agreeing to hear their case, and that we received such an early court date. Cases like this usually take months, if not years to be heard."

As their lawyer went back to looking at his papers, the opposing party walked in. One of the plaintiffs glared at June as if she wanted to slap her.

Her name was Drusilla Lepel. Despite her intimidating glare, she was so thin that her hot pink dress hung on her like a flag, while her costly white high heels looked as if they were going to fall off. Drusilla's brown eyes appeared heartless and cold. She had always had a narrow face, but she had become so thin that her face seemed elongated like the face of a fox or coyote. She was so thin that she seemed to be a walking skeleton covered by a thin layer of skin. Each time her family members saw her, which wasn't often, she became more and more unrecognizable. Her scrawny lips were painted with a bright coral lipstick which did not complement her brown skin.

Standing next to Drusilla was her husband Victor Lepel. Victor had rich honey-brown skin. His face housed a large nose dividing a pair of very angry-looking brown eyes. Victor's face was clean-shaven. On his head, he had short curly hair that had been dyed blonde. He was dressed in a dark blue three-piece suit with a light blue shirt and a dark blue tie.

The plaintiff's attorney rushed past them. He was dressed in an orange three-piece suit covered with pictures of ducks. The Lepels' attorney was a very old male fairy by the name of Oscar Whitfield. His green wings were faded. Noticeably instead of a dress shirt, he appeared to be wearing a red T-shirt underneath his very orange suit coat. His face was accented by a very long white beard that stretched to the center of his chest. He had a head filled with thick silver hair matching his beard. He wore no socks, and his feet were covered by a pair of red sneakers.

However, the feature that stood out the most on this day were his eyes- deep emerald green eyes, with one eye looking very sad. The other eye had been punched so hard that it had swollen up to a point where he could not open it.

As the plaintiff's attorney started to nervously sift through several papers in his briefcase, Drusilla walked over to June.

Drusilla looked at June and said, "Big sister, are you ready to stop playing games? Because I found out your plan for the brat. It makes me sick our brother is cold in the ground dead for only a week, and already you think you can take advantage of his kid like this."

June started to respond when Bartholomew said, "Mrs. Wilds, do not respond. The plaintiff is only trying to antagonize you so you will say something you regret."

Drusilla smiled as she said, "It does not matter what my sister says. She and the others like to play the role of a loving family, but I know the real reason why you want the kid."

In a stern tone, Wanda said, "That is enough out of you, Drusilla. You have already caused enough trouble for this family. Go sit with that good for nothing husband of yours."

Drusilla glared at her mother as she said, "Of course you only stand up for your favorite child." Then she strutted over to the plaintiff's table.

Wanda took a breath before saying, "I just don't know why she turned out this way."

June responded, "It's ok, Mama. She will not get her way."

Akeem looked at June. He said, "I don't even know why they are even trying to take Violet. It's not like they ever made an effort to come and see the child in her entire life."

June responded, "Drusilla criticizes me, but they weren't even at the funeral."

Wanda said, "I hate to say this, but I'm more than a little glad they weren't. My poor boy."

Tears started to fall from her eyes. Akeem held up his right hand and whispered something. Out of nowhere a white handkerchief suddenly appeared in his hand. He gave it to Wanda, who buried her face in the cloth.

In a tearful voice, she said, "My poor Mathew. He and Ivy did not deserve to die like that. Damn those investigators. They try to blame little Violet for their deaths instead of trying to find the people who killed my son and his wife."

June offered to take her mother outside. Wanda told her it would not be wise for her to step out of the courtroom, so she would go alone. Akeem told Meg to go with her grandmother.

After the two of them left, Akeem said, "The only good part about this is that once this trial is over, we will never have to see your sister and her husband again."

June said, "I just don't get them. When Drusilla and Victor somehow flew here from Brazil despite the travel restrictions, I assumed that they had taken that risk to honor my brother by trying to help the family. But when they started to demand we let them take Violet, I, I nearly fainted."

"Yeah, that was one fucked up day."

"You know, June, despite their past successes with promoting pro boxers, I suspect they have gone belly up."

"Why?"

"Violet's inheritance is the only reason they would want her."

8

Just then May returned with Violet. Violet was still visibly upset, but she seemed to have calmed down a bit and was sucking on a lollipop. June told May it was smart to get Violet a piece of candy.

To which May responded, "I didn't. Anas is part of one of the news teams covering the trial."

Akeem said, "Dammit, his network has a lot of nerve making him cover this trial."

May said, "What can you do? The studio knows that he is dating me. So, they are obsessed with trying to get him to report on anything involving our family."

"You make a good point, but I was thinking about how he got hurt."

June said, "Let's not talk about the demon voids. Those things have been getting worse after those South American Eden witches were killed fighting those monsters."

May said, "Before I left the courthouse, I called him to see if it was even safe for us to go outside."

June stated, "This is a private family matter. Why the fuck does the media not keep their asses out of it?"

May replied, "I agree. He helped us avoid the press and bought Violet a sucker to help her relax a little bit."

Akeem said, "That was nice of him."

Meg returned and sat down next to May.

She looked at her parents and said, "Grandma says she is feeling overwhelmed right now, so she is going to wait in the car until the trial is over."

June said, "You can wait in the car, too, if you want."

Meg replied, "It's ok. I want to stay because this whole thing is scaring Violet."

Akeem started to say something when the bailiff shouted, "All rise for the honorable Judge Hendrickson."

Everyone stood up as the judge's chair started to abruptly shake. When it stopped shaking, the judge appeared in it as translucent as a ghost.

Akeem whispered to June, "That is a dramatic way to teleport in a room."

June whispered, "It's foolish, too. It takes way too much magic power just to teleport four miles, so why is he using double that power just to appear in a fancy way?"

"I bet you he is going to be tired as soon as he fully teleports in."

"I'm not taking that bet. I know he will be."

When the judge finally appeared to be solid, his face looked like he had just taken a six-mile hike. Judge Hendrickson was an old man with wrinkly peach skin, green eyes, and thinning silver hair on his head. He had a traditional black judge's robe covering his clothing. He told everyone to sit down, and as he sat down, he rubbed his eyes.

He said, "Today the court will be hearing from the Wilds and the Lepels regarding the custody of six-year-old Violet Evergreen. Also, the court must decide whether the minor child Violet Evergreen shall be placed under level twelve extended custody, which means that until she reaches the age of twenty-five her life will be controlled by her guardians. Then the topic of whether or not she needs to remain under someone else's custody will fall under review. Also, the court will decide who will control the inheritance of the minor child Violet Evergreen."

The judge then noticed the Lepels' attorney's clothing. He said, "Mr. Whitfield, what in the Sam Hill are you wearing, and what happened to your eye?"

Oskar's right hand started to shake as he said, "My good suits are all at the cleaners, forcing me to put on this oh so fashionable attire. I got it at a thrift store back when I was a young attorney. As for my eye, I was running a little late when I was leaving home. I was moving so fast I wasn't looking where I was going, and I hit my front door face first. At the time, I thought I was alright. It wasn't until I got to the courthouse and people began asking if I had been attacked, did I realize the bruising."

Akeem whispered to his wife, "I bet Victor punched him. He was probably pissed at Oskar for failing to get what they wanted in mediation."

The judge did not seem suspicious of Oskar's response. He said, "Alright, I understand. Have you prepared your opening statement?"

Oskar replied, "Yes, your honor."

"Very well, proceed."

Oskar said "Your honor, the tragedy little Violet caused in her home that night was truly the stuff of nightmares. If you had spoken to me before little Miss Evergreen murdered her parents and said that she was capable of such a thing, I would have called you a liar. But as we now know, she buried them alive."

Violet, who was sitting next to Meg, started to shake. Meg hugged her and whispered, "We know you didn't do such a mean thing. He's just stupid."

Violet slowly stopped shaking and seemed to calm down a little bit.

11

Madam Crystal Butterfly

Then they heard Oskar say, "But despite her horrible crime, we need to remember that she did not kill them because she wanted to. Poor little Violet has UMD, more formally known as unstable magic disorder. Because of its rarity, there was no way anyone could have known she had it. But either way, she has it, and steps must be taken to ensure nothing this terrible happens again.

The Wilds may love Violet; however, they are far too unwilling to do what is necessary to help someone with Violet's condition because they are in perpetual denial about her plight. This is why the Lepels should receive level twelve extended custody of little Violet. They are willing to raise her with the restrictions she needs to function in society, which will make it possible for society to never have to worry about little Violet losing control of her power and hurting anyone again."

Oskar sat down as Bartholomew stood up.

Bartholomew said, "This is very sad. It is sad that Mathew and Ivy Evergreen were killed. It is sad that their only child saw them die. It is sad that the police decided to falsely accuse poor little Violet of killing her parents. It is sad that the Lepels are attempting to take a child from people who love her. But the saddest part is that this court is hearing pure lies as if facts. What makes me so bold as to call the plaintiff's entire claim a lie? I will list the reasons right now.

First, when police arrived on the scene, they did not even attempt to look for the culprits little Violet said shot her parents and their household staff. Evidence from the coroner's office that shows the Evergreens and their employees were shot has been ignored. The police office has even refrained from attempting to charge Violet with the murder that they publicly said over and over she committed. And that's because they do not have even one shred of evidence proving that she did it.

I would like to add that the fire spell Violet accidentally conjured out of fear was a grade E fire spell, and basic magic training teaches that spell

12

cannot burn skin or even produce smoke that can suffocate someone. Any adult with state-mandated magic training can get rid of grade E fire without a blink. Second, the other side states that the Lepels, complete strangers to Violet, can take better care of Violet than the Wilds, and that is absolute poppycock.

When Mathew Evergreen married Ivy French, his younger sister Drusilla Lepel sent him a letter begging him to divorce his wife. If he was unwilling to do that, then she wanted him to get a vasectomy because according to her any child Ivy gave birth to would be a crime against nature. This action terrified Mathew Evergreen to the point that the very day he discovered his wife was pregnant, he specified in his will that Drusilla Lepel and Victor Lepel were never to be allowed anywhere near his child.

Third, the Lepels are very well known to have stated they wanted nothing to do with Violet. So, why would they suddenly show up out of the blue demanding custody of Mrs. Lepel's niece? Unless, and I do realize that this is supposition on my part, they were trying to get ahold of little Violet's inheritance.

Finally, the Lepels have had several charges brought against them for their involvement in underground boxing. Mr. Lepel has even served three years in a Brazilian prison. Why? He nearly murdered a young boxer in his employ for losing an underground boxing match. There are also several other allegations against him for violent behavior.

Mrs. Lepel is no different. She has been arrested several times for violent outbursts. She also spent a year in jail for nearly murdering a man. Why? Because he made a negative comment about her shoes. So, the question before the court is whether either Mr. or Mrs. Lepel are fit people to care for a child."

As Bartholomew sat down, the judge said, "Mr. Whitfield, it is my understanding that your clients, in addition to level twelve extended custody, wish to have magic restrictions placed on Violet. If this request is granted, then you do realize even though she is set to receive her inheritance at age twenty, the state will not allow her to have it until these restrictions are removed."

"Your honor, my clients were hoping to negotiate the restrictions on the use of little Violet's inheritance in order to allow the Lepels to get access to a third of the inheritance."

The judge raised an eyebrow as he asked, "Why do they want access to the inheritance?"

"Sadly, my clients suffered a huge expense to come to the United States. They are worried that they will not be able to provide Violet with what she needs in Brazil without the extra money."

The judge thought for a moment before responding, "I will take your claim into consideration."

Akeem whispered to Bartholomew, "Why is he even considering that? The will is airtight."

The judge said, "Mr. Samson, do you have anything to add?"

Bartholomew replied, "Yes, the Lepels' request is very suspicious. They are insistent they are the best ones to care for Violet, but they are asking for money for her care. Also, they want to take her to Brazil, a nation currently plagued by demons after the deaths of two of their Eden witches. That does not sound like a safe place to raise a child."

The judge said, "I agree it is unwise to take her someplace unfamiliar after what she has been through, but considering what happened, the Wilds family is unfit to care for her. So, I am granting level twelve extended custody to the Lepels."

June grabbed her chest and started hyperventilating, and Akeem nearly fell out of his chair. May was tightly holding Violet who had taken her sucker out of her mouth and was crying. Meg just looked at the judge as if he punched her in the stomach.

Bartholomew quickly said, "But your honor, you need to consider..."

The judge said, "Silence. I understand there is no hard evidence that young Miss Evergreen accidentally killed her parents; however, it cannot be argued that she lost control of her powers, causing the Evergreen's mansion to burn down. Since we have no idea how bad her UMD is, I am ordering that the Lepels take her to a specialist to see how strong of a magic limiter Violet needs to keep her magic under control. Also, because she has UMD, it is dangerous not to know where she is at all times. So, a magic tracker will be placed on her to ensure the state always knows where she is."

Bartholomew said, "Your honor, the assertion that she has UMD is unproven and uncalled for. She has been tested for the disorder six times, and all the results came back negative."

In a stern tone, the judge said, "Mr. Samson, one more word out of you, and I will hold you in contempt."

In a whisper, Bartholomew said, "What kind of shit is this?"

The judge continued to say, "However, the Lepels are forbidden from taking Violet to Brazil. The late Mathew Evergreen set up specifications to ensure not a dime of Violet's inheritance could be touched. I considered ignoring these specifications for the sake of her care.

However, the only way to get around them would require a ruling by a higher court. So, the Lepels are going to be required to find a place to live locally- a decent home to show that they can afford to care for her. Otherwise, Violet will be sent to live at Greenages facility. It is not the most

15

suitable place for a child, but it is the only place that can handle a UMD case."

Violet screamed, "MOMMY!" as she began weeping inconsolably.

The judge said, "Victor and Drusilla Lepel, you have three weeks to meet my specifications. It is so ordered."

He slammed the gavel before ordering the bailiff to give Violet to the Lepels. The Lepels fist bumped to celebrate their victory, while everyone else in the courtroom including the Lepels' attorney, looked as if they were going to pass out from shock.

In response to Violet's tears, Meg screamed, "You can't take her away. You just can't!"

May hugged Violet tightly as she cried. Akeem slammed his fist on the table while he shouted, "THIS IS NOT JUSTICE!"

The bailiff, who looked ill after hearing the judgment, took a minute to collect his nerves. He walked over to May and asked her to give him Violet. A tearful May just shook her head no as she continued to hold a hysterical Violet.

In response, the bailiff said, "Ma'am, I'm very sorry about this."

He then ripped Violet from May's arms, causing Violet to panic and scream. May tried to grab Violet, but the bailiff pushed her back. He carried Violet over to Drusilla. He started to hand the child to her until Drusilla told him to drop her on the floor.

The bailiff looked disgusted as he gently sat Violet down. Drusilla immediately took Violet's candy and threw it across the room. She called Violet a little fat ass and then screamed at Violet, telling her to stop crying.

The bailiff said, "Ma'am, she is a scared little girl. You need to be more patient with her."

Drusilla looked at the bailiff as if he were nothing. She said, "You have no business telling me how to handle a worthless child."

Shocked by what Drusilla said, the bailiff looked at the judge. He asked, "Your honor, are you sure about this?"

The judge sat up in his chair and said, "This may seem cruel now, but trust me it's for the best."

Akeem looked at the judge dumbfounded before running over to Drusilla, who was still screaming at Violet. Drusilla's husband, Victor, immediately got in front of Drusilla.

He looked Akeem in the eyes as he said, "Just walk away, Wilds. We have custody, and there is nothing you can do about it."

Akeem told himself to remain calm as he said, "I know, but I have an idea you and my sister-in-law might like."

"What could you possibly give us?"

Akeem answered, "A place to live for starters."

Victor snapped, "We will find a place tomorrow."

Akeem continued, "I can tell you it is better than the roach motel you expect to pass off as a suitable living environment."

"Get out of my face. We are not…"

Drusilla interrupted and said, "Wait, let's hear him out."

A throng of reporters had gathered outside the Fulton County courthouse. The courthouse was a huge building constructed of marble

17

both inside and out. The atrium of the building was filled with large windows and two marble staircases- one on the left side of the atrium and the other on the right- that made that part of the building feel bright and open.

A throng of reporters were outside of the Fulton County Courthouse. Among them were Leonard Beck and Anas Amodako. Leonard was a man nearly 6 feet tall. He possessed a head full of short blond hair, piercing blue eyes, and his skin was a soft peach color. He was wearing a dark gray suit with a black shirt and black tie, along with a pair of black shoes.

Anas had curly black hair that was styled in a low taper fade with a juice cut and short beard. Both his rich dark brown skin and eyes were complemented by his dark blue suit with matching blue pants and a black shirt. He was also wearing a pair of black shoes and a dark blue tie to complete his outfit. His left arm was wrapped in a white bandage. His right hand had scratches that went all the way up his arm. There was a bulge in his right pants leg, where unseen there was a deep scar where his flesh from his knee to the center of his ankle had been cut to the bone.

Leonard looked at Anas who seemed to be struggling with his microphone and asked, "Are you having any trouble with the microphone?"

Anas, in his heavy Ghanaian accent, said, "The bandage made it a little hard to attach it to my shirt, but I've almost got it."

"Seriously Anas, you need to stop letting the network send you to report on demon voids."

"I admit reporting whenever the demons enter our world is risky, but someone has to do it."

"Anas, I see your point, but you almost died last time."

Anas took a breath before saying, "I understand where you're coming from, but it's fine. After that thing nearly killed me the last time they sent me to cover a void, the network is not going to let our boss force me to get super close to the monsters."

Just then a leprechaun wearing a blue T-shirt with a pair of beige pants and green tennis shoes walked over to them.

The leprechaun was short with peach skin, and he had flaming red hair and large sky-blue eyes.

He looked at Anas as he said, "Anas, you are not going to like this. The Lepels were granted custody of Violet."

Both men looked at the leprechaun in shock. Anas's mind started to race, and it took him a few minutes to collect himself.

When he did, he said, "George, you have got to be joking."

George shrugged as he said, "I thought it was a huge joke, too, when I heard the judge give his ruling. But he thinks that the Lepels will be able to provide Violet with more structure because she supposedly has UMD. I find the whole thing fishy. It's clear he didn't take into account anything the Evergreens' attorney said or even the late Mathew Evergreen's will. Also, he did not say anything when Mrs. Lepel started screaming at the child for no reason."

Leonard asked, "Isn't Mrs. Lepel the girl's aunt?"

George said, "She is, but you would think the kid was the spawn of the devil. You should have seen how she yelled at the kid."

Anas said, "Shit, poor Violet."

Leonard said, "Should we feel that bad for her? Like Anas, I get she is your girlfriend's niece, but the kid did commit parricide just a few months ago."

Anas glared at Leonard while George rolled his eyes before saying, "You believe that?"

After reminding himself to stay calm, Anas said, "We were on sight covering the story the night she burned down her house. She started the fire only because she was scared of the intruders who killed her parents and all their staff."

Leonard replied, "We were reporting across the street from the house because the fire department was trying to keep the flames from spreading. Plus, you were so shocked by what can only be described as horrific events that evening, so I don't believe that you were in any mental condition to fully grasp all that was going on that night."

Anas responded, "That doesn't change the fact that we heard that bullshit reasoning the police chief gave, claiming that little Violet was responsible for the murders. He didn't even take time to fully investigate. He just arrived on the scene and pronounced Violet guilty of parricide, and not just parricide, but the murders of the entire household staff."

George yawned before saying, "Speaking of that, I want to see if we can get an exclusive with the Lepels' attorney."

Anas asked, "Why?"

"He was sh…"

Just then someone shouted, "They're coming out!"

In response, Anas and Leonard immediately raced to get in position to hear the statement from the Lepels.

Both Anas and Leonard noticed that their cameraman was not back from getting coffee. So, George cast a spell to make the camera hover in midair. Then he gave the two men the signal to start the broadcast. Anas and Leonard greeted the audience.

Anas said, "The custody case for little Violet Evergreen has just ended. Our studio was informed that the case resulted in a surprising win for her estranged relatives, the Lepels- despite it being a very stupid idea."

Leonard gave Anas an irritated look for a split second before saying, "Anas, this is not the time for jokes."

"I was not joking."

"Oh, it looks like the families are coming out of the courthouse now."

The Lepels were the first to come out of the courthouse. Victor walked out beside Drusilla, who was dragging a tearful Violet by the arm. Violet, whose eyes were completely red from her tears, was begging Drusilla to let go of her, not only because she wanted to be free of this strange evil woman, but because Drusilla was squeezing her arm so tightly that it hurt.

In response to Violets' plea, in a harsh tone, Drusilla said, "You should have thought of that before you decided to murder my brother."

In a sad voice, Violet responded, "But the bad men kill my mommy and daddy."

Drusilla rolled her eyes as she told Violet to shut up.

Just then Meg ran out of the courthouse and rushed over to Drusilla. In a nervous voice, she asked to be responsible for Violet until the press conference was over.

In a cold tone, Drusilla said, "Just stand there and be quiet. Otherwise, I will reconsider the deal your father proposed."

Not wanting to make things worse, Meg stood there quietly. After a few minutes, the rest of the family except for May started to walk out of the courthouse. Once everyone was gathered behind a podium that had been set up, Victor whispered something in Drusilla's ear. She shook her head yes then he walked up to the podium.

Victor cleared his throat before saying, "As you all know, the youngest member of our family murdered her parents. All of us know that little Violet did not mean to do such a horrible thing. The entire incident was out of her control because she was unaware she had UMD. However, because she has UMD, Violet needs to be raised differently than other children. The judge understands this, and my wife and I understand this. That is why we were awarded level twelve extended custody of Violet.

I know it sounds harsh to hold custody over someone for most of their young adult life, but you all must understand that Violet's condition means she is going to require a lot of care. Many of you know my wife and I currently live in Brazil. However, with demon voids frequently opening up in that nation, due to the failed efforts of the Eden Witches, we agreed it would be best to raise Violet in the United States."

Anas whispered to Leonard, "I wonder why he is lying about the efforts of the Eden witches. Better yet, I don't care right now. At least Violet gets to stay in the U.S.A."

Leonard replied, "You're right. We should probably worry about why he was taking a jab at the Eden witches. But I am wondering if maybe he said that to hide the real reason they are coming back here."

Victor continued to say, "Also, after conversing with my brother-in-law, we agreed that after recent tragic events it would not be wise for Violet to be separated from the family members she is used to. So, my wife

22

and I will be moving into the Evergreen estate with my wife's family. I know that that news is surprising, but we will not be answering any questions about this or anything else. My family members including myself are all very tired, so we are all going to go home now." After that, Victor and Drusilla started to leave.

June ran over to them and said, "Um, since we agreed you guys were going to move into the family house, will you allow Violet to ride home with me and the rest of the family?"

Victor laughed at June while Drusilla screamed, "Violet is not going anywhere with you, our stupid sister, your husband, your daughter, or our bitch of a mother! She is staying with Victor and me at the hotel until we are ready to move into the family estate!"

Drusilla's declaration shocked everyone, and reporters who were being held back by the police started to demand answers.

June said, "But, wouldn't it be better for her to stay at the house while you guys are packing up your house in Brazil?"

In a harsh tone, Drusilla said, "We have already begun the process to sell our home without needing to head back. Besides, she has been spoiled by you and everyone else for too long. She needs to understand her place and help her fat ass lose some weight."

In a shocked voice, June said, "I told you before. Violet is at a perfectly healthy weight for her age."

"Please, you and that bitch our brother married turned her into a fat little piggy. I am going to get her to a healthy weight so that she gains better control over her magic and hopefully gets married at sixteen."

Surprised by her sister's statement June said, "What do you mean by that?"

As June followed her sister and brother-in-law, Akeem began walking toward her. Meanwhile, the family security team escorted Meg to their car. As for Anas and Leonard, they started to walk toward the news van.

Leonard said, "What the hell just happened?"

Anas replied, "I told you something was not…"

Just then George rushed over to them. He said, "Anas, bad news- looks like you and I are going to Colombia."

"Why?"

George announced, "A demon void opened near Bogotá, and it let a bunch of really nasty monsters on the loose."

Anas remarked in an angry tone, "What happened to the network's promise to not send me into the field until I finish my recovery?"

George, in an effort to explain, "I don't know what to say about that man. I think because you're well enough to report on local events, they feel you're more than ready to get back into the field despite what your doctor said."

Leonard asked, "What about me?"

George replied, "What about you?"

Leonard said, "What I mean is, I should be the one covering the demon void story."

Anas thought for a minute before saying, "If you can get the network to give me some time off, then I will help you try to convince the higher-ups to send you."

A smiling Leonard said, "Let me guess, you want to hang out at the Evergreen mansion while you finish recovering. Wow, you're lucky. I hear their estate is nicer than a luxury hotel."

In a quiet tone, Anas said, "I don't know how nice my stay will be with the Lepels there."

George started to give Leonard advice on how to stay safe near a demon void, while Anas decided to get a cup of tea at a nearby coffee shop before heading back with them to the studio.

Anas was almost at the coffee shop when he walked by a sandwich shop and noticed his girlfriend inside. Within a second, he could tell she was ordering everything under the sun. Out of curiosity, Anas decided to see if he could find out why she was ordering so much.

The inside of the shop was nothing special. There was black and white tile on the floor and white painted brick walls. There was a display case near the front of the room full of desserts and a black chalkboard on the upper wall behind it. A store clerk was standing in front of a register that was next to the display case. He had peachy skin, green eyes, and thick brown curly hair. He was wearing a dark green uniform. May, who was on the other side of the register, was ordering more food as Anas walked inside.

She said, "I also want to get ten ham sandwiches and a large strawberry chocolate cream cake."

The clerk said, "Miss, I know it's none of my business, but are you sure you want to get your niece another cake?"

In a panicked voice she said, "Just give me the damn cake!"

Anas walked over to her and said, "May, are you alright?"

May didn't look at Anas when she said, "Oh, hey." Then she started looking at the menu.

"May, I get why you're worried, but buying every cake and sandwich in this shop is not going to help Violet."

May looked at Anas with watery eyes. She said, "We did not even walk out of the courtroom before Drusilla and her husband started calling Violet obese. Drusilla even called the child an ugly little piggy before saying they are going to have to spend a lot of money to hopefully make her a little pretty.

They even talked about not letting her have any dinner tonight. Anas, Violet was so sad this morning that she barely touched her oatmeal. Then we were in court for so long that she has not had her lunch yet. I doubt my sister is going to let her have any lunch if she is talking about not giving her dinner."

Anas kissed May before saying, "Calm down. I know which hotel they are staying in. Later I will have my contact help sneak us in. Then we can give her some roast beef for dinner."

"Why a roast beef?"

"She told me that it is one of her favorites."

"How are we going to get the food to her if she is in the room with my sister and her husband?"

"Don't worry about those two. They were gloating about how they were going out partying as soon as they got custody, remember? More than likely, they will leave Violet alone every night at the hotel."

"At least we have that blessing. Oh, my poor little Violet. How is she going to survive my sister and that husband of hers?"

Chapter 1
A Very Bad Date

Many years had passed since the day of the custody battle. Violet had grown into a lovely eighteen-year-old woman who was so skinny that she almost looked like a walking skeleton. This was made more apparent by her thinning dark brown hair, which she attempted to hide by having her hair pulled back and tied into a tight bun. Despite her effort, having her hair pulled back made the skeletal structure of her bony oval face more apparent. Her soft lips were painted with red lipstick.

On the other hand, she was fortunate enough to be blessed that her glorious violet eyes still sparkled like amethyst. She was dressed in all white, including a pair of expensive white high heels on her feet. The one exception to an otherwise all-white outfit was a thick braided black leather belt. On someone of normal weight, the black belt would have complemented the outfit that Violet wore. But on her, it was unattractive because it only accentuated her anorexic figure.

Violet, sitting on a brown bar stool, stared at the glass shelf against the wall across from her. Sitting on top of the shelf were several different bottles of alcohol of varying shapes and sizes. She carefully scanned each of them from where she was sitting, in an attempt to try to read their labels.

Madam Crystal Butterfly

When she read the last label that she could make out, she looked down at the wooden bar in front of her. She stared at her glass of water for a moment, wishing it was food. Violet thought, *I was hoping reading those labels would take me a while. Now how am I going to distract myself from thinking about food in a damn restaurant? I could always stare at the floor and see how many tiles I can count. Guess it's worth a shot since doing that would be more effective than paying attention to him.*

She then looked at her date who was sitting next to her. He was tall with rich honey-brown skin. His head was covered with thick, spiky bleached blond hair. His dark brown eyes were divided by a large pug nose, which sat above a pair of lips covered with so much clear lip balm, that whenever she looked at him all that she could see were those shiny lips. He was wearing a gray suit with a white shirt and a striped green and gray tie. A pair of black shoes covered his large feet.

Her date was oblivious to the fact that she was not paying close attention to him. He smiled as he was saying, "So, as you can see, Emilia Devonshire simply ruined the Hendersons' garden party. Honestly, what kind of woman eats three peppermints in public …"

After hearing him say the word public, Violet went back to listening to her thoughts. *Counting tiles will definitely be more interesting than hearing this guy prattle on about nothing.* She then proceeded to count floor tiles in an attempt to distract herself from her stomach's uncontrollable growling. However, she quickly realized how foolish her efforts were when she could no longer focus on which title she was counting.

As her hunger began to grow worse, she thought, *I was hoping the salad I had when I got here would at least tide me over. Guess it was very silly for me to think that way because I'm always hungry.* Every day she was hungry and every day she wished that she could have more than the one small salad she was allowed to eat each day.

Hmmm, I have a little cash, and it's not like my date is paying attention to me. Maybe I could order a small appetizer? Am I crazy?

She knew even if her date did not care if she ordered more food, her guardians had their watchdog watching her making sure that she did not sneak extra food while on this date. *Just be good and ignore the cries my stomach is making. That's hard to do with so many delicious smells in the air and so much yummy food around me.*

Desperate to silence the overwhelming hunger pangs, Violet grabbed her glass and drank all the remaining water in it. Sadly, the water was not enough, and her hunger pangs raged on.

Stop thinking about eating and get through this date. I'm sure the rest of my family saved a few scraps for me to help me get through the night. After a moment, the realization that Violet only had a few scraps to look forward to hit her like an icy cold shower.

It's not fair. My family is not even close to being poor, so why do I...

Suddenly, Violet's date laughed very loudly, which shocked her back to reality, causing her heart to beat very quickly.

In an excited tone her date said, "You have truly proven yourself worthy of my company."

I'm glad his sorry ass is happy, but I hope he's ready to call it an evening so I can go home.

Her date continued to say, "Actually, now that I think about it there is one problem I would like to address."

Worried her date had a problem with her, Violet asked, "Did I do something to displease you?"

"No, your dietary control along with your clear fascination with everything I had to say was excellent."

He's happy I'm starving. Son of a, no, don't think negatively about him. After all, he's happy, meaning I won't get punished.

Her date continued to say, "I'll contact your guardians to set up the date for tomorrow around twelve. However, I'm meeting my tailor at that time so you're going to have to be good and wait patiently outside the tailor's shop. You're also going to have to exercise some patience. It will probably take about five hours for me to get fitted for several new suits."

"Wouldn't it be better if we meet up after you finish at the tailors?"

"The restaurant I want us to go to is down the street from my tailor, and I don't want to wait for you to arrive."

You piece of, calm down. I impressed the asshole enough to get him to want to go out with me again. That's the whole reason why I'm here, and besides, it's not like I have a say in the matter. I hope he is ..."

Her thoughts were suddenly interrupted when the bartender walked over to Violet and placed a plate along with a fork in front of her.

The bartender was a man with peach skin, short brown hair, and green eyes. He was wearing a black shirt and pants. Violet looked down at the plate. She saw that it contained a pasta dish that had white sauce, fettuccine noodles, bacon bits, spinach, diced tomato, and sliced green onions.

As her eyes started to glitter at the very sight of the pasta the bartender said, "A gentleman ordered this for you."

Violet was only half paying attention. She thought, *dear god almighty, thank you for creating the man who was sweet enough to buy me food.*

Without a second thought, Violet quickly picked up her fork. As she stuck the fork into the pasta, her date snatched her fork from her hands. He threw the fork onto the ground. Before anyone could blink, he picked up the plate of pasta and threw it across the room.

The moment the sound of the plate crashing to the ground permeated throughout the restaurant, almost everyone in the room went silent.

Violet's date shot a nasty look at the bartender and started screaming, "How dare you try to force my date to eat that crap!"

The bartender, who was clearly aggravated, took a breath before he calmly said, "Sir, a gentleman purchased the pasta carbonara for the lady. I just brought it to her. I never attempted to force her to eat it. Also, she was fully within her right to reject the pasta if she wanted to. More importantly, this kind of behavior is not allowed here. Please calm down, or I'm going to have to escort you out of the restaurant."

Enraged by the bartender's response, Violet's date started to scream at him. As for Violet herself, she was completely unaware that her date was yelling at the bartender or anything the bartender was saying to her date. She just kept staring at the empty spot on the table where her plate of pasta once sat.

Her body started to shake as she asked herself, *why? Someone was kind enough to see I was hungry, and he just threw it away. Why did he do that? This does not make any sense. Why, why, why, why, why? Dammit, just someone tell me why?*

Suddenly Violet's expression went completely blank as her heart started to beat slowly deep within her chest. Slowly, she turned in the direction of her date who was still screaming at the bartender.

As if possessed, Violet got off her barstool and then slapped her date so hard that he fell to the ground. When he hit the floor, the realization of what she had done hit her.

Oh no, why did I just do that? I bet this guy is pissed at me now. Shit, my guardians are going to make me regret upsetting him. Maybe there is some way I can smooth this over. Why am I trying to fool myself? I'm probably going to get the crap beaten out of me for messing this date up.

Her date, who was pissed off, picked himself off the ground. When his eyes finally settled on Violet, he yelled, "What the hell is wrong with you? I stood up for you when that son of a bitch tried to force you to eat fattening food!"

Forced me to, no, just apologize he most likely won't forgive me for slapping him. But he may be flattered enough to go easy on me when he complains to my guardians. She took a breath to calm her nerves.

Then she looked her date in the eyes and barely whispered, "I'm sorry."

Her date glared at her as he said in a very authoritative tone, "What did you just say?"

I screwed up again. Stop panicking dammit. Just say you're sorry and get it over with. She then attempted to apologize again but even though her mouth moved, no sound came out. *What is with me? I need to apologize?* Not wanting the situation to escalate she told herself to just blurt out an apology.

Quickly she said, "I'm sorry you're a dumb ass."

The moment the phrase you're a dumb ass escaped Violet's lips, she felt as if she hit herself in the stomach.

Oh shit, why did I just say that? Quick, just say you did not mean what you said.

She then quickly blurted out, "I'm sorry you're an asshole."

Violet's heart raced from the shock that she had insulted her date twice when trying to apologize. Her date on the other hand looked as if he had had enough of her and anything that she had to say.

In a very stern and disappointed tone, he said, "It's sad. I thought after our next outing that I would want to make plans to marry you. Clearly, I was wrong and you're nothing more than some psychotic witch."

After everything she had been through that night, his insult caused a well of anger to swell up inside her. It was so bad that her body started shaking.

Suddenly, without a second thought, she screamed, "You threw away my food for no reason, and I'm crazy?! Hell, you even thought about marrying me when you don't know one thing about me."

Her date rolled his eyes before responding, "You're just a woman. I don't need to know you when your only job is to care for my home, raise my children, and entertain me. At least that would have been your function if you weren't a crazy bitch."

"Excuse me?"

"Stupid girl, isn't it obvious…"

Just then Violet's date halted in his words because the bartender who had walked out of the bar came up to them.

In an annoyed tone, the bartender said, "Both of you are disturbing the other guests. You both need to leave this instant, or I will have to escort the two of you out of here myself."

When the bartender brought up how they were bothering other patrons, Violet looked around, and for the first time realized people were staring at them.

Violet, filled with regret, thought *great, this got out of control fast. Shit, I bet a bunch of people recorded us and put it on social media. Why didn't I…."*

Violet's date suddenly screamed, "I've had enough!"

Then he extended his right arm, with his palm facing the bartender.

Quickly he said, "Eit," and a green ball of light shot out of his hand toward the bartender.

The moment the green ball made an impact with the bartender, it exploded and made him fly back halfway across the room. In an instant, he crashed hard on the ground. After the bartender hit the floor, several people started to scream while others pulled out their phones to either call the cops or livestream what was happening. A few people rushed over to see if the bartender was alright, as many of the restaurant's other patrons started to gather their things so they could leave.

Violet looked at her date and yelled, "What is wrong with you?!"

Her date laughed at her as he said, "You're upset about a peasant. Wow, I was right. You are crazy."

"My goodness, I can't beli…"

Out of nowhere, a fast-moving slap made contact with Violet's face. The impact, combined with the shock, caused her body to slam into the bar. As she started to fall to the ground, someone grabbed her arm and yanked her upright.

Once she was back on her feet, Violet heard a British male voice say, "Stupid little rich bitch. Look at what you started."

She then looked at the person holding her arm, only to see a familiar yet unwelcome face.

The person holding Violet's arm was a middle-aged very red-faced plump man. His eyes were dark green, and he had a large fat nose in the center of his face. His chin was home to a long gray beard. He was wearing a green baseball cap which covered the bald spot in the center of his head, yet revealed long greying brown hair hanging from the sides of his head. The rest of his clothing consisted of an old worn-down brown jacket, faded white T-shirt, raggedy brown pants, and a pair of worn black boots.

The moment Violet realized who was holding onto her arm, any courage she had completely drained from her body.

She started trembling as she said, "I'm sorry, Winston. I know I messed things up."

Winston replied, "You think you're sorry now. Wait until your guardians learn about this."

He then proceeded to take a large gulp of a beer Violet noticed that he was holding.

After that, Winston looked at Violet's date and said, "Sir, I am so sorry about her behavior. Her guardians thought being in the company of someone as distinguished as you would help improve her behavior. Sadly, it appears that they were wrong."

Violet's date looked disgusted as he fanned the overwhelming smell of booze away from his face.

Violet's date replied in a condescending tone, "When I was approached about meeting with her, I thought her unstable magic was going to be my only problem. But it looks like her mind is unstable as well. If her guardians are smart, they will stop trying to marry her off and have her institutionalized."

Without another word her date left. Winston let go of Violet's arm then yelled, "You stupid bitch! What possessed you to insult your date?!"

Even though Winston was yelling at the top of his voice, Violet had difficulty paying attention. His breath reeked of alcohol, and Violet's cheek was very sore from being slapped. As she massaged her cheek, she thought, *he's drunk again.* Winston finished his drink before throwing his glass on the bar so hard that it shattered.

In a shaky voice, Violet said, "You really shouldn't do things like that."

Winston looked at Violet with a murderous gaze. He screamed, "Your guardians already paid this shitty restaurant for the damages you caused!"

"But the bartender tried to…"

"Tried to what? Take your side?!"

"No, he just tried to…"

Winston shouted, "Exactly! He wasn't trying to help your crazy ass! If anything, I should have your guardians demand a refund because that bartender forced your date to defend himself."

Just then a bald man walked up to Winston.

The man had brown skin and eyes. He was wearing a polo shirt with black pants and brown shoes.

The man said, "You need to cool it."

Winston yelled, "Mind your own business."

In a serious tone, the man replied, "No, I won't. Now step aside and leave the poor woman alone."

Aggravated, Winston pulled out his gun and pointed it at the man who was terrified.

In a cool tone, Winston said, "As I told you before, mind your own damn business."

Despite his obvious fear, the man stood firm. In a calm voice, he stated, "Listen, there is no need for violence. Just put the gun down and let the restaurant call the lady a cab."

Without a word, Winston pointed the gun in the air and fired one shot.

The sound of the gun firing caused several of the people remaining in the room to scream and run out of the restaurant.

Winston pointed the gun back at the man who looked even more frightened. He said, "For the last time, mind your own business."

After that Winston motioned for Violet to follow him. She quickly grabbed her purse, and the two of them started to walk out of the restaurant. As they walked Violet saw several patrons rushing quickly to leave, while a few stood their ground videotaping her. She could also hear several others on their phones with the police.

Slowly she turned her head forward while she thought, *all I had to do was keep my date happy so he would think about marrying me. Instead, I fucked it up, causing a man to get hurt and another man was almost shot. Why do I always mess everything up?*

Violet gripped her clutch tightly under her arm as she walked slowly behind Winton, while they navigated through the parking garage on their way to the car. As they walked, Winston would occasionally take a drink from a whisky flask he had in his pocket.

Violet was thinking to herself as they walked. *Winston is seriously drunk. I hope that he's sober enough to drive.* Thomas, the man charged with driving her, had quit his job earlier that afternoon. So, that evening when it was time for her to go on this blind date set up by her guardians, Violet hoped that they would cancel. Instead, the Lepels insisted that Winston drive her to the restaurant. Every member of the household staff knew that by 4:00 p.m. every day Winston was legally drunk. He is an alcoholic, a fact that the Lepels must also have known. He was in fact a mean drunk, which as Violet reasoning with herself realized for the first time, is probably why her guardians kept him in their employ.

The sound of Winston's loud gargled voice interrupted her thoughts. Winston shouted, "Dammit, where the hell did you make me park that fucking car? I'm in no mood to be wandering around this fucking garage all damn night!"

Returning to the solitude of her thoughts, Violet reasoned, *seriously he's blaming me because he's too drunk to remember where he parked the car? Don't know why I'm surprised. He always compulsively blames me for every tiny thing when he's super drunk.*

Winston stumbled a little bit before taking another large swig from the flask. Seeing him continue to drink made Violet more scared than she already was. *I don't want to get into the car with him. But my guardians will be upset if Winston is not the one who brings me home. Funny, that thought feels like an oxymoron. How sure can they be that I'll even get home? When they had a known drunk driving me?*

After wandering throughout the garage for about twenty minutes, the two discovered the silver Prius they had arrived in. Winston polished off the remainder of what was in his flask before searching in his pocket for the car keys.

Violet's thoughts raced in her head. Everything in her being told her not to get into the car and have this too drunk man drive her home. *He was a little drunk when he drove me here and we got here alright. What am I thinking? Just because the drunk got me here ok does not mean I'll get lucky twice.*

Violet watched him struggle to get the keys out of his pocket. She thought, *I've got to convince him not to drive. How do I do that? He won't listen to me about anything.*

As Winston started to unlock the car door, he accidentally dropped the keys. He got down on his knees to look for them. Violet thought, *he's distracted. I could try to run. That's stupid. If I run away, how am I going to get home?*

She suddenly remembered the ride app her Aunt May put on her phone. Violet started rummaging through her purse, searching for her phone. She thought about how May told her she was putting a ride app on her phone. May had Violet promise to not share that she had it and to only use it in case of an emergency. When she found her phone, she searched the screen for the app.

The moment she found the app she could hear Winston once again drop the keys.

Running away is starting not to sound so crazy. He could never catch me. Not only is he stinking drunk, but he is out of shape. Damn my guardians. Why couldn't they just let one of the other staff members drive me. Way were they so obsessed with Winston driving me all of a sudden?

Winston finally picked up the keys and said, "Finally, time to get the fuck out of here."

He then tried to stand up so he could unlock the car door. But his inebriated state caused him to stagger so badly that he dropped the keys before falling against the car door.

Frustrated, he shouted, "Dammit, why did that bitch buy a fucking car without automatic locks?"

Violet thought, *Auntie June is not a bitch, and the damn thing does have auto-locks, you drunk shithead.* After that thought Winston finally retrieved the keys once again; however, he started having an absurdly hard time unlocking the car door.

Violet looked at the app again while thinking, *he is not even in good enough condition to unlock a car door. If I let him take me home, I know I will die in a crash. My only options right now are death or getting in trouble. Death might be the better option. My life is absolute shit, and my family is suffering because of it. If I were to die, then all the pain I cause would come to an end and…"*

Violet's phone started to ring, forcing her out of her train of thought. It was set to play silent night whenever a member of her family called, and she soon realized her Aunt June was calling.

In response to the noise, Winston shouted, "Dammit bitch, shut up that fucking cat. Honestly, do you realize how late it is?!"

Cat sound, this fool is drunk if he can't tell the difference between a cat and a ringtone.

For whatever reason, at that moment Violet felt her legs move very quickly away from Winston. Despite his drunken state, it did not take Winston long to realize that Violet was quickly walking away. He threatened to hurt Violet if she did not come back immediately, but that only caused her to start running.

As she ran, she thought, *"What am I doing? I need to turn around now or I'm going to be punished.*

Almost out of breath Winston screamed, "Stop running. I promise to make sure your guardians don't beat you too hard!"

In response, Violet ran faster. *I'm making everything worse. I need to stop running.*

Despite her continued plea with herself, she could not get herself to stop, and after turning the corner she heard a loud thud, causing her to stop dead in her tracks.

Why did I keep running? Maybe my will to live is just that strong, or maybe I'm dumber than my guardians say I am. I guess now I have to..."

Her thought process was interrupted when she heard someone vomiting. Quickly, Violet turned around and saw Winston throwing up and then hitting the concrete floor as he passed out. Instead of meditating on what she saw, Violet figured her only option was to run and hope that when she got home her guardians would not be too angry. She started to leave, but she turned back around and walked over to the passed-out Winston.

Violet looked at him for a moment and saw that he was breathing. There was a large bruise on his forehead, and his face and hair were covered in vomit.

She continued to stare while thinking, *he's breathing so I guess he's alive. I should just march out of this garage now. No, unlike him I have a soul. So, I can't stand back and do nothing. The restrictions on my magic may have weakened me, but I think I'm strong enough to do a simple healing spell.*

She extended her right hand over him and with her palm facing down she said, "Restere." Her hand glowed bright purple for a moment. After the glow was gone, all the vomit had disappeared along with Winston's bruise.

Figuring she had done her good deed for the day, Violet started to leave. However, she barely got a few feet before stopping again. She did not look back as she stood thinking. *A lot of people were calling the cops in the restaurant. Knowing the influence my guardians have, the cops will let the whole thing go. Even with several witnesses and all that video people were taking. Hmm, Winston is probably going to be out for a while. If I take his ID, it will take a little while to locate him.*

She turned around and stared at the still unconscious Winston. A minute passed before she thought, *is doing what I am thinking the best idea? If Winston is gone even a day, my guardians will have a hard time finding a temporary watchdog. Why am I debating whether this is a good idea?*

She looked down at the phone in her hand, remembering that her aunt had called. Figuring it would be best to hurry and call the police, she decided not to call her aunt back and dialed nine-one-one.

A male voice answered, "Nine-one-one, what is your emergency?"

Violet replied, "There's a man passed out on the ground on the third floor of a parking garage, and he has a gun."

"Ma'am, where is this parking garage located?"

"It's located at midtown Atlanta next door to a restaurant called Four-Eighty Grilled."

"Thank you, ma'am, I just need to ask a few more questions before I can send dispatch."

"Alright, whatever you need me to do."

"Can you please tell me whether or not you have been drinking?"

"No, I haven't."

"Are you sure you have not consumed any alcohol?"

42

In a slightly annoyed tone, Violet said, "Yes, I am."

"Ma'am, I need you to please stop attempting to argue with me. I am only trying to help."

Violet thought, *why is he determined to say I'm trying to fight with him?*

The nine-one-one operator said, "Ok, Miss, just calm down. Are you on any illegal substances?"

She took a breath before answering, "I'm not using drugs of any kind. Can you please send someone to help this poor man? It looks like he was roughed up pretty bad."

"Miss, I understand. But you need to stop attacking me and just explain the situation."

In a forced calm tone Violet said, "I've told you more than once that there is a man passed out in a parking garage. He's very beaten up and has a weapon. I'm unsure if he's involved in anything illegal. Now please, please send someone to help him."

"Very well, ma'am. Several officers are already headed to the Four-Eighty Grilled. I will have one of the officers check out the parking garage. Please stay where you are. Understand that the officer is going to have to take your statement. Also, you will be expected to take a drug test as soon as the officer arrives."

"Ok, I understand."

"Thank you."

After the operator hung up Violet thought, *I need to hurry and get out of here.*

She then proceeded to reach down and take Winston's wallet out of his pocket. Violet also remembered Winston still had the car keys. Not wanting him to have access to her aunt's car, Violet decided to hurry and take the keys. After that, she put the keys in her purse before looking for the garage's elevator. As she walked, she looked through Winston's wallet. Inside she found his ID, several credit cards, the key card to enter Buckhead, the key card for the gate to the estate, the key for her garage, and six hundred dollars.

I shouldn't use his credit cards. I guess I'll just throw them and his ID in a trash can. But what should I do with the cash?

She paused for a moment and scheduled a car. When the app said a car would arrive in fifteen minutes she looked around until she saw an elevator. After making her way to the elevator and pressing the button, Violet felt strangely relaxed.

When the elevator arrived, and she got inside, as it went down her heart jumped. Violet thought, *when my guardians realize Winston did not bring me home, they're going to beat the shit out of me.*

The elevator arrived at the parking deck's bottom floor. When she stepped out of the elevator, she continued to think, *calm down. Remember they are trying to marry me off. No man wants a woman with a black eye.* As her heartbeat started to slow down, she walked up to the garage's exit, where there was a trash can sitting close to the exit.

Violet checked her phone and saw she still had thirteen minutes until the car arrived. She decided she had time to quickly dispose of Winston's cards. First, she put the cash in her purse. Then she went through the cards again to make sure she did not accidentally throw away a card she needed.

As Violet ditched the unnecessary cards into the garbage, she thought, *I don't understand my guardians. They are not going to get any money for keeping me. I'm legally an adult. Why are they so determined to keep extended custody of me? I've been asking these same questions since I was a child, and I never get any answers.*

Violet put the cards she needed into her purse. After which she threw the wallet, along with its remaining contents, into the garbage. She then checked the time to see how long she had until the car arrived. She smiled nervously to herself- only had six minutes left.

After walking out of the parking garage, she decided to walk up the street a little bit because she didn't want to be too close to the parking garage, should the cops arrive before her car. As she walked, she started to walk past Four-Eighty Grilled.

The restaurant was at the bottom level of a very tall concrete skyscraper. Its large rectangular windows had a large red outdoor curtain hanging from them. Above the curtains were the words Four-Eighty Grilled written in red cursive letters. Violet stared into the brightly lit restaurant window while she walked. She saw a bunch of restaurant staff scrambling in a panic, but there were no police officers.

The law enforcement budget was raised. So, the police should be here by now.

When she got halfway up the block she spotted a section for temporary parking, so she figured it might be a good place to wait.

Just as quickly she noticed what appeared to be several families in a dark alleyway trying to light a fire in a round metal trash can. At first, she told herself to ignore them since she was by herself, and it would be stupid to walk up to a group of people she didn't know. Suddenly she heard a baby cry, drawing her attention to the fact that there were children within the group.

I really shouldn't get involved. But I can't let a baby go hungry when I can help.

As Violet approached the people in the dark alleyway, she realized that the people making up the group appeared to be made up of two families. One of the men's eyes were a rich chocolate brown. He was

45

sporting a thick curly black afro on the top of his head. Also, like Violet, it was more than a little obvious that he had not seen a good meal in quite a while. He wore a raggedy blue suit and a pair of worn leather shoes.

Next to him was a woman sitting on the ground, her back leaning against the wall of the nearby building. She had rich dark chocolate brown skin, dark hazelnut eyes, and very short thick black curly hair. The woman was wearing a dirty worn blue dress. On her feet were a pair of very worn-down sneakers. In her arms, she was holding a little girl who looked to be about three years old. The child had dark chocolate skin and eyes, along with thick dark brown hair that was styled in plaits with tiny pink ribbons on the ends. She was wearing a dirty white and pink dress. She, like her mother, wore a pair of dirty white sneakers. The child had her face pressed against her mother's shoulder as she cried little tears.

There was another woman with long unkempt red hair. Her skin was a rosy pink, her eyes a deep ocean blue. She was wearing a basic old red T-shirt and a pair of shaggy brown pants. She wore no shoes on her feet. Just like the other members of her group, her frame was so thin that it was amazing her clothing stayed on her.

The second adult male among the group, although thin, was nowhere near as thin as the rest of them. His large green eyes looked even bigger due to his thinning oval face. His skin was so pale that he almost looked like a ghost. The thinning short dirty brown hair on top of his head did not do much to help his sickly appearance. His left hand appeared to have been cut and was wrapped in an old rag. He was dressed in a ratty gray T-shirt, baggy black pants, and like the woman with red hair, he had no shoes.

Sitting on the ground next to the man was a little boy who was holding a value pack of creamy chicken flavored Ramen noodles. The child appeared to be around ten years old with short brown hair, peach skin, green eyes, and like the others in his group, was way too thin. He was dressed in a ratty yellow and blue polo shirt and a pair of very baggy blue jeans. Just like the very pale man and the red-haired woman, he possessed no shoes on his feet.

The little boy looked up at the man with brown skin before saying, "I can't believe you were able to buy two whole big packs of Ramen, Mr. Ace."

Ace replied, "No problem, little guy. Just be glad I stumbled across three dollars this morning. But the real hero of the day is your dad. If he had not shielded me earlier, I would have never been able to get those noodles back here for us to eat."

The man with the injured hand said, "Ace, it is no big deal. You're the only reason my family and I will have any food tonight."

"It's not that big a deal, Parker."

Parker continued, "Yes, it is. Because you did not have to share with us at all. I can't even begin to express my gratitude for that."

Parker's eyes started to swell up and Ace patted his back as he said, "It's all right, man. The temp job recruiting is in the morning, which means food might not be a problem for three whole months."

Parker calmed down and said, "You're right, buddy."

Then he looked at his son and said, "Speaking of that, Matt. While all the adults are at work, we are going to drop you kids at the park. You know it's your job to look after little Emmanuelle."

Matt smiled at his dad and said, "No big deal, Dad. I still have my baseball. I wanted to start teaching her how to play catch."

The redheaded woman who was trying to start the fire in the metal trash bin looked at Matt. She said, "Matt, sweetie. Remember Emmanuelle is still a toddler, so don't throw the ball too hard."

In a slightly annoyed voice, Matt responded, "I know that, Mom. If she could handle a fastball, I would be teaching her baseball instead."

Ace said, "Baseball, now that's…"

Just then the group noticed Violet walking up to them. Emmanuelle's mother, who was still comforting her daughter, asked, "Can we help you, Miss?"

Violet replied, "No, but I think I can give all of you a little aid."

She then gave Parker and Ace three hundred dollars each. The two men stared at the money and almost simultaneously told Violet thank you. Violet told them it was no problem.

Before she could turn to leave, Ace said, "Miss, as much as we appreciate you helping us, you really shouldn't do things like this by yourself. With the economy the way it is, a lot of people are desperate. Just a few hours ago some guy tried to stab me when I was bringing back a twelve-pack of Ramen from a dollar store. My buddy over here even got hurt bad just for trying to help me."

Violet, who had not noticed, looked at the inside of her left arm for a second. She thought, *the judge may have had a limiting spell on me, but I used a simple healing spell, and it did not set off. I bet I could do it again.* She then asked to see Parker's injury.

Parker responded to her request by saying, "Don't trouble yourself. You have already done more than enough for us."

Violet said, "I insist. My relatives taught me some basic healing magic, and you really should not risk your injury getting infected."

Parker thought for a moment then said, "Alright, but do you mind checking Ace's injury too? It's not as bad as mine, but we don't have any clean water, so he might be risking infection as well."

Violet responded, "Of course, but since yours is worse, let me see it first."

Parker then gave Violet his injured hand. She carefully untied the cloth covering his wound, revealing a deep bloody gash in the center of his hand. There was also visible damage to the bone.

Violet said, "I'm surprised you're not in more pain with an injury this bad."

Parker replied, "Both Ace and I were in pretty bad pain at first. However, Cindy over there was able to cast a spell to remove the pain. Then she patched up our injuries as best she could. As you can guess, there aren't a whole lot of bandages in the streets."

Violet asked, "Who is Cindy?"

Parker pointed at the woman holding the baby.

Ace said, "None of us have had anything to eat for a while. So, casting that spell took a lot of energy out of my wife. We were hoping that after she has a little cold Ramen, she might start feeling better."

Surprised, Violet said, "You were going to eat the Ramen cold?"

Parker's wife said, "Cindy is the only one who can cast a decent fire spell. Plus, it is really hard to get matches at this hour."

"Why?"

Parker said, "Before you came along, we did not have any matches. But now the only problem is that the only general store we can get to is closed."

Violet thought, *I might be able to get away with lighting a fire if I only conjure a small spark.* She then started to take a closer look at Parker's wound and continued to think. *His wound is pretty bad. I'll have to use a spell to mend the broken bone before I even consider fully healing it. His friend is hurt, too, and I don't know how bad his injury is.*

She then placed both of her hands over Parker's injury and said, "Os fix."

A bright purple light emitted from her hands. After a moment, the broken bones in Parker's hand began to re-set into place. After that, Violet used the spell she had used on Winston to fully heal Parker's hand. Parker thanked her for her help, then Violet turned her attention to Ace's wound.

Ace rolled up his sleeve, then he removed his shirt and then the ratty cloth around his injury. Once the cloth was removed, it revealed a deep cut in Ace's shoulder. But thankfully, unlike Parker, none of Ace's bones were damaged.

Violet asked, "How did the assailant hurt both of you?"

Ace answered, "It's the same story that happens all the time these days. I bought some food, and a very desperate soul saw me, and then he decided to try and take it. When he attacked, he used what looked like a hunting knife to cut my shoulder. Before he could use the knife to cut my neck, Parker put his hand in the way of the knife. I don't know how he was able to then use his injured hand to push that guy out of the way, but he did. After that, either the attacker came to his senses or got scared because he immediately ran away."

Violet finished healing Ace's injury and then said, "Wow, that sounds scary."

Parker said, "It was, but being homeless these things happen. Not that our current representatives care."

After everyone, including Emmanuelle, expressed their gratitude to Violet, her phone suddenly pinged. When she checked it, she realized her ride was going to arrive in thirty seconds.

After quickly saying goodbye, she rushed over to the portion of the sidewalk where she had been standing. At the very moment she reached that spot, six police cars raced by on their way to the restaurant. After the police went by and parked in front of the restaurant, two of the police cars drove into the parking garage.

A black Toyota pulled up next to her. The window rolled down and Violet could see that the driver was a slightly plump old man with wrinkly peach skin with short white hair on top of his head and baby blue eyes. He was wearing a green T-shirt, gray pants, and a gold chain around his neck.

The driver asked, "Are you Violet Evergreen?"

Violet said, "Yes."

Then she proceeded to get into the back of the car.

Chapter 2
How was the date?

After Violet fastened her seatbelt, the car started to move. She stared out of the window. For the first time in her life, she noticed just how many poor people occupied the streets of Atlanta. Many were huddled on corners, others in alleyways.

Some people were hanging out or sleeping on the sidewalks. She thought, *I wish I could help all those people. But I don't have enough power to cast any more spells. I'm being foolish. Even though I used magic to help those families, I can't help anyone else.* She looked at her left arm as she thought, *all because of this.*

Violet could no longer bear the sight of so many poor people on the street, so she turned away. She told herself to try and think of something pleasant. Sadly, fear of what her guardians would do to her started to overcrowd her mind.

My guardians may kill me, but tonight I'm not going to regret anything I did. She sat forward in her chair as she continued to think how she could help people like the families she just met. *I should be trying to help people, not going on expensive dates with men who don't give a crap about me. But my guardians for some reason want me to marry into a high-ranking family; actually, not high ranking so much as a member of the monarch class. What's so special about them other than they have money older than my family's money? Or maybe all of this has to do with…"* Suddenly her stomach growled, and she was reminded of how hungry her body was.

She thought, *I have to eat something, and Winston is not here to stop me. But the tracking spell the court put on me might. Or will it? I am technically on my way home. So, as long as I get food from a place on the way home…*

Her stomach growled again. In response, she figured she might as well take a chance on getting something to eat. Once again, she stared out of the car window, this time searching for the names of the different restaurants. She looked at the places within her view to decide where she wanted to eat. As the car passed a restaurant called Snail Pie Train, Violet cringed in response to seeing the sign.

Taking the name on the sign literally she thought, thankfully I'm not that desperate. Her stomach roared painfully. *Fine, I'm desperate. But my Uncle Akeem gave me some money for emergencies. So where can I…"*

Suddenly she noticed a red neon sign that had a giant V. As she read the words Varsity, her eyes glittered as if she had found her salvation. Quickly she asked the driver to stop at the Varsity for a few minutes. He agreed and soon turned into the Varsity parking lot which was as it always is, crowded.

Violet realized that she was extremely excited to get a meal from the Varsity. At first, she thought it was because she hadn't had a decent meal for at least four months. Then a memory that her mother had once taken her to the Varsity flowed into her mind. She knew she was around four years old when it happened. Her mom had been talking about how she was going to take Violet to get a Varsity hotdog for a week.

Finally, the driver found a spot near the restaurant's entrance and parked the car. As she exited the automobile, Violet could smell the food cooking inside. This made her think more about how excited her mom was about her getting a Varsity hot dog.

Back then mommy and I were supposed to go inside and have lunch. But thanks to that sudden issue at our family's hospital, mommy had to change plans about us going in. It's funny, she got so panicked about me at least getting to try one of the hot dogs. She was shouting at the driver to order for us while on the phone with an investor. Funnier than that was how even after we got our food, she kept promising me we would sit and have lunch inside one day. Too bad we never got the chance.

Her stomach growled as she walked inside and thought, *I don't have time to sit and eat as mommy wanted. But I can still hurry and grab some food.* After walking inside the building, she immediately noticed a wall with pictures that seemed to be a chronicle of the restaurant's history. As much as she wanted to take time to look at the photos, she reminded herself she had limited time and decided not to take time to look at them.

Remembering she had to hurry home made her panic and think, *oh darn, I don't have a reservation. They might not even seat me. Even if they do find me a table, how am I going to get them to pack up my food? Wait a second, at the bar a lot of people said they were getting their food to go.*

The bartender brought them their food boxed up. I'm being silly. It was the same way when the driver brought mommy and me our food all those years ago. So, if I ask this place for that to go thing, then I can get some food to bring home with me. Crap, how am I going to eat it when I can't take it with me in the house? Let me think. I've been using magic all night. One more spell probably won't hurt.

She walked into a large open room. In front of the room was a massive metal counter that had several cash registers on it. Violet also noticed that there were several lines of people in front of the counter, who were either walking away with red trays of food or red and white boxes with the label Varsity on top.

Violet recognized the boxes as similar to the ones the driver picked up when she was little. She then noticed several people lined up to get food in front of the metal counter. Violet decided to get in the shortest line she saw. The line started to move, and she began to feel nervous about ordering anything from the restaurant. She knew that her feeling of discomfort came from the fact that she had never ordered food for herself before.

I know my date always orders my tiny salad for me. Ordering food doesn't look like it is something hard for me to do. I'll watch the people ahead of me order and maybe I'll feel less worried about ordering. She also began to read the restaurant's menu posted on the wall behind the counter.

When she got closer to the front of the line, she noticed the view of the kitchen. It was a large kitchen where several people were wearing funny hats with the word Varsity printed on them. In addition to the hats, they were also wearing red T-shirts, plastic gloves, and white aprons while they were running around preparing food and shouting orders. Violet liked watching the people in the kitchen, and part of her wished she could work there too.

A minute passed and she noticed that she was almost at the front of the line. She decided to watch and listen to the person in front of her, a little plump woman with smooth dark brown skin and long brown hair tied up into a ponytail. She was wearing a pair of tennis shoes along with a dark blue sweatshirt and matching pants. Hugging the woman's leg was a little girl who appeared to be about three years old. The child had dark chocolate skin like her mother. Like her mother, the child was dressed for comfort in a yellow t-shirt, blue jeans, and a pair of tiny tennis shoes.

The child looked up at her mother and said, "Pemo chee mama."

In response, the girl's mother looked down at her child and said "Don't worry Cynthia. I will get your pimento cheese."

Then the mother said, "I need four chili dogs, with two orders of fries, a pimento cheese sandwich, and three frosted orange drinks- two medium, one small."

The person behind the counter replied, "Alright, do you want that for here or to go?"

The woman replied, "To go."

Surprised, the child said, "I want my pemo chee now."

In response, the girl's mother said, "Sweetie, we have to wait till we get home so we can eat dinner with your daddy."

Upset, the child squealed, "No, my pemo chee get cold."

In a stern tone, the woman said, "Cynthia, calm down. The nice man is going to put a spell on our food. That will make it stay warm until we are ready to eat it."

The girl looked at her mother with a shocked expression and said, "No way."

The cashier replied, "Your mother is right. It's standard procedure for all restaurants to put a spell on takeout to keep it warm until you get home."

Excited, the child said, "I wanna see spell."

The cashier smiled as he said, "Ok."

The woman paid for her food, and the cashier retrieved the three boxes and a cup holder containing three drinks. Then he held his hand over the three to-go boxes and said, "Donec fermentum manent aperiuntur."

The boxes shined bright orange for two seconds. He then looked at the woman and said, "Alright, these should stay warm until you open the boxes, and you don't have to worry about your drinks melting for three hours."

The little girl squealed. Then in an excited voice said, "Mama, mama man did magics."

The woman laughed and said, "Of course he did. Alright, are you ready to go home and eat?"

Excited, the little girl started to jump up and down and said, "Yay."

As the woman and her daughter turned to leave, Violet realized she felt both excited and terrified at the thought of ordering. She didn't have time to dwell on her feelings because it was her turn to order.

She thought, *alright, don't let fear get to you. The sooner you order the sooner you get to eat.*

Violet forced herself to bury her fear, and she walked up to the cashier. He smiled at her and said, "Good evening, Miss. What'll ya have?"

Violet's hands twitched slightly. She forced herself to calmly say, "I would like to get one naked dog, one chili dog, a pimento cheese, onion rings, and a small frosted orange."

The cashier rang up her order before asking, "Do you want it for here or to go?"

"I want that to go."

After that she paid for her food, and he gave her two dollars and forty-five cents in change. As he went to retrieve her order Violet exhaled as her body started to feel a whole lot lighter.

I never thought I could get away with buying food. Oh crap, not out of the woods yet. I'm going to be in huge trouble when I get home for what I did to my date. Don't think that way. If I can get away with buying food, then there has to be some way for me to get out of trouble for being mean to my date.

The cashier enchanted her food the same way he did with the previous customer, in addition to casting a spell to keep her drink cold. As Violet headed for the exit, she felt a little sad that she had to leave so quickly because of how much her mother wanted them to eat there together.

I don't know why, but I get the feeling that this place has opened new opportunities for me. Or I'm just being dramatic because I'm about to get away with defying my guardians for the fourth time tonight. I need to hurry and get back to the car, and at least I finally got to see the inside of this place.

As Violet walked back to the car, she made a point to sit her bag of food on the seat next to her. That way her dress would not smell like her dinner. She got back into the car and after closing the door she thought, *I need to..."*

Just then her phone rang, and she remembered she had not called her aunt back. She pulled her phone out of her purse, but instead of seeing her Aunt June's name on the caller ID, it was her cousin Meg.

When she answered the phone, she heard her cousin say, "Violet, are you alright?"

Violet answered, "I'm fine, Meg."

"Oh, thank God. Hattie May called my mom. Told her that the driver quit, and you were forced to let that sad drunk drive you to your date."

Hattie May deserves a pay raise. Her contract may state all she has to worry about is cooking and cleaning the kitchen, but she always goes the extra mile to do whatever she can to try and help me.

She replied, "Don't worry. I got a ride home using the app Auntie May put on my phone."

Meg sounded more than a little relieved as she said, "I am so happy to hear that. How did you get Winston to let you use a rideshare app?"

"He didn't get to have a say in it."

May questioned, "What do you mean by that?"

Violet told her cousin about everything that happened when her date went south. Then she explained what happened after Winston passed out in the parking garage.

Meg responded, "I'm really glad you didn't give in to pressure and let him drive you. And I got the bonus of your date going to shit."

Violet stated sadly, "You know my guardians are going to be pissed."

Meg asked, "Violet, did you like that jackass?"

"No."

Meg continued, "Then it is good your date didn't work out. Besides, the worst thing they'll do is yell at you."

"Are you sure?"

Meg stated, "Violet, why do you even feel the need to ask that question? Those two assholes have been trying to marry you off since you were sixteen. Meaning they can't afford for you to show up on your next date bruised and beaten."

Meg's comment made Violet remember that she had had the same thought earlier, which helped her relax a little bit.

"Meg."

"Yes?"

"Do you think they are going to be mad about Winston?"

Meg responded, "Aunt Drusilla doesn't like Winston. So, I don't think she'll be mad about you coming home using the ride app. As for Uncle Victor, as long as you don't tell him you're responsible for Winston getting in trouble, nothing is going to happen."

"Aren't they going to figure out it was me?"

Meg in a reassuring tone said, "With Winston's track record with the cops, they are more than likely going to think he made another drunken mistake. I would have assumed the same thing if you hadn't told me otherwise."

"Ok, cause I am also worried the tracking spell that's on me will tell them I went to the Varsity."

Meg explained, "Hun, the tracking spell only reacts if you go somewhere, you're not supposed to. You're allowed in restaurants. If you were to try to leave the city or go into a building you were specifically told not to, then it would trigger itself. Wait, did you say you picked up Varsity?"

"Yes."

"Oh, thank God almighty. I have been worried about you getting enough to eat after Aunt Drusilla reduced how much salad you can have. Oh, who am I kidding? I am always worried about you getting enough to eat."

Violet questioned, "How am I going to hide my dinner?"

"Good question. Let me, what the hell? Violet, did Winston pull out a gun on someone?"

"Um, yes."

Meg laughed, "Shit, I wish you told me about that first. There is a video of what happened to you on the internet."

Violet's heart raced as she remembered the people who were videotaping the incident. As she began to criticize herself for not even considering that what happened could end up on the internet, she could hear Meg laughing very loudly.

In a giggly voice, Meg said, "The Lepels are so going to have to kiss our asses."

"Why do you say that?"

Meg informed, "Uncle Anas's news show is on now. He's using the video to talk about how crazy the Lepels are. There are even people calling in saying you and that guy Winston threatened were very brave. Also, your date's family is trying to save face and failing at it. Oh, shit. They are interviewing the guy Winston pointed the gun at."

"My ass is grass."

"Calm down, Violet. Ok, so the guy just called Winston crazy and is threatening to sue him. I need to have my assistant contact the guy to say thank you. Hold on, this started because of a plate of pasta? Who bought you pasta?"

Violet answered, "I don't know, just some guy. Like the dude who stood up to Winston, I never got to thank him."

Meg plotted, "Hmm, don't worry. I'll track the person down so we can thank him then. Also, I believe that I know a way to use this situation to our advantage. I'll do a little internet trolling myself and make sure that the whole incident is blamed on the Lepels. Then I will call my dear auntie with a proposition in exchange for clearing their name and protecting their image. I get to do your hair from now on. No more perms for you."

"Meg, what are you talking about?"

"What I am going to demand in exchange for helping the Lepels save face."

"Why would they agree to that when Aunt Drusilla considers natural hair undignified?"

"Just let me work on them. Then I can have you looking good for your birthday. Maybe you will attract a real man, one that you pick out."

Violet remarked, "I don't want to think about dating. Wait a second, I forgot my birthday is tomorrow."

"I'm not surprised, considering how bogged down with dates you have been lately."

"It's like my guardians have been getting more desperate to match me with someone."

Meg changing the subject said, "Back to your food problem. Hide it under the old willow tree. A protection spell to keep bugs off your food is not a lot of magic, so you can get away with it."

"I don't know. I might have used too much magic already?"

"What did you do?"

Violet told Meg about her encounter with the homeless families.

Meg chastised, "Violet, I know you only want to help, but never do that again. They could have been dangerous."

"I know."

Meg complained, "Damn, why do politicians want to build fucking walls instead of trying to help displaced citizens get back on their feet? The number of people losing their homes is growing every day."

"I thought the wall project kept demons out."

"No, the president and the majority of congress think that if they build walls around important areas, then they will keep the poor and homeless outside the wall. The demons will just munch on the poor and leave rich people like us alone, which obviously doesn't work. Those shits will never admit that their sick plan doesn't work. One of the results of this selfish policy is it is destroying the middle class and increasing the poverty rate."

"Is that why so many people are out of work?"

"It is part of the reason. The main issue is that the demons blew the shit out of Europe, The Middle East, and the majority of Asia. Many of the African and South American nations would be in the running, too if, hold on Violet."

A moment passed before Meg said, "Violet, I have to go. But before I hang up, eat half of your pimento cheese sandwich. Then, cast that spell over your food."

Violet questioned, "How did you know I got a pimento cheese?"

"You made a big deal about that when you were a kid once, when I tried to get you to eat a regular grilled cheese. Anyway, I'll save that story for another day. I have to go. I will let my mom know you're ok, and I'll try to get home in ten minutes to help you deal with the Lepels."

After they hung up, any leftover tension Violet felt washed away. She was left with nothing but an overwhelming sense of joy that her cousin Meg was such a great big sister.

She looked outside the window and realized that she was almost in Buckhead, and the driver was turning down the street that led to the Buckhead entry gate. *Stay cool, Violet, and just eat part of your sandwich.*

When she was about to reach for her bag, the driver asked, "Hey, you got a key or something to get in this place?"

She closed the Varsity bag and then rolled down her window to scan the key that would open the gate into Buckhead. As the car went through the gate, Violet started to look for the card to her front gate.

While thinking, *After what Meg told me, I see why almost half the neighborhood wants to tear the wall down. This whole time I thought it was because the damn thing is an eyesore.*

They pulled up to her gate just as she found the key card. After opening the gate, Violet realized she never touched her sandwich. Figuring she didn't have enough time to eat, she decided to just wait until after she spoke with her guardians before eating.

When the car stopped in front of the house, Violet checked to make sure she had everything before getting out. She wished the driver a safe night before closing the car door. The car sped off as Violet stared at her house.

Violet's home was a massive mansion completely constructed out of gray stone with a Spanish-style roof and a lot of arched windows. The front of the house had a small but very wide staircase constructed out of gray stone with a landing shaped like an octagon, which led to a red arched door with a black arched gate that had a vine-like design in front of it. There were large topiary trees in cement pots on each side of the door.

A little way from the right side of the house was a massive lake that had a fountain encircled with small lights. On the edge of the lake was a very old willow tree whose trunk was crooked and had a trunk that

64

partially bent, causing some of its vines to delicately caress the lake's surface.

She told herself that it might be wise for her to hurry and hide her food. Violet placed her hand above the bag of takeout and said, "Hastam in locum consolatory sumus." Suddenly, the bag of Varsity food was encased in a large floating clear blue orb. She started to carry the orb over to the willow tree when a pain shot through her left arm. It caused her to drop the orb, and it rolled a little way from her. She fell to her knees in pain as she looked at her arm. Violet noticed a glowing blue symbol in the shape of a male ram in the center of her arm.

Fuck, fuck, fuck I set off the limiter spell.

Just then she heard Drusilla scream from inside the house, "VIOLET! GET YOUR STUPID FAT ASS IN HERE NOW!"

As if possessed by a spirit, Violet grabbed the orb. Her left arm started to throb more and more as she ran as fast as she could towards the willow tree. The pain became so bad that part of her wanted to scream. But she bit her lip and told herself to keep quiet as got closer to the tree.

When Violet reached the willow tree, she quickly placed the sphere underneath a portion of the tree trunk that was partially exposed. When she was certain it was tucked safely underneath the exposed portion of the tree trunk, she stood up. She tried to rub her arm, but the moment she touched it, it stung even worse. Once again, she heard Drusilla shout for her to come inside. She gulped as thoughts of what Drusilla might do to her flowed into her mind. Violet told herself it would be worse if she didn't hurry and face the music. She quickly headed towards the house.

The estate's entryway was an open space with light gray walls and white marble floors. All the walls had white crown molding. The ceiling housed two large silver chandeliers that hung from opposite sides of the space. Each chandelier had four swooping handles that pointed upwards, and both held lights shaped like lotus blossoms on the ends of the handles.

There were two large swooping staircases on opposite sides that lead upstairs. Underneath the staircase were the entrances to hallways that lead to the rest of the downstairs. The family room was also underneath the staircase, along with a window that took up the majority of the lower-level back wall.

The moment Violet closed the door behind her and turned around, she saw her Aunt Drusilla Lepel. Her aunt was standing in the center of the room next to a round wooden coffee table that had a glass vase full of pink roses on top of it. Drusilla was wearing a very tight, light orange dress that was definitely way too young for her, and a pair of blue high heels that were too small for her feet.

Violet forced herself not to cringe in pain as she noticed Drusilla had a cigarette holder with a lit cigarette in her right hand. Violet hated the smell of tobacco. She knew Drusilla was smoking in the house to piss off June and Akeem, who had strict rules about no smoking in the house, not only because smoking was unhealthy, but mostly because June was an asthmatic.

Drusilla took a big puff of her cigarette before looking Violet in the eyes.

In a cold voice, Drusilla said, "What is that on the twenty-thousand-dollar dress I bought you?"

Violet looked down at her skirt and realized that she had gotten a little dirt on it. She looked at Drusilla trying to quickly think of an excuse.

Drusilla said, "It is alright, child. I know now that the limiter spell was activated because you tried to use magic to make your clothing presentable. So, I won't punish you for using your powers."

Drusilla snapped her fingers, causing the pain in Violet's arm and the glowing mark to disappear.

She continued to say, "After I saw that video on my computer, I'm not surprised your dress got messy by Winston pushing you into the street, trying to run away from the problems he caused. Pathetic drunk, where is he? I would like to hand him over to the police myself."

In an almost whispered tone, Violet asked, "The cops are here?"

"No, I was waiting for you to get back before I called them and the press."

"Why?"

Drusilla in her usual cruel tone said, "Obviously, you stupid fat ass, I want the media to know we handed him over. Then I don't have to deal with any negative press."

Violet wished Drusilla would stop always looking for an excuse to be cruel.

Drusilla took another puff of her cigarette. She smiled as if she were in heaven before saying, "My husband wished for me to hide Winston until everything that happened tonight calmed down, but I am done covering for that lard ass. Besides, if he is not around, you might feel more influenced to finally lose some weight."

Violet began to speak, "I, I need to tell you that…"

Before Violet could finish her sentence, Drusilla held her left hand forward, signaling for Violet to be quiet. Violet's heart started to race as she stood in the disapproving aura of her Aunt Drusilla, who took another huge puff of her cigarette. Drusilla stood in silence for what felt like five minutes before she put her hand down.

She glared at Violet before saying, "I have had time to think things over, and I understand your other problem."

Drusilla took another puff, and a smile appeared on her face. She said, "Yes, absolutely yes. I understand everything."

She then started to pace back and forth saying, "Ok, ok, I get it."

A perplexed Violet wanted to inquire as to why Drusilla was acting so strangely, but she knew better than to ask.

Suddenly, Drusilla stopped pacing and paused for a moment and then looked at Violet.

She asked, "Do you know why my husband and I became your guardians?"

In a shaky voice, Violet answered, "No, Aunt Drusilla."

"What did you just say?"

"No, Mommy Drucilla."

No sooner did the words Mommy Drusilla escape Violet's lips that she felt a little nauseous. Sure, she had been made to call her aunt mommy and her aunt's husband papa all the time. Yet, no matter how many times she was forced to say it, she always felt sick. At first, Violet thought her sick feelings were from the idea that she was betraying her parents. Later she realized her discomfort from uttering those words was actually from calling the two people who hated her real papa and mommy that was just painful. She even questioned why her guardians were desperate for her to refer to them as mommy and papa. But she knew that she would be punished if she ever tried to find out the answer.

In a stern tone, Drusilla said, "That's better. Where was I? Oh, right, when you killed my brother and his bitch wife. It was because you lost control of your powers. I knew my sisters would be too sentimental to do what was necessary for you, meaning making sure you were raised with a strict hand fell to me."

Violet's heart raced even faster while in a shaky voice she said, "My parents did not die from my magic."

Drusilla took a breath then said, "Violet, let's not play that game where you pretend to not be responsible for the death of my brother. As I have told you so many times, you have to take responsibility for your sins. Honestly, your refusal to accept that truth makes me wonder what you learned when I let June take you to that church.

But I guess I will worry about that later. Anyway, when my husband and I made our decision to be the ones to provide you with the type of environment you need, we knew it would be hard. Sadly, no matter how hard we work and how hard we try, you always prove to be a huge disappointment. Now, explain to me why you messed things up with that nice young man I set you up with?"

In a shaky tone, Violet said, "He just wasn't really interested in me."

Drusilla laughed very loudly before saying, "Please. You may be a very ugly little creature, but Oliver Smith is not stupid."

"Who is Oliver Smith?"

"The young man you had the privilege of going out with tonight, you little dumb ass."

Violet responded, "It's not my fault you never tell me the names of the men you set me up with. Not to mention those jerks have their heads so far up their own ass, they don't think I need to know their name."

Drusilla walked up to Violet very quickly. Before Violet could react, Drusilla slapped her so hard, she fell to the ground. As Violet hit the icy floor, her mind was not thinking of the stinging pain in her cheek. Violet was not thinking about the throbbing headache she had from being hit. She was not even thinking about how much her sides ached from the impact. The only thing on her mind was how much she wanted to hit Drusilla back. She knew she would never be able to do it, but oh how she wanted to slap this bitch of a woman.

Violet slowly got back onto her feet as Drusilla said, "We always tell you the name of your dates. Your ears are just too fat to hear properly."

Violet thought, *lying bitch.*

Drusilla took another puff of her cigarette. Then she said, "I hope you're happy with your behavior. Now I have to stay up late getting you another date for tomorrow. But maybe I don't have to."

Drusilla reached out and quickly snatched Violet's purse from her hand. Drusilla opened it and started searching for Violet's phone.

Drusilla demanded, "You are going to call him right now and tell him you're very, very s…" Some of Violet's change fell out. When they hit the ground, Drusilla became deathly silent.

Drusilla stared at the coins as if they were part of some great sin that had been committed against her. Violet, who was also staring at the change, felt her heart drop in her chest.

Shit, why did I forget to hide my change in the bag with my food? I've been so careful not to hide my emergency money in my purse. Why did I forget to do that tonight?

Drusilla quickly slapped Violet for a second time. She looked at Violet enraged and then screamed, "You little slut, did you take up fucking people for money?!" Violet tried to come up with a response, but her head hurt too badly for her to think clearly.

Drusilla yelled, "I'm waiting!"

Violet quickly blurted out, "I found it on the ground outside the restaurant."

Drusilla glared at Violet as she said, "You liar. I know you pickpocketed someone."

Violet started to shake while she thought, *she is insane. If I was ..."*

Suddenly, Drusilla kicked Violet very hard in the stomach, causing her to fall to the ground once again. As Violet gripped her stomach in pain, Drusilla screamed, "Stupid little bitch. You shouldn't be borrowing money. It makes the family look poor."

First, she accused her of prostitution and then stealing. Violet realized as she lay on the ground that she was not being beaten because she had money. She was being beaten because Drusilla was angry; about what she had no idea.

Drusilla glared at Violet for what felt like the world's slowest minute before shouting for her to get up. Every part of Violet's body throbbed with pain. Fearing another kick from Drusilla, she forced herself to remove her hands from her stomach before slowly standing up. The very second she was back on her feet, Drusilla kicked her in the side. A horrible burning pain filled Violet's body that made her want to scream, but she held it in. Overwhelmed, she lost her balance, once again finding herself on the floor.

All emotion seemed to drain from Drusilla's face as she said, "Puerum pergit Etiam capillus tuus."

Violet shouted, "No, please, not my hair, please don't!"

Yet sadly, her plea was answered by no one. The next thing Violet knew, her hair was being pulled upward. As her hairclip fell to the ground, she screamed while her whole body was hoisted off the ground by her hair. As she hovered a little bit off the floor screaming in pain while trying to free her hair, Drusilla just stared at her.

Suddenly a female voice shouted, "Creatura enim peccatum dimittere!"

Instantly, Violet found herself crashing onto the floor. As she groaned in pain, she felt someone carefully touch her shoulder. She looked up to see Hattie May looking at her terrified.

Hattie May Jonson was an elderly woman who worked as the family cook. She had honey brown skin with short curly gray hair. Her eyes were a glittering maple brown, and she had chubby chipmunk cheeks. Hattie May was wearing a white silk nightgown with a lace overcoat. Also, her feet were protected by a pair of cotton slippers.

Drusilla screamed, "Hattie May, stop interfering! This cow needs to be punished!"

Hattie May glared at Drusilla. In a very stern tone, she said, "Put out that damn cigarette."

Drusilla froze for a moment before saying a spell that made the cigarette disappear. At the same time, Hattie May cast a healing spell on Violet. This made Violet's pain disappear. As Violet started to get up, that strange feeling that she had had all night as if things really would be ok, returned. Violet knew that unless Victor was with her, Drusilla would never challenge Hattie May. She didn't know why, but Hattie May had some power to control Drusilla in a way that no other member of the family possessed.

Once Violet was on her feet, she heard something crash to the ground. When she looked to see what fell, she saw her phone crushed on the floor.

Her good feeling vanished just as quickly as it had arrived. Even though her phone had restrictions on it allowing her to be able to only call family members and download certain apps, she had loved the fact that it gave her a way to get help when she was in trouble. Violet stared at her broken phone, resisting the urge to cry. No, she wouldn't give Drusilla the satisfaction of seeing her tears.

Hattie folded her arms while frowning at Drusilla. She said, "You beat her for no reason. Then you broke her phone. Does that make you feel better about being a failure?"

Drusilla snapped, "Shut up, Hattie May."

Hattie May snapped back, "Don't you dare think that you can disrespect me like that. You evil woman. It's more than obvious you need this girl to have a place to live, so why the hell do you think it is a good idea to hurt her?"

Drusilla acted as if she didn't hear a word Hattie May said. She glared at Violet and screamed at her to get ready for bed. Then she conjured another cigarette. Hattie snapped at Drusilla to get rid of the cigarette, but she ignored her again. Drusilla used a lighter to light it before heading towards the family room.

Hattie stamped her foot before she said, "She thinks she is smart. But it's never a good idea to piss off the person who makes your food."

Violet questioned, "You're not going to poison her, are you?"

"No," Hattie May replied, "but she is going to have some bad indigestion for a while. Maybe even a bad rash, too."

The two women shared a smile. Violet announced, "Thanks. She deserves it."

In an apologetic tone, Hattie May said, "I'm sorry I didn't arrive to help sooner. I assumed she wasn't at home."

"Why?" Violet asked.

Hattie May continued, "After she and her husband made you leave with that drunk, they departed for a boxing match. I think it was for that boxer that they sponsor. He probably lost, which would explain Drusilla's mood. I'm not happy with this forced dating and marriage crap your guardians have been trying to pull, but I was happy that it prevented them from abusing you. That leads me to wonder if the boxer lost an important match and that's why she decided to risk hurting you."

"Probably, and that's why she risked smoking in the house."

"Sweetheart, that isn't really a risk. She knows she can get away with it as long as she threatens to send you to the facility. But once she does, she loses all the leverage she has."

"What do you mean?"

Hattie May explained, "Mrs. and Mr. Wilds tolerate the Lepels for your sake, which is good for the Lepels because they don't have anything but a failed boxing promoter business."

Violet said, "I thought the guy they were promoting was bigtime."

"You only think that because the Lepels severely restricted your internet access and never allow you to watch tv. Otherwise, you would know their boxer is a loser. Tonight was his last chance to stay in the ring. As I already said, he must have lost, which also means the Lepels are not going to get any more money from sponsors. Now that I think about things, at this point, all they have is what they suck out of the Wilds. Your aunt and uncle pay the Lepels to allow you to live in this house."

Violet, shocked at the information she had just heard, questioned, "They are being paid so that I can live here?"

"Initially, right after the custody battle, they used to pretend that they would ship you off if they weren't given money, so Miss June gave them a few million. However, after the Lepels blew through every penny, they demanded more money. By that time, it became clear to the Wilds that the Lepels were desperate for cash and a place to live. Since you were the only reason that they were allowed to remain in this house, the Wilds made it clear that if you were shipped off, then the Lepels would have to leave. Until they're able to get cash or whatever for marrying you off, they will never send you to some institution.

Anyway, those dummies who work for the Lepels are all upstairs playing poker. Let's sneak into the kitchen, and I'll whip you up something sensible to eat for once."

Violet confided to Hattie May, "That's ok. I was able to grab a little food on the way home."

"Where did you put it?"

"Under the willow tree, and there is a shield spell around it."

Hattie May laughed, "Well look at you, Miss Sneaky. In that case, I will make sure that those jerks stay upstairs and don't come looking for you."

"Thanks, Hattie, but what should I do about Aunt Drusilla?"

"Knowing that woman, she is going to sit in her room and drink all night."

Violet agreed with Hattie May. Then she told her good night before heading outside.

As Violet went to retrieve her dinner, she started to wonder why Meg was not home. She figured something serious must have happened at her office. Violet proceeded to retrieve her food from underneath the willow tree. She figured since she did get away with casting most of her spells, that meant Meg was wrong and that the last spell she cast was too powerful, which was why the limiter spell triggered itself.

She used magic to remove the protection spell around it. Then she held up her free hand and said, "volitant."

A small glowing white orb of light appeared, and it was hovering a few inches above her hand. As she put her hand down, she removed the container of food. The orb continued to hover in the air. When Violet began to walk toward the nearby woods, the orb followed her like an obedient puppy.

After navigating her way through the woods, she entered a small clearing. This spot was filled with happy memories; it was the spot where as a child she used to play with Meg. *I'll stay here and eat my food in peace.* Violet sat her bag on the ground and clapped her hands together before saying, "linteum litore."

Just then there was a small cracking noise, and a red and yellow beach towel suddenly appeared on the ground. After fixing the towel, she put her takeout bag along with her purse on top of it. She sat down on the blanket before grabbing the bag and pulling out her frosted orange and a straw. After un-wrapping her straw then placing it in her drink as she took a sip, she was surprised how happy the sweet taste of the drink made her.

After she opened one of the Varsity boxes and ate a few onion rings, she picked up her naked dog and poured a packet of mustard on it.

Once she was done with her first hot dog, she thought, *I just can't get over what happened. The more I replay events in my head, the harder I find it to believe that I am really about to get away with having dinner.* Tears began to fall down her face as she continued to think, *this is not right. I should not be forced to go hungry.* Not wishing to be overwhelmed, she told herself to try not to think about it. Using one of the napkins from her takeout order she wiped her tears away and sat in silence, forcing herself to think of nothing as she ate, except how delicious her food was.

Chapter 3
Another Date

Violet smiled from the joy of actually being full. She stood up and dusted herself off.

Hattie May made a good point earlier. It makes me wonder if maybe they are trying to marry me off for money. It would explain the types of men they have been setting me up with. According to the rules of the arranged date, the family not in the monarch class is responsible for paying for the date, the engagement, and the wedding. So how would my marriage benefit them? They have to be up to something shady. I just can't..."

Just then she heard a loud pop like thunder. She knew that sound could only mean someone teleported to the house very quickly. Figuring it was Meg, she decided to hurry back to the house.

Violet pointed at the Varsity bag full of garbage and said, "ad quisquiliarum."

The trash turned to dust, and she picked up the beach towel. *This is a nice towel. I want to keep it, but if my guardians or one of their people find it, I'm in for another beating.* She started to cast an incineration spell but stopped herself long before uttering a single word. Violet looked at the towel for a moment, feeling that the towel she created was just too nice to destroy. She was also unsure if the spell that would destroy the towel was strong enough to set off the limiter. So, she decided to take a chance on keeping the towel.

After folding it, she picked up her purse and put it under her arm. Violet then started to walk back to the house.

Ok, so how do I get this towel inside without getting in trouble? Maybe if I get caught with it, I can say Meg bought it for me. No, Aunt Drusilla might get mad at her like she did when Meg bought me shampoo. Aunt Drusilla is weird. I mean who gets mad at someone for buying a family member shampoo?

She suddenly started to feel very dizzy, forcing her to come to a halt. A surge of pain shot through her stomach, causing her to grip her waist with both hands. The pain began to grow, and in response she fell to the ground while still gripping her stomach. Eventually, the pain became so bad that she tried to scream for help. The moment that sound started to escape her lips, her entire torso started to feel as if it was on fire, forcing her to give up.

Five minutes passed and Violet still couldn't get herself to move. With fear growing inside her, Violet began hyperventilating. Once again, she attempted to shout for help. As she did, her whole body erupted in a searing pain, which led to the hyperventilating growing worse.

Violet felt as if she couldn't breathe. *I'm really going to die here. Damn it, why did I have to continue to be worthless up until the very ..."*

Just then Violet felt a surge of pain so bad she was forced to scream. Her pain reached the point where she could no longer bear it. Feeling completely defeated, the world started to dissolve around her. When things looked as if they were about to go completely black, she heard a female voice call out, "Violet, where are you?"

Violet recognized the voice as belonging to her Aunt June, but she was too delirious and in too much pain to respond to her aunt's call. Despite

Violet's forced silence, her aunt kept calling for her. As her voice got closer and closer everything went black.

Violet woke up in her bed, drenched in sweat. Violet's bedroom had white carpet floors surrounded by four light brown walls. Hanging from the high ceiling was a large crystal chandelier that lit up the entire room. Four large rectangular windows on the left wall revealed the night sky. Each window had a decorative white curtain that stretched almost to the floor. On the right side of the room was the door which led into the hallway.

The back wall had a door on its left side of the wall and in front of the center of the wall was a king-size brown wooden sleigh bed. Sitting next to the bed on the left side was a dark brown nightstand that had only a tiny alarm clock sitting on top of it. The bed's mattress, covered with a white sheet, housed a slowly awaking Violet. Her whole body felt very sore as she forced herself to sit up in the bed assessing her surroundings.

Violet still felt a little drowsy as she propped her sore body up against her pillow. She looked around her room, and she noticed a broken camera in the middle of her floor.

Aunt June must have broken that stupid camera my guardians set up. I can't figure out why they keep putting cameras in my room. Whenever Aunt June finds one, she breaks it.

Of all the rooms in the house, Violet hated her room the most. This room was never meant to be her room. When the Wilds and the Lepels made their deal for the Lepels to live at the family house with Violet, Violet was forced to give up the room the Wilds had prepared for her after her parent's death- a beautiful bright cheerful space that Violet had loved.

Oddly at this moment, Violet's memory went back to the stipulations for the agreement of the Lepels being allowed to live in the family home. The Lepels were permitted to have their own staff. They were also given the east wing of the house, which originally was reserved for guests. No one was allowed to be on the east wing except the Lepels, Violet, and the Lepels' staff. Violet also moved into this room on the east wing, a room that became a prison, because she was not allowed to be in any other part of the house without permission. Therefore, most of her days had been spent alone in this room.

She usually sat in her room, bored until the Lepels needed her to do something. School proved to be Violet's salvation. She made friends easily. During her school years, the parents of her friends used to make up excuses about Violet needing to come over for the weekend to work on a school project with their children. The Lepels agreed, provided her friends' parents adhered to the rules they put in place for her.

The parents of her friends would agree, then proceed to break practically all of the Lepels rules. They would use the time she was at their home to make sure Violet received the proper amount of food. It was during these visits that Violet had ice cream, cake, pie, and cobbler. Those afternoon study dates and weekends kept Violet from going insane under the Lepels' abusive control. During the summers when she was at home, the rest of her family and their staff would sneak Violet food. Sometimes they would even sneak small games for her to entertain herself.

Sadly, all good things must come to an end. The Lepels figured out what was going on. She was stripped of her right to visit friends, and they had a security camera installed in her room, along with listening devices placed in her bathroom and closet.

Despite this, June and Akeem would use magic to break the devices whenever they wanted to sneak Violet food. The Lepels often threatened to send Violet away when the devices were broken; however, due to the incompetence of all but one member of the Lepels' staff, the Wilds were able to trick the Lepels into thinking the devices were not installed properly. However, the Wilds knew breaking the devices wouldn't always work. So, they would use more complicated methods to give Violet food. But this was also risky, and some days they were unable to give her anything.

The door to her room opened, and June walked in holding a cup emitting blue steam. Violet's aunt was wearing a white doctor's jacket, a light blue shirt with black pants, and a stethoscope around her neck.

Violet, who had finally pieced together what happened, looked at her aunt with very grateful tired eyes and said, "Auntie June, thank you so much for saving me."

June took a breath of relief when she noticed Violet was awake.

June said, "Thank God almighty you're all right."

Violet warned, "Auntie, you can't be seen here."

June replied, "Don't worry. The Lepels won't care if I'm not here for long, seeing how you are in bad shape after my sister hit you."

Violet with pain in her voice asked, "How bad is the damage?"

"You'll be fine. I used a very strong healing spell on you before you could be brought inside. Then I had our new maid Emma help me change you into your pajamas and put you to bed. I need you to drink this potion I mixed up for you. It will get rid of the last of the bruising."

Her aunt walked over to the bed and handed Violet the cup she was holding. As Violet drank the potion, she noticed it tasted like turmeric. When she was finished, her aunt took the cup from her.

Violet asked, "Was there turmeric in that drink?"

"Yes, but can you tell me what else you tasted."

Violet thought for a moment then said, "Turnip root, aloe oil, fairy cane, and I think fish oil."

"What kind of fish oil?"

"Codfish oil."

Her aunt smiled as she replied, "Very good."

Violet yawned before saying, "I guess the turnip root combines with the oil from the cod, along with the turmeric, to create an anti-inflammatory medicine. The other ingredients help stimulate the main ingredient, which will heal my bruising and cause me to fall asleep within thirty to fifty-five minutes."

"Very good. Your elixir skills are still sharp. But you didn't recognize that the elixir also makes it impossible for you to be transported long distances for at least eight to nine hours. So, don't try to go anywhere other than the bathroom for now. Actually, since your body is going to be so weak for a few hours, I'll call one of the female staff to help you make it to the bathroom."

Violet commented, "The healing effects from the elixir must happen so fast that the body needs time to rest."

June yawned before saying, "Yeah, that's pretty much what it does. I'm lucky Hattie May did a few healing spells on you. Otherwise, you would have been in worse shape."

"Violet, can you lift up the top of your pajamas partially for me to give you a quick check?"

Violet pushed her bed sheets off her torso and lifted her pajama shirt enough for her stomach to be exposed. After her aunt examined her for a minute, she had her put her shirt back down and tucked her back into bed.

June said, "Alright, looks like the elixir worked and all your bruising is gone. How do you feel?"

Violet smiled, "Much better. That was really quick. Thank you, Auntie June! You've saved my life."

June replied, "I thank the Lord that I found you when I did. Usually that potion completely heals a patient in under a minute, but there have been a few instances where it takes longer."

"Auntie, let me ask this before I forget. Why did you want to know if I knew what was in the elixir?"

June said, "I had to see if you could think clearly after passing out. It has been a while since I have challenged you to examine and identify a potion. So, I figured there would be no harm in testing your elixir knowledge while at the same time seeing if you were feeling better. After my initial examination, I used the iniuriam lustro exire spell to scan all your injuries. I discovered Hattie May's spell did not completely heal a major wound."

Violet stated, "I was hurting, but I didn't think my injury was that bad."

"You should know better than to underestimate my sister. She may be thinner than a snake, but she is very strong. Her sudden willingness to attack you when she is trying to marry you off makes the whole situation even odder."

"Hattie May said the same thing. She suspected it had to do with the boxer Aunt Drusilla is promoting. But I have a hard time believing it was because of the boxer."

"I think Hattie May is right. When you think about what kind of boxing the Lepels are involved in... At least they consider it boxing. I wouldn't call it that."

"What do you mean?"

"My sister's whole boxing…"

Suddenly, Drusilla flung the door to Violet's room open.

June said, "Great, the killjoy is here."

Drusilla glared at her sister as she screamed, "Don't talk about me that way in front of the little bitch!"

June responded, "How many times do I have to tell your sorry ass to stop cursing at her!"

Drusilla, using an arrogant tone said, "And how many times must I remind you, you are not allowed in this wing of the house. Only my husband and my staff are allowed in the east wing."

June stated, "I go where I please. This is my home, and since we are jogging each other's memories, please let me remind you if you kill our niece, then you, your husband, and your staff are no longer welcome in this house."

Drusilla ignored her sister and shot a dirty look at Violet. In a harsh tone, she said, "Your adoptive father and I are going to L.A. for a meeting in the morning. I was able to arrange a date for tomorrow at ten thirty. Don't mess it up."

Violet thought, *I was hoping Aunt Drusilla was not going to find me another date this soon. Great, looks like my birthday is going to be ruined. But maybe it was stupid of me to expect her not to ruin it.*

Pissed off by what her sister said, June shouted, "She's not wasting her time going on one of those foolish dates tomorrow."

In a calm, almost threatening tone, Drusilla looked directly at Violet and stated, "She will because I say so."

"Drusilla, I filled out the paperwork. You and your husband agreed."

Drusilla questioned, "What paperwork?"

"The paperwork stating that I could throw Violet a birthday party."

"So? The party is in the evening, and her date is scheduled for 10 in the morning."

Exasperated, June said, "I have to take her to the hospital in the morning."

Questioning her sister's motives, "Why do you need to do that?"

June took a breath, struggling to hold back her anger, and said, "You beat her so badly that she passed out. Even though I was able to heal her wounds, I need to use the hospital's x-ray to make sure she doesn't have any other problems."

Drusilla replied sarcastically, "If she isn't fine after the examination that you already gave her, then that medical degree you spent all of those years in school for was a huge waste of time."

Angrily June shouted, "Damn you, Drusilla! You injured her. Now you want her to go on some stupid date instead of getting further examination to make sure she is alright?!"

Drusilla shrugged while saying, "If you're so worried about her going to the hospital for more tests, then why aren't you trying to take her there now?"

June tightly balled her fist as she answered, "Gee, I don't know. Maybe just maybe because I had to give her powerful medicine and that makes it unwise for me to move her immediately."

I appreciate auntie trying to get Aunt Drusilla to not force me to go on a date tomorrow. Knowing Aunt Drusilla, hell will freeze over before she lets me skip out on one of her dates.

In response to her sister's comment, Drusilla shrugged and said, "Whatever. Her date cost me two million, so she is going. Now get out of this room."

"No, this is my damn house."

Drusilla threatened, "Must I remind you of our agreement again? Also, you are paying to replace that damn camera. You better not have damaged any of the other surveillance equipment in the rest of the room."

June replied, "I am not replacing anything, and I'm not going anywhere. Not once did I ever agree to allow any of your surveillance shit in Violet's room. So, I will break that shit if I want to."

Drusilla in a frustrated tone said, "You know what? I'm tired. I am just going to have Ollivander deal with you."

Damn, I really don't want to see him right now.

After that, Drusilla left the room and June slammed her foot on the ground. She said, "I can't stand her."

Violet yawned before saying, "Me either, but there is nothing we can do about her or this situation that I am stuck in."

87

Seeming not to have heard what Violet said, in a calm tone June said, "Violet, I want you to ruin your date tomorrow."

Shocked by what her aunt said, Violet responded, "Auntie, I know you're upset, but you know I can't ruin my date on purpose. I'm lucky I got away with yelling at that arrogant prick that she set me up with earlier this evening. But I don't think I'll get lucky twice."

June instructed, "Violet, none of your dates ever work out. At least not the ones my sister sends you on. Anyway, Ollivander is going to most likely walk in here in a few minutes. So, I want you to listen. When you get up in the morning, make sure you are alone and then look inside your vanity drawer."

Violet looked in the direction of her vanity. It was on the left side of the room with a large rectangular mirror hanging above it. The vanity was made of dark brown wood with a single drawer underneath the tabletop.

June continued to say, "Alright, Violet, I will let you get some rest. But don't forget to …"

The door opened and the Lepels' head butler Ollivander walked in. He was a very tall muscular man with brown skin and brown eyes and not a strand of hair on his head. The man was wearing a black suit and tie, a white shirt, and a pair of well-polished black leather shoes on his feet.

Ollivander smiled at June. It was not a welcoming smile. Instead, it sent a message that something very bad was going to happen.

June looked at Ollivander as she quickly said, "Don't worry, Ollivander. I am leaving."

Ollivander replied, "I am very grateful for your cooperation."

Once June was gone, he looked at Violet and said, "Good night, Miss Violet. I expect nothing but good behavior from you tomorrow."

After that, he left. Violet took a big exhale as she thought, *that went a whole lot better than I anticipated. Usually, he tells me not to mess up my date in a threatening way. Dates, dates, dates… I am so fucking sick of dating.*

Violet lay back down in her bed. She continued to think about how much she wished things would change. Eventually, she made herself stop thinking about her problems and fell asleep.

It was very early as Violet lay in her bed and watched the sunrise peek through her blinds, painting the walls of her room with orange light. She still felt groggy as she slowly rolled over in the bed and looked at the clock and saw that it was six-thirty.

Suddenly, she heard an angry young woman's voice say, "Miss Evergreen, stop being lazy. Get the fuck up so you can get ready for your date."

In response, Violet sat up, wiped the sleep from her eyes, and looked at the woman and said, "What do you want, Kinya?"

Kinya was a thin woman wearing a green maid's uniform. Her skin was a smooth dark brown, and she had long, straight jet-black hair on top of her head which was tied up into a ponytail. Her face was void of makeup. Kinya's brown eyes had a natural cruel glint which always made Violet uncomfortable in her presence. Violet just wanted Kinya to leave her room.

Kinya had her hands on her hips. She said, "Your adoptive mother sent me here to wake your lazy ass up."

Violet responded, "Alright, I'm going to get ready."

"Whatever."

As soon as Kinya was gone, Violet slowly sat up. She thought, *Auntie June told me to look in my vanity.* She stared at her vanity for a moment. She thought, *I know she told me to ruin my date, but will that really help my situation? Auntie is the type of person who never takes a risk without the cards being lined up. At the same time, it is not like she and the others have not been trying to get me away from my guardians. Nothing ever worked.*

Violet climbed out of bed thinking while on her way into the bathroom, *just go through with what my guardians want. This new guy they found might not be so bad.*

Violet's bathroom had white tile floors, and the walls were covered with beige stone tiles. A marble two-person sink sat on top of a white cabinet against the right end of the right wall. Next to the sink was a large glass rain showerhead. Near the left wall was a giant white porcelain tub with jets. In the center of the back wall was a white door that led to her closet.

As Violet approached the sink, she noticed a white cloth on the floor. After picking it up she realized it was her dress from the night before. Her mind told her to just put it in the dirty clothes hamper, but for some reason she just kept staring at it.

After a moment she realized why she was staring at it. The dress looked similar to the dress she wore under her robe at her high school graduation. No sooner did her graduation pop into her mind did she wish it hadn't. Violet started to feel her body tremble. That day all the graduating class had white robes with gold sashes. She remembered how happy she was to graduate top of her class. Despite all that she had been through, she would graduate as valedictorian. Her family sat proudly in the audience, at least the ones she loved. Her guardians thankfully chose not to attend.

After giving the valedictorian speech, she felt that she was onto bigger and better things. As she was talking to her friends after the ceremony, her guardians arrived with Ollivander. They told her to tell her friends goodbye because she would never see them again. The family had made arrangements to take her for a celebration dinner at a restaurant called Cuts. It was one of those rare days in her life when she was genuinely happy. When Violet reminded the Lepels of her planned celebration at Cuts, Drusilla laughed, and they immediately demanded that she return home.

Victor told her that she was too fat to be eating such rich food. This insult was followed by him telling her she needed to be on a stricter diet so they could get her married in the next few weeks. When she said she was not going to do what they wanted, Ollivander punched her in the stomach.

Violet touched her belly as the memory made her insides churn. After losing her balance from the impact of the punch, Ollivander threw her over his shoulder. He carried her off as her friends screamed for help.

Her eyes began to water as she remembered how much worse her life had become after that day. All she was allowed to do was sit in her room while waiting to go on another bad date. On top of that, Winston was constantly berating her now even more than he had in the past.

Violet fell to her knees as she thought about how miserable her life had been since the day the Lepels gained control over her life. As a child, she would always lay in her room hungry even though there was a refrigerator full of food downstairs. She was only allowed two very small salads a day made of iceberg lettuce. Even then her family and members of the staff who were nice had to sneak her scraps.

Violet slammed her fist on the ground as she shouted, "Why?!"

After that, she took a moment to calm down, thinking, my *life has been hell ever since those people killed my parents. Why don't the police give a shit about who killed them? Why am I stuck with these horrible people?*

She made herself get off the floor. Then she turned on the sink and cleaned her face. Violet stared at herself in the mirror. She thought, *what is wrong with me? I should be getting ready so I won't be late.*

As Violet turned on the tub water she thought, *maybe this guy will be nice.* While the tub was filling up with water, Violet walked over to the sink and picked up her toothbrush and started to brush her teeth. As she scrubbed her teeth, she thought, *even if he is not, it will still get me away from my guardians. That would be good. Not to mention I bet he has a house so big I'm never going to see him.*

Violet finished brushing her teeth, and then went to check the tub water. She opened one of the cabinets underneath the basin to get some bath soap. Violet picked up rose-scented soap before returning to the tub. After pouring soap into the tub water, she put it back before turning off the water. She then removed her pajamas and climbed into the tub. As Violet washed in the warm waters she thought, *this is the same speech I always give myself before one of these dates. Why do I keep pretending things will work out? Nothing good is ever going to work out for me.*

She told herself to relax. As she leaned back in the tub her mind kept buzzing. Violet wished she would stop stressing. Suddenly, the bathroom door opened and Kinya walked into the room holding some voice recording equipment.

Violet said, "Do you have to do that now? I am trying to take a bath."

Without looking at Violet, Kinya said, "Shut up. If you're unhappy about me being in here, then blame that bitch June. She broke all of the listening devices."

Violet, in a stern tone reprimanded, "Don't talk about my aunt like that."

Kinya snapped back, "What's your dumb ass going to do about it? In fact, I don't want to hear your voice anymore today. So, be fucking quiet while I set this stuff up."

Violet clenched her fist wanting to scream at Kinya. But fear of Ollivander or her guardians punishing her for shouting at Kinya scared her. So, she sat quietly in the tub until Kinya finished setting up the surveillance equipment.

Once Kinya was gone, Violet covered her mouth as she screamed. She wished she hadn't been scared to tell Kinya off, even though she knew that for her own safety, she had to stay quiet.

Violet quickly gave up on trying to relax in the tub. After quickly getting out, she reached over to the shelf next to her tub and grabbed a towel. As she dried herself, she felt her body temperature rising. Once she was dry, Violet screamed into her hands again. Her attention soon set on the listening equipment Kinya just set up.

As if some unknown force took over her body, Violet dropped the towel as she rushed over to the device. Quickly, she ripped it out of the wall and smashed it on the ground. She picked it up and smashed it again and again. Once there were no more pieces to break, she just stared at the broken device.

I don't care if they hit me for this. I don't care if I lose my tiny salad privileges for this. Hell, I don't give a flying fuck if they kill me for this. I am tired of being scared. I am tired of being nervous. I'm tired of starving when I should not fucking have to.

Violet felt a huge smile form on her face. *Wow, this feels good. I don't know why I didn't act sooner, especially with what I got away with last night.* After that thought, she decided to get dressed.

Violet's closet could only be described as a debutant's dream. The two-story room had white walls along with a white carpet floor and a beautiful crystal chandelier hung from the center of the ceiling. Both floors of the room were connected with a curved staircase. The staircase started at the bottom floor's back wall. It then proceeded to meet the center top floor in a way that formed a semi-circle.

The top floor had a massive shelf that took up the entire left wall. It was filled with designer purses. Hanging on a long rail connected to the right wall was a large assortment of designer coats. The coats were organized from summer to winter. Underneath the coats were an assortment of designer heels organized from boot heel to regular heel. In the center of the bottom floor was a large white island with a white marble top. Inside the island were all of Violet's undergarments and jewelry. The left wall had all kinds of designer dresses organized from formal to casual. Lastly, the right wall of the bottom floor was home to Violet's pajamas and bathrobes.

After putting on a white cotton robe, Violet looked at some of her dresses before finally pulling out a strapless pink dress that had a frilly skirt. As an accessory, she chose a black belt with a gold buckle. She placed the dress on top of the island to change into in a little bit. Violet decided she might as well finish planning her outfit before she checked to see how much time she had left to get ready.

She picked out a pair of pink heels to go with her dress. After sitting her high heels next to the island, she began to get dressed. As she put her clothes on, she thought, *I wonder how long it will be before they notice what I did? Who cares? There is nothing left they can do to me.*

Just then she heard a loud beep followed by Ollivander's voice over the house intercom system.

He said, "Miss Evergreen, please come to the dining room. Your father wishes to have a word with you."

Violet took a breath before saying, "Time to face the monster."

Chapter 4
Cursed

The long open hallway had white marble floors and high gray walls. Several white doors led to different rooms, while photographs of Violet's family from both current and past generations hung on the walls.

Violet walked down the hallway for a while before reaching the section of the hall that led downstairs. A grand staircase led to the lower level of the house. As she walked down the stairs, she started to feel an uncomfortable tingling feeling running all over her body. Despite her discomfort, she forced herself to keep moving.

While Violet continued down the stairs, her vision was slowly becoming blurry. The loss of clear vision combined with anxiety caused her to begin hyperventilating. To calm herself she began to repeat, *I will be fine. I will be fine. Just tell him it was not installed properly or something.* Her panicked mind eventually caused her to feel so sick that she was forced to stop her descent and sit down.

As Violet continued to hyperventilate, she closed her eyes in an attempt to stop her growing dizzy feeling. With her eyes still closed, she focused on trying to steady her breathing. Her mind buzzed with every disconcerting scenario of what would happen if she could not fool Victor and Ollivander. She thought, *I'm not going back to being afraid.*

And after that thought, she started to feel her breathing steady. Violet slowly opened her eyes and then continued her descent.

The main area had the same hardwood as the staircase, and the walls were painted a light blue. Just like the upstairs hallway, family photos were hanging from the walls, along with doors that led to different rooms. Without a second thought, she walked into the dining room.

The dining room was large with dark brown hardwood floors and four white walls. Against the left wall was a massive square window. The window had several square panels that allowed a good amount of sunlight to brighten the room. The large windows also afforded a fantastic view of the lake. In the center of the room sat a rectangular dark wooden table that had eight dark wooden chairs with red cushions. Underneath the table was a large red, green, and beige rug with several different circular patterns in the center. Against the right wall on the left side were white doors that led to the kitchen. Hanging in the center of the same wall was a painting of the Serengeti, depicting animals and trees as shadows with a dramatic orange twilight behind them. Sitting at the head of the table was Violet's uncle.

Victor Lepel was enjoying a breakfast of country-fried steak, three fried eggs, bacon, cheese grits, two large Belgian waffles drowning in maple syrup, a cup of white chocolate coffee, and a cup of freshly squeezed orange juice. Ollivander stood in the left corner holding a dishtowel.

Looking at all that food made Violet realize she was hungry, which made her look at her uncle's breakfast with envy until he asked, "Violet, what happened to the microphone in your bathroom?"

Without another thought, she looked him in the eyes as she responded, "I do not know."

"Why don't you know?"

97

With cool efficiency, Violet lied, "I was in my closet getting ready when it fell. My only guess is that it was not installed properly."

Victor looked at Violet with a suspicious gaze. He said in a very calm tone, "So you want me to believe it just fell?"

"No one was in my room, so that is my only guess."

Victor thought for a moment before saying, "Alright."

He ate a little bit of the grits before saying, "There is another problem I wish to address. Last night Ollivander received a call. It was from the young man we paid to go on a date with you. He said he never wanted to see you again. Now, explain what happened."

Immediately, Victor's stare felt completely void of any joy or kindness. Violet had seen this look on her Uncle Victor's face before. She knew if the next words she said did not trick him, then things would get worse for her quickly.

In a calm tone, Violet said, "He was upset because I was not falling for his trick."

Victor slammed his fist on the table, which made Violet jump. "What kind of lie are you attempting to sell me?"

Calmly Violet said, "I'm not stupid enough to try to try to lie to you."

Victor cut into one of his eggs. As the runny yolk spilled out, he said, "You have five seconds to give me a good reason to believe you, or the consequences will be worse than that beating my wife gave you last night."

Violet's heart began to race. *Shit, shit, shit, he is willing to hurt me even though I have a date in a few hours. What am I going to do? No, stop thinking negatively. It never helps you.*

Victor took a sip of coffee before saying, "I'm waiting."

Scared, Violet said, "He was plotting to just go on dates and never consider me for marriage."

In a calm and intimidating tone, Victor said, "Why do you believe he was going to do that?"

"Because he told me that was what he was going to do."

"Explain to me why I should believe you."

In a very confident tone, Violet answered, "Believe what you want. But I'm telling you, that guy you and your wife set me up with told me he was only going to date me and never consider marriage. He even laughed when he told me he was going to have you guys buy him a new suit."

Victor glared at Violet while asking, "Why would I buy him a new suit? The contract for your date stipulates that I only pay for him to go on a date with you and for the date itself?"

Without any hesitation, Violet answered, "You were going to pay for his suit because the first half of our date was going to take place at his tailor, where he was planning on getting several new suits. You have to pay for the date, so you would be responsible for paying for the suits."

Ollivander said, "The young man did say something about Miss Evergreen losing out on waiting for him at his tailor."

That dumbass felt the need to cry about me not waiting at the tailor's? I'm very grateful he's stupid. Now Ollivander's suspicious. If he is suspicious of that guy, then Uncle Victor will be suspicious too.

Victor thought for a moment before saying, "Leave."

As Violet walked out of the room, she felt as if she wanted to dance. For the first time in her life, she had outsmarted one of her captors.

Once she was back in the hallway she started to head upstairs. *I wonder what else I can get away with? I better not jump the gun. Otherwise, they might…"*

Just then she heard Victor scream, "Drusilla, get your fat ass in here now!"

Violet wondered, *why he was mad at her? Better yet, I don't give a shit. If I'm lucky those two will fight all the way to L.A.*

Just then she heard Drusilla scream, "I don't give a damn what she said. If he was not planning to consider her, then we are running out of time. If the deal…"

Victor shouted, "Drusilla, keep your fucking voice down!"

Violet realized, *I need to try to hear what they are saying.* She started to head back downstairs. Before she could reach the bottom step, she heard a male voice say.

"Where do you think you are going, Evergreen? You're supposed to be in your room."

Violet cringed as she turned around and saw the Lepels' other butler Harold standing at the top of the stairs. Harold was a young troll who was the same height as Violet. His skin was blue and very wrinkly. He had a huge nose, and his ears were large and twisted with white hair sticking out of them. Harold had small unwelcoming gray eyes. His head had thin patches of almost nonexistent gray hair. His small hands had very sharp long claws.

He was dressed similar to Ollivander. The only difference other than the outfit size was that he was wearing tennis shoes.

I need to get away from him quickly if I hope to hear anything. But I can't listen at the door with him here. I can try going into the room next door to the

100

dining room. But I need to make sure he doesn't follow me. He does get distracted when he is mad. I'll make him angry, but I must be careful to keep him from clawing my face. If I piss him off, he will attack or stomp off in anger.

She said, "I was on my way back to my room, but I am a little thirsty. So, I was going to head into the kitchen to get some water."

Harold replied, "You are not allowed in the kitchen. You eat too much, fat ass."

Violet replied with anger, "Dumb shit, how am I supposed to get into the fridge when there is a spell on it to make sure I can't touch it? Get out of my way so I can have my water."

The second she called Harold dumb, she felt her whole-body tingling. No matter how mean they were to her, she had never been harsh with her guardians' staff. It made her feel like she was taking control of her life.

As for Harold, he looked at Violet as if she had just slapped him. He squeezed his fist as he hissed, "What did you just say?"

Violet snapped, "You heard me, fool. Why don't you get back to cleaning or whatever the hell you do around here? If I catch you lollygagging any longer, I'm going to let my guardians know."

Harold gritted his teeth as he extended his claws. Violet noticed his eyes slowly turn red. She knew that meant he was about to strike.

Out of nowhere, a familiar female voice said, "Harold, what has gotten into you?"

Violet then saw the daughter of the Wilds' head butler. Janet was the same age as Violet, and they had been friends since they were small. Yet another painful chapter in Violet's life; she and Janet were not allowed to chat.

Janet had smooth dark chocolate brown skin and hazelnut eyes. Her hair was full of thick black curls that had been picked out into a small afro. She was wearing a powder blue headband and a black suit and tie. A pair of comfortable black leather flat shoes adorned her feet.

Knowing how much Janet hated wearing non-colorful clothes, Violet took Janet's attire as a sign Janet had joined the household staff and was working with her father. To take over his role one day was something Violet knew Janet always wanted to do.

In a harsh tone, Harold said, "Shut up, Janet. Miss Evergreen's attitude is going to stop right now."

Janet folded her arms and smiled. Her reaction seemed to surprise Harold because he retracted his claws for a split second.

He said, "Stop this smart-ass behavior or I..."

Janet snapped, "You will what? Hit her? She has a date in a few hours. Do you think the man the Lepels' paid for her to go out with wants a woman scarred? I'll tell you right now, no. Now get the hell out of her face."

Harold looked as if he was about to say something. Instead, he stomped off.

Violet wanted to stay and chat with Janet; however, she knew that she had to hurry if she wanted to hear what the Lepels were saying. She started to open her mouth when Janet quickly said, "You're welcome. Now hurry and grab a bite before the Lepels get out here."

Knowing she didn't have time to explain, Violet quickly headed towards the kitchen without a second glance.

The kitchen had a marble floor. The walls were painted a light gray color. All the kitchen cabinets were a dark gray, and against the front wall was a stainless-steel stove. The stove sat proudly in between two cabinets that had quartz countertops. On the end of the left wall was a gray door that led to the pantry. Sitting in between two cabinets with white quartz countertops was a large three-door stainless steel refrigerator. In the center of the room was a gray island with a countertop made of gray quartz in its center was a vase filled with daffodils.

Please, oh please, let them still be talking about whatever they are trying to hide.

Her heart started to beat rapidly as she quickly put her ear to the wall. It was tough to hear, but eventually she could make out the muffled voices in the other room.

Drusilla said, "But we only have till the end of this year."

Victor replied, "I know that. You don't have to keep repeating it. Thankfully, the brat is still in the dark, so we don't have to worry about our plan getting spoiled."

Drusilla continued, "I know she doesn't remember her aunt or the others. I just keep stressing out about how much time we have left to marry the brat off."

I have another aunt? At least I think that is what she means. Who are these others?

Victor said, "After your blunder last night…"

Drusilla laughed as she interrupted, "My blunder? You're the one who hired Winston after I warned you not to."

"I admit giving Winston another chance to prove himself was a mistake."

Drusilla continued, "You're fucking right it was a mistake. Now I've got to let Meg handle the little bitch's hair."

Victor questioned, "What are you talking about?"

Drusilla explained, "I had to agree to let Meg be the only one allowed to control styling Violet's hair from now on. Otherwise, the family won't help us save face after what happened last night."

"Why does that upset you? It's one less thing you have to worry about."

In an exasperated tone, Drusilla said, "When Meg begins spending more time with Violet, the brat will start becoming more defiant. You know the family is always looking for ways to make Violet rebel against us."

"If you're worried Violet getting more family time will make her misbehave, then why did you allow them to give her a phone?"

"I thought that would be obvious to you. Winston's drinking was getting more and more out of control, so I had to let them give her the cellphone."

Victor shouted, "Bullshit! You could have given her a cellphone that only allowed her to speak with us."

"Victor, she is rightfully scared of us. If Winston got her in trouble, the brat would have taken a chance on wandering around the city alone at night. Rather than ask us for help."

Victor snapped, "That's crap. The tracker would activate if she tried something like that."

"No, it would not."

"Why?"

"At Violet's last checkup the tracker spell was removed."

In a shocked tone, Victor snapped, "Why the fuck didn't you tell me?"

In a calm tone, Drusilla explained, "I was worried you would have told Winston, and he might have told Violet in one of his drunken stupors."

Victor agreed, "Fair point, but why did the tracker get deactivated?"

Drusilla continued, "Violet's magic has gotten stronger. It started to weaken the tracker to the point that she would be able to remove it on her own. I spoke to Judge Hendrickson, and he told me if it wasn't removed by a doctor, then Violet would figure out she has the power to remove it on her own."

"Why not just put another tracker on her?"

"There is no magic wielder on our side strong enough to put a more powerful tracker spell on her."

"Hmmm, I guess as long as she doesn't know what we know, then it is fine. Can we get back to the real problem? Drusilla, just trust me. No matter what, she will be married before time runs out."

"How are you so sure?"

Violet heard Ollivander's voice, "Sir and madam, I am sorry to interrupt, but the two of you should be getting ready to leave."

Drusilla said, "He's right. We need to go."

Violet heard what she assumed was them walking out of the room. She thought, *dammit, I wanted to hear Uncle Victor's plan.*

105

Violet then walked over to the counter and sat down. *How did I not know the tracker spell had been taken off? Forget it, I need to tell the family about it. They could probably use this knowledge to hide me somewhere safe.*

An uncomfortable tingling feeling started to sweep through her body. It made her feel a little dizzy, so in response she put her hand on her forehead and laid her face on the counter. After a minute she continued to think, *I always thought about getting far away from this house. But for some reason, I don't wish to go. I guess I just don't want to leave everyone. Really, if someone should leave, it's the Lepels. This is my home, not theirs. I'm being stupid. If I just take off, then I can get away and not have to worry about marrying some bastard that I don't know or love. But if I run away, then my family might get in trouble.*

She tried to think about what she should do, when Hattie May walked into the kitchen. She was holding the dirty dishes from Victor's breakfast. Hattie May looked at Violet and asked what was wrong. Violet sat up and looked at her. Part of Violet wanted to tell Hattie May everything she heard. But something told her to keep quiet about Victor and Drusilla's conversation. Instead, Violet told her how she tricked Victor.

Hattie May smiled as she said, "Good. That dummy deserved it for eating your breakfast."

"That was for me?"

"Of course! It's your birthday, girl."

"Oh, right. It's my birthday."

Hattie May questioned, "How did you forget?"

"The Lepels are very good at making my birthdays miserable."

"Are you remembering how until the Wilds started selling your gifts for charity, Drusilla and Victor used to set your presents on fire?"

106

Violet replied, "No, I don't really care about presents. It's because they ruin my party, or at least make it worse. I'm always so hungry that I barely have any fun."

Hattie May put the dishes in the sink as she said, "Let's put an end to the hunger problem."

"Miss Hattie May, you're not supposed to feed me. They nearly got you arrested the last time you tried to give me food."

Hattie said in an exasperated tone, "Violet, a young woman needs to eat. Plus, I'm angry with Victor for tricking me. I was really mad about what Drusilla did last night, so I told him I was going to retire because they make my job too difficult."

"I would miss you, but it makes sense. The Lepels have made it almost impossible for you to enjoy cooking on the property."

"I hate having to always let the Lepels inspect how much food I make, just so your family won't sneak you a proper dinner. That makes me not enjoy cooking for them, but I can't risk them cutting off your salads again. If they do, they are not getting one more bite of anything I cook."

"It makes me wonder why they threatened to have you arrested for making me chicken soup."

"Sweetheart, that whole attempted arrest was just a cheap scare tactic."

Hattie May pulled some eggs out of the fridge. She continued to say, "Anyway, Victor begged me not to retire. He even told me he would make it up to me by letting me make you a birthday breakfast. After I cooked a practical feast, Ollivander came in. He told me the nice breakfast I made was no longer for you because you had been bad. I knew it was crap, but as you know, it isn't a good idea to fight with Ollivander."

107

Violet chimed in, "The Lepels need to learn they can't keep intimidating people."

Hattie May started cutting up vegetables as she said, "I know. Right now, there is not much we can do."

A thought popped into Violet's mind. If she had become powerful enough to disable the tracker, then *maybe I can get rid of the limiter spell as well. If I can do that, they can't hurt me anymore.* Doubt crept into her thoughts. *Or am I just assuming things?*

They also mentioned the judge. Why is he the only judge who gets to rule on my case? My family has gone to court over my situation twelve times. I wish I knew who could answer all the questions I have. My mind is cloudy, and I can't think clearly.

Hattie May said, "Don't worry, kiddo. The food will be ready in a minute."

At that moment Violet could smell sausage cooking, which made her realize her stomach was growling.

Hattie May said, "You look like you're trying to figure something out. I'll tell you right now, no one can think with an empty belly."

A little more time passed before Hattie May gave Violet a large plate with an omelet, sausage, and bacon.

Hattie May smiled as she said, "Happy birthday."

Violet's eyes glittered as she thanked her. She cut into her egg before she delighted in the taste of her fluffy omelet. Meanwhile, Hattie May was playing lookout in case anyone who would try to stop Violet from eating showed up.

As Violet took a big bite of bacon, she thought, *the judge. Aunt Drusilla said he was the one who told her to have the tracker secretly removed. Oh, shit, my doctor was the one who secretly removed it. He has been my doctor since I was born. The man even lectured the Lepels to be nicer to me. If he is involved in helping them keep me captive, who else is involved?*

Violet finished her bacon and began polishing off her omelet. Hattie said, "Crap, it's that Kinya bitch."

Quickly, she rushed over to Violet and collected her plate. She sat it next to the sink before filling a glass of water. She handed it to Violet before starting to rinse off some dishes that were in the sink.

Violet took a sip of water while thinking, *dammit. I really wanted to finish that. Oh well, at least I ate enough to hold off till I can get something else.*

Kinya walked into the kitchen with a smirk on her face. She looked at Hattie May for a second. Then she turned her attention to Violet.

In a cold voice, she said, "I heard you like to be a little smart ass."

Wanting Kinya to leave, Violet said, "What kind of crap are you trying to start?"

Kinya continued, "I'm not trying to start anything. You were the one harassing poor Harold."

"It is not my fault the moron was trying to stop me from having water."

"As fat as you are, you should be avoiding water."

Violet raised an eyebrow as she said, "What are you talking about?"

Using a smug tone Kinya spoke, "You'll gain a ton of water weight from drinking water, dumbass. And believe me, water weight is harder to lose than fat."

Violet wondered to herself, *how stupid are you, Kinya?*

Hattie May folded her arms as she looked at Kinya with a puzzled expression. Hattie May said, "Kinya, were you just born crazy?"

Kinya stuck her tongue out at Hattie May, which made Hattie May frown while Violet started to think Kinya had the mind of a four-year-old.

Kinya said, "Whatever. I'm only here because Mrs. Lepel wants the brat to go to her room."

Hattie May asked, "Why?"

Kinya stated, "The hell if I know. It is just what I was told to do. So, get moving, brat. Or I'll get Ollivander in here."

Violet clenched her fist as she thought about attacking Kinya. She told herself to keep her cool. The conversation she heard left her with a lot to think about. So, it wasn't the best idea for her to teach Kinya a lesson right now, but she promised herself the next time Kinya was a bitch to her, she would make her regret it.

Violet got up from the counter. As she headed out of the kitchen, Kinya smiled as if she had won something. Kinya's smug expression made Violet yearn even more for the day when she would put Kinya in her place.

After walking into her room, Violet checked her clock. She still had three hours before she would have to leave for her date. So, she lay down on her bed to try and think. After a few minutes, she started to realize her mind was all over the place.

Who is this aunt? What is the judge getting out of this? Why do I have to be wed before the year is out? There is also that cause Uncle Victor mentioned.

Violet turned her attention to her vanity. She hadn't forgotten her aunt's plea for her to check her vanity, where she could collect the plan to ruin her date. Earlier, Violet let fear stop her from challenging her guardians. But after what she had heard, she realized that she had some power. She didn't fully understand how much power or how to use it, but she had it. That meant that for her not to begin taking a more active role in fighting back was stupid. After her dear aunt almost killed her last night, she had to learn to protect herself. More importantly, she had to find out the Lepels' secrets and get rid of them.

She jumped up and looked in the direction of the camera monitoring her room. Violet noticed that while she was downstairs it had been replaced. She headed into the bathroom. Once she was in her bathroom she sat down on the edge of her tub. She looked around and saw that the listening device hadn't been replaced.

I'm glad I checked to see if they replaced the camera. I can try to use weak magic to knock the camera down. That would probably get Kinya in trouble, so I should do that.

She took a breath before whispering a spell to knock the camera off the wall. After a few seconds, she heard something fall. She got up and walked back into her room.

Violet looked at the broken camera on the floor. She wondered if the point of all the spy equipment was not about watching her. Her aunts, uncles, Meg, and Meg's husband were always breaking them when they snuck into her room. Maybe the whole point of the surveillance equipment was just to intimidate her. It made a lot of sense. As long as she thought they were watching her, she wouldn't leave her room without permission. Nor would she attempt to sneak in friends. More importantly, she wouldn't practice her magic and learn that her powers were becoming stronger.

Violet turned her attention back to her vanity. She walked over and opened the drawer. Her heart raced with excitement as she opened the drawer to find it was completely empty. She reached into the drawer thinking that her aunt June had placed an invisibility curse on her instructions. However, when she reached inside the drawer, she couldn't feel anything.

Where are the instructions? Aunt June said she was going to leave details of her plan. Shit, my guardians' staff must have found them. I bet it was Harold who did it- his way of getting back at me- petty bastard. The thought that her guardians knew about Aunt June's plan caused Violet to feel a twinge of panic.

At that moment her bedroom door swung open, and Ollivander raced in. He quickly grabbed Violet's left arm. He squeezed her arm so tightly Violet feared he was going to break it. She begged him to let her go, but he ignored her plea. He scanned her arm for a moment then pushed her as he finally let her go.

The second Violet hit the ground, despite the pain, she quickly got up. She saw Ollivander feeling around in her vanity drawer. After a minute, he slammed it shut.

He glared at Violet as he shouted, "Did you break that camera?"

Violet's voice shook as she told him she did not. Ollivander took a breath before saying, "Alright, alright." Then he stormed out of the room.

Violet sat down on her bed. *What the fuck was that? No one ever rushes in that fast when the spy equipment breaks.*

112

She then remembered what Drusilla said about her powers getting stronger, which made her wonder if they were scared. Violet wondered if Ollivander knew that her powers were growing. Did he know that she was strong enough to break the limiter spell? Her thought process quickly turned to Ollivander digging through her drawer.

Violet walked over to her vanity. She reached into the drawer to see if she was somehow mistaken about it being empty. She had learned over the years that her Aunt June was always two steps ahead of her guardians and their staff. When she reached inside, this time she felt something inside of the drawer. She still didn't see anything inside, believing now that she had been correct in her thinking earlier that the object had been made invisible. When she felt the edge of the object, she pulled it out. The very moment she pulled it out the object became visible. This shocked Violet despite her realization that a spell had made the object invisible.

As she took a better look at the object, she noticed it was a rectangular pink box with a silver bow on top. After opening it, she saw a new cellphone and some red capsules. She took the phone out of the box. When she turned it on, she immediately looked in her contacts. Her family, along with her friends' numbers, were programmed in the phone.

A tear fell from Violet's eye. When she wiped it away, she thought, *I never expected this. My guardians said I wasn't allowed to have friends anymore. I thought I would never get to talk to any of my friends again.*

Her attention turned back to the box. She noticed a note and a black card. After removing the paper from the box, she began to read it.

Violet, after you read this note, destroy it immediately. If you're wondering why you did not find this box immediately, it was because I was worried that someone else would find this box before you. So, I cast a spell not only making it invisible, but that it would not become solid until you reached into the drawer a second time. You have most likely noticed the new cell phone and onyx card. I know you heard me scream this at my stupid sister, but you are an adult now and since my sister and that idiot she is married to insist on sending

113

you on dates with strange men, you really need to always have a cellphone. The credit card is your birthday gift from the family- yet another privilege that goes with turning nineteen.

Violet quickly picked up the black card. While she examined it, smiling, Violet thought, *hallelujah! I can get used to a no-limit credit card. Well, it does make sense. Meg got her card when she went to college.* Once again, she turned her attention to the note.

Make sure to always keep both your phone and new credit card hidden. More importantly, I want you to hide the pills in the box in your purse. Be very careful with them. Those pills are fake blood capsules. During your date, chew the capsules to make your date think you have hemophilia. Knowing the type of man my sister will set you up with, fooling him will not be hard. After your date leaves, demand to be taken to the family hospital. When you arrive, we are going to have to have a serious talk. Also, do not worry about the new driver. He works for us, not my bitch sister and her husband.

Love, Aunt June

Violet performed a spell to incinerate the note with the envelope. *I wonder what Auntie June wants to tell me. Then again, she might be able to answer some of the questions spinning around in my head concerning the conversation that she had heard between her guardians earlier. More importantly, how did they get a driver who wasn't blindly loyal to my guardians?*

Chapter 5
It's Good to have Friends

Deciding that it would be wise not to carry her new credit card, Violet hid it in one of her purses in her closet. When she returned to her room, she picked up the cellphone. She started to wonder how she could hide it on her person. Because Drucilla had found her last phone in her purse, she knew that it was too risky to keep her new phone in the same location. While she tried to decide on what to do, she started to download a few apps. She figured whenever she wanted to use the apps, she could do it in her closet. As long as she kept the phone on silent, she didn't have to fear anyone hearing it ring. While the apps were still downloading, she checked the time. She still had two hours and a half before she had to leave. Normally it annoyed her that Kinya would wake her up way too early. But, after everything that had happened so far, she was more than a little grateful that the idiot had gotten her up early.

As she looked through her apps, a notification from her news app popped up. Because her knowledge about what was going on in the world had been restricted for so long, she decided to click on the notification. When the article popped up, she read.

The ongoing demon crisis has hit a new high as Australia becomes the fourth country to be overrun. Their prime minister has stated that he fully intends to take their country back from the demon surge. Despite his declaration, many Australians blame the prime minister for the demon takeover because it was the prime minster who deported the nation's five Eden Witches. Many survivors even say that the prime minister forced the Eden Witches to leave because they were determined to prioritize protecting the lower and middle classes. The prime minister on the other hand says that the Eden Witches he deported were the ones opening demon voids. His only evidence of this is his statement that because the Eden Witches were Aborigines, they were plotting to use the demons to chase true Australians out of Australia. Many Australian citizens, including the Eden Witches of Australia, say that the prime minister is lying. They claim that the prime minister told the Eden Witches that if they exclusively protect him and many of his associates, then they would not be deported. Currently, many Australians who escaped the danger in their own country have escaped to England and New Zealand. As for the Eden Witches of Australia, three have stated that they plan to sneak back into Australia to eliminate the monsters. They also said that their sisters that were not at the interview had already gone back to Australia. The interviewer asked them if they thought it was wise to publicly state that they were heading back to their home country. In response, they said the prime minister was not and in fact could not do anything to stop them. He himself had already escaped from the country in hopes that the military would take care of the problem. At best, despite the army's efforts, without the help of Australia's Eden Witches, the military will most likely be eliminated by the demons in a month.

Violet stopped reading and put her phone down. The article reminded her of what Meg told her about the walled cities last night. This made her wonder why so many world leaders were trying to get the Eden Witches to exclusively protect them. Violet like everyone else knew that this group of Witches were needed on the front lines. They were the world's last line of defense against the demons.

Feeling overwhelmed by all the information she had consumed in the last few hours, Violet decided to search through the game apps on her phone, figuring that playing a game for a while would help her to relax.

Violet then heard a tapping noise at her window. She looked away from her phone to see what was causing the noise. The sound was coming from a small bright pink light shaped in a circular ball. Violet thought for a moment before she realized the glowing pink ball outside her window was her friend Zhang Li. Immediately, she rushed over to the window and as soon as she opened it, the glowing pink ball rushed inside.

Violet closed the window. As she turned around, she heard a small pop. Zhang Li appeared before her in human form wearing a pink sequin dress. Zhang Li was a fairy with lovely violet, pink and blue-colored wings. Her wings were like those of a butterfly, but much larger. Her hair was jet black and tied up in a ponytail held together with a pink butterfly clip. Zhang Li's eyes were an exquisite shade of black that always appeared to glitter in the light. Her eyes complemented her warm skin tone. The tiny nose on her face hung above a smile that could bring joy to the saddest person.

She hugged Violet while saying, "Happy birthday!"

Excited to see her friend after such a long time, Violet hugged her as she replied, "Thank you."

After the hug Zhang Li said, "I know it's been a while, but how have you been holding up. Your guardians haven't been too cruel, have they?"

Violet responded, not wanting to think of her guardians at such a happy moment, "Don't worry about them. How have things been going for you?"

"I'll tell you all about that at your party later, but first, presents."

Violet thought, *my friends, are coming to my party.* This news made her smile.

Zhang Li clapped her hands, and a small pink cloud appeared for a moment before popping and turning into a large circular metal box hovering in the air. As the box hovered silently in the air, Violet quickly reached for it to see what was inside. The moment she touched it, the box felt so cold it stung her fingers, and she immediately pulled her hands away.

117

Zhang Li said, "Careful, my grandmother put an ice enchantment on it so that the food would stay cold."

Violet's smile widened, and with anticipation she asked, "There's food in there?"

Zhang Li replied, "Since you're not allowed to come over to my house anymore, my grandmother is terrified that your guardians have you at death's door. To be frank, now that I can see how skinny you've gotten, I guess she had good reason to worry."

Violet, in an effort to reassure her friend, said, "Don't be scared. My family and several members of the staff, who don't work for my guardians, still sneak me food."

Zhang Li complained, "Violet, it is still not enough. So, anyway, the tin has three compartments. The first compartment is full of both leek and mushroom pan-fried buns. The second compartment is stuffed with vegetable dumplings."

"Really? Yum."

"I'm glad you're excited about it. And finally, the last compartment is filled to the brim with homemade peach-vanilla ice cream."

Violet clapped, laughed out loud, and said, "Great! Tell your grandmother I said thank you."

Zhang Li reminded Violet, "No problem, but we need to find a place to hide it."

Violet suggested, "I guess I could enchant it to look like one of my handbags."

Zhang Li, unsure, questioned, "What if one of their servants touch your handbags?"

"They won't. About two years ago one of the Lepels' servants stole several pieces of my jewelry. After that Ollivander ordered them not to touch anything in my closet."

Zhang Li responded, "I'm surprised he is protective of your things."

Violet smirked, "He's not. When I am married, the Lepels want to sell all of my belongings."

Zhang Li continued, "Oh, don't bring up them and marriage. Their crazy is sucking the excitement of my own wedding plans."

"Sorry. How is the wedding planning going?"

"Don't apologize. It is not your fault they are crazy."

Part of Violet felt that if she spoke to Zhang Li about what was going on, it might help her figure some things out. But once again something told her to keep what she learned to herself.

Zhang Li continued, "Anyway, you have no way of knowing. Jin and I decided to put things on hold till after college."

"Why?

"Not for any big reason." Zhang Li, using her regular tone signifying to Violet that the information she was about to share was no big deal, "Trying to plan a wedding while going to college was causing problems for our relationship. So, we decided to push things back till we graduate." Zhang Li smiled as she continued, "After we decided to wait, our love was renewed, and things got really good again."

Knowing that she should hide her gift, Violet said an incantation. However, Zhang Li stopped her. She told Violet to let her do the spell to ensure the limiter would not activate.

Zhang Li snapped her fingers, and a pink ball of light engulfed the metal box. It dissipated very quickly, revealing a red hoop bag. Violet picked up the bag, which felt cold as ice. As she placed it on her bed, Zhang Li told her if she opens the bag, it will turn back into the box. When she closes it then the box will turn back into a handbag.

Violet said, "Thanks, Zhang Li. I appreciate it."

"No problem."

"I was wondering, how did you sneak onto the property," Violet asked. "My guardians altered the security spell on the property to keep my friends out."

"It was hard to get around the security spell," Zhang Li said with pride. "But you know, girl, your friends', geniuses that we are, found a way."

"What do you mean by we?"

Zhang Li explained, "Sorry, I forgot to mention that Jackson, Tawanda, and Janet helped me get past the security spell. If I'm being honest, it was mostly Tawanda who found the solution. She discovered a spell that can bypass home security spells."

"You're lying!" Violet said she couldn't believe how many things seemed to be lining up in her favor.

"I know the whole thing feels like a deus ex machina. She found the spell when she was searching for a cleaning spell."

Curious, Violet questioned, "Why did she need a cleaning spell? It is not like cleaning enchantments are very effective."

"No big reason. Her little brother accidentally knocked over a tiny Meyer lemon tree on her coffee table. He was playing with his toy cars while waiting for her parents to pick him up. You know how five-year olds can be when they get lost in their imaginary worlds. She had to clean up the mess because it was the staff's day off. Tawanda said that her vacuum is a piece of crap. In truth, she probably didn't know how to work the vacuum. I love the girl, but let's face it, Tawanda has never done a day's house cleaning in her life. Anyway, when she found the spell in her family's grimoire, she asked her folks about it. They were more than a little shocked to see it in there."

"Why were they surprised?"

Zhang Li explained, "Her dad's family is the one that owns the grimoire. As you know, all the wealthiest witch and warlock families have grimoires. Tawanda's family grimoire was created for the construction spells and cleaning spells, and that made her family rich. Apparently, no one noticed there was a third type of enchantment."

Violet responded, "Interesting."

Zhang Li continued, "After she found the spell, she said that she immediately thought of you. So, she called our crew together to help her test it out. We figured we could surprise you before the party. But the opening the spell created was a very small opening. Since I'm the only one who can shrink, it was obvious that I would be the only one to come inside. Besides, I had to deliver the food my grandmother made for you…"

Violet smiled, "I'm amazed all of you were able to pull that off."

Zhang Li said, "Me, too! The entire time I was sneaking in, I was scared of getting caught."

Violet began, "Speaking of that, one of my guardians could…"

Out of nowhere, both women heard Drusilla scream, "Violet, where the hell are you?!"

Before Violet could blink, Zhang Li turned back into a pink ball of light and snatched Violet's cellphone, before flying under her bed. Without warning, Drusilla swung open Violet's bedroom door so hard the knob left a hole in the wall.

She looked at Violet with a murderous gaze in her eyes. As she pointed at her she said, "Et semen maledictum proles et anima dissoluta richus punsment omnium aeternum."

There was a flash of yellow light, followed by Violet feeling so dizzy she fell to her knees.

In a smug tone, Drusilla said, "I bet you thought you were so smart when my husband fell for that pack of lies you fed him. Well, guess what, bitch. I'm not as dumb as he is. That ass beating I gave you clearly didn't teach you anything. Now, I must take extreme measures."

A very nauseous Violet said, "What did you do to me?"

Drusilla walked over to Violet and knelt so she could meet her at eye level.

She stared at Violet for a moment with a blank face before saying in a cold voice, "The name of your date is Patterson Westing. My spell will make you do whatever he says no matter what it is. You'll be forced to be polite to him, you can't willingly try to run away from his companionship, and you can never hurt him even if it's in self-defense."

Violet, with fear in her voice, asked, "Why are you doing this to me? I don't deserve this."

Drusilla laughed hard at Violet before saying, "You are nothing more than the unholy seed. That woman who tricked my brother into marriage created you, the devil's spawn. Before I go don't even think about running down the hall to get help. My spell prevents you from telling anyone about it."

After that, she stood upright and looked down at her adoptive daughter with pure disgust. Drusilla then kicked Violet hard in the side. Violet rolled over in pain from the kick, while Drusilla laughed as she headed out of the room.

When she was sure that Drusilla was gone, Zhang Li came from under the bed and returned to human form. She then helped Violet get into her bathroom. Zhang Li examined Violet who sat on the edge of her tub. Zhang Li thought for a moment before running to get Violet's phone. After a few minutes, she came back into the bathroom.

She stomped her foot before saying, "I tried calling for help, but no one picked up. Now I really wish I had brought my phone with me."

She then started to pace back and forth, trying to think of a way to solve the problem. Violet, who was both dizzy and nauseous, remained quiet trying not to throw up.

Frustrated with the situation Zhang Li said, "Dammit, I'm a pre-med student- I should know how to fix this."

In a soft tone, Violet replied, "Zhang Li, you only have one year of college. You probably won't learn how to counter complex curses until you're in med school."

Zhang Li answered, "I know, but I feel that I should know how to counter this."

Violet in a soft tone replied, "Don't worry about countering the spell. Just try to call for help again."

"Alright."

After using Violet's phone four times to get ahold of someone, Zhang Li gave up on her efforts to call for help. Frustrated, Zhang Li suggested she try to find Violet's aunts June or Meg. But Violet reminded her that it was too risky. If she was caught, her adoptive parents or their staff would have her arrested for trespassing.

Zhang Li said, "Dammit, it will probably be time for you to leave soon. By the time I can get help, your date will have you signing a marriage contract, or worse."

Violet in a hopeful tone stated, "He, he may not like how I look and abruptly leave."

Zhang Li said, "Violet, I don't want to leave whether or not you're forced to marry to chance. Let me think. There must be a way to get you out of this. Unless, maybe, the way she said that curse it sounded like she was combining multiple small hexes."

Violet stated, "Maybe, I feel too ill to think clearly."

Zhang Li said, "Even if I'm wrong, it's probably still worth trying."

Violet asked, "What's worth trying?"

Without a word, Zhang Li placed her index finger onto Violet's forehead before saying, "Stabiliendum."

A bright pink light flashed from her fingertip for less than a second. After that, she put her hand down as Violet felt her dizziness and nausea begin to quickly go away.

Zhang Li asked, "How are you feeling?"

In a more relaxed tone, Violet answered, "The sick feeling is starting to vanish."

Zhang Li in a congratulatory tone said, "At least I was able to ease the side effects of her spell before you throw up."

Violet said, "Please don't make me think about that. I still feel a little sick."

"Sorry."

In a grateful tone, Violet replied, "It's ok. Besides, I guess having to deal with this is what I deserve. I should have just sucked it up and not upset my date yesterday."

Zhang Li in a somewhat hesitant tone said, "I admit I was not going to bring the video up because I was not sure how that incident affected you. But come on Violet, these people torment you for no damn reason. So, if last night stopped them from getting what they want, then that's really good."

Violet suddenly remembered how her aunt mentioned giving Winston a chance for a cause. She had already had a feeling that whatever the cause was it was bad. It also made her suspect that her getting married was a big part of it.

Violet said, "I guess you're right, but it doesn't change the fact that I just got cursed to obey my date. That bitch even made it so I can't defend myself if he tries to force himself on me."

"I know. Anyway, we don't exactly have time to ponder the insanity of your guardians. Let me try something else really quickly."

Zhang Li placed her palm on Violet's forehead and said, "In hoc quod humilem puer dimittere sigillum Dei omnipotentis."

Zhang Li's palm glowed pink for a moment. After which she removed her hand and Violet asked, "What did you do?"

"Your aunt cast a spell lock when she cursed you. I just tried casting a spell to try and remove it."

"Did it work?"

"I don't know but we are about to find out."

"What ar…"

Zhang Li held up her left hand and snapped. Out of nowhere a small golden rod with a pink gemstone at the top appeared in her hand. Before Violet could react, Zhang Li pointed her staff directly at Violet's face and said, "Hanc maledictionem injuste dejectus."

An overwhelming pink light shot out of the top of the crystal that was so bright it shined throughout the entire room. Violet was forced to close her eyes. After a minute the light finally dissipated and Zhang Li tossed the rod in the air, and it instantly disappeared.

Once her rod was gone Zhang Li said, "Violet, the spell is finished. You can open your eyes."

A slightly annoyed Violet asked, "Zhang Li, why did you not warn me you were going to use your fairy scepter?"

"Sorry, Violet. But unlike witch magic, fairy magic is more potent when the person having the spell cast on them is unaware."

"What kind of spell did you cast?"

"I cast a spell to try to take that curse off you, silly. Anyway, what do you think of Patterson Westing?"

Violet frowned while thinking. *He most likely is a pretentious prick who will cry for his mommy when he does not get his way.*

Then she answered, "I think Mr. Westing is most likely a delightful man."

As soon as Violet finished her sentence, she was shocked by what she said. *Why did I just say something nice about him?*

Violet said, "I have no idea why I said that. What I think of this Patterson Westing guy I'm going out with later, is that he's a wonderful human being. I'm very lucky, no, privileged to have the chance to be in his presence."

Surprised by her continued praise of the man she was being forced to go out with, she said, "Why did I just say that?"

In a frustrated tone, Zhang Li answered, "That stupid curse is still on you. So, you can't give an honest impression of how you currently feel about Westing. However, there is hope you didn't call him your unquestioned master. Looks like the counter spell I just cast has weakened the curse, enough for you not to have to agree to whatever he wants. You might also be able to tell people about it now."

Violet thought, *I'm glad I can tell him no. But my inability to be rude to him may prevent me from..."* suddenly she remembered her Aunt June's instructions. In an angry voice she shouted, "Crap!"

She stood up and retrieved one of the blood capsules. Violet paused for a moment before attempting to put the capsule in her mouth. As her hand moved closer to her lips her body suddenly started shaking and she dropped the pill. In response, she knelt down to retrieve the pill but found herself unable to grasp it in her hand.

Zhang Li walked over, asking as she retrieved the pill from the floor, "Is this some kind of medicine?"

Violet responded, "No, it's a fake blood pill."

"Why are you trying to eat it?"

"My Aunt June gave it to me to help me ruin my date."

"Oh, I see. Your aunt is starting to get bolder when it comes to interfering with your guardians."

A frustrated Violet announced, "Doesn't help when I can't go through with her plan."

Zhang Li asked, "Do you have nail clippers?"

"Yes, why?"

Zhang Li thoughtfully said, "I am going to have to take some of your nails to your family hospital. Your Aunt June, or my dad if he is there, can hopefully take the rest of that curse off you."

Violet got her nail clippers from the bathroom. After clipping all her nails, she put the clippings into a plastic sandwich bag that was in one of the bathroom drawers, and she gave it to Zhang Li.

The two women then went back into Violet's bedroom. Zhang Li opened the window to leave. Before Violet could thank her friend, Zhang Li turned back into a ball of light and flew out of the room.

After Violet closed the window, she thought, *it's probably going to take my aunt the whole day to make a serum to get rid of this curse. Dammit, why does Aunt Drusilla have to be so evil? Keep it together. I can't let myself fall to pieces over this.* Violet looked at the clock and saw that she needed to start heading to her date.

Chapter 6
The Driver

After retrieving her small pink clutch and hiding her new phone and credit card in her bra, Violet was ready to go. As she walked to her bedroom door, she thought, *it will be ok. Remember what the note said about the driver.*

As Violet walked down the hall to get to the garage, she said, "Patterson Westing is the smartest man in the world."

In response to what she said, Violet took a breath. *Darn it, that wasn't what I wanted to say. Why can't this curse just wear off?*

Violet reached the section of the house that had an elevator that led to the garage which was underneath the house. As she waited for the elevator, she continued to think, *I wonder why Aunt Drusilla took the time to curse me. I would just blame it on her weird desire to marry me off.*

The elevator arrived and after Violet got inside, she pushed the button for the garage, which was located on the bottom floor. *I know she said that cursing me was to stop me from screwing up my date, but knowing the initial effect it had on me, I don't think that was her goal. I felt so sick I could barely walk. If Zhang Li hadn't been there and done what she did, then I would probably have stayed lying on the floor of my room until someone walked in.*

The elevator arrived at the bottom floor and as she stepped out, she headed for the garage entrance because that was where the chauffeur was supposed to be waiting for her. The garage was like a second mansion Violet's family had built for their cars. The top floor of the garage housed a car wash along with a station to either scrub the outside of a car or vacuum it.

All the other floors of the garage were made to house specific cars from the family's collection. The cars on the second level of the garage were all high-end sports cars. Only a few were driven regularly. The third level housed expensive cars that could carry several people such as different types of limos, SUVs, and four-wheel drives. On the bottom floor were different hybrid cars that Violet and her family members used for transport, except for her guardians.

Suddenly, she heard an unfamiliar man's voice ask, "Miss, are you finally ready to leave?"

As soon as she heard the question, she looked in the direction of the voice and saw an elf standing in front of a red Prius.

The elf had dark brown skin, and he possessed a pair of very pointy ears. His long hair was a dark blue styled in dreadlocks. Like many elves, his hair was long and stretched to the center of his back. He had kind looking deep brown eyes, which were divided by his curved nose. His thin frame was clothed in a black suit and a pair of fancy black leather shoes along with a black chauffeur's hat.

Violet asked, "Are you the new driver?"

The elf responded, "Yes, madam. My name is Arkell. Your guardian Mr. Victor Lepel recently hired me to be your watchman and chauffeur whenever you have a social engagement. "But," Arkell smiled and continued, "your uncle Mr. Akeem Wilds paid me to go against the orders of my employer. Mr. Wilds has instructed me to look the other way if you choose to eat at the restaurant. Should your date take an interest in you? I'm not supposed to keep you from scaring him away."

Violet thought, *Uncle really did pay this guy off.*

Arkell continued to say, "Madam, if you will please get into the car so we can make our way to Taste of Magic."

In a confused tone, Violet said, "Taste of what?"

Arkell informed, "I'm sorry. I thought you had been informed. The name of the restaurant where your date will be waiting is a restaurant called Taste of Magic. I must admit, I find that name to be a little bit of a cliché."

Arkell opened the door to the back seat of the car so that Violet could get in. After closing the door behind her he proceeded to get into the driver's seat. A minute passed then he started the car.

The car sat in the middle of a huge traffic jam, and Violet noticed that Arkell was becoming more and more annoyed at being stuck in traffic. She on the other hand didn't care. She knew her current date just like most of her other dates would show up late. The later he arrived the less time she would have to spend with him. The misery for her was waiting, her stomach growling and aching with hunger while she smelled the wonderful smells coming from the kitchen. Worst still was to see the delicious plates of food being consumed by the other patrons and her date while she was only allowed a small salad. She would try to order some food today hoping that Arkell would follow her uncle's instructions and look the other way. Maybe for once she would get something out of one of these dates.

She was also debating with herself about telling Arkell about the curse. Part of her thought it wouldn't be a good idea. But another part of her still wanted to make sure she could trust him.

Arkell on the other hand was becoming more and more irritated, and he honked the car horn several times. With his efforts wasted since the traffic still didn't budge, he said, "Dammit, why won't these cars move?"

In response, Violet said, "Honking the horn isn't going to make traffic move any faster."

Arkell ignored Violet and honked the car horn again.

Traffic remained stagnant, which pissed Arkell off to the point he hit the steering wheel before saying, "My predecessors never had this problem. So, why am I dealing with it?"

Confused, Violet asked, "What do you mean? Winston and the former drivers got stuck in traffic plenty of times."

Arkell replied, "I'm referring to the fact that we are already late thanks to all this traffic. When I was hired, Mr. Lepel went into great detail about how that Winston person handled everything perfectly."

Violet said, "The only thing he was good at was scaring me or trying to almost kill me."

"I don't understand what you mean by that."

Violet decided to tell Arkell the truth about Winston. She replied, "What I'm trying to say is, Winston is a sad drunk. He sometimes put me in danger when he was very drunk, or he degraded me for the sake of keeping me in line."

Arkell groaned before he remarked, "Members of the Lepels staff told me Winston had been your watchdog, and in rare cases your driver since you were a sixteen."

"Yes, and?"

"Oh, come on. You can't possibly expect me to believe that a drunk was allowed to drive you on occasion for several years."

Violet smirked, "Believe what you want to believe, but I'm telling the truth."

"Alright, if you're telling the truth, then explain why."

"Explain why, what?"

"Explain why your guardians would let someone drive inebriated with you in the car."

Feeling as if she was being put on trial, in a slightly irritated tone, Violet said, "It's because they hate me. Any other questions?"

In an almost mocking tone, Arkell replied, "Yes, I do have more questions. You just …"

He was interrupted when a man holding a baby boy knocked on the car window.

The man looked as if he was in his early twenties with peach-colored skin and messy short blond hair. His narrow face was home to a pair of very sad aqua blue eyes, eyes that sat in between a large, pointed nose that sat above his cracked lips.

Sleeping in his arms, the infant had his head laying on the man's shoulder. The child's skin was so milky white that he looked abnormally pale. He was also too thin, with no baby fat on his body, and the blue romper he was wearing made it more obvious because it was hanging on him like a sheet on a laundry rope.

Arkell rolled down the window. In a very desperate voice, the man said, "Sir, can you please give me a few dollars? I need to get my nephew some formula."

In response, Arkell handed the man some money and after the man thanked him, he rolled the window back up.

In response to his kindness, Violet said, "That was very sweet of you."

Arkell replied, "I guess. If that man was smart, he would drop that kid off at one of the new orphan shelters."

In a shocked tone Violet responded, "Why would you say that? Those places are underfunded and understaffed. For shit's sake, they even have a reputation of being responsible for the deaths of a lot of children."

"Whatever. That lazy moron should get a job and stop asking for charity."

Arkell's statement shocked Violet. "That's a closed-minded way to see things. After the economy entered a downward freefall, jobs have been getting harder to find, and the increase in businesses going under didn't help matters."

Arkell responded, "All I know is I have a job. Even that Winston person you insisted is a drunk, had a job. So, there is no excuse not to have a job."

"The only reason Winston had his job was because he is an old friend of my Uncle Victor."

"Just because Winston was Mr. Lepel's friend doesn't mean he would let the man be your chaperone or occasional driver."

"My uncle hates me, so having a drunk man drive me wasn't a big deal to him."

Arkell using a cynical tone, "Yeah, right."

"I'm telling the truth."

"Please. Even if Mr. Lepel hated you, he would not be crazy enough to let an alcoholic put his luxury vehicles in danger. You know better than me that many of those cars are worth close to a million dollars."

"So?"

Arkell in disbelief stated, "So, why would he throw away millions letting a drunk crash his cars just to kill you? Not to mention if someone was injured, the Lepels and Winston would have been hit with a lawsuit for endangerment. Not to mention all the other possible charges and court costs. Hell, that's only a few reasons why your claim is stupid."

"He never drove me in one of my guardian's cars."

Traffic started to move as Arkell asked, "Then whose cars was he using?"

Violet clarified, "The cars Winston drove and crashed with me inside belong to my Aunt June, not my guardians."

Arkell thought for a moment. Then he said, "Alright, let's say he did destroy a bunch of Mrs. June Wilds' cars. Why would she be alright with him doing that?"

"She was never alright with him destroying her cars.," Violet's tone changed to one of annoyance, "especially now that she goes the extra mile of only buying eco-friendly vehicles."

Arkell started to drive down a narrow street as he asked, "If she was never alright with it, then why would she let him get away with it?"

Violet groaned as she said, "It's like this. Because my guardians have extended custody of me, they have the right to send me to the Greenages facility. This facility is full of mentally ill criminals whose crimes go beyond murder. When they demanded my aunt let Winston drive me in one of her cars, she said no. In retaliation, my guardians threatened to send me to the facility. My aunt quickly changed her mind and begged them to let me remain at home. After that, she let the drunk man drive me only whenever he absolutely had to. Luckily, my grandmother made me a charm so I would not die if he crashed. But the charm lost all its magic three months ago. Thanks to the demon problem, my grandma can't get the items she needs to make another one."

Arkell thought for a moment before asking, "Did your guardians really almost send you away because your aunt didn't want you to be driven by a drunk, or did they almost send you to the Greenages facility because your condition got worse?"

Violet snapped, "I don't have a condition."

Arkell turned to drive down another street as he responded, "Don't worry about it, Miss Evergreen. Your guardians told me you have UMD. I know you're sensitive about having this condition after it forced you to cause the fire that killed your parents. But you need to remember it's not your fault you lost control. Having UMD means you have almost no control over your magic."

Violet's body temperature started to rise, and she felt her fists clench. She desperately wished to curse Arkell. But she told herself not to. After all, what would it accomplish, except make her seem mentally unstable?

Violet thought to herself, *this son of a whore is just evil. What kind of shit rag says you killed your parents… well do not feel too bad about it since you're mentally unstable. Damn this fucking curse and damn my shithole of a life.* She forced herself to calm down.

After a few minutes, they arrived at the restaurant. When Arkell parked, Violet asked, "My uncle Akeem Wilds paid you not to obey my guardians' orders. Do you have any intention of doing what he paid you to do?"

Arkell took a breath before saying, "We are at the restaurant aren't we?"

"That doesn't answer my question."

"I was told you were a simpleton, but I could never imagine you were this foolish."

Violet felt as if Arkell had just spit in her face.

Without looking in Arkell's direction Violet asked, "Why did you decide to tell me that my Uncle Akeem paid you if you had no plans of going through with a single thing he asked you to do?"

"I'll tell you in a minute."

Arkell's response sent a jolt throughout Violet's entire being. She clenched her fist while in a harsh tone she said, "No, you are going to start answering…"

Arkell quickly interrupted as he said, "Enough, there is something I need to show you."

He climbed out of the car. Violet thought, *I'm starting to think getting Winston arrested was not the best idea. At least he never tried to hide the…*"

Her thought process was interrupted when Arkell knocked on her window. He shouted for her to get out of the car. Violet rolled her eyes as she opened the door and climbed out of the car. After Violet walked around to the back of the car where Arkell was standing, the two of them stood in the parking lot for a moment.

Arkell said, "The rules your guardians told me were very thorough. As you already know, you are to eat nothing during your date, and that includes fluids."

"That's not right. I've always at least been allowed to have a glass of water."

Arkell snapped, "Maybe in the past you were, but many of the staff and Mr. Lepel are concerned you're getting fatter due to water weight."

Fucking Kinya, I bet she planted that idea in Uncle Victor's head, stupid bastards.

Arkell continued, "Personally, that does not make any sense to me, but I'm not being paid to understand their logic. However, since I am being paid to make sure you follow your guardians' instructions, I will levitate you every time you try to break the rules and...."

In an aggravated voice Violet said, "No."

"No, what?"

"No, you are not levitating me."

Arkell smiled, then snapped his fingers. The very second Violet heard the snap, her body started to lift off the ground. Violet's heart raced as she went higher and higher into the air. Very quickly she reached the point where she was hovering very high above the parking lot, but not so high Arkell needed to shout for her to hear him. Panicked, she began to thrash around in a futile effort to get back to the ground.

Arkell laughed as he shouted, "I would stop that if I were you! The whole world can see your underwear!"

Embarrassed, Violet clenched her skirt so no one would see her panties, while shouting for Arkell to let her down.

He laughed at her again before shouting, "I'm not going to let you down until I'm sure you understand who is in charge here. Now where was I? Oh right, in addition to levitation I will incinerate your menu if you try to order. Also, don't think about asking the server for food suggestions. Because I will use my magic to incinerate any food they bring you. So basically, if you keep ordering, all you will be doing is wasting food. Finally, even though you are under a curse I am aware of how crafty your family is. So, I'm not surprised if they weakened the curse."

At least he can't sense the difference between fairy magic and witch magic.

Violet questioned, "How did you know about the curse?"

"I'm an elf, stupid. My kind can sense when a curse is set, when a curse is weakened, and when a curse is lifted. But despite my ability, I can't tell how strong your curse is. If you're capable of doing anything mean or nasty to Mr. Westing, for your sake, don't."

Violet shouted, "Why not? All you can do is levitate me!"

Arkell shrugged as he said, "I can also take away your voice."

Violet started to shake as she responded, "You can't do that."

"I was given permission to take away your voice temporarily. So, I will if you don't do as I tell you."

Arkell started to pace back and forth. Violet, who was becoming more and more afraid, started to silently pray he would sit her gently on the ground.

Suddenly, Arkell stopped and said, "I think that's everything."

He snapped his fingers, and Violet started to fall towards the ground very quickly. During her descent Violet started to scream franticly.

Right before her face made contact with the black pavement, her whole body stopped in midair. Her heart raced as her body shook.

As she tried to steady her breathing, she thought, *it's ok I…"*

Suddenly, Violet hit the ground as Arkell said, "I just sent you screaming several feet in the air. I left you scared hovering in the air for as long as I wanted to. I made you drop from the sky. So fast that if I had not acted when I did, you would have been soup on the tarmac. We are even standing in the middle of a restaurant's parking lot. No one from the restaurant or any of the surrounding businesses came to help you. There are even cars driving down the street and none of them stopped to even try to intervene. Shit, you were even screaming at the top of your lungs and not one person moved an inch to see what was going on.

I bet you're asking yourself why, why, why didn't anyone at least try to help you. I'll tell you why right now. It's because other than being a plaything for some rich brat, you're worthless. Tiny grains of sand have way more value than you. No one is ever going to come and save you. So, just give up and accept your place."

Violet continued to lie on the cold pavement while her heart beat very fast within her chest as she breathed very quickly.

In a cruel tone, Arkell said, "Get your ass up. I don't have all day."

He then looked disgusted as a shaky Violet picked herself up. While trying to calm her nerves she looked at Arkell, who in a serious tone started to say, "Despite the truth I just showed you, I still see that there is some speck of hope still inside you. To make sure you understand that you have no hope of successfully rebelling against the will of your guardians, let me introduce you to my ace in the hole."

He then held out his right hand and said, "Verum vision."

A bright orange light glowed in his hand for a moment. As the light started to dissipate, a floating green eye with tiny bat wings and a devil tail was hovering above his hand.

Arkell said, "This is the Eye of Esca. Now even though it's my job to keep watch over you, your guardians wanted your date to take place in one of the restaurant's private rooms. Because of that, I'm unable to watch from a nearby table. This is where my little friend comes in. You see, the Eye of Esca can show me everything without me being in the room. It will also make a recording for your guardians. Now that you understand the position, let's head inside. We are already late."

A still-shaky Violet started to steady her breath as she followed Arkell through the restaurant's entrance.

The restaurant was a rectangular brick building designed to resemble a small house. There were two windows on either side of a dark blue door that led inside. To the right of the left window, there was a very large green ivy growing on the side of the building. In front of the door was a small concrete staircase with a black railing. Sitting above the door was a sign with flashing yellow lights that said, "Taste of Magic." There was an image of a small blue flame that looked like a real fire.

Violet, who was still traumatized, stared at the fire and felt for some reason it was very familiar. She started to wonder if she had seen it before. Her curiosity didn't last long because Arkell snapped at her to hurry. He held the door open, and Violet slowly walked inside.

The inside of the restaurant had a strange, homely feeling. In the restaurant's front entrance there was a black hostess stand. Sitting on top of the stand was a bell, but the hostess seemed to be missing in action. Violet, trying to calm herself, surveyed the restaurant's interior. The walls were painted maroon while the floors were made of brown parquet wood. There was a large crystal chandelier that added a lot of brightness to the space. On the left side of the room, there were several round wooden tables. Each table had a white tablecloth with a small lit purple candle in a glass sitting in the middle. All the tables had four wood chairs parked against them. The other side of the room had several booths. Each booth had the same

141

tablecloth and candle set up as the other tables. Except for the booth seats, which were covered with bright red fabric.

While Violet attempted to calm herself, Arkell compulsively rang the bell to summon a member of the restaurant staff. After a few minutes, the hostess arrived. The hostess had lovely dark brown skin and eyes. Her brown hair was styled in a poofy afro while her lips were painted with gold lipstick. She was wearing a silk white top with a black vest with gold buttons. Her pants were black, and her shoes were white high heels.

The hostess looked at Violet and Arkell. She said, "I am so sorry, but the restaurant is closed for a private event."

In a slightly annoyed tone, Arkell responded, "I know. I am the chaperone for Miss Violet Evergreen. She is here for the reservation made by Mr. Lepel for her assigned date with Mr. Westing."

In a surprised tone, the hostess said, "Oh, please forgive me. Because the reservation was for an assigned date, we assumed that the party would not arrive for another hour."

Arkell questioned, "The reservation was set for eleven, so why would you expect us to arrive late?"

The hostess, in a somewhat surprised tone explained, "Well, usually with assigned dates neither party arrives on time. They usually arrive an hour after the reservation is up. No one wants to seem desperate."

Arkell snapped, "That's no excuse. Mr. Lepel paid for the reservation to begin at eleven. Ergo, this establishment should have been prepared for our arrival."

"I understand, and don't worry about the private room where Miss Evergreen will be..."

The hostess stopped in mid-sentence. At that moment she noticed Violet was shaking with a fearful look on her face. She walked over to Violet and placed her hand on Violet's shoulder.

She asked, "Miss Evergreen, are you alright?"

Tell her what happened! All you have to do is tell her what happened. and she will call the police for help! At the same time, a conflicting thought raged shouting. *What is the point?! Even if the cops are called, they will do nothing. No one is coming to save me.*

Arkell removed the hostess's hand from Violet's shoulder. When he let go of her, in an authoritative tone he said, "She's fine. Now, will you please show us to the private room that was reserved for her date?"

The hostess gave him a disgusted glance before saying, "Follow me."

They walked through an archway, then navigated their way through a narrow hallway until they reached a red door. As Violet stared at the red door she wondered if it was meant to symbolize her impending descent into a more hellish existence. The hostess opened the door, and Violet and Arkell walked inside.

The private room was small with maroon-colored walls and dark hardwood floors. In the center of the ceiling, there was a light shaped like a small dome emitting a warm bright light throughout the entire room. On the right side of the room a brown hardwood door led in and out of the kitchen. In the center of the opposite wall was a large painting depicting a winery. In the middle of the room was a circular hardwood table with two hardwood chairs. In the center of the table, there was a small button emitting a red light that was used to call for assistance.

The hostess told them a server would be with them in a few minutes.

Arkell looked at the hostess with a pissed-off expression as he said, "Do not send any waitresses in until Mr. Patterson arrives. Also, when he does, only bring orders for him. Miss Evergreen is attempting to shed some weight, so she won't be eating or drinking anything."

The hostess shot a very concerned look at Violet, then looked at Arkell for a moment. She looked as if she wanted to say something, but she chose not to and silently left the room. A minute after the hostess left, Arkell summoned the eye of Esca and cast an invisibility over it so its presence would not bother her date when he finally arrived. After that, Arkell told Violet to remember what would happen if she did not behave herself. He left, taking a seat in the main dining room. After he left, Violet, who was still having trouble collecting her nerves, managed to regain enough control to stop herself from shaking. When she realized that she was standing in the middle of the room, she walked over to the table and sat in one of the chairs.

Chapter 7
The Date from Hell

Violet was grateful that her blind date had not arrived. The quiet time gave her time to think.

Dammit, I should have been suspicious about Arkell the moment I saw him. What kind of elf is poor and has to work? When he started that weird interrogation why did I even waste time answering him? Stop asking yourself questions you know you won't get an answer to.

Violet started to sigh. *Dammit, that fucking Arkell. Thanks to him the guardians won. No, all he did was just rush their inevitable victory. Maybe married life won't be so bad. I won't be living with my guardians anymore, and I guess that's pretty good. What kind of bullshit logic am I trying to trick myself into believing? I know what kind of man they picked out for me. Bastard won't give a damn about me. I'll always have to let him push me around like a slave and rape me whenever he feels like it.*

She leaned back in her chair as she continued to think, *even when I'm married. It is not as if my guardians won't maintain their custody of me. Instead of two captors, I'm going to have to deal with three. No, that's not right. The bastard's parents are going to get to control my life as well. I even bet the rest of my family won't be allowed to visit, and I can forget about seeing my friends. No, I take that back. I'll probably get to see them at the wedding, but most likely that's it.*

Suddenly, a voice inside Violet screamed, *so Arkell shows off his powers, it's still nothing important.*

As her nerves calmed, Violet began to think with more clarity. *That's right. Arkell said he has to prove himself to my guardians. Meaning he really can't afford for this date to go wrong. Causing me to become pavement jelly is definitely a major turn off to a lot of guys. I bet making me fly up to the sky then dropping me was nothing more than a ruse to make me obey him.*

That realization made Violet feel dramatically better. She felt even more confident as she continued to think of a plan.

Violet sat quietly for ten minutes, trying to think of a plan. The more she tried to concentrate the more she wanted to eat something. After several minutes her hunger reached the point where she could no longer ignore it. She turned her gaze to the glowing red button in the middle of the table.

As she stared at the button, she thought about how she had a card with no limit. All she had to do was press the button to order.

Violet sat up in her chair thinking to herself, *if I press the button to call the waitress, then Arkell will stop me from ordering. At least he will if I try to eat here.*

Violet stared at the door that led out of the room. *I know leaving will cause my guardians to sic the police on me. But it might be the perfect way out of this mess. If I leave, I can try to ditch Arkell. I'll probably need to cast a blocking spell to keep his weird magic eye from following me.*

Casting a spell like that might activate the limiter. Whatever, some things are worth taking a chance on.

Violet smiled, then jumped out of her chair. She quickly rushed over to the door.

146

She reached the door handle, and as she started to open the door her whole body instantaneously levitated off the ground. Panicked, Violet started to swing her arms and legs around hoping she would be able to pull herself down to the floor. Still thrashing around Violet thought *shit, shit, shit,* before she could scream for help. She was quickly flung back into her chair so hard it was amazing that the chair didn't break.

With her heart still racing deep in her chest, Violet thought, *Arkell must have levitated me again. No, if it was him, I would have sensed a concentration of elf magic. If it wasn't Arkell, then how? Crap, it was the curse. I guess not being able to run from Patterson Westing includes me trying to run away before he gets here.*

Her attention then turned back to the glowing red button in the middle of the table. As she intensely stared at the button Violet thought she was just going to have to call the waitress. She knew it was a risk, but she didn't care. After being terrorized her whole life, she decided it was her birthday, so she deserved a treat.

Without a second thought, Violet pressed the button. She looked nervously in the direction of the door, and she wondered if Arkell was going to charge in. Or was he going to wait till she had the menu to incinerate it?

Just then the door opened, and Violet's heart jumped while she mentally prepared herself for Arkell to attack. Happily, it was the waitress who walked into the room.

The waitress appeared to be a few years older than Violet. She had lovely soft peach skin, and green eyes. Her long straight brown hair was tied into a ponytail. Her uniform consisted of a black shirt that had the words Taste of Magic embroidered in gold letters on the upper left corner of the breast pocket. Underneath the gold letters were a small picture wood log with a blue flame. She was also wearing a plain black hoop skirt and bulky black serf safe shoes.

147

The waitress walked over to where Violet was sitting and asked, "Ready to order, Miss?"

Violet's heart started to steady itself as she replied, "Yes."

"Alright, I will be back with a menu in just a second."

A few minutes passed after the waitress left the room. *Arkell still hasn't shown up to stop me from ordering.*

She thought about her aunt's note. *When Arkell started making fun of me I thought he had fooled Uncle Akeem. What if he was trying to trick me? Why would he do that?* As Violet pondered on whose side Arkell was on, the waitress came back with a menu.

She handed it to Violet and told her she was going to be back in a few minutes to take her order. After the waitress left the room, Violet started to look at the menu.

Arkell still hasn't busted in to stop me. So, I might as well order something.

As Violet scanned the menu, each tasty dish advertised made her think. She had been on over a hundred arranged dates. This was the first time she looked at a menu. This made her feel a strange sense of joy. Eventually, she found herself fixated on the ribeye steak the restaurant had for one hundred dollars. She also fancied a drink called the tropical lemonade that the restaurant had for thirty dollars. After a minute the waitress returned, and Violet told her what she wanted to order.

As the waitress took down the order, she smiled at Violet as she said, "I'm glad you decided to go ahead and order. I was told that this room was reserved for an assigned date. But considering how long your date seems to be keeping you waiting, it's good you're treating yourself."

Once the waitress left the room Violet leaned back in the chair. Still wondering if she was wrong, and Arkell was going to try to stop her from eating.

Her thought process was suddenly interrupted when the waitress came back. She was holding a tray. The waitress sat a large plate of zucchini fries and a small bowl of a strange, orange-colored sauce on the table.

Before Violet could say anything, the waitress said, "The chef made those for you before you ordered. He felt bad about how long your date is taking to arrive, so he whipped those up for you free of charge."

Violet smiled at being reminded that there were still kind people in the world. "Oh, I want to thank him before I leave."

The waitress left the room once more while Violet stared at her zucchini fries. Her stomach suddenly roared, reminding her how hungry she was. She thought, *there's food in front of me that I need to eat. I'm just staring at it like a crazy person.*

Violet picked up a fry and dipped it in the sauce. The moment the flavor of the zucchini mixed with the sauce hit Violet's tongue, she thought wow this is delicious.

Without a second thought, she placed her white cloth napkin in her lap and proceeded to eat all her zucchini. When the last one was gone, she licked what remained of the sauce out of the bowl. After the sauce was gone, Violet wiped her face with a napkin while thinking, *Arkell didn't stop me. I guess he's not going to be a problem.*

The door to the room opened and the waitress came in with Violet's order. Despite being full, Violet's mouth started to water the moment she smelled the steak. The waitress sat Violet's drink and her plate down on the table. Impatient to dig into her food, Violet quickly reached for her utensils. As she laid a clean napkin in her lap, the door opened, and a man walked into the room.

Patterson Westing was tall, but not super tall. He had extremely smooth brown skin and brown eyes. His hair had been permed, dyed blond, greased, and styled into spikes. Patterson was dressed like a wannabe rapper. He had gold plated teeth with the letters of his name spelled in tiny diamonds. His fingernails were also painted gold with his initials on his index and ring finger that was also written in diamonds. He was wearing a very baggy black shirt and pants and a pair of red sneakers on his feet. Patterson proceeded to sit down at the table and Violet realized he must be her date.

In response to Patterson sitting at the table, the waitress said, "Good afternoon, Sir. I'll get you a menu in just a second."

Patterson laughed as he said, "Are you some kind of dumb shit? Why would I need a menu when my date was kind enough to order for me?"

Before either woman could react, Patterson picked up both Violet's plate and drink.

As he proceeded to place the food and drink in front of himself, Violet concluded, *this is one of the most self-absorbed men I have ever been forced to go out with.*

Patterson started to unroll his napkin. He then paused before looking at Violet and saying, "I can't do this. You were kind enough to order this steak for me so I would not have to wait to eat when I arrived. I know you're going to tell me not to get you anything. Your guardians already informed me you were not going to eat because they have you on a very strict diet. However, I just can't be alright with you seeing me eat this beautiful steak when I know you most likely only had a little rabbit food today."

Does this mean he is going to let me get away with ordering food?

Patterson turned his head to look at the waitress and said, "Please bring my date a glass of sparkling water with crushed ice."

The waitress looked at Patterson dumbfounded, while Violet thought, *should have seen that coming.*

She glared at Patterson as she said, "I don't want sparkling water. I want my steak and tropical lemonade."

In shock, Violet thought, I just spoke my mind. Does that mean the curse is gone? I don't think so. What I said was not exactly cruel. Maybe that is why I got away with it.

Patterson responded, "I know sparkling water is not allowed on your diet, but seeing you were sweet enough to order for me, I'm getting a feeling that things are going to go well. I have so much faith that this date will go well, that I'll pay for the water."

This mother fucker thinks paying for a single glass of sparkling water is some kind of treat for me?

The waitress looked as if someone slapped her. In a slightly perplexed tone, she said, "I'll go and get that right now."

As she started to leave the room Patterson said, "Don't forget- sparkling water with crushed ice- my girl deserves the best."

With a worried look on her face, the waitress looked back and said, "I won't forget any of this."

Meanwhile, Patterson was chewing a piece of steak with his mouth open as he said, "So, Evergreen, tell me about yourself."

Surprised her date asked her about her, Violet figured she might be able to drum up some sympathy from Patterson. She said, "I'm being forced to be here and…"

Patterson interrupted and started to say, "Oh, that's very fascinating. As for myself I always had things pretty hard. My parents weren't always rich like they are now. So, I only got a two million dollar a week allowance. I know that idea is pretty shocking to you, but not everyone gets everything handed to them."

As he talked and ate with his mouth opened, a piece of meat escaped Patterson's lips, flew across the table, and hit Violet on the cheek. Violet cringed as she used her napkin to wipe the meat off her face.

Violet looked at her date who was still talking with his mouth full. She said, "Talking with your mouth full is disgusting."

Patterson was too into his own world to hear a word that Violet uttered. She then noticed he was almost done with the steak, and she wondered how he could eat so quickly. Once he was done, he wiped his mouth before saying, "Well, that was the worst steak I've ever eaten."

What is wrong with this idiot? Patterson stole her steak, ate it to the bone, and wants to pretend it was bad? Violet wondered, *why is he lying?*

Patterson pressed the button to call the waitress as he said, "Violet, I know you were only trying to make me happy with that steak. Don't feel bad about it not being enjoyable."

He leaned back in his chair as he said, "You have been fun to be around, so I've decided we should get married next week."

The moment Paterson declared that he planned to marry Violet, she jumped up and shouted, "We can't!"

He smiled as he replied, "I understand your shock," His tone took on a flare of arrogance as he continued, "the sudden realization that you are worthy of marrying a man of my caliber. That's like winning the lottery a billion times in a row."

Violet's heart raced as she said, "We do not know each other."

"I know enough to be sure about my decision."

"No, you don't. I would make a terrible wife."

Patterson in a reassuring tone said, "The fact that you say that only reflects how humble you are. Now I am even more certain I have made the right decision."

I have got to do something quickly. Think, Violet. There has to be something I can say to get through to this guy.

She said, "I'm sure there is a woman you would like better out there."

Patterson agreed, "Most likely, yeah. But whoever she may be, can be my mistress. The person I marry must come from a very distinguished background. You, like me, come from a powerful family. So, I know you were raised to know how to behave around other bourgeoisie. Unlike some girls, you eat less than a bird. Now, calm down. You're clearly a good pick for a bride."

What do I have to do to get rid of this guy? He only hears what he wants to hear. Maybe if I stop being polite and give it to him straight.

She took a breath then said, "Listen to me. You're an incredibly beautiful man."

Violet's heart jumped and she cringed upon realizing that the curse had not worn off. But she told herself to finish what she was saying because she still hoped she would be able to get through to him.

Violet continued, "I do not wish to be your wife although you are incredibly smart and handsome. I'm not interested in marrying you."

Patterson chuckled as he said, "Your humility is wonderful. Anyway, I'll call my driver so that we can meet with your guardians. We can begin making arrangements for the wedding."

In a frustrated tone, Violet said, "My guardians are not in town right now."

"Strange, I was told they would be available if this date was successful. Oh well, I guess we will just head over to my estate to let my family know the good news. This is pretty fortunate. You will be able to start working with my mother who will inform you of what your household duties will be. In the meantime, I will contact your guardians about drawing up the necessary paperwork for our engagement."

PAPERWORK! Why would we need paperwork to be engaged? The hell with that, I need to get myself out of this. Shit, I need help.

She said, "Can I be excused for a moment to call my family about this?"

"Why would you need to do that?"

"Marriage is a big step I feel that I should talk to them about it first."

Patterson said, "Don't be silly. Any concerns you have about our union can be handled during the prenuptial negotiations."

"But we…"

"Stop talking. I've already decided how we are going to handle everything."

I don't care what the extended custody law says, or what my guardians will do. I'm not putting up with this shit.

She took a breath before saying, "I am grateful you have taken such a strong lead in making decisions for me." Violet corrected, no that isn't what I want to say. What I mean is you are so brilliant in how quickly you have planned our engagement. Darn, that isn't what I am trying to tell you."

Patterson rolled his eyes as he said, "I have a lot of things to do today. So, get on with it so we can leave."

Violet said, "I only wish to make you happy. Can we get married tomorrow?" *Damn this fucking curse! That is not what I want to say!*

Patterson smiled as he replied, "It's ok. I should have realized sooner the idea of marrying me made you extremely happy. Don't worry your pretty little head with such silliness. Your feelings are…"

Violet shouted, "That is not how I feel!"

Patterson, using a calming tone said, "Calm down. I told you I understand your frustration. You know what, let me check on that sparkling water I ordered for you. That lazy server should have brought it by now, and it will calm your wedding jitters."

Violet started to rub her forehead. Before Patterson could press the button to call the waitress, the door opened, and a man walked in.

The man had glittering aquamarine eyes that complemented his silky milk chocolate skin. His thick long black dreadlocks were tied into a ponytail. He was wearing a white chef jacket with black pants and a pair of black serf-safe shoes.

The moment Violet saw the man she felt the blood rush to her cheeks. Quickly, she covered her face to prevent anyone from noticing her embarrassing expression. Despite her effort, neither of the men noticed her or her reaction to the man who had just entered the room. Violet assumed that the man must be the chef.

155

The man looked at the splattered food on the table while trying to hide his disgust.

He turned his attention to the couple. He said, "I am the owner of Taste of Magic as well as your chef for this afternoon. How are the two of you enjoying your stay?"

Paterson scoffed as he responded, "The food was vulgar. Also, my fiancé has not received her sparkling water."

"In a frustrated tone, Violet shouted, "I am not your fiancé. I donnnnk likddd yo asjjjj!"

Both men looked at Violet shocked. *I almost got what I wanted to say out. The curse must be wearing off.*

Patterson said, "My goodness this place must have you stressed. Don't worry yourself any longer. I will call my driver, and we will leave right now."

Violet replied, "Listen, dammop. I deso want tog bay youred fiancé Id don'ts likddddd youb."

Patterson got up while saying, "Don't worry. I am getting the driver now."

The chef on the other hand looked very worried. He looked at Patterson as he quickly said, "Sir, I do not believe you are interpreting what she's trying to say."

Patterson glared at the chef as he said, "If you are smart you will stay out of our business."

He then looked at Violet and said, "Come on, we are leaving now."

In response, Violet folded her arms and said, "No."

The second the word escaped Violet's lips, Patterson's brows furrowed. He glared at Violet while saying, "I'm going to have to do something about your attitude."

Violet snapped, "Don't talk to me that way. Also, jackass, if you took half a microsecond to listen to someone besides yourself, you would have noticed that I don't like you. You're so full of yourself and overall, you are a jackass. I want absolutely nothing to do with you."

At that moment Violet felt a surge of joy shoot through her. *I did it. I told him off. My fucking guardians are going to kill me. Oh, fuck it all. It was worth it.*

Patterson said, "So you have gone from ecstatic to be my wife to rejection in about a minute. I was warned by your guardians that you sometimes have mood shifts because of your UMD. But that is alright. I knew what I was getting into when I agreed to this date."

The chef said, "Sir, I do not think you understand what is going on. The lady doesn't wish to be near you. So, I feel you should just call it a day and go home."

Patterson shouted, "Do not interject when I am speaking to my fiancé!"

He then looked at Violet and said, "As for you, I thought the wedding contract was all I needed to work with today. Now that you are exhibiting this attitude, I see that there is a need to have you mentally corrected."

Violet's heart jumped, while the chef looked at Patterson as if he just kicked him in the stomach.

Patterson continued to say, "After our wedding night I am going to have you committed to an upscale mental facility. We will find a lovely place where you can get treatment to get your mood swings under control."

157

Violet jumped up and said, "You have no right to do that to me."

Patterson laughed as he said, "I'm the only man willing to marry you, so I can do whatever the hell I want to you."

Suddenly the chef shouted, "Alright, that is enough. Sir, if you don't step away from the lady and leave now, I will be forced to call the police and inform them that you are harassing her. Now please go."

Patterson shouted, "How dare you speak that way to me. Do you realize who I am?"

The chef replied, "Another spoiled little brat struggling with hearing no for the first time."

Patterson said, "I'll teach you your place."

Out of nowhere, all the color disappeared from the room. Everything looked like an old black and white movie. Patterson started to say, "t bedicat ibi sem e inds qu nem pum lius…"

Violet's heart was racing. *Crap, crap, crap. This level of distortion of color only means Patterson is going to place a powerful curse on this poor man. I don't even sense a lot of magical power from the chef. Dammit, he can't defend himself. This is my fault. I should …"*

As Patterson was about to finish his curse, the chef punched him so hard, he was unconscious before he hit the ground. Violet's heartbeat steadied as she stared at Patterson in absolute shock. They stood in silence for a moment before the room returned to normal. The chef looked at Patterson before turning his attention to Violet.

He asked, "Madam, are you alright?"

Violet shook her head yes. She then gulped before saying, "I'm surprised that you were able to get away with punching him. I was always told that hitting someone cursing you instead of using a powerful counter curse would cause an even worse spell to be cast."

The chef responded, "Under normal circumstances, yes. But when your magic is as powerful as mine, some magic rules do not always apply."

Violet said, "Interesting. I did not know that someone with strong magic could do that."

"I'm not surprised. Most people only learn that little factoid if they take magic philosophy in college."

That was scary. I'm glad the owner knew how to handle the situation.

She said, "Thank you so much for helping me. I would have been in real trouble."

"No problem, Ma'am. I'm just sorry you did not have the best dining experience here today. I hope that your unfortunate experience today does not make you wish never to dine here again."

Violet looked at the still unconscious Patterson before looking back at the chef. She smiled while saying, "I have a feeling this place is about to become my favorite restaurant."

"I'm very happy to hear that. Now, if you'll please excuse me, I need to contact the authorities about this little incident."

They said goodbye, and the chef walked out of the room. Violet, who had just realized her clutch was on the ground, knelt to pick it up. *I'm really lucky things worked out. But it didn't work out the way auntie planned it.*

Chapter 8
Family Hospital

When Violet stepped out of the restaurant, Arkell was standing outside waiting for her. He clapped his hands while saying, "You handled that train wreck very nicely."

Violet clenched her fist as she snapped, "You ass. You did all that awful stuff to intimidate me into not messing up my date. Now you're happy my date went wrong. Dammit, either tell me the truth, or don't say anything and take me home."

"I understand your frustration, but I need you to understand why I had to do that."

"Then start explaining."

"Let's take a little walk."

Violet had no desire to go anywhere with Arkell. But she wanted answers, and she knew he was the only one who could give them.

They started to walk down the street. After they turned the corner Arkell said, "Where do I begin? When I showed you the Eye of Esca it was watching us before I revealed it to you. It has the power to act like a drone and send live feed. Ollivander was watching that feed. Now, originally, I was banking on Mrs. Wilds' plan.

I believe that if Ollivander saw a recording of blood pouring from your mouth, he would inform your guardians of what happened. They would probably react to this news by not sending you on dates for a while. Sadly, you had that curse on you. Part of me hoped when you ate the zucchini the curse would wear off immediately. Sadly, as it took a while to work, I feared I would have to incite plan B."

"Why would the zucchini have helped?"

"Cooked zucchini is good for removing most low-level curses. The owner of Taste of Magic is an old friend of mine. When I told him your situation, he wanted to help."

"What is plan B?"

"Telling you might make you an accessory."

Violet smirked, "Accessory to what?"

Arkell remarked, "All you need to know is your family is rich and rich people get away with things."

"What is that supposed to mean?"

"Stop worrying about it."

"Fine, then can you tell me how any of the footage that eye sent helps?"

"I can see why that confuses you," Arkell began to explain, "Earlier when I was desperate to get to the restaurant on time, it was not just because of my act. If I leave the eye of Esca in a room for an hour, I can alter the feed I send three times. To put it in more basic terms, I can alter what a person watching the feed sees. However, despite that little bit of information, the only benefit I got was to alter the image of you eating zucchini so that Ollivander would think you were sobbing on the table. I made them see the same image of you crying when you tried to leave the restaurant and when you started speaking your mind. As far as the Lepels know, before Patterson arrived you sat quietly and cried until Mr. Westing arrived."

"Why?"

"Patterson Westing had become too big of a wild card."

"I do not understand."

"Think about this. I can alter what Ollivander saw. I cannot alter what Mr. Westing tells your guardians. If everything had gone according to Mrs. Wilds' plan, then Mr. Westing would have just complained about being set up with a hemophiliac. So, there had to be a dramatic change of tactics."

"Why does having to change your methodology involve dropping me from the sky?"

"I was always going to do that."

Violet in a burst of anger said, "Seriously?!"

Arkell laughed, "Sorry, I had to do that to gain Ollivander's trust."

"It's not funny. We were in traffic for at least an hour. You could have altered what they saw and warned me that you planned to levitate me. I was terrified!"

Arkell apologized, "Sorry. There are three problems however with your assertion. First, I have no assurance you would be able to act terrified if you knew you were safe. Second, both your garage and the car have spy cameras. Those cameras were also sending Ollivander a live feed of our actions. I couldn't officially take over all live streaming until we stepped out of the car. Third, I forgot to mention even though I can alter what the eye shows a person three times, I can only do that once a day. I could not take the risk of a scenario of things going south. Specifically, something I didn't want them to see happen."

"There were cameras in the car?"

"Yes, there are. I'm surprised you did not know that. Back to Patterson- I needed a way to chase him away without you facing repercussions."

Violet responded, "Well, that plan failed."

"No, it didn't. I told you before, I am friends with the chef who owns that restaurant. Since he was forced to call the cops on Mr. Westing, like many in his social circle, he is not going to want anyone to know he was in jail. No matter how much gangster rapper posing he does."

"Can that eye record?"

"No, it is an artifact century's old."

"Then how can we keep him quiet without proof?"

"My friend has a secret camera in the private rooms to ensure people don't try to have sex in them."

"Really?"

Arkell smiled, "What can I say? Some people think they can fuck anywhere. Anyway, there will be video evidence showing the cops arresting Mr. Westing. When Mr. Westing gets ready to leave prison, I am going to contact him.

When I do, I am going to tell him that if he doesn't want his friends to know he was in jail, then he needs to tell your guardians that he thought you were nice. And that sadly, he is not interested in marrying you. He feels that he is too young to be tied down and has changed his mind about looking for a wife at this time."

Violet was impressed, "You can get away with that?"

"If I couldn't, then your grandmother would have never hired me. For the most part, your dates will be easy to handle. The real challenge is going to be getting the extended custody removed."

"That's only because it is impossible."

"It's not impossible. I just need to find a rat."

"What do you mean by that?"

"I will tell you on the way back to the car."

As the two of them started walking back to the car, Arkell asked, "Tell me how much you know."

"How much I know about what?"

"How much do you know about why your guardians were able to get extended custody?"

Part of Violet thought she should mention what she heard about Judge Hendrickson. But once again she decided to keep quiet because she was still unsure whether she could trust Arkell.

"Only that Judge Hendrickson is convinced that I have UMD. In his mind, it's necessary for me to be in a strict household."

"You know all of that is nonsense, right?"

"Yes, my Aunt June showed me in a medical book that if I had UMD, I would have only lived to see the age of three at max if I had it."

"Someone is profiting off you being under your guardians' custody."

"How could anyone profit off of me being in the care of my guardians?"

"I do not know, but clearly someone is. I just need to find out who."

"Ok, Mr. Private Eye. How come you're the first person to figure that out?"

Arkell continued, "I'm not. Your family suspected foul play the day your guardians got extended custody of you. It's odd to hand a child over to strangers when they have other relatives they are familiar with, who are rich, and who want the child. Even if the strangers are relatives, you also have to consider your parents specified that you were to be under Mr. and Mrs. Wilds custody until you turn eighteen."

Violet questioned, "I was joking, but you mean that you really are a private detective? Tell me, how long ago did my grandmother hire you?"

Arkell answered, "Yes, I am a PI and your grandmother hired me two months ago, when the person investigating your case went missing. Apparently, I'm the tenth investigator to be hired. Sadly, whoever took out my last predecessor also took some kind of key information he acquired."

Violet stated, "I had no idea anyone was investigating my custody case all these years, and hearing that the last PI went missing is more than a little scary."

"Yes, but it does give me more motivation to solve your case."

The restaurant's parking lot was in view when Violet suddenly stopped. Without looking at Arkell she asked, "If your predecessors could not help, why should I trust you to be able to help me?"

"I understand why you would feel that way. Your case is not an easy one to solve, but I believe I'm getting close to what the previous investigator found. Which, Miss Evergreen, may lead to finding some answers to the many questions that surround you. Now, let's head to your family's hospital."

"But you could not make it look like I coughed up blood."

"It's ok. Ollivander was told you needed an examination to see if you're alright after the brutal event you suffered last night."

Violet thought, *that is a polite way to say I got my ass handed to me.*

"I imagine after meeting me there are several things your family wants to tell you. I also imagine that you have questions for them as well. We all know that this conversation cannot happen at your home."

They silently headed back to the car. After getting in and driving off, Violet stared out the window and thought, *I just don't know.*

The Evergreen hospital consisted of a group of five buildings that were clustered like a small city. Each of the buildings was painted white and like most buildings, contained multiple windows. All but the three largest buildings were devoted to research. One of the largest buildings was devoted to the research and treatment of rare illnesses, while the other two were devoted to standard hospital care. The one exception was built exclusively for rich patients, and the other one was built for the middle class with four floors being dedicated to caring for the poor and indigent.

Arkell started to pull up to the building for the rich. There was a massive circular fountain in front of the building, and there were yellow and white flowers planted around the fountain. In the center of the fountain was a marble statue of a swan with its wings outstretched. As the car passed the fountain and pulled up to the front of the hospital, Violet unfastened her seatbelt. When the car stopped in front of the hospital entrance, Arkell told her that he would pick her up later that day. After she got out of the car, she stared at the glass doors leading into the hospital. She thought, *I feel like I'm standing in the middle of a typhoon.*

As Violet went inside, it hit her that she had not been inside of the family hospital in years, mostly because her guardians were worried that she would get the silly idea of helping with the family business. The front lobby of Evergreen hospital looked like the inside of a hotel. The floors were made of white marble and the walls were painted egg cream white. The half-moon shaped front desk made of oak wood sat in the center of the room.

Violet walked up to the front desk. She looked at the secretary sitting at the desk and said, "Hello Mandy, how have you been doing?"

Mandy was a young woman with honey brown skin and light auburn brown eyes. Her thick black hair was fashioned into a tight bun that sat in the middle of her head. She wore a green tank top, a blue-jean jacket, black pants, and blue sneakers.

Mandy replied, "I'm good, how have you been doing?"

"I'm doing alright."

"Your cousin is in your aunt's office. She is waiting there to do your hair."

Surprised, Violet responded, "She what?"

Mandy smiled as she responded, "Your cousin didn't say specifically, but she came in here with a big bag of hair. I asked her what she was planning to do with all that hair. She smiled and told me she is sick and tired of you being forced to have your hair done with that unhealthy chemical perm. Then she rushed over to the elevator, telling me that when you arrived, I needed to send you to your Aunt June's office."

Violet remembered Drusilla's complaint that morning. Part of her felt excited to get a fresh hairstyle, but another part of her was scared Drusilla would get angry and try to rip the hair out of her head. This had happened twice before. On one occasion she had been saved by Meg who tackled Drusilla, allowing Violet to run away and hide until dear momma Drusilla calmed down. On the second occasion, Violet had attempted to style her own hair. When Drusilla saw her, she grabbed Violet by the ends of her hair and dragged her from her bedroom, down the hallway, down the staircase, and into the living room. Violet only escaped when Hattie May freed her. She hid in the kitchen pantry for nearly twenty-four hours, her head throbbing.

She told herself to calm down. Mandy noticed Violet's discomfort and quickly said, "Don't worry, Miss Evergreen, "I don't think your guardians will be angry if your cousin does your hair."

An unsure Violet questioned, "How are you so sure?"

Mandy, smiling, said, "Your birthday party will be a huge event; it's being covered by all the newspapers and television stations."

"Really?" Violet wondered to herself why anyone would be interested in her. Then the thought that it was her reputation for having murdered her parents that was probably the reason for the attention.

Mandy spoke the words aloud, "The ongoing controversy surrounding your guardians getting extended custody of you is hot news."

Exasperated, Violet responded, "Seriously? That happened almost thirteen years ago."

Mandy clarified, "Actually, your birthday and the extended custody issue is big news because of your date last night."

Violet took a breath then said, "I forgot about that."

Mandy continued, "That date is still being talked about on every news network, especially all the gossip network shows. It's making your guardians and that guy you went out with look really bad. People are cussing them and him out all over the internet. There is even a huge campaign to hunt down that guy who forced you to leave the restaurant."

Violet then thought, *If the story is that big, it is surprising that his arrest has not been made public. Hmm… my guardians didn't sound concerned about where Winston was. Either they don't care, or they don't know.*

Mandy continued to say, "With all that bad press, your party has to be perfect for everything to die down."

"What does that have to do with my hair?"

Mandy smirked and said, "Your guardians need for your party to be perfect, so when you arrive you must look perfect from head to toe."

"I hope you're right. Anyway, I should hurry up and head upstairs. Have a good one."

Mandy smiled, "You, too, Miss Evergreen."

Violet headed for the elevator and when she entered, she pushed the button for the sixth floor. After leaving the elevator, Violet walked to the end of the hall reaching her aunt's office. She noticed the words written in gold letters, *Dr. June Wilds Chief of Staff*. As she entered her aunt's outer office, she saw that June's secretary was missing. She continued walking into her aunt's office. Sitting on a black leather couch in the center of the room was Meg.

June's office in its own way almost resembled a small loft apartment. The walls were navy blue, and like the rest of the hospital, the floors were made of white marble. There was a 60-inch curved television on the front wall playing a soccer game between Atlanta United and the Chicago Fire. The back wall behind her aunt's massive mahogany desk was made up almost entirely of windows, which had a great view of a beautiful garden surrounded by a small park that lay in the center of the hospital complex. The left wall was filled from floor to ceiling with a massive bookcase filled to the brim with medical books and binders filled with medical research information.

Violet walked over to Meg who was asleep on the couch. Meg was wearing a pair of jeans and a black lace shirt with a tank top underneath. Her legs crossed at the knees, and she had a pair of black tennis shoes on her feet.

Violet gently nudged Meg. Her cousin groaned as she slowly opened her eyes. After blinking twice, she started to sit up. As she wiped the sleep from her eyes, she asked, "How long was I out?"

Violet replied, "I'm not sure. I just got here."

Meg mentioned, "I guess I was still really tired from last night."

Violet asked, "How late was it when you guys got home?"

Meg informed, "I don't know about my dad, but TJ and I didn't get home until about two-thirty. Then all of us had to get up at six to get to the hospital."

Violet inquired, "Why did you guys have to come in so early?"

Meg began to explain, "The board is being a pain in the ass. To be honest, I was pretty pissed about it until your friend suddenly arrived and told us you had been cursed. What happened to you?"

Violet began recapping the events of her day. She started with the conversation she had overheard between the Lepels, getting cursed, and culminating with the details of her date. Meg looked at her, shocked for a split second.

170

Once she regained her composure Meg said, "What is this cause they were talking about? Better yet, who is this aunt?"

"I don't have any answers, only questions. I was hoping you might have at least heard about this mystery aunt."

Meg remarked, "I don't have any answers. My mom is in the lab right now working on a potion to get rid of your curse. Maybe she can shed some light on all of this later. I am going to do your hair. Sit so that I can get started."

Meg took one of the throw pillows from the couch and dropped it on the floor between her legs. Violet sat down on the pillow. While Meg searched through a bag of hair that was on the floor, Meg pulled out some hair oil and a black comb from the bag.

Violet asked, "So, my hair."

Meg said, "Needs a new look very badly, yes. Seriously, I don't know why Aunt Drusilla was so desperate to perm it. It's going to take a while for your hair to grow back strong."

"I'm more worried about Aunt Drusilla or her husband ripping my new hairstyle out of my head."

"Don't worry about that."

Violet reminded Meg, "You told me not to worry about my date going bad last night, and I got my ass kicked."

Meg started to comb Violet's hair while saying, "I know. I should have brought it up after you woke me up. I'm sorry, Violet. I honestly didn't believe either of them would hit you."

"It's ok, Meg. It's not like you could have known that she would attack me."

Meg started to oil Violet's roots as she said, "I know. I can't speak for the rest of the family, but it is weird you could not reach me on the phone. I should check your phone when I finish your hair."

"Ok."

The two cousins sat quietly listening to the soccer game as Meg styled Violet's hair.

Violet asked, "I wonder how is it that with everything going on how can we still have sports games?"

"It's because all sports are held in the same highly protected stadium."

"Don't demon voids just pop up anywhere?"

Meg said, "Almost anywhere. They never show up on or near a place of worship. But the reason for that is still highly debatable."

"A stadium is not a place of worship."

"I don't know. People have a habit of loving their teams as if they were gods. Anyway, the stadium is special because it is protected by the army and two Eden Witches."

"Let's not talk about the Eden Witches."

"Why?"

Violet explained, "I was reading about what is going on in Australia, and all this stuff with them and the demons makes no sense. People are always talking about demon voids opening up every five minutes. Then we hear all about how the Eden Witches are being thrown out of a country, or a state, or put in prison. How on earth is any society even functioning if things are this bad?"

172

Meg educated Violet as she rubbed the hair oil into Violet's scalp, saying, "I understand how you might draw that conclusion. The truth is that in the past only one or two demon voids would show up on a continent every year. Thirteen years ago, the number of demon voids increased to five per continent per year. This scared a lot of people. Now I can't speak for other countries, but in the U.S. a lot of wealthy families began hiring private protection from Eden Witches."

As she began putting leave-in conditioner into Violet's hair, Meg continued to say, "Violet, now that I am in charge of your hair, I'm buying you some hair oil. I don't know what is wrong with Aunt Drusilla or that hairstylist of hers. Your scalp is too dry."

Violet said, "I know, but the last time I asked for hair oil Aunt Drusilla slapped me. Then she started screaming about how hard Miss Adams works to keep my hair nice."

"Please, that woman doesn't know one damn thing about hair. She is bald for shit's sake, and I doubt that is on purpose."

Meg had Violet bend her head forward. As she started putting the first braids in Violet's head, she said, "Next time I do your hair, I am going to have to give you a deep condition."

"Why didn't you give me a deep conditioning today?"

Meg said, "It would take too long. I want it to sit in your hair for several hours, and we don't have time to do that today. Back to what I was telling you before, so when members of the upper class started wanting private protection the majority of the Eden Witches said no. This led to several laws, likely illegal, to regulate the Eden Witches."

Violet questioned, "How can an illegal law get passed?"

Meg responded, "Corruption and for the most part, the government has gone to shit. Most of the members of the current party seem to only serve their own self-interest, which as you can assume is very problematic especially when they choose supreme court justices."

"Ok, so the court upholds laws specifically passed to hurt Eden Witches. So, you are saying that the court is corrupt and under the control of our corrupt ruling party."

Meg confirmed, "Yes, anyway, even with all that crap, the Eden Witches are still able to handle the demon problem. The real issue in this country and the world is the rising poverty. Unfortunately, it is easier to push the wall-building program than it is to solve the rate of poverty."

Meg finished a few more braids as Violet said, "That is hard to believe."

In a serious tone, Meg said, "Some problems that seem simple are very convoluted. Then they get worse when they go unaddressed. Speaking of that, should we probably talk about the information you overheard this morning?"

Violet, in a defeated voice, said, "Why? It is not like we can do anything?"

Meg said, "We don't know that yet. When you told me about all that stuff, I admit the information overwhelmed me a bit, especially since I was just told about Arkell this morning."

"I thought you would have known about him for a while."

Meg announced, "No, only grandma, my mom, and Auntie May knew about Arkell. My mom told me, my dad, and my husband about Arkell when we got to the office this morning. Dad and I were angry at first, but after a minute we accepted that Arkell's role in our family drama had to be kept as secretive as possible."

"Well, explain the reason to me," Violet stated in a slightly angry tone.

Meg continued, "As you most likely suspect, Aunt Drusilla and her husband are involved in something not good, maybe even criminal. It probably has something to do with that cause you mentioned earlier. I'm surprised I didn't think of that before. I must still be a little tired from last night. Anyway, Arkell has been trying to find out what they are involved in. The only thing that my mom told me was that he has recently made some important discoveries and is getting closer."

"That's it?"

"I know that's very anticlimactic, but knowing that Aunt Drusilla…"

The office door opened, and June walked in. She was wearing blue scrubs and a white lab coat while holding a cup. June looked at Violet and Meg as she asked, "What are you two doing?"

Meg answered, "I'm doing Violet's hair."

June asked, "Why are you doing her hair? You know Drusilla will have whatever you do to it taken out."

Meg, using a coy tone, "Don't worry, Mama. I made a deal with my dear aunt this morning before leaving for the office. I told her if she let me do Violet's hair from now on, then I would work my magic and clean up the events of last night, getting it out of the limelight."

Violet asked, "How?"

"I will just release some hidden footage I have of a few famous people."

In a stern tone, June said, "Meg, that is a horrible thing to do."

Meg started to braid more of Violet's hair while saying, "Normally I would agree, but the footage I'm going to put out is going to be from a major Hollywood star who did something super bad. If I am being honest, I was going to put it out anyway."

June asked, "Who is this person and what did they do?"

"Mama, I would rather talk about it after the party."

June frowned as she said, "Fine. How long is it going to take you to do Violet's hair?"

"Probably another two hours."

June said, "In that case, let her have a mini break from braiding so I can give her this potion. I want to get the remainder of the curse off her before the party."

Violet said, "Auntie, Arkell told me since I ate a lot of zucchinis the curse should be gone."

June replied, "You ate zucchini fries, not raw zucchini. When you are trying to break a curse, you have to eat the necessary items raw."

"Did Arkell tell you about the zucchini fries? Also, the curse is not affecting me right now."

"Yes, he did tell me. As for that curse, the zucchini only weakens the curse. It does not remove it."

"I'm still cursed?"

June reassured, "You won't be after you drink this potion that I just made for you. Thank goodness your friend Zhang Li let me know what happened."

Meg finished another braid before telling Violet to get up. Once Violet was on her feet, she walked over to where her aunt was standing. June handed Violet the potion to fully free her of the curse. The moment the substance touched Violet's tongue, she savored the sweet taste of peppermint. This was followed by the feeling of her muscles relaxing. When she finished with the potion, her aunt threw the cup in a nearby trash can.

June asked, "How do you feel?"

Violet replied, "Relaxed. I feel as if all the stress in my body just washed away."

June replied, "Good, that means the curse is gone. Now all I have left to do is figure out how to stop my sister from sending you on more dates for a while."

Meg told Violet to sit back down because they only had so much time before they had to leave to get ready for the party.

As Violet sat down June said, "Alright, girls, there are some things I need to tell you."

"Auntie, before you start, there is something I want to talk to you about."

After explaining the events of that morning again. June's body seemed to stiffen. Violet, who could not see her aunt's expression, sensed that something was not right. When she asked her aunt if she was ok, June, who was sitting down at her desk, told her she was fine.

After a moment June said, "I felt a little dizzy for a moment, but whatever it was seems to be gone. Your doctor being involved in all of this doesn't surprise me."

"Why did Doctor Dawson do that?" Violet asked.

"He quit working for us as soon as your parents died. Dr. Dawson stated that he was disgusted by our family because we were allowing someone with UMD to run around unchecked. But he then continued to see you as a patient. It made no sense unless he was in league with the Lepels. You're also too old to be going to a pediatrician. Yet, he's still your doctor. I feel this information gives us a lead to some answers. All these years I've wondered why the judge gave Violet to the Lepels. I've also been perplexed why we were sent back to the same judge every time the case was reopened."

Violet asked, "Did you request a new judge to hear the case?"

"Yes, your uncle and I did. But our request was always denied. Arkell did inform me shortly after he was hired that he suspects someone very influential was keeping your case with Judge Hendrickson. Sadly, he could not figure out who it was. What's got me puzzled is this aunt, ouch!"

Violet and Meg both quickly asked if June was alright. June told them she was fine. She just had a headache and probably needed to take some medicine. June started to search her drawer for pain killers as Violet reflected on all the information that she had learned in the last several hours.

Auntie June was questioning this information about a mysterious aunt. If she is surprised by this supposed aunt, then something strange is going on.

A little bit after June took some painkillers, she sat quietly for a few minutes. Then June said, "I wonder if this aunt must be a member of your mother's family."

Violet responded, "You know that my mom didn't have any family. That's why she grew up in an orphanage."

June remarked, "I know, but if my sister is saying you have an aunt we have not met, then that is the only logical answer. However, ouch!"

"Auntie, are you alright?"

"Yes, this stupid headache will not leave me alone."

Meg said, "You probably need to rest for a while."

"I'll be alright."

Meg asked, "Maybe we should take another look at Uncle Mathew's will. It might mention who this person is."

"I doubt it, but it wouldn't hurt to look. To other matters, it is well past time I fill both of you girls in on what has been going on before Ollivander gets here."

Violet asked, "Why is he coming?"

June answered, "You know neither Victor nor my sister like you being around any member of the family by yourself for a long period of time."

"But Arkell is here, and they think he works for them."

"True, but Arkell is nowhere near as intimidating as Ollivander. June continued, "Victor probably thinks Meg and I will be more willing to challenge him because of that. Also, their only real use for Arkell is his ability to use that eye thing to spy. But the hospital has a very powerful spell on it to make sure that no spy devices will work anywhere on this compound."

"Why?"

"There was an incident fifty years ago where a husband tried to use spy equipment to set up his wife. I'm not clear about all the details since whatever happened really bothered your grandpa, but the resulting lawsuit nearly got the hospital shut down. So, your grandpa had that spell put on the building.

Anyway, back to business. The judge from the custody case is under investigation. I don't hold out much hope that he will be convicted because he and the governor are old friends."

Meg said, "Seriously?"

"Yes, it is true the governor is the one having the charges dropped. But he is not doing it out of friendship. The governor of all people is obsessed with making sure Violet is married as soon as possible."

Violet quickly said, "Why the heck does he care about that?"

June took a breath before saying, "I have no idea. But I do know that he isn't the only high-ranking official involved in this."

Meg said, "They must all be a part of that cause Violet heard about."

June said, "I assume so. The real problem is that I can't bribe anymore of Violet's dates to pass on her."

Violet quickly said, "You what?"

June continued, "Violet, you are a pretty girl with a very big inheritance. Don't you think it is more than a little strange that every man my sister picked, passed on you?"

As the realization of what her aunt said felt like a punch to the gut. *I'm really stupid. I should have known. All the men my guardians picked for me were clearly more interested in my inheritance than in me. Who would propose to a woman less than an hour after meeting her?*

"Violet, I know what you're thinking and do not be too hard on yourself. There is no way you could have known the family was interfering with your dates. Until we were able to succeed in giving you a cellphone, you barely got to talk to us. Even when we snuck you scraps and took you to church."

Meg asked, "Why did this most recent guy and the dude from last night not take the money?"

June answered, "I'm not sure. My only guess is my sister and that husband of hers are getting better at who they pick. Also, I should mention to you both that none of the men Violet had gone out with know about this conspiracy."

Meg took a breath before asking, "How do you know that, and why are they only picking men who don't know what they are up to?"

June said, "Arkell informed us that the men are not involved in this conspiracy. I also don't know why they pick men oblivious to their plan, but Arkell thinks that…"

Just then the door opened, and Ollivander walked in. His usual unwelcoming smile on his face as he asked, "I hope you ladies have not been up to anything."

June looked at Ollivander as she said, "We were going over the guestlist for tonight's party."

Ollivander remarked, "I understand a lot of very important people will be at tonight's event. Have you explained to young Miss Evergreen how she must behave during tonight's event?"

Meg said, "Don't worry. We had a long talk about ladylike behavior, and which forks to use with what."

Ollivander in a slightly surprised tone said, "What are you talking about? It was my understanding that young Miss Evergreen was to have no food or drink today, to help her lose all that weight the salad she had yesterday put on her."

In a stern tone June said, "Violet gets to eat and drink as much as she wants at tonight's party. I have a contract with your employers stating that fact. And if anyone prevents her from doing so, then I get a fine of thirty-two thousand dollars."

Ollivander frowned as he pulled out his cellphone and started to make a call. Meanwhile, June picked up the remote control for the television and clicked through the channels.

As Violet turned her head to the right so Meg could finish braiding her hair, Ollivander reached someone on the phone. After saying, "Thank you, Mrs. Lepel," he hung up.

After ending his call, Ollivander turned to June and said, "It appears that what you were saying was accurate. Arkell will be dropping her off at the party venue."

In an aggravated tone June said, "I know."

Then she turned and looked at him as she asked, "Can you go somewhere else for a while?"

"I'm sorry, Mrs. Wilds, but I am under strict orders to watch Miss Evergreen while her hair is being done. Then I am to escort her home so she can…"

Just then his phone rang, and without a word he rushed out of the room.

June waited a moment before checking to see if Ollivander was in the hallway. Then she left the room in a hurry.

Violet frowned as she wondered what just happened.

Meg retrieved the remote and turned to the news. As she sat down and went back to work on Violet's hair she said, "Uncle's on the tv."

Violet couldn't turn her head in the direction of the screen, but she heard Anas' voice say, "After months of fighting, Atlanta mayor Rebecca Franklin has lost the fight to prevent Atlanta from becoming a walled city."

Meg said, "Shit. I was hoping she could stop them from building that stupid thing."

Violet asked, "Are we going to ignore what just happened?"

"Violet, it's not safe to talk about things when Ollivander is in the building."

"Why?"

"I will tell you eventually."

Suddenly, June burst back into the room. She quickly closed the door then rushed over to her desk and sat down.

Meg said, "Mama, what's wrong?"

June replied, "Just focus on Violet's hair."

They heard Anas say, "This loss for the mayors of several major cities came after Federal Court Judge Nancy Wallace ruled in favor of President Andrews' demon wall plan. Governor Jerry Pine immediately gave the order to build a wall around Atlanta, Macon, Marietta, Savannah, and 20 other Georgia cities that have been dubbed by the governor as successful. Locally, many believe the governor forced the mayor's hand in a desperate attempt to comply with the president's new keep out the demons initiative. Instead of only enclosing wealthy sectors of a city, now President Andrews is attempting to build walls around every profitable city in the United States, despite criticisms saying that the president's plan secretly includes the relocation of poor citizens.

The poor and unemployed will be relocated to areas outside these cities once the walls are built. This plan will turn the inner cities into havens for the rich and upper working class. Unnamed sources also shared with this network that the contracts to build these walls will not be given out in the usual manner. Instead, all contracts for this project will be given exclusively to friends of the president's, who just happen to be in the construction business. A spokesperson for the White House denies this report saying there is no plan to relocate American citizens, nor is there any conspiracy to award construction contracts to the president's friends. President Andrews holds firm that the walls are nothing more than a protection measure against the demon voids."

June said, "Andrews is a lying sack of shit. How the hell is a wall going to ..."

Just then Ollivander walked back into the room with a pissed off look on his face. When he noticed June looking at him, his expression softened, and the uncomfortable smile returned.

In a stern tone, he said, "I think it is time to turn off the television and change subjects. Politics is too overwhelming a topic for someone with Miss Evergreen's condition."

Meg told Violet to turn her head to the left. After Violet did, she heard June say, "Don't you think it would be best for Violet to at least be a little aware of what is going on in the world?"

As Ollivander started to disagree, Violet heard Anas say, "We are about to switch over to the White House lawn where the president is giving his second address of the day."

Violet heard her aunt say, "I do not want to hear anything this fool has to say. Where did I put that remote?"

Meg stopped working on Violet's hair to take her mother the remote. Violet lifted her head and massaged her neck a little bit. She looked at the television as the president started to make his announcement. President O'Donnell Andrews' balding, very greasy black hair seemed to shine in the sunlight. While the president's peach skin looked as if it was sunburned, his emerald green eyes glittered like a cat about to pounce on its prey.

He was wearing a black suit with black leather shoes. After he adjusted his dark blue tie, he walked up to the podium.

The president said, "Good news! The courts have ruled in our favor, and construction of walls around all of America's great cities will begin immediately. I just got off the phone with Governor Pine of Georgia. He sends thanks from the people of his state, and he assured me that the wall will provide protection to Atlanta and other great Georgia cities. This is real good, folks. Atlanta will no longer be a shithole slum waiting for demons to invade it. No, folks, like all the other walled…"

June quickly changed the channel to a music talent contest while Meg had Violet turn her head so she could braid the hair on the back of her head.

Ollivander asked, "Why do people like these silly music shows?"

As Meg continued to work on Violet's hair she said, "Because people like having fun."

Ollivander shot Meg an annoyed look, but she ignored it.

Meg continued, "Anyway, this wall is going to be a huge waste of money."

June said, "I know, but as we already know, he would rather waste tax money on those stupid walls instead of what's needed now that the economy has collapsed. You know, I thought things got bad when

Buckhead and other rich areas opted into the wall program, but now that it has extended to the entire city, I know things are going to get worse."

Ollivander asked, "Mrs. James, are you almost done with Miss Evergreen's hair?"

Meg told him to be patient, that she was going to be finished in a few minutes. Then June told them both that she was going to have a car meet them at the front. Violet felt her neck start to get sore. While she massaged it a little bit, she thought, *I'm glad my aunt and Meg are going to ride home with me. I'm not all that comfortable with Arkell, and I always hate being anywhere with Ollivander.*

She asked Meg if she could lift her head up for a minute.

Meg replied, "I'm almost done. Just try to hold out for a few more minutes."

Violet groaned while saying, "All right."

A few more minutes passed before June looked at Violet. She smiled while saying, "Violet, your hair looks very pretty."

Violet's heart leaped as she said, "Really?"

Meg told her, "You can see for yourself in the mirror in mom's restroom when I am done."

Violet felt a grin form on her face while impatiently waiting to see how her hair looked.

A few more minutes passed before Meg said, "Violet, I'm done. Take a look at yourself in the mirror."

When Violet quickly got up, she noticed her scalp felt sore. She told herself to ignore it as she walked into her aunt's private bathroom. Violet looked at herself in the mirror over the sink. A huge smile formed on her face as she admired her long braids in the mirror. She felt overwhelmed at how beautiful her hair looked, and in turn, it made her feel beautiful.

As she walked back into her aunt's office, she felt her eyes begin to well up.

June said, "Violet, don't cry."

Tears began to fall down Violet's face as she replied, "I can't help it. My hair is gorgeous."

She looked at Meg who was turning off the tv. Violet said, "Meg, tha…"

In unison, Meg and June said, "Don't say thank you."

"Why?"

June answered, "Your great grandma always told me that if you say thank you to someone for doing your hair, then all of your hair will fall out."

Violet said, "Yikes, forever?"

Ollivander walked over and looked at Violet's hair for a moment. Then he turned to Meg and said, "Mrs. James, you did an adequate job with Miss Evergreen's hair. But next time, it would be wise to allow her usual stylist to handle her hair."

Meg looked at her mother and asked, "Is the car ready?"

June replied, "Yes, let's get going."

Chapter 9
Party Time

After arriving back in her bedroom, Violet tied a silk scarf around her head. She lay on her bed and decided to try and get a little rest before her big event. The more she lay there staring at the ceiling, the more she thought about the events of the day. What was happening to her life and why would someone as important as the governor care about what happened to her? Why were her guardians so desperate to marry her off? Her mind swirling, she decided to take a quick shower. After drying off she sprayed herself from head to toe with her favorite perfume, put on her undergarments, stockings, and makeup.

Then she put on her new dress, another birthday gift from her Aunt June and cousin Meg. The dress was a soft silver-gray color covered with sequins that sparkled in a way that reflected different colors depending on how it caught the light. Her stiletto heels matched her dress. They too, sparkled in the light. Next, she placed silver bracelets on her right wrist. Looking at herself in the mirror, she understood why Meg chose the silver color for her nails. She lingered in front of the mirror for several minutes, admiring how lovely she looked. Violet twirled around in her new dress as she giggled. She was happy, and more importantly, she felt pretty for the first time in her life.

Before her happiness could sink in too deep, insecurity crept its way into her thoughts. Suddenly a voice in her head said, *don't get too excited. You know everything is going to go to shit at the party.*

Violet shook her head before saying, "That's not true. It's my birthday, and I am going to have fun."

The voice replied, *like everything went ok after you bought food? Face it, anything good that happens to you is followed by something bad.*

Violet stomped her foot as she said, "Shut the fuck up. I promised myself I was going to stop always giving into negativity. That is what my guardians want."

Just then Violet heard her Aunt May ask, "Violet, is everything ok?"

Violet's heart leaped at the sound of her aunt's voice. Her hands began to shake. Violet looked at her hands as she said, "I'm fine. Just double checking my makeup before we leave."

She continued to stare at her hands. As she wondered how to get them to stop trembling, May asked, "Are you sure you're ok?"

Without thinking, Violet turned on the cold water in the sink and placed her hands under the running water.

As she stuck her hands under the water she said, "Yeah, I'm almost ready."

"Ok."

After a moment her hands stopped shaking. She dried them while wondering why she was shaking and why the cold water helped. Violet took a deep breath as she told herself to calm down before opening the bathroom door and walking out.

May had grown plump from her pregnancy. She was wearing a dark blue maternity dress that had blue sequins sewed into it. Wrapped around May's neck was a long gold chain that had a green pendant attached to it.

May smiled as she looked at her niece's hair. She gently touched it while saying, "Meg did a really good job with your hair."

Violet smiled as she said, "I know. It's nice to finally have my hair done properly."

"Violet, you always had beautiful hair. It just got ruined when my sister decided to put that perm in your head."

"You're right."

"Ok, missy. Your uncle and your grandma cannot join us tonight, but they both told me you are under strict orders to have fun."

"Why aren't they coming to the party?"

"Your grandma had to go to the dentist today. He drilled into her gums to prevent her from losing her teeth, and her face is going to be numb until tomorrow. It also made her sleepy, so she just wants to rest tonight. In your uncle's case, he has to bail for the usual reason."

Violet announced, "Work? I saw him on television today."

May replied, "Yes, work as usual."

Violet asked, "Why is he never allowed any time off unless he gets hurt or sick?"

May answered, "He started refusing to report from locations known to be demon voids."

"I'm glad he stopped getting close to those monsters when he found out about the baby."

"We may be happy about that, but his bosses are not. The studio heads seem to be annoyed with him for his refusal to continually put his life in danger. They don't want to fire him either, so his bosses are punishing him by having him work crazy hours. Mind you, everyone in this city knows that tonight is your big birthday party."

Violet, with sympathy in her voice, said, "That sucks."

"True, but there is nothing we can do about it. He loves being a reporter, so no matter what he has to go through, he refuses to quit." May's phone dinged. As she looked down at her phone, she smiled and commented, "I could live without him texting every hour."

Violet wondered, "Why is he doing that?"

"He is in perpetual worry about me and the baby. I'm close to my due date."

"Not surprised, this is your first baby."

May smiled as she informed her niece, "Sweetheart, I have a feeling he is going to act this way with every child we have. Enough about that, are you excited about your party? I don't remember the last time we got to throw you a nice event.

My stupid sister or that husband of hers would always find a way to ruin every birthday party we tried to give you. But tonight isn't the time for sad memories. It's your B-Day, girl, and this party is going to be non-stop fun!"

Violet, still feeling nervous, said, "Do you believe that my guardians will honor the contract that they signed with the family, agreeing not to interfere with the party in any way?"

May replied in a reassuring tone, "Yes, they won't interfere thanks to that debacle date they sent you on last night. It's all-over social media. Not wanting to be publicly seen as terrible guardians, they are desperate to save face. So, they want tonight's event to be a success as much as we do."

Violet, in a nervous tone, remarked, "Meg mentioned that to me earlier. I guess I'm just nervous."

Violet wanted to question her aunt about the family's interference with the dates she had been forced to go on, but she reminded herself that all the surveillance equipment in her room had been reinstalled that afternoon.

The door opened, and June walked in. She was wearing a gold dress and black heels.

June uttered a quick spell that caused the camera to melt a little bit. They heard a strange popping noise for a second. June smiled as she turned to look at the partially melted camera as it looked as if it were about to fall.

June looked at May as she said, "Little sis, before Ollivander runs in here, Violet told me she overheard Drusilla say she has an aun...OUCH!

May asked if June was alright. Meanwhile, Violet took notice that June's head seemed to hurt every time she was about to start talking about Violet's supposed aunt. Sadly, she didn't have long to think about the matter because Ollivander walked in.

Ollivander made his usual uncomfortable smile as he looked at May. He said, "Mrs. Amodako and Mrs. Wilds, I must remind you both that neither of you are allowed to be in this room alone."

May quipped, "We're not alone. Violet's here"

Ollivander, using a deep tone, stated, "Madam, you know what I meant."

To avoid confrontation, Violet quickly said, "Anyway, we are wasting time. We need to be going."

Violet, June, and May were reunited with the rest of the family in the garage. After they shared compliments, they climbed into one of the family limos. As they headed to the venue for Violet's party, Ollivander rode shotgun in the front seat next to Arkell, who was acting as the chauffeur.

Violet sat in the back of a limo next to her Aunt May. Sitting across from them were June and Akeem. Akeem was wearing a dark blue three-piece suit with a white shirt and a gray tie with a pair of black leather shoes protecting his feet. Meg, wearing a tight red dress and red heels, sat next to her husband Theodor James, nicknamed TJ, on the seat directly behind Ollivander and Arkell.

TJ was a tall, very muscular man with rich mocha skin. The long thick black hair on top of his head was styled in corn rolls with a braided bun. TJ had deep brown eyes that glittered in the light, which were complemented by the large ears on each side of his head. He was wearing a tan three-piece suit with a light blue shirt and tie. On his feet were a pair of dark brown leather shoes.

TJ was looking down at his cellphone as he said, "The Yellow Stars won."

Meg looked at his phone while saying, "Impossible. When I was watching the game, they were behind six throws to one."

TJ shrugged before replying, "Sky ball has never exactly been a predictable game."

May asked, "Is that the one people play on broomsticks?"

Meg answered, "No, it's that ball game where five people on each team are suspended in the air, and they are attached to a bungee cord that is connected to a helicopter."

June took a breath as she said, "I thought they outlawed that stupid shit."

TJ replied, "You would think that, but like any other sport, as long as it's making money for rich assholes like us, it won't be going anywhere."

Akeem said, "We should get a sky ball team."

June quickly replied, "Absolutely not, they are…"

Violet's attention wandered away from her family's conversation. She couldn't help but think about all the events of that day.

May said, "Violet, did you hear me?"

Violet quickly replied, "Sorry, Auntie May, I was lost in thought."

May responded, "Not surprising after the day you had."

Suddenly, the car stopped at a red light. As TJ stared at his phone, Meg inquired as to what he was looking at now.

He responded, "Nothing. I was just checking the stock market. Our shares have gone up again. So, I was debating whether…"

Ollivander cleared his throat very loudly, signaling that TJ should drop the topic.

In response, June folded her arms. Then in what seemed to be an act of defiance, she said, "I'm not surprised our stocks are going up. I'm planning to take advantage of it to start a new venture."

Violet asked, "What are you going to do?"

June answered, "For a while, some of my friends and I…"

Suddenly, Ollivander said, "Mrs. Wilds, I must remind you that there will be consequences if you discuss the Evergreen company with young Miss Evergreen."

At that moment all conversation in the car ceased. Violet folded her arms. *I wish Ollivander didn't have to be here.*

After a few minutes, Meg broke the silence when she said, "How much longer till we get there?"

As Arkell began to answer, "We have…"

Ollivander interrupted as he said, "A driver's only job is to drive, not engage in chitchat."

What the h-e double hockey sticks just happened? Ollivander never jumps on the drivers when they are answering a basic question. Does he not like Arkell?

May said, "We are passing the Fox Theatre, so we should be there in twenty minutes."

TJ replied, "Darn, I was hoping we were closer."

Violet asked, "Tired of sitting in the car?"

"Yeah, but it's more about you getting to see this place. The whole club is nice, but seeing the entrance will take your breath away."

Meg said, "He's right. We go there almost every…"

Arkell suddenly slammed on the breaks, which made Violet slam into May. Her heart raced as she asked if May was alright. May had one hand on her belly as she steadied her breathing as she responded to Violet by saying that she was fine.

Meanwhile, Ollivander was yelling at Arkell about how he should have been watching the road. Arkell was apologizing profusely as he stated that a man came out of nowhere.

Suddenly, they heard someone hit the window on the driver's side of the limo. Violet looked in the direction of the noise. She saw a man with a very angry look on his face. The man had brown skin with short curly hair that had been dyed bright red. He had a large, curved nose and dull aqua blue eyes. He was wearing a baggy white shirt.

The man punched the window again before screaming a few profanities and storming off.

Ollivander shouted at Arkell to start driving. As the car started to move, Ollivander said, "You should have just run over that moron."

June said, "Ollivander, don't say something that awful."

Ollivander stated in a matter-of-fact tone, "How is that awful? The light was green, and he ran out into the middle of the street. If Arkell had hit him, it would have been that man's fault."

June responded, "I am not saying the man was smart. What I'm saying is that we should be grateful that the moron did not die."

Ollivander's tone remained cold and indifferent as he said, "I beg to differ. He looked and behaved like a vagabond. So, there is no doubt he has no money, meaning if this car crushed him, it would not matter."

Violet said, "That is a sick thing to say."

Ollivander laughed and then said, "Miss Evergreen, you are truly still a child. That man is nothing more than a bottom feeder who is a waste on society."

Akeem said, "You are truly a sick man."

The car went silent after that. Violet thought about what Ollivander said. She wondered how many people thought like Ollivander. Even worse, how many people closed their eyes and let people like Ollivander get away with treating human beings with such complete disregard. As she meditated on that topic, she wondered why she had chosen to be one of the people with their eyes closed for so long.

She continued to reflect on the situation until the car stopped and Arkell announced that they had arrived. Before anyone began to get out of the car, Ollivander said, "Miss Evergreen, do not forget that you are representing the Lepel's tonight. I may not be accompanying you inside, but remember if you do anything to humiliate them, then you will be made to regret it."

Violet didn't look at Ollivander or respond to anything he said. All she wanted to do was get away from him.

After TJ helped May slowly climb out of the car, Violet immediately rushed out. The second she was outside, Violet stared at the large gray building, a little disappointed.

TJ kept saying my jaw would drop at the sight of this place. But I don't get the appeal.

May walked over to Violet and said, "What are you waiting for? Everyone is already inside."

Violet noticed that the car and the rest of her family were gone. May urged Violet to follow her, ushering her inside the building.

Chapter 10
Happy Birthday

When Violet walked into the club, she was hit by an amazing sight. The outside of the club looked like a boring gray building, but the inside was practically breathtaking.

She was standing in a massive outdoor open area with a fountain in the center. The fountain was full of pink lotus blossoms. As the music played, shoots of water sprung up from the fountain. The water shoots would fly into the air before transforming into doves made out of water. The water doves flew around in different patterns to keep up with the beat of the music until they eventually flew back into the fountain.

The floor was constructed out of flat, smooth white tile. There were two long rectangular tables both covered with white tablecloths on either side of the room. Each table was covered with beautifully covered boxes with bows of every color and size. Sharing the same space were elaborately decorated gift bags with tissue paper of every hue sticking out of their tops. The site of her gifts filled Violet's heart with mixed feelings. She imagined all the happy hours she would spend discovering what each package contained; however, she knew that she would not be allowed to keep any of them. All the contents of the packages, all of her gifts, would be taken away and sold- the money would be given to charity by her family.

As Violet continued to stare at the beautiful assortment of packages in every shape, size, and color, she smiled remembering that Zhang Li had snuck into her room to give her a gift earlier. At least she had been able to keep one of her gifts.

May said, "Violet, come on. Hurry up, let's get inside."

It was at that moment that Violet noticed the back wall of glass doors. She assumed they led to the section of the club where her party would be happening. As they walked toward the doors, May told herself that despite how the room looked, they were actually inside. Magic had been used to make the ceiling reflect the sky outside.

Violet thought, _I never knew magic could make a ceiling look like that._

When they reached the doors May said, "Violet, I just remembered something. I wanted to double-check with security about transferring the gifts to the auction house."

Violet questioned, "I thought you guys sold them for charity money."

Aunt May responded, "We do, but mind you, these gifts are from some of the wealthiest people in Atlanta and from across the country. Having them sold through the auction house will fetch the best price. What they can't sell at auction will be sold online."

Violet thought of the families that she had met on the street a few nights earlier. She asked May, "Which charity do you guys send the money to?"

May said, "I thought you knew. Most of it goes to aiding the poor. We use the rest to fund the suicide hotline. Anyway, that's enough chit chat. You need to go in and start having fun. This is your party."

May walked away in the direction of one of the security guards. Violet approached the glass doors. They opened, and she entered the next room.

199

The room was so dark Violet could barely see. After a minute she figured it would be wise to double-check to see if she had walked into the right room. Before she could turn around, multicolored club lights suddenly turned on. The light revealed that she was standing at the top of a small staircase with a view of the room below.

The room had dark wooden floors with black painted walls. In the center of the ceiling were the multi-colored lights that added some brightness to the space. Against the right wall were white couches. The couches were grouped into sections of three, one in the center of each group with the others on either side of the center couch, and a small square glass table in the center of each grouping. The opposing wall had several large round tables filled with food, except for one table that had utensils, napkins, and cups. Next to the table with the utensils was a bar with six bartenders serving guests.

She heard an announcer say, "Happy Birthday, Violet Evergreen!" Violet saw her family cheering as they stood in front of a large crowd of cheering and applauding guests.

Confetti started to rain down as music began to play. Violet couldn't stop smiling as she began to descend the staircase. When she reached the bottom of the stairs, she was greeted by her family. After each of them gave her a hug, she thanked them for throwing her such a wonderful party.

Meg said, "You're welcome, Violet. Now go ahead and hang out with your friends. We don't know when you will be able to see them again."

That's an odd thing to say. Zhang Li was the one who told Auntie June I was cursed. Then again, we didn't talk about Zhang Li getting onto the property earlier. I don't know why I didn't discuss it with Meg and Auntie June. The more I reflect on this, Auntie June may not have wanted to talk to me about it. Probably since Ollivander was on his way, and she had to talk to me about the things she didn't feel she had the time to talk to me about.

200

Meg put her hand on Violet's shoulder and asked if she was alright. Violet said yes and that she was going to do as she suggested and find her friends. However, she barely took three steps when her friend Tawanda popped out of nowhere and hugged her.

Tawanda had rich dark brown skin and hazelnut eyes. Her lips were painted with gold lipstick while her eyelids were dusted with silver eyeshadow. Tawanda's dark brown hair was styled in long diva curls. Both of her arms had thick gold bracelets around her wrist, and she was wearing a glittery strapless red dress with gold high heels.

As soon as Tawanda let go, Zhang Li rushed over to hug her. She squeezed Violet very tightly as she said, "Thank goodness that curse is off of you."

Tawanda said, "Zhang Li, you're about to crush her."

In response, Zhang Li let go as she said, "Sorry, Violet."

Violet replied, "It's ok. You didn't squeeze me that hard. I love that dress."

Zhang Li was wearing a noodle strap dark blue sequin dress. She smiled as she thanked Violet.

In a snarky tone, Tawanda said, "You didn't say anything about my outfit."

Violet giggled as she replied, "As always, your outfit is amazing."

Just then a few more of Violet's friends walked over. Her friend Lucius was a very tall vampire with rich dark brown skin. His eyes were blood-red while his fingernails were long, sharp, and painted black. He had short curly black hair and a very distinctive curved nose. Lucius was wearing a black suit with black leather shoes.

Standing next to Lucius was Janet. Janet wore a strapless gold sequin dress, and she was holding a gold shawl across her left arm. On her feet were a pair of gold high heels.

As Violet greeted Janet, her friend Bell tapped her on the shoulder. Bell had smooth chocolate brown skin and sparkling hazelnut eyes. Her hair was styled in dreads, and there was a decorative plastic pink lily in her hair. Bell was wearing a green dress with red high heels and a gold necklace hanging around her neck.

Lastly, Violet's friend Demetri hugged her as he commented how long it had been since they had seen each other. Demetri was the youngest member of the group, having just completed high school earlier that month. His emerald green eyes glittered while his dark brown skin was smooth as silk. His hair was dark brown and very curly. His nose was round. Demetri was wearing a navy-blue suit with dark brown leather shoes.

Janet said, "Zhang Li told me that madwoman cursed you. How much more crazy shit do those two assholes have to do before the cops finally accept that they're not right?"

Violet shrugged while saying, "At this point, I think my guardians pay them off."

Bell stated without hesitation, "I'm inclined to agree."

Lucius chimed in with, "We have forever to talk about those jerks. Right now, I think we need to eat and dance till it's time to cut the cake."

Violet agreed, and she and her friends headed in the direction of the buffet tables. While they walked, Violet and her friends chatted about how life after high school was going. Violet listened attentively to her friends' stories. She enjoyed their stories and wished that she could have half the freedom and fun that her friends had. She wondered for the millionth time what her life would be like if her parents were still alive and if she had a normal family. Catching herself wishing for things that could never be, Violet reminded herself that at least for tonight she was in the company of friends and family who loved her and only wanted to see her happy. So, she began to talk and laugh with her friends; friends that she had not been allowed to see or communicate with since her graduation ceremony.

When they reached the buffet table, Violet's jaw almost dropped. There were giant plates of roast beef, rack of lamb, sirloin steak, chicken marsala, crab legs, lobster tails, salmon, cauliflower steaks, beef kebobs, and probably every other food on the planet. There was also a dessert table nearby with tons of treats Violet could not wait to try. She said to herself that this is one night when she won't go to bed hungry.

Lucius looked at Violet while saying, "Enough staring, more eating."

Standing near the prime rib, Lucius placed a plate in her hand, and she immediately reached out to the meat carver who placed a large slice of meat on her plate. Violet couldn't hold back her smile as she filled her plate. Once her plate was full, Isabel found a spot where they could sit and eat. That was when Violet noticed there were a few white couches in the center of the space. When she finally sat down, she started digging into her plate without a second thought. Violet was happily eating to her heart's content.

Janet then said, "Ok, now can we tell her what we did?"

Zhang Li, who had just swallowed a ginger roasted carrot, paused for a second before saying, "I told her what we did to the security barrier this morning."

Bell replied, "I'm not talking about that. I'm talking about where we are all going to start meeting up."

Demetri said, "Shit, I literally forgot all about that."

Violet asked, "What are you guys talking about?"

Excitedly, Bell said, "We found a way for all of us to meet, and it won't get you in trouble."

Violet said, "How?"

Bell continued, "Ok, so when Tawanda made the hole in your home's protection barrier, we knew that it would still be a hassle for us to meet one at a time. So, we figured out a way that we can sneak you out on occasion."

Violet swallowed a piece of salmon while thinking, *they must have forgotten about the tracking spell. What am I thinking? They don't know about the tracking spell. I never told them. Not like any of that matters anyway.*

She asked, "Tawanda, did you ever find out why that spell is in your family's magic book?"

Tawanda said, "Sadly, no. The only way to find out is to contact a government magic scholar. My parents want to hold off on doing that since the scholar may deem my family's grimoire as giving us too much power. Then the courts will have the spell removed."

Lucius said, "That makes sense. Grimoires are only supposed to contain two types of spells at max."

Tawanda told me her grimoire only contained building and cleaning spells, so it's strange it has a security spell. The spellcaster who made her spell book must have been extremely powerful, or insane. People who create a grimoire sign away their lives in the process. I know I have a family grimoire that led to our wealth. I just don't get why someone would give up their lives and happiness just to create a grimoire.

Bell said, "It would be nice if the grimoires didn't only work for one or two different types of spells, seeing how super powerful they can make spells someone cast from them."

Lucius replied, "As good as that sounds, being aware of how strong a grimoire spell is, it's probably smart there are only two spell types in them. Combined with the fact that they only work for someone from the bloodline of the book's creator."

Demetri said, "That was a thorough explanation of something we all know."

Lucius explained, "I was just trying…"

Demetri interrupted, "Don't worry, man, just messing with ya."

Tawanda said, "Alright, I think we can work sneaking you out like this. Violet, because we know that spell limiter gets in the way of you casting high-level magic, Lucas and Zhang Li will sneak onto your property."

"Why?" Violet asked.

"They are the only ones with the power to change their size."

"Oh, right."

"Ok, so, they will wait for you at the window just as you open it. Then Zhang Li will cast a spell to mess up your room's security."

Violet wondered, "How?"

Zhang Li said, "I'm going to cast a spell to make the camera see an image of you in your room."

Violet questioned, "What happens if someone comes into my room?"

Janet said, "I'm going to put a distraction spell on your door. It makes anyone who touches your door think they need to do something else and leave. But the spell will only last three hours, unfortunately."

Violet shrugged as she replied, "Better than nothing."

Demetri said, "After all the spells are cast, Zhang Li and Lucas will help you exit via the window. And all that's left is to leave through the woods area of your property. Then we all take off in my car."

Violet's eyes welled up as she said, "Thanks. I appreciate this."

Bell said, "You're welcome, Violet. We know it has been a rough year for you with all those crazy dates."

Janet asked, "What were those dates like? It's driving me nuts that we live in the same house, and I am never allowed to talk to you or even come into your room."

Violet told her friends about a few of her dates, including her date from earlier that day.

Demetri smiled while saying, "Damn, I wish I could have seen that."

Bell giggled as she said, "Me, too. Bet that son of a bitch sailed when he was punched."

Violet and her friends talked for a little while. Soon she realized that her throat was dry. After asking her friends to watch her food, she went to get something to drink.

She had just gotten herself a cup of berry punch as she turned to head back to her friends. She noticed a large plate of zucchini fries. Violet knew she was more than a little full at that point, but she figured a few zucchini fries wouldn't hurt. She put a few fries on a plate when she heard a man giggle behind her.

This was followed by a familiar voice saying, "You really love zucchini."

Violet turned around to see the chef from Taste of Magic standing behind her. He was still wearing his chef's uniform, and he was smiling at her.

Violet froze as her heart and mind raced. *What is he doing here? Is he one of my family's business partners? No, they would never get involved in fine dining unless there was some kind of outbreak. Wait, why am I even feeling nervous? I don't exactly know him that well. He is really cute. I can't believe I just thought that. Wait, how long have I been standing here? Say something, dammit.*

Quickly she said, "How you. Um, I mean, how have you been doing?"

That was such a stupid question. I'm so dumb.

The chef said, "Thanks for your concern, but you don't have to worry about that guy getting back at me. He woke up when the cops arrived. The idiot tried to bribe the cops into arresting me. Little did he know that the police chief, the mayor, the governor, both state senators, several state representatives, their backers, and their friends love my restaurant. Darn, I wish I had taken a photo of the look on his face. He looked like someone slapped him twice."

"I'm glad it worked out."

The chef then said, "Thanks, you will find this a little hard to believe, but when I called the cops, the operator thought I was pulling a prank."

"Why?"

The chef chuckled as he voiced, "It was the twelfth time I had to call over a dispute that started with a date."

Violet smiled as she responded, "If I hadn't had to go on so many assigned dates, I probably wouldn't have believed you either. I did not get your name earlier."

The chef responded, "It's Cinder."

She felt her palms get warm, and she told herself to stop being nervous. Violet asked, "That's an interesting name. How did your…"

Just then Akeem rushed up to Violet and said, "There you are. We have been looking all over for you."

Before Violet could react, her uncle grabbed her arm. She quickly said goodbye to Cinder as she was pulled away.

When they reached the rest of the family, in an aggravated voice Meg said, "Dad, you should have waited."

Akeem replied, "What are you talking about? You know we only have so much time."

Violet asked, "What are you guys talking about?"

No one seemed to hear her, and Meg mumbled something Violet couldn't hear very clearly. June asked Violet to give her the plate and cup Violet was holding. As Violet handed the items to her, she started to ask her aunt why she needed them. Before June could respond, the music suddenly stopped. Several people stopped what they were doing and started to inquire why the music was gone.

What is going on?

TJ looked at Violet before looking at the cake.

The birthday cake was six massive tiers. It was covered with white fondant and multicolored frosting flowers with the words *Happy Birthday Violet* written on the front.

A few minutes passed and people started to complain. May said, "Ridiculous, simply ridiculous. As much money as we gave this place, we should not have this problem."

TJ said, "I don't think it's the club's fault."

Violet asked, "Is there something wrong with the cake?"

TJ replied, "No, but I want you to take three steps back."

Violet shrugged before stepping back three times. Suddenly, all the lights went out. A spotlight suddenly shined on Violet. She felt blood rush to her cheeks as she saw everyone staring at her. Before she could even try to think about what was happening, she heard a man singing. As his voice became clearer, he emerged from the crowd.

The man had brown skin and short curly bright red hair. He was wearing a black suit around his neck. He wore a yellow tie, and on his feet were a pair of expensive tennis shoes. The man, in a lovely jazzy tone, sang "Happy Birthday to ya."

Violet couldn't help smiling as he walked up to her and took her hand. He was singing happy birthday to her as he led her over to the cake. The man was still singing as all the candles on the cake lit up. Once the song was over, people started cheering for her to blow out the candles. Violet looked at the candles and a single tear fell down her eye. She started to breathe in to blow out the candles when she heard her Aunt May shout, "What the hell?!"

Violet quickly turned in the direction of her aunt. She was shocked to see TJ helping her aunt pull out a couple of crab legs from her hair. Before she could devote any thought to what was happening, her heart stopped as she heard her skirt rip, and this was quickly followed by someone grabbing her arm very tightly. When the person began to yank her arm, she looked in her direction. Her heart leaped when she realized it was her Aunt Drusilla.

Chapter 11
Oh Boy

As Drusilla began to pull Violet, June quickly rushed over to her sister. June separated them before saying, "What is wrong with you? I can't believe you would rip her dress and try to drag her out."

Upset, Violet looked down at the lower part of her dress. Thankfully, her undergarments were not showing. But the dress was ruined.

Drusilla folded her arms as she responded, "I made this piece of crap you have her in look better. Anyway, she is leaving since you violated the agreement."

Akeem walked up to them and shouted, "Bullshit!"

He collected himself, continuing to say, "We filled out the necessary paperwork, and both your and our lawyers went over it before either side signed it. Also, what are you even doing in Georgia? You told us all that you were going to California."

Drusilla said, "None of your business. I'm just here because I know that you and my sisters violated the agreement."

May shouted in anger, "No, we did not!"

Drusilla, in a dry cold tone, replied, "You have food that is not allowed on Violet's no fat diet. Now, I am going to have to cut how many calories she is allowed a day in half."

People started to stare while others began to whisper. May, who had just been freed from the crab leg, threw it at Drusilla. Sadly, Drusilla was able to shield herself from the incoming projectile.

May shouted, "Why are you such a bitch?!"

Suddenly, she lost her balance, and TJ caught her in time to keep her from falling to the ground. Concerned for her aunt, Violet attempted to walk in May's direction to make sure that she was alright. But Drusilla quickly grabbed Violet's arm once again and began to drag her away.

Violet thought, *I should have known this would happen. In my life nothing good ever lasts for long. Fuck it all. I don't care if I am sent to the facility. Nothing is worth this kind of suffering.*

Violet began to fight against Drusilla's grip. In a harsh tone, Drusilla snapped at Violet. She raised a hand to strike her when Akeem rushed up and grabbed Drusilla's hand. Drusilla immediately pulled her hand away while gripping Violet's arm tighter.

Akeem glared at his sister-in-law as he said, "Tell me right now. How did you get in, and why are you here?"

Drusilla stared blankly at him for a moment. She quickly said, "I told you. You went against the agreement by having all of this fatty food at this party. So, Violet must come home now."

Akeem spoke in a harsh tone, "Stop lying. We specified what was going to be served tonight in the paperwork. Ollivander even confirmed the food allowed. Now answer my question."

Drusilla answered, "I don't need to tell…"

Drusilla's hand was hit by a tiny fire spark which made her let go of Violet. Violet quickly ran back to where her family and friends were standing. Drusilla suddenly yelled, "Ouch."

Lucius asked Violet, "Are you alright?"

Violet rubbed her arm while saying, "No. Were you the one who made her let me go?"

Lucius said, "As much as I would like to take the credit for freeing you, I can't."

Violet asked the others if they were responsible, but everyone was clueless as to who singed Drusilla. Meanwhile, Drusilla was demanding whoever hit her with that tiny ember to come forward, making it easier for her to punish them for it. The lights of the club were suddenly turned on. Violet noticed a man talking to her Aunt June and TJ.

She asked Lucius, "Do you know who that man is talking to my aunt?"

Lucius replied, "That's the owner, I know because we used this place to give a surprise birthday party for my cousin last year.

The owner was a short bald man with milk chocolate skin and eyes. He was wearing a white suit with a black tie. As her aunt and TJ assured the owner there was not going to be any trouble, Violet noticed her Aunt May sitting down as Meg handed their aunt a glass of water. Worried, Violet walked in the direction of where her aunt was sitting.

She barely took two steps when she heard her uncle shout, "Drusilla, leave, or I will have you escorted out!"

Violet turned in their direction to see an angry Drucilla.

Drusilla frowned as she screamed, "Not unless Violet comes with me!"

Akeem shouted, "No, this is her party!"

Drusilla turned her attention to the cake. In less than a blink, she cast an enchantment on Violet's birthday cake, causing it to float high above the crowd.

Violet shouted at her aunt, "You have already embarrassed me enough. Put my cake down!"

Drusilla frowned as she said, "Your ass should know better than to sass me."

She then flicked her wrist and before anyone could react, the cake slammed into the middle of the room.

As people stared, Drusilla shouted, "Violet Evergreen, get your ass to the car now! Or I will send you to Greenages tonight!"

Violet folded her arms as she shouted, "No!"

Janet put her hand on Violet's shoulder and said, "It's not worth it. Remember, she doesn't know you can't be isolated anymore."

Violet grudgingly agreed, then headed toward the club's exit. When Drusilla noticed Violet heading towards the exit, she groaned as she said, "Finally."

Drusilla started to leave as Akeem shouted, "Drusilla, we will sue you for this!"

Without looking back Drusilla replied, "Go ahead. It doesn't matter. You will never get rid of my custody over her."

Violet, who had just made it to the door, looked back. She stared at the ruined cake that was being cleaned up by the staff. Her heart cried as she thought that she didn't even get to blow out her candles. The music and the colorful club lights were suddenly turned back on. She heard some of the guests laughing and others headed back to the dance floor. Others were still huddled together talking about what happened. Just like the night before, several guests were videotaping what happened. The rest started to collect their things and their gift bag so they could leave.

She could hear TJ apologizing to the club owner, while Meg appeared to be trying to keep May from getting even more upset. Violet also noticed her Aunt June was staring at Drusilla. Meanwhile, Akeem was shouting at someone on the telephone. Violet thought another day that should have been filled with joy was ruined. Drusilla snapped at Violet to hurry up, and the two of them left.

Drusilla was driving her car while Violet sat in the passenger seat next to her. During the ride, Drusilla screamed non-stop at Violet. She called Violet obese, which was followed by a lecture on how people with weight problems as bad as Violet's should not eat fancy food. The abuse continued with constant taunts about how stupid Violet was, how she was ugly and needed plastic surgery, and just how much she was a burden on everyone.

A few minutes passed and Violet started to question why she was not crying. Normally when Drusilla or her husband would scream at her, she always started to cry. But this time was different. The panic and tears were gone.

Her body felt tense as she clenched her fists. *I always ask myself why. Why do these horrible people have control over my life? Dammit, for once I'm going to get an answer to my question.*

She glared at her Aunt Drusilla and asked, "Why do you want me?"

215

Drusilla snapped, "I don't. You're just the burden Mathew left me with."

Violet screamed, "No, you and your husband want me around. Is it so the two of you can stay at the house? Or, do you think if I am under your custody the both of you can somehow get my inheritance?"

Drusilla in a mocking tone said, "Stupid girl, why the fuck would I or my husband ever want you?"

Violet, near the point of rage, shouted, "You spent money to get extended custody of me. You spent money to keep the extended custody. You spend money on making me go on expensive dates. No one invests that much cash unless they think they are getting something out of it in the end."

Drusilla snapped, "I am tired of hearing your voice. Just shut up."

Violet shouted, "No, bitch."

Violet felt herself tremble the second the word bitch escaped her lips. Oddly enough, she didn't feel any worry about how Drusilla would react. Drusilla on the other hand looked as if she had just been slapped in the face.

A moment passed before Drusilla shouted, "What the fuck did you just say?!"

Violet didn't know why, but Drusilla's wrath only made her feel more emboldened to say what she wanted.

She glared at Drusilla as she replied, "You heard what I said. Just answer my fucking questions. You owe me the truth."

"Ha, I raised you, so I don't owe your little ass one fucking thing."

"You didn't raise me. All you have ever done is make my life hell and tormented the people who did take care of me."

Drusilla shouted, "Bullshit, you only say that because the rest of the family lets you do whatever you want, just like they encouraged Malcom to choose that thing over me."

My dad chose who over her? Hold on is she talking about my mom? Still, that sounds messed up as hell.

Violet asked, "What did you mean by that?"

Drusilla quickly replied, "I didn't say anything. Just shut up."

At the top of her voice, Violet screamed, "Just fucking answer me!"

Drusilla suddenly stopped the car. Violet realized that they had arrived back home. Drusilla started to race out of the car, and Violet followed her.

Once both women were outside, Violet shouted, "We are not done yet! Answer my question!"

Drusilla glared at Violet as she said, "Just shut the fuck up and go to your room."

Violet stomped her foot as she screamed, "Answer my question, dammit!"

Suddenly, purple flames shot out of the old willow tree. Violet's heart started to race.

It's just like that night. I was scared when those people killed mommy and daddy. Then somehow, I, I just..."

Drusilla shouted, "See that?! You're incapable of keeping your magic in check! That is why I am burdened with your care! That is why you need

217

a man who will keep you in check! That is why you are responsible for the death of your parents!"

Violet shouted, "You're wrong. I didn't kill them!"

Drusilla laughed very loudly before saying, "Bullshit. You can deny it all you want. You're nothing more than the unnatural seed that ended the life of Malcolm Evergreen and his bitch wife."

Before Violet could react, a blue Fiat pulled up on the property. It was being followed by a red Porsche. The Porsche's top was down, and Violet could see that Janet was in the driver's seat.

When both cars came to a screeching halt, Janet sat in her car staring at the fire. June jumped out of the driver's seat of the Fiat, and she was followed by May, who was getting out of the car slowly.

June looked at the fire and said, "De igne." The flames quickly dissipated.

May looked at Drusilla and said, "This is your fault."

Drusilla folded her arms as she replied, "No, it is not. That little bitch just cannot control her powers or her temper. You know she had the nerve to cuss at me."

May snapped, "If she was swearing, then I can tell you right now you're responsible for it."

June looked at her little sister and said, "May, you need to get back in the car. I don't want this crazy woman upsetting your baby."

As May sat down June said, "Violet, sweetie, I want you to head into the house. The three of us need to have a conversation."

Violet didn't wish to leave, but she was also not willing to disrespect her Aunt June. So, she quickly raced inside.

218

The house was dark when Violet stepped inside. As she headed toward the stairs, Kinya stepped in the way. She started to demand Violet tell her what was going on outside. Violet was about to scream at Kinya when the lights suddenly turned on, and she noticed The Wilds' head butler Williams.

Williams was a tall man with a little mustache and rich dark chocolate brown skin. He had graying short curly hair. He was wearing a black suit with a blue tie. Oddly enough, he wore no shoes. Violet knew that if Williams was not wearing any shoes, then he was most likely about to go to bed. She knew this because he made a big deal about shoes in bed. He threw a fit one day when he had to wake TJ up after he noticed TJ had gotten into bed with his shoes on.

A clearly tired Williams demanded to know what was going on. Before either woman could open her mouth, Janet rushed in.

She quickly said, "Papa, Kinya has been stealing from the house again."

Williams glared at Kinya while saying, "Give back what you stole."

Kinya snapped, "I didn't take anything. Your brat is a liar."

Williams put his hand on his temple as he said, "Do not talk about Janet like that. You're an unwanted guest who stole from this house multiple times. Janet and the rest of the real staff have caught you on several occasions. I suggest you hand over whatever it is that you stole."

Williams always went out of his way to never acknowledge the Lepels' people as a part of the staff. This attitude always made Violet happy because she felt as if his rejection meant the Lepels' staff would one day have to leave.

Williams looked at Violet. When his eyes met hers, he could instantly tell that she was upset. He suggested she go up and rest. He would deal with Kinya's thievery himself.

Violet thanked him. As she quickly rushed upstairs, she could hear the three of them shouting.

I'm glad Janet was willing to lie and Williams was willing to go along with it. I really can't deal with Kinya's sorry ass tonight.

Once she got to her room, Violet grabbed her pillow and screamed. Afterwards, she felt tears start to flow down her face as she thought, *I'm so done with this shit.*

Chapter 12
The Gamble

Violet had gone into the bathroom to clean her face. After her makeup was washed away, she didn't recognize the woman staring back at her. Her eyes were completely bloodshot from tears, while the rest of her face was completely blank.

Tonight is the last night I let either of the Lepels ruin my life. Why was Drusilla even here? Why did she humiliate me in front of so many people? There must be some kind of angle to all of this.

There was a knock on her bathroom door, followed by her Aunt June saying, "Violet, I know you're upset, but we need for you to come out."

Violet wiped her eyes before taking a deep breath. After exhaling, she figured that the person with June was Drusilla. Drusilla was the last person she wanted to see. But she also knew there was no getting rid of Drusilla unless she spoke to them.

She forced herself to head into her room. As Violet entered her bedroom, she saw her Aunt June standing next to her bed. Her Aunt Drusilla was standing next to the window with an angry expression. Violet noticed Drusilla had the beginnings of a black eye, which made her think Drusilla must have had another conversation with June's fist.

June looked at Violet and asked, "Violet, how are you…"

In a harsh tone Drusilla interrupted, "Just tell her what we discussed, and get it over with!"

June shot her sister a nasty look, which Drusilla ignored.

Despite how tired she was from the events that had transpired earlier, Violet knew that if she wanted answers she would have to talk to Drusilla. She looked at Drusilla and said, "At least tell me why you're not in California."

Drusilla groaned before she said, "My husband changed his mind."

"So, you both decided not to take the trip?"

"No, he just decided I didn't need to go with him."

"Why?"

"That is none of your concern."

"You ruined my birthday. I deserve an answer."

"Well, you killed my brother, so you owe me more."

June snapped, "No, she did not. You should just tell her the truth."

Drusilla snapped, "Shut up, June. Or I will change my mind about letting you on my wing of the house."

June, in an exasperated tone, said, "It's not your wing of the house. This is just where I allow you to stay until I can throw your ass out."

Drusilla snapped back, "Trust me, I can't wait to leave."

June continued in an angry voice and said, "Then why don't you? You can just leave Violet here. Then you and your bitch ass husband can get the hell out. I have heard the demon situation in Australia is getting super bad. You two should move there. I bet you'll get a great deal on a house."

"Enough, June, just tell the brat our decision."

June took a breath before looking at Violet. She said, "My sisters and I had a talk a..."

Violet thought, *meaning you kicked Aunt Drusilla's ass.*

June continued to say, "We agreed that the assigned dates that you have been subjected to are extremely stupid."

Annoyed with her sister, Drusilla shouted, "The dates were for her own good!"

In a pissed-off tone, June responded, "Bullshit." June turned to Violet and in a calm voice said, "Anyway, since your Aunt Drusilla is still determined to send you on a date tomorrow, we made a deal. If it works out, then you're getting married with no objections. However, if it fails, you will be spared from going on any more of these silly dates. You will also get to attend the college of your choice."

Violet's entire being was filled with hope. She wondered if college meant the extended custody would be lifted.

Drusilla said, "Tell her the rest."

June's eyes looked as if she wanted to cry. Violet thought, *here it comes.* Drusilla smiled as she said, "What's wrong, June? You were all ready to do this just a little while ago."

June took a breath before saying, "I have to put a curse on you. Otherwise, Drusilla will not agree to the deal."

Violet's heart started to beat very fast. She started to cry, "Please, Auntie, don't put a curse on me."

In a mournful tone, June said, "I'm sorry, Violet. I just can't deal with fighting with my sister and her husband for the rest of my life."

Violet began to feel a large knot in her stomach as her whole body began to shake. Meanwhile, June closed her eyes before kneeling on one knee. June looked toward the ceiling with her arms stretched above her head.

In a commanding voice she said, "Vivamus deprecor vos pius. Usque ad occasum die in animo et corpore eaque."

Suddenly, there was a bright blue light flashed throughout the room. As the light began to dissipate, Violet felt as if there was a heavy invisible cloth covering her entire body very tightly. Once the blue light was completely gone, June started to get up while Drusilla asked if the curse was working.

June yawned as she said, "My spells always work. Just test it out if you don't believe me."

Drusilla said, "Violet, Donny told me that he only likes women who wear yellow dresses."

Violet felt her face being forced into a smile. She felt as if she were about to say something but started to fight the urge. Sadly, her resistance proved to be futile.

She felt as if she was vomiting as she blurted out, "To make Donny happy, I will wear yellow dresses every day."

Violet felt sick as Drusilla said, "Your curse is effective, sister."

June replied, "It doesn't matter how effective the curse is. This date will fail just like all the others you wasted your time on."

Drusilla laughed as she replied, "She may be an ugly little bitch, but her date needs a wife badly."

Drusilla walked out of the room while saying, "I think I should start looking for wedding venues."

Once she was gone, June said, "Violet, I know…"

Violet interrupted, "Auntie, this has been the worst birthday I have ever had. Just please go away."

June looked as if she wanted to say something. But instead, she slowly walked out of the room.

Violet lay on her bed staring at the ceiling. She hadn't changed out of her party clothes. As she continued to stare at the ceiling, she thought, *how could Aunt June hurt me like that? It's just not like her to be so mean. Maybe this is a part of some convoluted plan.*

Or, she has finally given up. I can't be mad at her if she did; after she has spent years wasting money on lawyers and overly complicated contracts. She even spent heaven knows how much money on my birthday, only for it to be a massive financial loss in the end.

Violet sat up while she continued to think, *maybe Auntie June and even Auntie May just want me gone. Heck, I bet the whole family wants me gone. I'm nineteen, and I'm not exactly doing anything with my life. When my mother was this age, she was working two jobs and going to college. Me, on the other hand, I just sit around in this room all day.*

Suddenly, she slammed her fist on her bed as she said, "I can fix this."

She then remembered how her friends told her about the spell Tawanda found in her grimoire. Violet figured if Tawanda can find an unusual spell in her book, then maybe she can find one in her family's grimoire, too. But the grimoire was protected by a glass seal connected to several levels of security. Even if she managed to leave her room unchaperoned, only her Aunt June knew how to remove the glass seal to the grimoire. Knowing that she had to do something to change her life, Violet stood up and walked to her bedroom door.

Opening the door just enough to stick her head out, Violet looked around the dark hallway. She suddenly remembered the camera. Someone will know that she's not in her room. Stepping back into her room, she looked to the spot on the wall where the camera usually hung and was relieved to find that it had not been replaced after her Aunt June's spell had melted it before they left for her party. Feeling free to leave her room, Violet walked to the door and left her bedroom.

As she walked down the hall, she thought, *last time I saw the book it was in the aquarium when I was a kid. I doubt it has ever been moved, so it should not take me long to find it.*

She then focused on how she was going to get out of the east wing unnoticed. If she could make it to the main family wing of the house, then she would not have a hard time getting to the aquarium. At least she assumed so.

The last time she had been on the family's wing of the house was when she was getting ready to leave for court, where later the Lepels were granted extended custody.

Violet eventually turned down a corner, where to her dismay, she saw Harold and Kinya. Thankfully, they had not noticed her, so she quickly hid in the massive hallway. She figured it would be wise to just take a different route to the aquarium; however, at the same time, she was curious as to why they were up this late. She decided, since they were always in her business, that it was only fair for her to get into theirs.

Kinya said, "True, but you know it's not going to be easy."

Harold said, "Yeah, but the damn things are worth over a million. So, it is worth it."

Kinya, in a doubtful tone said, "I know, but maybe we should just stick to the plan, and wait for the wedding. Then, we get our money without having any problems. If we take all the black pearls, then we risk getting caught. Ollivander said he would not protect us if we stole anything else. So, if we get caught, we'll get fired and probably end up doing some jail time."

Violet couldn't believe her ears. *Are they talking about stealing Meg's collection of black pearl jewelry? Oh hell no.*

Harold said, "There is not going to be a wedding. Every time we think the little spoiled bitch is going to meet a man who is fool enough to marry her, he runs away, and we are stuck cleaning a house we should own."

Kinya said, "I know, but the bosses have a fool-proof plan this time."

Harold, in a doubtful tone said, "Really, what?"

"Ok, so they only let the brat have her birthday at that club to fuck up the Evergreen fortune."

"I don't get it?"

"There were a lot of important investors at that birthday party. Those investors know when the brat turns twenty-six, she will inherit eighty-five percent of all their business."

"How come she gets so much?"

227

Kinya explained, "Their family still believes a man has to run things. Her father got a huge chunk of the business when his dad died. Now, get this. Since the brat's dad didn't have any other kids, he decided to leave her everything. The only reason she has to wait till she is twenty-six to get anything is because he thought she would be done with school by then. Ok, this is how everything gets fucked up. Those family members who always try to help her don't like her. This whole time they have been getting in the Lepels' way so they could manipulate the brat."

Harald questioned, "I don't understand."

"Think about it, Harald. If she trusts them, then they can trick her into signing over her shares. But, thanks to the extended custody, she can't touch her shares until she turns twenty-six."

Harald said, "So, that's the real reason they are so nice to her?"

"Yeah, ok, so originally the Lepels were going to find her a husband with fat stacks so they could get a sizable dowry for her and then split it with us and Ollivander."

"Does Ollivander deserve anything? All he does is lecture the brat on occasion."

"He watches the video feed."

"Sometimes he does. Most of the time he's just ordering us to clean."

Kinya snapped, "Enough about him. Mrs. Lepel ruined the party, and now the Evergreen business may be in trouble. Those sisters, June and May, decided to finally call it quits. They don't care about controlling the business anymore. They're just going to try to get their money and get out. June agreed to curse the brat so the date will go well. Then, once she comes of age, her husband will take over what is left of the Evergreen business. He'll liquidate the remainder of the assets, and then he and the brat's aunts will split the money four ways."

"As long as we get our money, I don't care."

Just then Ollivander walked up. He said, "I am guessing the two of you were updated about tomorrow. Mr. Lepel is setting everything up. When he gets home, we need to start getting the house ready for the family pre-engagement meeting."

Harold said, "They really found a man for the brat?"

Ollivander replied, "More like a small-minded boy, but yes."

Kinya yawned as she said, "I'm gonna get some sleep."

The others agreed that they should do the same. Once they were gone, Violet started to walk toward the hallway that would take her to the family wing.

Her eyes welled up as she thought, *my family doesn't want me. I knew it. Why else would Auntie June curse me. I bet she only mentioned college to make me think she was still on my side.*

She wiped her eyes as she continued to walk in what felt like a daze. After some time passed, she suddenly realized she was standing in the middle of the aquarium.

The Evergreens' private aquarium consisted of one large room filled with brightly lit glass walls and glass floors. Behind the glass walls were tanks full of different kinds of tropical fish. The floors had four separate tanks full of jellyfish. In the center was a massive tank shaped like a pillar that was full of tiny sharks. In front of the center tank, was a stand with a glass top protecting a book. Violet walked over to the book.

She stared at the beautiful leather-bound book that had the word *Evergreen* written in glowing green letters on the front. Underneath there was a picture of a flower known as the Amazing Grace Creeping Phlox. As

Violet touched the glass, she heard her Aunt May say, "Violet, what are you doing?"

Violet quickly turned in the direction of May's voice. There, she saw May sitting on a bench eating a beef rib.

Violet's heart was beating fast as she said, "I'm um, um…"

May said, "Surprised to see me? I'm staying over tonight because your uncle is afraid for me to be alone in our apartment at night, so close to my due date."

She then looked at the book before holding up the plate next to her and asking, "Want a rib?"

Realizing May didn't care that she had come to search through the grimoire, she thought, *does this mean I can still trust her? Or maybe she is just trying to trick me into continuing to think she is nice. Just take her up on her offer to try and gauge things.*

After agreeing to eat a rib, Violet sat down next to May. May said, "Violet, I know you want to get that stupid curse off of you, but next time tell someone if you want to look at the grimoire. The glass is connected to an alarm. Use the wrong spell to open it, and it will set it off."

Violet wondered, "You're not mad at me for looking for a way to take the curse off?"

"Why would I be? I wasn't ok with June putting it on you to begin with. You just got that last curse removed. My dear sister is just insistent it's a sacrifice we must make to get you out of this mess."

May's words made Violet feel almost as if she was about to win something. Sure, she was still cursed. But it was only done to help her. At least that was what she was hoping.

Violet asked, "What exactly is Auntie June's plan?"

May answered, "I wish I knew. She's refusing to tell me. That curse she put on you can only be removed by her, so I'm pretty aggravated with her right now. If I wasn't hyper-paranoid about using powerful spells with my pregnancy, I would have put a gossip spell on her to get her to spill her plan."

Should I believe her? You know what, yes. Sure, what those assholes said is scary. But now that I have had a little time to think, it doesn't make sense. At the same time, I guess the only way I am going to be able to do anything is to tell Auntie May what I heard.

Part of Violet felt it would be stupid to say anything, but she also knew with the curse and the extended custody that there was no way she could pull herself out of the hole she was in on her own.

Violet then told her aunt everything. When she was done, May stared at her with a half-eaten rib in her mouth as if she was in total shock. After a moment, May put her rib back on her plate and pulled out her cellphone.

She called a number, and when the person on the other end picked up, she said, "Hey, sugar. We're in trouble. No, I'm not at the party. Drusilla ruined it. I'm at June's house like we talked about. Yeah, she is upset, but sadly that is the least of our problems. The baby is fine, just listen."

May then told the person Violet assumed was her uncle, the whole story. Violet finished her rib and put it in the bag May had for the bones. While still on the phone, May told Violet she could have another one. Violet let her aunt know she was full, which made May smile.

Suddenly, Violet heard her Uncle Anas shout, "Shit! May, I am going to have to look into the trip Victor took. I will call you back tomorrow afternoon!"

Anas hung up, and May took a breath. She looked at Violet and said, "Kiddo, your uncle and I have some concerns. Where do I begin? I guess that stuff Drusilla's servants said is a good place to start. I don't know who fed them that fake story about the family. Hell, I don't even know why they would believe it. They have met your grandma and know she doesn't go for that men should run everything crap."

Violet, in a thoughtful tone said, "I know. After I had a little time to clear my head, I realized it didn't make any sense."

May said, "Violet, you should also think about this: If that load of crap they were saying was true, wouldn't it have been easier to just take advantage of you being declared unstable? Then we could have seized your share of the business."

Violet commented, "I didn't even think about that."

May continued, "You have a lot to think about after a night like tonight. Speaking of that, I probably should call Meg about those pearls. Your grandpa gave her a lot of them, and I know she will be devastated if she loses even one."

May started to call Meg as Violet looked at the shark tank. While she watched the tiny sharks swim around, Violet thought more about what she overheard. She started to wonder even more why her guardians were going to share a dowry with their servants. The more she thought about it, the more she started to get a feeling that something wasn't right.

May hung up the phone as she said, "Glad I called your cousin. Anyway, outside of that concern, I should let you in on a little information. June overheard Ollivander talking to Drusilla about messing up your party. Apparently, Victor decided at the last minute that he didn't want Drusilla to come with him to California. Something to do with him feeling she would mess up some kind of negotiation. Drusilla was upset that she had been uninvited to go on the trip to L.A, so she decided to take out her rage on you and the family by messing up your party. She pretended she went to California with her husband. That way, she could sneak into the party and ruin it. We gave the club's security strict orders under no circumstances to let Drusilla or any member of her staff inside. Clearly, for some reason that didn't work. This means the club where we had your party is going to have to give us all our money back.

At any rate, even before all this nonsense happened, we did entertain the idea of everything going to crap because when have the Lepels ever stuck to an agreement? So, your Aunt June and I hatched a plan. We invited several of the upper scale families who are the type to have sons you would be forced to go out with."

Shocked, Violet announced, "So, you guys were hoping my birthday was going to go to shit?"

In a calm tone, May replied, "No, and we had a secondary plan to make sure their sons would never consider you. Even without that, you have to admit it is suspicious for the Lepels to agree to let us have a party for you at a club. Normally, the menu alone would have been the reason that they would have rejected our attempt at giving you a birthday party. But we decided to take a chance anyway because it was your birthday."

Violet said, "I understand. I guess I'm still pretty mad about what happened."

"I am still pretty pissed myself. Your Aunt June and I went to twelve different cake shops to find the perfect cake. Then Drusilla's dumb ass just had to ruin everything. I wish Malcolm never brought her here. Ouch!"

May started to massage her head. Violet inquired if her aunt was alright.

May said, "I'm fine. A migraine appears to have snuck up on me."

"What did you mean by my dad brought Aunt Drusilla here?"

233

"What are you talking about?"

"You just said you wish he never brought her here."

"I'm not sure why I would say that. Unless maybe, OUCH!"

May's head suddenly started hurting again. Seeing her aunt get a headache made Violet remember June also getting a strange headache. She started to feel their sudden headaches were a little too strange. Why did they get headaches when she asked questions about her mysterious aunt and then about Drusilla? Violet dismissed her thought. She was reading too much into the headache. She knew that she was just desperate for answers.

May looked confused for a second before saying, "Sorry, kiddo. I think I'm just tired and talking nonsense. Back to my point. Those people who walked out were only from the families who participate in arranged dating. So, after tonight you will not be able to get another arranged date."

"Then how am I going on a date tomorrow?"

"The date must have been made long before the party. Whoever they picked can't back out, and that's assuming he knows what happened."

"So, my birthday didn't hurt the family."

"No, if anything, you standing up to Drusilla the way you did may have increased profits. Plus, everyone else was either family or family friends, and they expect Drusilla to act that way."

"How did me standing up for myself make us money?"

May explained, "It provided our investors with proof that you are stable. Also, the investors received insurance. Should the extended custody be removed, you will not allow Drusilla to have any part of the company."

"Wow, I'm glad I didn't lose my cool till I got home."

May asked, "Do you still want to take a look at the grimoire?"

"You know how to remove the security spell?"

May laughed and said, "I might have decided to take my husband's last name, but I'm still an Evergreen. I also want you to know how to access the grimoire. You should have learned how to do that when you were fifteen."

"Why fifteen?"

"That is the age a person is old enough to use a grimoire. I should tell you a few things before we take the book out. Do you remember how a grimoire is made?"

Violet said, "Yes, I don't understand why people were willing to kill themselves to make it."

May said, "I don't know all the details of how our grimoire was made. I do know that the ancestor who made our book, supposedly, made that sacrifice in the name of giving our family a chance to prosper."

"Clearly their wish was granted."

May informed, "Violet, unlike other spell books, all spells cast from a grimoire feel different."

A curious Violet questioned, "How so?"

"When you cast a spell, you get the same feeling as when you exercise."

"Yeah?"

May warned, "Using a spell from a grimoire will give you a surge of energy. It kind of feels like if you get an intense sugar rush, but that rush is followed by a major crash. Your muscles feel a little sore. That is why it takes time and practice to master casting a grimoire spell."

"I think I understand."

"I'm going to show you how to remove the security spell. After I do, I'm going to have you practice arming and disarming the security."

Violet, excited and nervous at the same time said, "Ok, I'm ready."

They walked to the glass case. May said, "Violet, you must never share what I am about to show you with anyone who is not a blood relative. You cannot even show this to your future husband."

"Why?"

May said, "There is a spell called Dco vois ara sret. It is a powerful spell that makes you tell all your secrets. Thanks to the protection spell all grimoires have, this spell will not force a person to say anything about their grimoire provided they belong to the bloodline of the grimoire's creator."

"Wow."

May put her hands on her face for a moment before raising her hands in the air. While still holding her hands up, she clapped twice. She then stomped her left foot three times. Finally, she clapped one more time. After a moment the glass case disappeared.

She looked at Violet. May took a breath before saying, "Pay close attention. I'm going to re-encase it.

May waved her hands over the book three times. She clapped once before stomping her right foot twice. This was followed by May jumping up and down three times before clapping one more time.

When the glass case reappeared, May looked at Violet. She said, "Now I want you to remove the glass case."

May moved so Violet could stand in front of the grimoire case. As she repeated the motions that she had just seen May perform, she felt as if her energy was being sucked out. Once the case disappeared, she felt very tired."

Her aunt said, "Feeling a little sleepy?"

"Yes."

"That is the power of the grimoire."

Violet questioned, "I thought it would not suck out my energy unless I cast a spell from it?"

"Even unsealing it will cause your energy to be drained. I forgot to tell you this sooner because I'm a little tired. When you open the book and look through the spells, you will have more energy drained from you. Also, as I told you before, when you cast a spell from the grimoire it will give you an energy jump before it drains energy from you. Even resealing the damn thing sucks the energy out of you. This happens because the book is draining magic from your body. It stores that power along with the power of others who have used it. This is how the book is able to magnify the power of anyone who uses it."

Violet understood, "No wonder it kills its creators."

"To be honest with you Violet, if you hadn't started to get some food into your system, I wouldn't allow you to mess with this book. Sadly, the book doesn't have a spell that can remove your curse. However, there are healing and protection spells in here. I want you to try a simple healing spell before you reseal it."

"Auntie May, Tawanda…"

"Say what you want to tell me after you cast your spell and encase the book."

"Ok."

As Violet opened the book, she began to feel even more drained. Each page of the book had words written in glowing green letters. Violet wondered if the letters were doing that because of the magic power of the grimoire. After turning a few pages May had her stop on a page labeled fever candy.

May said, "Cast this spell really quick."

Violet looked at the page. She saw the words *cia faubus eis muda t uasitem empr et. Um cpus pur cru tatem. D conso es.* While she read each word, she felt as if she had a huge jolt of energy. But the moment she read the last word, she felt so tired she wanted to lie on the floor and sleep. Suddenly, she heard a clicking noise. Before she could look to see what it was, May told her to quickly reseal the book. After performing the motions to put the book back in its case, May told Violet to grab a couple of candies.

Violet noticed her aunt holding a glass bowl full of round yellow candy. Without question, she popped a few in her mouth while May ate one as well. The moment the candy touched her tongue, she savored the sweet taste of lemon.

As she sucked on the candy, she started to feel a little more energetic. She and her aunt sat down on the bench.

Violet finished her candy before asking, "Are the candies from the spell?"

"Yes, the spell is meant to create a healing candy. It is good for recovering from an operation or from recovering from a near-death illness. It can help recover some of your energy after casting a spell from the grimoire. Also, it's not strong enough to set off your magic limiter."

"It didn't feel that way."

"Even a very basic spell feels powerful when cast using a grimoire."

"Auntie, Tawanda had her grimoire in her apartment, and she discovered a third type of spell in it."

"If it was in her apartment, she is doing more training to handle using it. Tawanda must have also been storing it in a special carrying case that seals its magic. As for the third spell type, ours has one too."

A surprised Violet said, "Seriously?"

May responded, "There is only one page with a third type of spell. However, we never alerted the government magic scholars about it. Only because it is a spell that can eliminate powerful demons. Sadly, no blood family member can use the spell."

"Why?"

"Anyone who has tried died in the process of using it."

"That's a pain. Before I forget, why did Meg start training with the grimoire at fifteen?"

May informed, "Because that is our family tradition. A lot of people do not like training blood family members to use a grimoire until adulthood for obvious reasons. I should also tell you, until you have trained using a grimoire for a while, never attempt to open it or use it unless one of your bloodline family members is present. Remember never open the grimoire in front of a non-bloodline member of your family. This book holds the power that is the foundation of everything sacred to our family. Speaking of spells, you need to start using magic more."

Frustrated, Violet asked her aunt, "How? The limiter keeps me from performing all but the most basic spells."

"I know you're not supposed to because of the rules of the extended custody agreement. But Violet, it may not be clear to you, but you have had the power to stop your guardians from beating you. You are a direct descendent of the Evergreen line, and at your age your powers have developed to the point where you are capable of some very impressive magic. I'm not saying you should barbeque them; however, giving your attackers a little shove back when they try to hurt you is not a bad idea." May yawned before saying, "I'm getting a little tired. I better go to bed. You should get some rest. Anyway, kiddo, you have presents to open in the morning."

"I thought we were selling my gifts?"

As she walked out of the room May said, "Not all of them."

Chapter 13
Unexpected Ally

Violet was awakened by the sound of Kinya screaming at her. As Violet slowly forced herself to get out of bed, Kinya said, "Hurry up. You overslept, and now you are running late for your date."

Aggravated with the unnecessary harassment, Violet glared at Kinya. She shouted, "Bitch, if I'm up late it's your fucking fault. Now get your stupid ass out of my damn face. If you don't, you're sure as shit going to regret it."

Kinya stared at Violet as if she had just been punched in the face. Violet was a little surprised by her own behavior, but she decided that it would be wise to capitalize on her momentum.

She climbed out of bed and yelled, "I said get the fuck out!"

As if being spirited away by Violet's will, Kinya rushed out of the room. After she was gone, Violet felt as if a weight had been taken off her. She decided that if she could make one of her tormentors run that fast, then maybe she could get through her date without a wedding ring. Knowing that she was running late, she decided to quickly dress for her date.

Violet turned on her shower and picked out her clothes before the water got warm. For some reason, she felt an overwhelming urge to wear yellow. As she reached for the closet door, she remembered her aunt mentioning someone named Donny who liked yellow. Figuring that was her date, she wondered if there was a way to fight wearing anything yellow. However, when she walked into her closet she almost jumped back. All her clothes were gone. She started to run around her closet, hoping to find a single article of clothing.

When she discovered that she did not even have a pair of shoes, she shouted, "What the fuck?!"

Were they hoping that I would go on my date in my pajamas? Seriously, what am I supposed to do?

As she looked around the empty room, she noticed a plastic grocery bag in front of her closet's island. Violet looked into the bag and was immediately greeted by a note. After pulling out the note, she read.

Violet, this is from your Aunt June. Destroy this note after reading it. I put a timed sleep spell on Kinya so that she would get up late. I figured after last night you deserved a little extra sleep. This outfit is the key to getting you out of this date without a wedding ring. So, make sure to wear it.

Violet felt a surge of excitement after reading her aunt's note. *I should have known.* After destroying the note, she figured that she did not have a lot of time to meditate on the matter.

The bag contained two pairs of new underwear, a yellow dress, yellow heels, and a yellow clutch purse. After taking a quick shower, Violet got dressed. Looking at herself in the mirror, she laughed thinking, I look like a yellow daisy. She wondered if this Donny person actually hated yellow. Is that the reason that her Aunt June left this outfit? Taking another look at herself in the mirror she commented aloud to herself. "Yellow may be my color. I would marry me." Instantly she snapped back to reality and asked herself, *am I crazy? The goal of the date was not to impress this guy.*

That thought made Violet rush to her bathroom sink, where she attempted to wash the makeup off of her face but found herself unable to do so. Knowing that the curse was preventing her from washing off the makeup, she decided she might as well just rip off the band-aid and head to her date. While walking into the hallway outside her bedroom, she could hear Ollivander screaming at Kinya for waking her up late. As she put her phone and credit card in her purse, Violet couldn't help smiling, knowing Kinya was getting what she deserved.

Later, as Violet was feeling relaxed and leaned back in the front seat, Arkell said, "The cameras in this car suffered Mrs. Wilds' wrath last night, so we can speak freely."

Violet said, "What about the Eye of Esca?"

Arkell smiled and responded, "Don't worry, I gave Ollivander a line about Kinya stealing and selling a potion I need to recharge the eye. Kinya must be on very thin ice because he believed me without question."

"That's kind of strange, seeing how he chewed you out yesterday."

Arkell said, "Yes, but unless I give him a reason to suspect that I'm plotting something, which I am, it looks like I'm in the clear. Anyway, did Mrs. Wilds provide you with any details about what her plan is for today's date?"

Violet answered, "Only that I am supposed to wear this outfit."

Arkell instructed, "That's what she told me as well. She also wanted me to tell you that the curse she put on you will make you be nice to your date. It will also force you to obey anything he tells you."

With some consternation, Violet said, "That doesn't sound good."

"I agree, but she told me it wouldn't be a problem. However, just in case it is, I plan to scare him off."

Hopefully, Violet asked, "How?"

"I should tell you, the curse you are under may force you to stop me, should I need to enact my plan."

Violet questioned, "Why would I stop you?"

Arkell explained, "Your curse is one of loyalty and obedience. Because you are going to be forced to do what your date wants you to, if you know what I plan to do, then you will be forced to use big magic to stop me. But because of the limiter spell you are under, you will get in trouble and it will cause you a lot of pain."

Violet said, "Ok, I get you. Wait, since I know you are going to get in the way of my date, won't I go ahead and try to stop you? Better yet, wouldn't I try to stop my aunt's plan?"

"I see why you would think that. You cannot stop me or your aunt because you do not know either of our full plans. So, the spell will not make you interfere."

"That only makes a little sense."

Arkell laughed and said, "I know it would take me several hours to fully explain all the details. I would have to get into very specific things about magic and a lot of loopholes. One of those loopholes explaining why you are allowed to wear that outfit if it means messing up your date."

They pulled up to the Taste of Magic restaurant. In a surprised tone, Violet said, "My date is happening here?"

"Yeah, the Lepels seem to be a little obsessed with this place because it's popular with the who's who."

Violet responded, "Cinder's food is really good."

Arkell continued, "True, but his place isn't just popular because of his food. When he first opened the place, he had a famous partner helping him in the kitchen."

With an interested tone, Violet said, "Really?"

"Yeah, she was responsible for several of the recipes on the menu."

Wanting to know more Violet asked, "What happened to her?"

"From what he told me she was killed in an incident with a demon."

"That's terrible."

"I agree."

Violet felt a teardrop from her eye. As she whipped the teardrop away, she wondered why what Arkell said made her tear up. She determined it might be because she felt bad for the woman. Then she told herself not to think about it.

Arkell parked the car as Violet asked, "Back to my curse, can you explain my outfit?"

"What about it?"

Violet wanted to know, "If my aunt left it for me to mess up my date, then why was I able to put it on?"

Arkell answered, "Hmmm… sure that part should not be difficult. So, I assume that you were told your date likes yellow."

She confirmed, "Apparently this Donny person is a fan of it."

"Hold up, did you say your date's name is Donny? And he apparently loves the color yellow?"

"Yes."

"And Drusilla says he needs a wife?"

"Yes, why is that important?"

"Crap, if your date is who I think it is, then this is going to be easier than I thought."

As Arkell parked the car Violet asked, "What do you mean?"

"I ..."

Suddenly, Arkell's phone rang. When he looked at it, he said, "Crap."

After answering it and speaking to someone for a few minutes, Arkell said, "I have to go"

Violet quickly said, "But what about the guy?"

In a reassuring tone, Arkell said, "Don't worry. If my suspicions are correct, then this will be the best date you ever had."

As she started to get out of the car, Arkell's phone rang again.

He quickly answered it and said, "I understand. I am on my way now."

Once Violet was out of the car, Arkell hung up. He rolled down his window and said, "It is going to be alright. Ask Cinder for a ride home. He owes me a favor, so he'll do it." After that, he quickly drove away.

Violet stood silently, not knowing what she should do. Part of her wanted to just run away. But she knew that things would turn out just like the last curse.

Why did Arkell have to leave so quickly? Worry about that later. I have to get through just one more date. Then I will be free. At least freer than I am right now.

Violet took a breath and told herself to just trust in whatever her aunt's plan is. As soon as Violet walked inside, she was quickly taken to her table.

To Violet's surprise, unlike her last date, she was not headed towards a private room. Also, unlike the first time she was there, the restaurant was full of customers.

As she walked, she thought *This place is pretty lively today. I guess my guardians didn't feel the need to pay for exclusivity like last time. They must feel really strong about this working out. Too bad for them, things are not going to go their way.*

Violet could not help smiling after that thought. She felt as if she was finally taking more control of her life even if she was under a curse. As Violet approached, the hostess recognized Violet from the previous day. After she greeted her, she said, "Miss Evergreen, we have been expecting you. Your table is ready, and your date is waiting."

When they reached the table, Violet's date glared at her. He was sitting next to an older woman who seemed angry. Her date was a pointy ear elf with peach skin and large blue eyes. His long hot pink hair was branded into three large braids and tied into a tight bun. Her date's nose had four piercings, which were outclassed by the five piercings he had on both his ears. He was wearing a black shirt, black leather jacket, black leather pants, and black leather boots.

The woman sitting next to him had a face that reminded Violet of a fox. She was clearly human with peach skin and very narrow blue eyes. Her makeup was pure black eyeshadow, and she wore black lipstick with matching black polish on her nails. The woman had a tattoo of a gold dragon that started at her forehead and stretched all the way down to her neck. She was almost as thin as Violet, with her graying brown hair tied into a ponytail. Her tight silk green dress had a skirt that was too short. If she had not been sitting down, Violet would have been immediately made aware the woman was not wearing any underwear.

Violet sat down at the table as she thought the man looked familiar. She also wondered why the woman was there. More significant, knowing her dating history she was confused as to why she was set up with another elf.

The elf, who was glaring at her, in a heavy British accent said, "I don't like this, Mira. You said that my date would be good for my image. But she ain't even wearing yellow. No date will end well unless someone is wearing yellow."

Confused, Violet thought, *what is he talking about?*

She then looked down at her outfit. Her heart felt as if it was about to leap out of her chest. Somehow, she was wearing Meg's old rocker outfit and a pair of lace high heel black leather boots on her feet. Her clutch bag had even changed from yellow to red.

What happened to my clothes? Auntie June must have put some kind of spell on Meg's old outfit. I wonder why she, oh shit. This is Meg's Donny Face shirt from when she was going through that rocker faze. This guy is freaking Donny Face McNight. Shit, I wish this wasn't a date. Then I could get Meg an autograph without it being super weird.

Mira rolled her eyes as she said, "Donny, for the last time, you're looking for a wife to revamp your image. Thanks to your nasty divorce, your popularity is down."

Donny folded his arms as he said, "No good relationship starts without the color yellow. Heck, she's even wearing an outdated look."

Mira looked as if she wanted to scream while replying, "What are you talking about? She is wearing a shirt from one of your concerts.

Clearly her style matches your look. She clearly can only be good for the brand."

Donny held up a finger as he said, "Correction, she is wearing my old look. Do you think it is smart for me to have a chick wearing a lifestyle I have disavowed? Fuck, I should be getting the hell out of here. If I'm seen considering marrying a chick with that style, my fans will think I am a damn hypocrite."

Mira criticized, "If your fans complain about her wearing what she is wearing, then we can say it was some kind of prank. Or that you're returning to that look"

Donny folded his arms as he said, "No, the rocker in red was nothing more than a pathetic fad. Personally, if I could go back, I never would have done it."

Exasperated, Mira said, "Whatever, Donny, the contract…"

Just then the waitress walked up and asked if they wanted to order. Donny told her they were all starving.

Faster than lightning, Mira told the waitress that neither she nor Violet were going to eat. In response, Donny's brows furrowed. Within a blink, he jumped up then slammed his fist on the table.

He screamed, "No Fucking Way!"

The whole restaurant went silent, and everyone started to stare at them. Violet began to wish she could hide as Mira told Donny to chill out. Donny glared at Mira as he slammed his fist on the table again.

He yelled, "I don't give a flying fuck, Mira! You can do your anorexia bullshit if you fucking want to, but I'm not about starving people to please the studio!"

Violet thought, *I was so worried about how I was going to deal with my date. But it seems like this woman is the one I need to fear.*

Mira took a breath before saying, "Her guardians informed the agency that she gains weight easily. So, she is on a very strict diet."

Donny plopped back into the chair as he said, "I'm not happy."

Mira picked up a slinky gold purse. In an aggravated tone she said, "I'm going for a damn smoke. Behave. You need this engagement if you want to make any more albums."

Donny watched Mira until she was gone. He exhaled dramatically before saying, "Good, the snake is gone."

He looked at the waitress and said, "Darlin', please give both of us a menu."

As the waitress handed Violet a menu, Donny said, "Sorry about earlier. My agency has decided that I need to get married again just to hype up my image. The entire plan is stupid. I may not have the numbers I used to, thanks to my divorce, but I'm still high up on the charts. I think you'll agree that I shouldn't be marrying someone who is probably younger than my kids."

Violet felt as if a heavy weight lifted off her shoulders. Donny noticed her relief and smiled. He said, "Glad to see you feel the same way. We need to figure out how to make this date go south without the curse you're under getting in the way."

A surprised Violet said, "You can tell I'm cursed?"

Donny remarked, "It's one of the benefits of being an elf. So, how did you get mixed up in this arranged dating crap?"

Violet told Donny a little bit about her situation, and he looked as if he was going to faint. He said, "You know, I heard about your case on the telly years ago. But I always assumed your money bags family got that crap overturned."

"They tried, but it never worked out."

In a sympathetic tone, Donny added, "That sucks. Right now, we need to worry about making sure we don't end up in an unhappy matrimony. Then we must go about getting you un-cursed."

"Can't you just reject me and call it a day?"

Donny explained, "I wish, but Mira makes all this complicated. She has some kind of leverage over my wife. Well, I should say my ex-wife. Whatever Mira has on her made her divorce me. If I don't get her to dislike you, then we'll have to get married, only because I can't let her use what she has to mess up my ex."

Violet said, "That's messed up."

"Yeah, when I saw you were wearing an outfit from my former style," Donny said, "I assumed Mira would let me get away with rejecting you. But she is being stubborn for some reason. We need something to…"

Just then Cinder walked up to the table. He said, "Donny, you may be one of my best customers, but I cannot have you being disruptive."

Donny replied, "Not now, Cinder. I have got to mess this date up."

Cinder frowned as he said, "Good for you. You and your ex better not start an incident. Cause if either of you even thinks about it, I will have you both thrown out."

Donny said, "What are you talking about?"

251

Cinder took a breath before saying, "Your ex-wife is at the table at the other end of the room. She has been spying on you this whole time."

Donny frowned as he said, "Darn it, I don't want Rose getting in trouble over this."

Violet decided not to try and see where Rose was. Part of her felt that doing so would embarrass the woman.

Cinder, who just noticed Violet was there, greeted her. He asked, "Miss Violet, I'm a little surprised you're on another date so soon."

Violet shrugged as she said, "My guardians want me married as soon as possible."

Cinder remarked, "If that is the case, you know you can do way better than this guy."

Donny said, "Hate to say it, but Cinder is right."

He seemed to think for a moment before saying, "Hey, Cinder, you want to help us make sure this date doesn't end in matrimony?"

Cinder took a breath before saying, "Alright."

Donny smiled and said, "Thanks, buddy."

Cinder stated, "I'm only helping you because I feel bad for Miss Violet. Plus, I need to get both you and your ex out of here before the dinner rush."

Violet asked, "Why do they need to be gone before dinner?"

Cinder answered, "Because catfish is on the dinner menu. When Donny and his ex-came for dinner and saw catfish was an option, they started a riot about me serving it."

Violet inquired, "What's wrong with catfish?"

Donny said, "It is wrong to eat our underwater friends."

In an aggravated tone Cinder said, "A catfish is not a type of merfolk. Dammit, Donny, we have been over this."

Just then, there was a loud crashing noise from what sounded like the kitchen. Cinder told them he would be back in a moment.

Violet said, "With Mira blackmailing her, I can see why Rose is worried."

"She isn't here because of the blackmail." Donny explained, "Despite her act when we were going through with our separation, I could tell that she didn't want to get divorced. My suspicion was confirmed after the divorce was finalized, and one of my friends found out about the blackmail. I confronted Mira about it, and she gloated to me about how she did me a favor. As far as she was concerned, Rose was too old to be my wife, and that was not good for my image."

"That's terrible."

Donny continued, "It gets worse. She threatened to expose whatever she has on Rose if I did not go along with finding a new young wife."

Violet stated, "I thought I did not like Mira when I first met her, but now I think she is a horrible person. To destroy a couple's happiness because the wife is getting older is sexist and an old-fashioned way of thinking."

Donny took a deep sigh and said, "That is one way to say it. After the divorce, Rose moved into an apartment in midtown. But I have caught her several times spying on my house. Our kids have caught her spying more than I have. They try to get her to come inside, but she just runs away as soon as any of us spot her."

"She probably feels bad for breaking up your family."

"I think that's what she thinks, but I know it was Mira's fault, and I told our kids that."

Violet felt a little sick after she heard Rose and Donny's story. She thought, *Mira is horrible.*

Donny continued, "I believe the reason Rose is spying on us is because she is terrified of me moving on. But I know if Mira catches Rose here, she's going to cause my poor wife more problems."

Just then Cinder came back. He said, "Alright, what do I need to do to mess up this date and get rid of you before you start another riot?"

Violet said, "Wait, if he started a riot over catfish, then why do you let him eat here?"

Cinder replied, "Three reasons: first, he paid for the damages. Second, his fans eat here a lot because he loves the place. Lastly, my wife and my brother-in-law are close friends with Donny. So, whenever Donny screws up, Arkell, my brother-in-law, will harass me nonstop to give him a second chance."

Violet's heart sank into her chest as she thought, *he has someone. What am I thinking? The last thing in my life I need right now is a relationship. Just focus on messing up this date. Wait, Arkell is Cinder's brother-in-law, and Donny is a friend of Arkell.*

She said, "Donny, Arkell didn't tell me he knew you."

Donny replied, "How do you know Arkell?"

Figuring it would be stupid for her to tell him Arkell was some kind of spy for her family, she just told Donny he was her new driver.

Donny said, "Seriously? Darn, Arkell is always doing some weird things. Tell me, is he still eating meat?"

Violet responded, "I only met him yesterday, so I don't know his dietary habits."

Donny continued, "Yeah, the crazy bastard; I'll bet he does. That habit got him in a lot of trouble with a lot of high-ranking elves. Anyway, I'll tell you more about Arkell's drama later."

He looked at Cinder and said, "I need you to give my ex a crowbar."

Cinder replied, "I don't have a crowbar."

Donny frowned as he said, "Great, now I have to figure out a better way for Rose to bust things up."

In a firm tone Cinder stated, "Oh, hell no, you are not breaking my fucking windows."

Donny smiled and using a calm voice said, "Don't worry, Cinder. I'm not trying to get her to mess up your place. I'm trying to get her to mess up Mira's car when Mira comes back in."

In a disgusted tone, Cinder remarked, "I should have known Mira is involved in this. You know, Donny, the only reason I let her in here is because your record company pays me a lot of money to do so. But after today, she is banned."

Thoughtfully Donny questioned, "Good, but I still must figure out a way to get Rose to bust up Mira's car. Crap, I can't exactly let Rose know I want her to mess up Mira's car."

Violet asked, "Why does Rose specifically have to mess up Mira's car? You said that you don't want to get her in trouble with Mira. Also, why can't you let Rose know you are the one who wants her to do it?"

Donny answered, "If she knows I want her to do it, then she won't do it. Rose is in an odd mindset right now thanks to Mira. She thinks it is her responsibility alone to fix the mess Mira has put us in. If I even offer to try to get her involved with my plan, she will just reject it. As to your other question, it's because if Rose beats the shit out of Mira's car, she won't get caught."

"Why?"

Donny smiled as he said, "She is very good at it."

Cinder said, "Understandable. I suggest that you just worry about ruining your date. I can get Rose to destroy that car the second Mira comes back to the table."

After that Cinder left. Donny took a breath before saying, "Ok, Violet, I need you to do something to give me insurance this date will not end in matrimony. But in all honesty, I don't want to ask you to do this."

"Why?"

"I need you to use Rose's spare phone to make an anonymous call to a Mr. Quintin Reed. He is the biggest shareholder of my record company, and he also has a big crush on my Rose."

Not understanding what she could do, Violet asked, "Ok, but I don't see how I can be useful if I am under a curse."

Donny explained, "If I'm reading it right, the curse you were placed under only forces you to be obedient to me. Whoever cast it on you probably expected me to be some kind of nasty rat who would try to control you. It was a smart move to ensure that they get what they want. To be honest, I'm surprised they didn't make sure you would wear yellow. Instead, they dressed you in one of my limited-edition T-shirts from years ago."

Violet inquired, "Why is the color yellow so important to you anyway?"

Donny answered with sadness in his voice, "Because it is important to Rose. She always believes the color yellow brings good luck whenever you want to start something new."

Violet thought, *this guy loves his ex-wife. Now that I think about it, it's strange that the two of us are in similar situations. I wonder how both of us ended up with crazy people trying to get us into bad marriages. Just as strange the more I think about this curse and the color yellow. Something is not right. If I'm supposed to be prioritizing whatever would make him happy, then why did I not feel an overwhelming need to change when I noticed my clothes changed?*

She decided to worry about the question of her clothes later and just try to focus on Donny's plan.

Donny said, "All you have to do is call this guy and tell him Rose is outside going postal. Then he'll rush over to try and calm her down. He'll also make a poor attempt to flirt with her."

Violet asked, "Why do you want this guy around your ex, and why do you have your ex's spare phone?"

Donny explained, "When she moved out, this was the only thing of hers I could snag. At the time I thought I would never see her again, which made me feel I needed something of hers just to have a way to keep her close. When I noticed her spare phone on what used to be her nightstand, I grabbed it. I know that makes me sound like a real nut, but I know if I hadn't, I don't think I would have been able to handle her leaving."

Violet sympathized, "I get it. You guys care for each other had a life together for many years. Then Mira, for whatever her reason, decided to destroy your happiness."

"To be honest with you, even if we get our way with this date, I may not be able to stop Mira from getting me to re-marry in the process."

Optimistically Violet said, "True, but it doesn't change the fact that we still have a chance."

"Maybe. Anyway, I should give you more details about Quintin before you call him. He is a super, how do I say this, he is sexually obsessed."

"Oh, so you need me to call a pervert." She cringed as she continued, "I guess if it's important to your plan, then it has to be done."

Donny said, "Thanks for understanding. I wish I didn't have to ask you to do this. But he's the only one who can give us the assurance I need to know that my plan will work."

"Why?"

"Quintin hates Mira more than I do."

"Why does he dislike her?"

Donny laughed as he explained, "The only thing I know about it is they had a one-night stand. At least it was a one-night stand for him. Mira must have felt it was more serious than quick sex. She turned psycho on him, harassing him, and she chased away women he wanted to have sex with. If she was not a top earner, he probably would have had her fired a long time ago."

The waitress came back and asked if they were ready to order. Donny told her they still needed time. After telling them she would be back in a few minutes, Donny told her to wait a moment. Then he requested she bring Violet the pomegranate sunrise and a small plate of zucchini fries. After telling her to charge it to him, she left.

Violet said, "Thank you."

"It is no problem. After a little consideration to the type of curse you're under, I don't believe I know a spell that can remove it. However, I can at least help weaken it. More important than that, no offense, you're a little too skinny."

Violet smiled and said, "None taken. My guardians are obsessed with the idea that I'm obese. They have restricted my meals to the point where I'm not allowed to eat anything."

Shaking his head Donny said, "That's insane."

"I agree. My family is always in a constant panic about me having enough food to eat. Also, do pomegranates have anti-curse properties?"

Donny replied, "No, but mandarins do. From what Cinder told me, there is a large amount of blended mandarin in the drink I ordered for you. Back to my plan, thankfully, Quintin isn't the wisest person. So, if he sees Rose freaking out over Mira. he is going to get in the way of whatever Mira is trying to do. He won't even think twice whether what he is doing is a good idea or not."

"Good, so do I make the call now?"

Donny handed Violet the phone while saying, "No, we must wait till Mira comes back. When she does, say you have to use the restroom. When you get to the restroom, make the call. Do not stay on the phone long."

Violet put the phone in her pocket as she said, "Is Mira going to get suspicious if I'm gone too long?"

"No, I just don't want you to have to endure talking to him for too long. When he hears a woman's voice, he can go from zero to very inappropriate subjects in a hot second."

Just then the waitress returned with Violet's drink and a small plate of zucchini fries with dipping sauce. When the waitress left, Violet started to sip her drink. When she put her cup down her body began to feel very relaxed.

Donny said, "The mandarin in that drink should be taking effect. So, the curse on you shouldn't be as strong as it was."

They chatted for a little while until the waitress came back. No sooner did they place their orders did Mira return to the table.

Chapter 14
Rock and Roll

As the waitress was leaving, Mira's attention turned to Violet's now empty plate and half-empty glass. She got an angry look on her face before mumbling something under her breath.

Wanting to get the plan in motion, Violet excused herself from the table. As Violet got closer to the bathroom, she noticed Cinder walking over to a table. Sitting at the table was a female elf with wild blood-red hair. Her eyes were a rich emerald green, while her skin was a soft shade of peach. She was wearing a yellow halter top with black leather pants and black boots. Her nose and ears had several piercings. Her lips were painted with dark green lipstick and housed two piercings.

Violet was not completely sure what Cinder said to the woman, but to Violet's surprise, the woman pulled out a bat with barbed wire at the top from under her chair. Then she flew out of the restaurant.

Violet thought that must have been Rose. *I wonder if she was planning to bust up Mira's car from the beginning. Or maybe she was just plotting to break something in general? Wait, did Cinder know that she had a bat the whole time?*

When she reached the restroom door, Violet began to worry if the cops would be called. She scolded herself for not thinking of that sooner. As she entered the lady's room, she reminded herself Rose is the one who is running around with a barbed wire bat. So, maybe she shouldn't let herself get worked up over the whole thing.

The restroom was nothing special. The floor and walls were covered in white tile. There was a large rectangular mirror hanging above a connected sink on the left side of the room, while there were three toilet stalls on the right side of the room.

Violet quickly pulled out the phone. As soon as she dialed the number, she heard a man who she assumed was Quintin say, "I knew it. I always told you the second you realized what a loser Donny was, you would come crawling to me."

Violet said, "I..."

Quintin interrupted, "Now that you finally accepted that I am the better choice, why don't you come over. We can have a little fun skinny dipping in my pool. Then, do it in the..."

Violet shouted, "No, you sicko!"

"Wait a minute, you're not Rose. What kind of sick game are you playing, lady?"

Violet continued to shout, "I'm not playing a game. This Rose person needs your help."

Quintin asked, "What did Donny do to her?"

"I don't know who did what to her. She is in the parking lot right now bashing in someone's car."

"Damn, Donny. I bet she is trying to get back at him."

Violet using her most persuasive tone said, "Buddy, I don't know what the hell you're going on about. I just picked up this phone after this Rose person threw it on the ground. This is the only contact in her phone, and right now she's bashing up a car. She's also crying while cussing some dude out. I guess it's that Donny person you mentioned. Anyway, she's at the Taste of Magic restaurant. Can you come down and help her before this whole thing gets out of hand?"

Quintin questioned, "I'm the only contact? She really has accepted I'm the best guy for her. I will be there in ten minutes. Thanks for letting me know. As a reward, why don't I have you drop by my place after I send Rose home?"

"Excuse me?"

"I'm just saying, we could have a little fun …"

Violet quickly hung up. *I'm glad I was warned not to stay on the phone with him for too long. That guy is strange. What a hypocrite. He seemed all obsessed with Rose but was willing to jump into an inappropriate affair with me, a woman he has never laid eyes on. Oh well, he's on his way, and that's what I need.*

She put the phone in her pocket before heading back into the dining area.

When Violet got back to the table, Mira was arguing with Donny. In a harsh voice, she said, "Stop complaining. You paid for it. Just use it so we can get this thing tied up quickly."

In an even harsher tone, Donny said, "I don't care. I got it for me and Rose."

Mira said in a harsh tone of voice, "It's over for you two, accept it."

Then she looked at Violet. She smiled as she said, "Miss Evergreen, you will agree with me."

Violet asked, "Agree about what?"

"Donny purchased a wedding package from the world-renowned wedding planner, London Skyler, right before Rose sprang the divorce on him. Since he is close to Mr. Skyler, he is letting Donny keep it until he is ready to use it. I was just telling him that since you two will be getting married, he should make use of …."

Without a second thought, Violet shouted, "Hell no."

In a stern tone, Mira said, "What is wrong with you? Everything was decided a little bit after your date started. What makes you think you can back out now?"

Violet said, "I don't know what the fuck you and my guardians talked about, but I didn't agree to any damn wedding. Shit, I already know Donny didn't agree to this crap. You can forget about whatever idea you cooked up. We're not going along with it."

Mira folded her arms as she smirked. She said, "I don't get what is wrong with you, you little bitch. You have no say in anything, and Donny has to do what I say."

Just then they heard someone with a New Jersey accent say, "Bitch, what makes you think you can run around making decisions for people?"

They looked in the direction of the voice only to see Rose and a man Violet didn't recognize. The man had slick black hair with skin that looked as if he had been in a tanning booth for too long. His blue eyes glittered while his lips looked like they had a little too much lip-gloss. He was wearing an expensive gray suit. On his feet, Violet noted a pair of alligator skin shoes.

Donny frowned as he said, "What's he doing here?"

This must be Quintin. He got here quick. Donny must be pretending so no one will suspect he set things up for him to come.

Quintin smiled as he said, "Don't be upset, Donny. Someone has to be here to help Rose after she had the courage to finally leave you."

In a harsh tone, Rose said, "I don't need your help, asshole. Just go back to your ivory tower and leave me alone."

Mira said, "What are the two of you doing here? We were planning Donny's engagement party."

Rose's jaw almost dropped, then her eyes filled with tears. She quickly ran away as Mira started to laugh.

Donny clenched his fist as he said, "Mira, what possessed you to say that to her?"

Mira shrugged as she said, "I don't know what you're upset about. You guys have been officially divorced for three months. And it's no secret she moved out a year and a half ago. It's time to get you connected with a new woman who can update your image."

Quintin said, "Actually, Mira, that won't be happening."

As if what Quintin said was like being burned with a hot poker, Mira jumped up. She shouted, "What the fuck are you talking about?"

Quintin frowned while responding, "I recognize this woman from a video that went viral. It would look bad if Donny married her."

Mira said, "But Quintin, right now we have his fans hyped on who he will end up with."

Donny interrupted, "Don't talk about me as if I'm not here. I told you this…"

As they argued, Violet noticed Cinder walking over. She thought, *Mira is going to get distracted dealing with those three. I wonder if whatever she has on Rose is in her purse. Stop speculating, just grab it now and find out.*

265

Without a second thought she grabbed Mira's bag. Her heart raced as she turned away from the direction where Mira was standing. Violet started to force herself to breathe slowly as she blurted out, "I have to go to the restroom."

She jumped up and started rushing back to the restroom.

Violet walked back into the restroom, her heart racing. She opened the bag hoping to find whatever Mira had on Rose. While she searched, someone asked, "How did you get that?"

Violet jumped. She looked in the direction of the voice and saw Rose. Rose's mascara had run down her face. She had clearly been trying to wash it off.

Violet quickly turned her attention back to the bag. At the same time, she said, "Sorry, I have to find something really quick."

"I don't know what Donny Face said to you, but you're not going to find it in there."

Violet looked at Rose as she asked, "How are you so sure about that?"

Rose tearfully explained, "Mira may be a bitch, but she is not stupid. If she trusted me, she never would have been able to get me to divorce my husband, move out of my house, or stop contacting my kids."

Violet questioned, "She won't let you talk to your kids?"

"Nope, that bitch had the nerve to tell me my kids are in their twenties. They don't need their mommy anymore. So, I shouldn't speak to them."

"That's cruel."

Rose reached for a paper towel to dry her face. She wiped her face while saying, "It's my own fault. I should have been more careful. Now, it looks like my foolishness is dragging you down along with my family."

Violet smiled and said, "How do you know I'm not some crazy fangirl, trying to marry her idol?"

Rose looked at Violet. She said, "I know what a crazy fangirl looks like. You weren't hanging on my Donny Face like a crazy person."

She must be the reason for the whole Donny Face thing. Why does she call him that?

Rose continued, "I saw the video of what happened to you at that restaurant. Just like Donny Face, you don't want to be here."

Relieved Violet said, "I'm glad you know that. To be honest, I was worried you'd claw my eyes out."

Rose advised, "The only person I want to damage is that bitch Mira. Speaking of her, you may want to head back to your table. She may notice her purse is gone."

Violet agreed. As she reached for Mira's purse, it tilted over, and as soon as she took a step, something fell. It slid across the room, and Rose picked it up before Violet could react. Rose stared at the object as Violet walked over and asked what it was.

Rose said, "It's a flash drive. It probably has her client info. Or, it may have more valuable information."

Violet, looking at Rose, suggested, "I guess you're going to have to take a little peak on your computer to find out."

Rose smiled, saying, "I guess you may be right."

Violet told Rose goodbye as she walked out of the restroom. When she arrived, Mira was slumped in her chair with her arms folded. Donny looked as if he was going to start dancing. At the same time, Cinder was glaring at Mira like he wanted to ring her neck.

The second Mira spotted Violet; she snatched her purse from her.

Violet said, "I am sorry. I grabbed it by accident thinking it was mine."

Mira snapped, "Whatever, Donny doesn't need a wife with a fucking bladder issue. It would be terrible for his image."

Cinder said, "You have your purse. Get out."

Mira snapped, "Fine, I don't want to eat at this garbage dump anyway."

Mira jumped up and started to march out of the restaurant. As she sat in her chair, Violet asked, "What happened?"

Cinder said, "Nothing. I said I was going to ban her from my restaurant."

Donny giggled as he said, "Don't be so coy, Cinder. That crazy lady almost busted up this place."

Cinder groaned before saying, "It is a relief to me to know that you would view seeing the destruction of my restaurant as wrong." Cinder leaned over to meet Donny at eye level and continued, "Well, at least if you or Rose aren't the ones destroying my humble place of business."

"Come on, Cinder, we never tried to hurt anyone like Mira did."

Cinder agreed, "Fair point."

Violet said, "She tried to hurt someone?"

Donny replied, "Here's what happened. Quintin put his foot down to the idea of us getting hitched, which pissed Mira off more than I even imagined it would. She slapped Quintin so hard he almost fell. Then, she grabbed your glass and hurled it at some woman who was just trying to eat her food."

Violet asked, "Was she always that violent?"

Donny said, "Yeah, it was why I have made so many requests to the company to get a new manager. As for Quintin, I think she scared him. Immediately after she threw the glass, he ran out. I'm happy that trying to seduce my ex wasn't that important to him. Otherwise, I would have had one hell of a time figuring out how to get rid of him without Rose knowing."

The waitress came with the orders, and Cinder bid them goodbye. Remembering what Arkell told her, Violet quickly said, "Um, Cinder."

Cinder looked at her and said, "Do you need something?"

Shyly Violet asked, "Arkell had to do something, and he told me to ask you for a ride home."

Cinder thought for a moment before saying, "Ok, just let me know when you're ready to leave."

After he walked off Donny asked, "Violet, how old are you?"

Violet said, "Nineteen, why?"

"I was hoping to order a bottle of champagne to toast our success. I guess we can use something else."

That very second Violet, Donny, and all the patrons in the restaurant heard a horrified scream. Donny laughed and said, "I guess Mira discovered the damage to her car." Violet joined some of the other customers who walked outside to see what was happening.

She saw Mira standing next to a red Porsche that had seen better days. Violet could see that all the windows were smashed, and the hood had been bashed in. She couldn't stop herself from smiling as Mira screamed and shouted into her phone.

Violet thought, *it's no fun when it's your life getting ruined. Is it Mira?*

Chapter 15
Demon Attack!!

After finishing her meal and sharing some delightful conversation with Donny, Violet wished him good luck stopping Mira's interference in his and Rose's life. She then headed to the front of the restaurant where Cinder had asked her to wait for him.

As she stood outside waiting, Violet thought, *that was oddly fun.* The date with Donny that she had dreaded so much had turned out to be one of the most enjoyable and interesting events in her life. Sure, this isn't a good situation for Donny and Rose, but I did get a little bit of a rush from swiping Mira's bag.

I wonder if I should become a detective. On second thought, work like that all the time would probably frustrate me and drive me crazy.

As she moved a little way from the restaurant door to wait for Cinder, Violet was suddenly hit with a realization. *Wait a moment, Donny's popularity took a hit after Rose left him. According to Donny, it has only gotten worse since the divorce. I find it hard to believe this whole wife search thing is popular with his fans.* Violet concluded that whatever nefarious reason Mira had for breaking up Donny and Rose's marriage, it was not to improve Donny's career. *I wish that I could help them, but I have to fix my own issues first. Once I do that, maybe I can help others.*

I should be excited right now. The date was fun, and the food was good. Per Drusilla's agreement with Auntie June, these stupid dates are done and over with. That doesn't mean that my fight is over. Knowing my dear guardians, they have some trick to get out of the agreement with Aunt June.

Just then a navy-blue Mercedes Benz pulled up next to Violet. The passenger window rolled down, and she noticed that Cinder was the driver. After getting in, Cinder started to drive.

He said, "I called Arkell, and he gave me your address."

"Did he mention what the emergency he had to take care of was?"

"Something about your guardian Victor Lepel being at the airport with a business associate. I guess he needed a ride, so he stole yours."

"Sounds like something he would do."

Violet started to feel nervous as the car drove, which made her wonder why Cinder made her feel this way. Maybe it was because she thought he was attractive. Or maybe she was just infatuated with him because he came to her aid when she was in trouble. Either way, he was married. Whatever romantic or most likely lustful feelings she was starting to develop for him needed to die.

Cinder said, "Arkell baffles me sometimes."

Violet asked, "Why?"

Cinder explained "I've known him for many years. He always finds a way to get himself in situations I have to assist him with. But I'm not complaining this time."

"Why?"

Cinder said, "Giving you a lift isn't exactly something I take as a negative."

Violet acknowledged, "Sorry about pulling you away from your restaurant."

Cinder replied in a soft tone, "Don't apologize. I'm happy to have an excuse to be away right now. In a way, you're doing me the bigger favor."

Violet wondered, "Do you not like running the restaurant?"

Cinder sighed, "I still love it. There are just days now and again when I just don't feel like being there. Thankfully I have a very good staff who can keep things running smoothly when I'm not there. Right now, I'm grateful for that because I don't want to be the one who has to stop Mira from trying to sneak in."

"She would try to get back in after what she did?"

"She more than likely will want to take revenge on me for her car."

"But Rose did that."

Cinder sighed and said, "True, but she doesn't know that. She called me after discovering the damage to her car. I refused to give her the parking lot video of Rose destroying her car, only because I suspect Mira is the reason Rose and Donny separated."

Violet turned her head away as she bit her lower lip. She thought, *Donny never told Cinder what Mira did. They probably never had a reason to talk about that I guess.*

She told herself not to worry about what she knew. After taking a breath she turned her head back in Cinder's direction.

Cinder continued, "Anyway, are your guardians planning another date for tomorrow?"

Violet smiled and said, "Thankfully, no. They are finally giving up, meaning I get to focus on college."

"Good. When I met you, I had a feeling your arranged dates were a waste of time."

"I agree."

"So, what are you planning to major in?"

Violet said thoughtfully, "Originally I wanted to major in medicine, but now I am thinking about doing something else, but I'm not a hundred percent sure what."

"You could always go into culinary."

"That might be fun. I always wanted to learn how to cook."

Cinder laughed, "That's not good. How about I teach you a few simple recipes?"

Excitedly Violet said, "Really?"

"Sure, I'll give you my number when I drop you off. Give me a call when you're free, and I will let you know when I can give you your first lesson."

"Wow, are you sure?"

Cinder continued, "I don't see a reason not to. With my brother-in-law as your driver, and the fact that he drops into my restaurant often to see his sister, I have a feeling you'll be stopping by a lot."

Violet felt a twinge of anticipation and happily remarked, "I guess if you think so, and thank you."

"You're welcome, oh due…"

Just then they heard a terrifying roar. Violet wondered aloud, what was that? Cinder stopped the car as Violet noticed that all the cars in front of him stopped also. The noise became louder and louder which made Violet begin to tremble.

Cinder looked back to see if they could take another route. Unfortunately, he realized that they were blocked in. He swore under his breath as Violet watched some people get out of their cars to see what was going on.

Cinder told Violet to wait there. Then he got out of the car.

The sound of the roar started to grow louder. Violet could not stop herself from shaking. Suddenly, the car shook so violently Violet screamed. When the shaking stopped, Violet bolted out of the car.

Chapter 16
The Shelter

Violet got out of the car. She saw screaming people running toward the right side of the road. Many headed down side roads as fast as they could travel on two feet. She heard the sirens of emergency vehicles become louder and louder.

Suddenly, she heard a recorded voice say, "a demon void has opened in the city. If you are not inside the Buckhead wall, make your way to a shelter. I repeat, make your way to a shelter."

She debated with herself whether to wait for Cinder to return to the car or to join the crowd and run for her life. Violet decided to run. She headed towards a group running down a side street where she assumed there must be a shelter.

As she followed the crowd, she heard another massive roar that made her insides churn. This motivated her to move her legs even faster.

Suddenly, there was a loud boom from an explosion, which shook the ground and caused Violet to lose her footing. She slammed to the ground face-first into the pavement. Suddenly, she felt the weight of two other people being forcefully slammed down on top of her.

Violet couldn't see the people who landed on her, but they quickly apologized as they righted themselves and climbed off her. As she heard them quickly run away, there was another massive roar louder than the previous one.

Violet lifted herself from the ground, rubbing her face and massaging her side. While she moved as quickly as she could, each step she took caused her pain due to her fall. Despite having not run a great distance, Violet began to breathe very hard. She suspected quick exhaustion was due to her lack of frequent activity but mostly because she was malnourished. Her body was bone skinny.

She knew no matter how uncomfortable she was, and no matter how much she wished to take a break, it would be bad news if she didn't get to that shelter soon. Another massive roar permeated throughout the air.

With each step, she cursed the Lepels. If they hadn't practically starved her for so long, she would have been able to move faster. Her body would not have felt fatigued so quickly. More importantly, she would have the strength to use magic to help her get out of this situation.

Looking ahead, she saw the end of the street. Her body burned, but she told herself to keep moving. She finally reached the end of the street. It was not a satisfying victory in the slightest. For at that moment, her body finally gave out, and she came crashing to the ground.

As she lay on the pavement, she begged herself to get up. Yet, her body had no strength to move. She could hear more explosions. More roars from the demon that sounded much closer to her than it had before.

Damn, what am I going to do? I, I can't move. That thing is getting closer, and I don't know what to do. Am I going to die here? No, this can't be it, not after what I've been through. If I can survive years with the Lepels, I can survive this.

Very slowly, she pulled herself back onto her feet. She forced her still burning legs to move. While people ran screaming, Violet tuned the noise out. She kept coaching herself to move. Suddenly, the ground shook violently again.

As expected, this caused her to lose her footing, only this time a pair of strong arms caught her.

She heard Cinder say, "Thank goodness I found you."

Violet's heart leaped as the blood rushed to her cheeks. Before she could respond, Cinder pulled her onto his back. As he pulled her up piggyback, he told her to hold tight. No sooner did she tighten her grip did he take off like lightning.

Violet was surprised Cinder was as fast as he was. He easily weaved through the stampede of panicked people. Realizing how much her head hurt from all the noise, Violet laid her head on Cinder's shoulder.

It was strange. At that moment, being close to Cinder, Violet felt safe. It seemed to her that Cinder was always saving her. Not just now, but three times in total in almost two days. However, she knew the main reason for this feeling was because she liked him. She knew it was wrong, but she couldn't help herself.

Cinder said, "Don't worry. We will be at the shelter soon, Miss Violet."

In a timid voice, Violet said, "You can just call me Violet."

Cinder agreed, "Alright."

No sooner had the words escaped her lips did Violet feel as if she wanted the moment to last forever. She was quickly snapped back to reality when she heard a massive roar.

Cinder said, "Oh crap, Violet, hang on tight."

It was then Violet noticed the danger in front of them. They were running through an area with a lot of construction. A huge concrete pole that had been connected to a crane had been loosened, and it was clearly about to fall.

Her heart started to beat fast as she said, "We need to get out of the way."

"No, it might hit someone."

Violet had no time to react when the pole fell; however, Cinder jumped high in the air like a rocket. Next thing Violet knew, Cinder was kicking the pole out of the way, preventing it from falling on any of the people running for their lives. After kicking the pole, Cinder backflipped with a screaming Violet, onto the side of a building.

From there he propelled onto the side of another building before propelling to another building and finally jumping to the ground. As Cinder continued to run, Violet attempted to grasp what had just happened.

That's impossible unless he is a sorcerer. But he isn't an elf. What can..."

Cinder shouted, "Hold on. We have to slide down if we want to make it on time."

"What?"

Cinder leaped up again, then landed on a stair railing. They slid down the railing until right before they reached the end, Cinder leaped up again onto another railing and they slid down again. When they finally reached the end of the rail, Cinder jumped to the ground.

Cinder said, "Sorry about that. I was taking a short cut. I'm afraid the shelter might close its doors early."

Violet looked around trying to see if the monster was near, despite hearing the devil's screams. She didn't see anything.

She asked, "Do you think that monster is getting closer?"

"No, I just think that the governor is most likely in the shelter, or he will be soon. If I am right, the moment he and his family are secured, the shelter will close its doors."

"How sure are you that he'll be in the shelter instead of behind the Buckhead wall?"

Cinder stated in a matter-of-fact tone, "That wall is the least secure place in the whole damn city. Right now, I'm hoping that thing is nowhere near it. If it is, practically everyone in that area will be trapped by that thing."

Violet thought, *Oh God, my family is in danger!*

Cinder said, "Thanks to the mayor, the shelter is still in good condition; however, it is the only emergency shelter in the city. So, the governor will go there. He is just like our current president in many ways- a complete coward. Even if the monster isn't close to the shelter, he will close it."

No sooner had Cinder finished speaking than he and Violet reached the shelter. The entrance to the shelter looked like a giant entryway to an underground parking lot, with giant flashing alarms above the entrance. As they entered the underground shelter, Cinder started to push himself to run even faster.

Towards the other end of the shelter was what looked like a massive garage door. Standing at each end of the door were twenty-armed soldiers. The military was ushering as many people as they could into the shelter.

Cinder said, "This is not good."

"What do you mean?"

"The army is not attempting to keep anyone calm and have us move inside in an orderly way. They are encouraging people to run, in order to save as many lives as possible. So, they are trying to rush as many people in as possible."

As Cinder and Violet got past the door, Violet thought she could breathe easy. Unfortunately, she quickly realized they were not out of the woods yet.

Violet said, "We are in the shelter."

Cinder instructed, "The entrance is just the first stop to get inside. We will not truly be safe until we get to the elevators that will take us underground. There is a lot of protective magic covering the elevators and the underground bunker. Once we are there, we'll be safe."

Cinder, like everyone else, continued to run as fast as their legs would carry them. Violet started to worry if her family was alright. She also worried whether or not she and Cinder would make it to the elevators. She clenched her hands tighter around his neck. When she did, she realized she had her purse, which meant that she had her phone.

She wondered how she didn't realize she had it until that moment, which didn't allay her fears for her family's safety. But at least if they made it underground, she could call them.

They continued moving for a few more minutes. Violet started to worry that Cinder was going to start wearing down. He had been running for a while. Not to mention the insane jumping around he did.

Violet said, "I'm feeling better. You can put me down, and I can run on my own."

Cinder declared, "Not happening, Violet."

"It's no trouble. We will be able to make it to the elevators faster."

Cinder announced, "No, we wouldn't. Violet, I know the sane people in your life have told you this over a million times. You're way too thin. In truth, the only reason you probably were able to get as far as you did is because of the big lunch you had. That doesn't make up for the lifetime of malnourishment you have undergone. It will be a long time before you can run at top speed. Not to mention you are wearing heels. I've seen enough horror movies to know that is a detriment, at least when running away during monster attacks."

Violet insisted, "But the extra weight is slowing you down."

"You don't weigh much of anything, which scares me. Have you ever tried drinking butter coffee?"

"What?"

"You may want to try drinking a cup every day for a while. It will help you get some calories in."

Violet's voice trembled while replying, "You can tell?"

Cinder told Violet, "Yes, but not because you're so skinny. Your guardians had a very thorough contract with me. It involved me not allowing you food in my establishment. I only signed the damn thing so I could defy it."

Shocked Violet said, "Really? They put that in a contract?"

Cinder continued in a defiant tone, "I'm a cook. Telling me not to feed someone is like ordering a priest to stop people from praying."

Violet, thinking of the good food that she had eaten at Cinder's restaurant, smiled and said, "Thank you, Cinder."

"You're welcome. Now that I think about it," Cinder said, "you probably never had the opportunity to try Kobe beef. I don't serve it in my restaurant currently. It's a type of high-quality Japanese beef. Sadly, Japan is under constant attack by lizard monsters. As a result, their meat vendors have jacked up the prices. Why lizard monsters are obsessed with attacking Japan is beyond me. However, should the opportunity to try Kobe beef come your way, you should give it a try."

Violet wondered aloud, "Why are we talking about Kobe beef?"

Cinder continued, "Food is my life. Besides, we should think about something other than what's troubling us right now."

"Umm… I'm not sure if I can do that. You said we don't have a lot of time to get to the elevator. Not to mention my family is in danger."

Cinder said calmly, "Exactly why I want to change subjects. Worrying about our potential impending doom doesn't help anything."

"Cinder, you're kind of strange."

"Thank you. It would be a crying shame if I was average."

Violet could not stop herself from giggling. This made her cheeks flush again. She was grateful that Cinder couldn't see her expression in case it gives away the sensations he caused her to feel.

Violet thought, *I can't believe I am laughing at a time like this. But Cinder may be right. He is doing all the running, so the most pressure is on him. I wonder…"*

Just then they heard a female voice over the intercom. "The shelter door is closing. Soon all elevator activity will be ending. Have a nice day."

Cinder snapped, "Fuck. Looks like I was right."

Violet questioned, "I don't get it. Why shut down the elevators when closing the shelter door?"

Cinder explained, "The elevators cannot be running if they want to use the shelter's protection spell at full power."

"That sounds stupid."

"It is for more reasons than you know. But we can talk about that later."

To Violet's surprise, Cinder started to run faster while many in the crowd screamed as they tried to reach the elevators as well.

Cinder turned down a corner so sharp Violet almost lost her grip. Thankfully when he did, they finally reached the level with the elevators. There were ten massive freight elevators where military officials were ushering people into the elevators.

Cinder dashed through the screaming crowd. As if possessed, he bolted for the left-most freight elevator. It took all of Violet's strength to hold on as he zigzagged through the screaming crowd.

When they got close to the elevator Cinder almost leaped into it. No sooner had they made it inside the freight elevator did Cinder finally slowed down. With Violet still on his back, he quickly walked to a corner of the elevator and stood there. They were sandwiched in by people rushing inside. Some people were practically crawling over each other to get into the elevator.

Then the sound of a gun cracked. This shocked Violet as she heard the officers shout for people to get back. She stared out at the crowd. Violet watched several people so terrified that they were trying to force their way past a wall of officers. In what felt like the world's slowest elevator closing, she saw the military officers stand firm. They pushed the crowd back, occasionally firing warning shots to get people to back away.

When the elevator closed and they started their descent, Violet prayed that all the terrified souls trying to survive this attack would somehow make it out alive.

Chapter 17
The Battle

When the elevator stopped, the people in front of them slowly exited the elevator. As they exited, Violet noticed people quietly leaving the other elevators. Once out of the elevator, Violet noticed that the space looked like a massive underground hangar. The space had grey concrete floors and there were folding chairs lined up against the walls.

Cinder slowly carried Violet out of the elevator where he finally put her down. Once back on the ground for the first time, Violet noticed he was drenched with sweat. She was about to offer to find him a rag or something when he quickly said they should find a place to sit before there were no seats left.

There were a ton of free spots to sit, which made Violet feel disgusted. If Cinder had not told her what he had earlier, she would have assumed that the demon had prevented the people left behind from getting inside. But to know the governor more than likely prevented people from getting into the shelter when there was still the chance for more people to be saved was just vile.

When they found a spot to sit down, Violet noticed Cinder seemed exhausted. He was breathing hard and using his wrist to wipe some of the sweat from his face.

She said, "Thank you. I know I wouldn't have made it without you."

Cinder looked her in the eyes and said, "You're welcome. It's funny we are being attacked by a monster now."

"Why?"

Cinder continued, "The president's wall program, or inactive wall city thing. Anyway, he is expanding it to Atlanta now. When that stupid thing appeared, it probably trapped a lot of residents inside the Buckhead area of the city."

Violet's heart leaped as she quickly took out her phone. *How did I forget to check to see if everyone is ok?*

No sooner had she pulled her phone out did she saw several missed calls, from almost every member of her family. She immediately dialed her Uncle Akeem because he was the last one to call.

Akeem answered, "Violet, are you alright?"

"I'm fine, Uncle. I'm in the shelter."

"Oh, thank the Lord you're alright."

"Are you guys ok?"

"We have…"

Suddenly, Violet heard June and May ask simultaneously, "Violet, are you alright?"

After assuring her aunts she was alright, Akeem somehow got his phone back.

Her uncle said, "As I was saying, we have a shelter on the property. Your Aunt June told me your grandfather built it a long time ago. It's funny I just learned about it. Oh, also some of your friends and their families are here, too. So, we are fine in case that thing comes back to our area."

Violet inquired, "It came near the house?"

Akeem informed, "It was running around Buckhead for a hot minute early in the attack. Thankfully, the demon was nowhere near our house. As I have always expected, the wall made it impossible for a lot of people to get away. So, there were many casualties. But the defense forces were able to expel it from the area; however, they haven't been able to take the darn thing out. According to reports, it's running around Old Fourth Ward."

Violet, relieved, stated, "At least you guys are safe."

"You don't have to worry about us. Also, look at the news. Your uncle is reporting."

Surprised, Violet said, "He's what?"

Reassuring Violet her uncle added, "Don't worry. He's reporting from the studio bunker."

Relieved, Violet said, "Good, he doesn't need to be anywhere near that thing."

They spoke for a little while until Akeem ended the call saying, "Ok kiddo, my phone is dying. After I charge it, I'm going to call you back."

Once she hung up the phone, Violet exhaled. At least her family was safe in a shelter, too. She asked herself why she never knew about it. But that was quickly answered by her remembering the Lepels' rules. One of which stated that she was not allowed to explore the mansion. She is to remain in her room unless instructed otherwise.

This made her thank God she was obsessed with the aquarium as a kid. If she had not, then she wouldn't have known how to locate it.

Thinking of the Lepels made Violet realize her uncle didn't mention her Aunt Drusilla. This made her wonder if Drusilla was not in the shelter with everyone else. The very thought of Drusilla having nowhere safe to be made Violet smile. Part of her questioned her morality for doing so. But another part of her felt that Drusilla was getting what she deserved for all the years of cruelty she had thrust upon Violet.

Drawn out of her thoughts and back into the sounds of her surroundings, Violet to heard Cinder say, "I'm so glad you're all right. I'll call back with an update of what's going on here when the officials let me know anything."

He hung up the phone. Violet's smile disappeared as she said, "I'm guessing your wife is safe."

Cinder used his hand to wipe his forehead before saying, "Yes. She was in a dangerous spot at one point, but thankfully she is safe now."

Violet counseled herself, *I need to get over myself. He's married and it is a good thing his wife is safe.*

After taking a breath, Cinder looked at Violet. He said, "I am glad we were not too far away from the shelter. Otherwise, I have a feeling we would be in serious trouble."

Seeking more information, Violet asked, "About that, I'm confused about something. My uncle told me about the route the monster took. We are downtown, but the monster was near Buckhead. Now it is supposedly in Old Fourth Ward. But it sounded way closer than that. It felt closer than that. The ground was shaking."

"From what I know, large devil demons can cause earthquakes. Those beasts are so loud I can tell you that people all the way in Cherokee County probably heard that thing. All of them probably will swear that the demon was in their town. I'm shocked and grateful that our ears did not rupture from the noise."

"That's interesting. Speaking of which, if these shelters are safer than the wall, why are there not more of them?"

"From what I've heard, the administration wants to prove the shelters are stupid. But I think they say that because one of the president's top donors owns the company that builds the walls. They and their rich friends have private shelters underneath their homes, or like our governor, they are rushed with their families to this shelter. The rich get richer while lying to and scamming the public. Of course, there will be no walls built around poor neighborhoods. "

Violet added, "Let me guess, if poor people are outside the wall and a devil attacks, they become collateral damage. The poverty rate goes down, making it look as if the economy has improved."

Cinder praised Violet's assessment of the situation, "Yep, you hit the nail on the head. Speaking of the demon attack, let's see if the news can give us any new details about what is happening."

They started to notice other people watching the news on their phones. Cinder suggested that he would use his phone to tune into the local news.

As Cinder opened the news app on his phone, Violet asked, "I noticed the shaking stopped. You think that is a sign that the demon is dead?"

"Nope, even before the final protection spell was activated, there is a spell on the shelter to keep the lower levels from shaking."

"You know a lot about this place."

Cinder articulated, "I do research on the shelters and demon attacks from time to time, out of curiosity. My wife, on the other hand, is always looking into this stuff. She is obsessed with learning all she can about demons and the Eden Witches. To be honest, if it was not for her, I wouldn't look at anything involving the monsters at all."

He then pulled up a live stream of the news. Cinder angled the phone so they both could see it. As Violet watched, she saw her uncle on screen. He was sitting next to his associate George in the studio. They were both wearing T-shirts with the station's logo.

Anas looked like someone had just slapped him. George asked him if he was alright. Anas took a deep breath. After exhaling, he thought for a moment.

He said, "I'm better. I just got confirmation my family is safe."

George reported, "At least we have some good news. Anyway, we are back everyone. To those of you just tuning in, a demon void opened up directly next to Buckhead. That's right, the place the wall was supposedly protecting. Sadly, several lives were lost in the beginning of the attack because the wall made evacuation nearly impossible. However, most of the damage was from the initial surprise attack.

Thankfully the security forces got the demon out of Buckhead. But unfortunately, they could not lead it out of a highly populated area."

Anas said, "There was an attempt to bomb the demon, but sadly, that only made it angry. I must admit, this is not surprising to me. Security forces haven't been thoroughly trained to handle high-level demon attacks. Otherwise, they would have known that dropping bombs on powerful demons, like the Hell Bishop we are dealing with now, only angers them."

George inquired, "Why?"

Anas informed the public, "A Hell Bishop is hard to kill and very methodical. To be honest with you, if there was not an Eden Witch fighting

291

it right now, I would be on my hands and knees asking God to give us all a quick death."

George questioned, "This Hell Bishop, how destructive is it?"

"I have seen firsthand Hell Bishops do worse than what we have seen so far. Hell Bishops in many cases are the main ones..."

"Anas," George interrupted, "hold on a sec. I am hearing the camera crew is on the scene."

Just then the screen switched over to a live video of the monster. Violet recognized the area. She passed that way on her way home whenever she went out.

The monster was massive with a fat gut. It had three large horns. One was in the center of his head while the other two were on opposite sides above the creature's ears. Its skin was wrinkled and colored a pinkish shade of pale orange. The devil had massive goat-like feet. Its only clothing was a loincloth that appeared to be made from some kind of red burlap. The monster also had a massive metal cannister with strange symbols strapped to its back.

It was standing in a defensive position, with its massive fist clenched, as if it was just waiting to punch something, while its eyes darted around searching.

They could hear George's voice say, "Why do they call this type of devil a Hell Bishop again?"

Anas answered, "It has to do with the cannister on its back. Watch the cannister on his back. If he can place the cannister on the ground and cast an incantation, a new demon void will open larger than the one it crawled through.

Violet asked Cinder, "Are there different types of demon voids?"

Cinder recounted some of the information he had learned about demons. "Yes, just like there are different types of demons. From what scientists and religious scholars have learned, there is some kind of barrier separating our world from the demon's world. What that barrier is, we are not a hundred percent sure. As of right now, most of the religious community believes the barrier is protection from heaven. Now, the usual monsters we see are very weak. However, they have the easiest time opening a void to get through the barrier."

Violet questioned, "Why is that possible if they are the weakest? This Hell Bishop is not one of the weak ones."

Cinder said, "Something about the barrier being more focused on keeping powerful monsters out of our world, via the fact that, oh shit."

Violet's heart raced as she started hyperventilating. At that moment, she saw the demon grab a woman and slam her to the ground.

As the woman was falling to the ground, Violet noticed something odd about the woman's feet. Her red high heels seemed very bizarre. The heels of the shoes looked like a gun with a barrel made of a strange pink crystal, while the gun's trigger resembled a spinning wheel.

Oh shit, that thing killed her. Crap, crap, crap.

Cinder put his hand on Violet's shoulder. In a calm tone, he said, "Don't worry, Violet. An attack like that is nothing to Cassandra Parker."

She steadied her breathing as she asked, "Who?"

Suddenly, they heard a loud pop from Cinder's phone. When they looked to see what it was, they saw the Hell Bishop. Gripping his wrist as blood flowed out of where his right hand used to be, Cassandra was standing across the street from the screaming monster.

293

She was drenched in demon blood, with a determined look on her face. Cassandra then pointed two blood-covered gold guns at the monster's head.

In a heavy Texas accent, she shouted, "You ruined my new outfit, you son of a bitch!"

At that moment she started to unload a swarm of bullets at the monster's face.

George said, "For those of you who do not know, that is Cassandra Parker, the sixth most powerful Eden Witch in the country. And she is giving that Hell Bishop one hell of a time."

The Hell Bishop began swaying around as if it was dizzy.

Cassandra said, "My, my, do you have a little headache? GOOD!"

Suddenly, as if being pulled up by the wind, she flew up into the air. She hovered in front of the creature's face, looking it dead in the eyes.

She smiled as she said, "Maybe this will make you feel better."

In less than a blink of an eye, a large sword suddenly materialized. It hovered in the air in front of Cassandra. She waved her wrist, and the sword slashed the monster's neck.

The creature started to fall back as it died, but before it's body could crash into the building behind it, Cassandra cast a spell that halted its descent. She descended back to the earth before casting another spell to sit the creature back on the ground.

Violet jumped when they heard loud cheering in the shelter and on the phone.

This was followed by Anas excitedly saying, "That takes care of that."

There was cheering in the shelter and in the background of the news studio. George said, "The president is having a press conference on the events that just occurred in Atlanta. We are switching to the White House."

The screen switched to the White House rose garden. The president was standing in front of a microphone with a big smile on his face.

President Andrew stated, "Let this be a testament to the effectiveness of the wall indicative. While the rest of Atlanta was in danger, the Buckhead area was safe. Now, I know I deserve credit for…"

"I'm not listening to that crap." Cinder said as he turned his phone off.

They then heard someone over the speaker say, "The demon threat is gone. You will all be free to leave in twenty minutes."

Violet said, "Good. I'm grateful that this shelter is here, but somehow I don't like this place."

Cinder agreed, "Neither do I. But I am glad the situation was not as bad as I thought it would be. But I don't feel we were spared completely."

"What do you mean?"

"I don't know any other way to tell you this." Cinder's tone was soft as if he was trying to comfort Violet. "But you should prepare yourself. What we're about to see will be heartbreaking."

Violet felt as if she had been punched in the gut. She knew what Cinder was talking about, which made her heart shatter into thousands of tiny shards.

Chapter 18
Loophole

During the twenty-minute wait, Akeem called Violet and she gave him the details. They agreed Cinder would still bring her home. They also agreed he and June would pick her up at the gate. Eventually, Cinder and Violet were let out of the shelter. When they cleared the shelter area, the two of them slowly walked back to Cinder's car.

The walk to the car proved to be one of the hardest things Violet had ever done. It was not because of the distance. It was because the two of them had to navigate through what felt like a sea of dead bodies.

Violet could hear the loud sound of sirens combined with the tears of those nearby. She had suspected that a lot of people didn't make it to safety. Either to her own arrogance or just not wishing to think about the truth, she didn't expect this many people to die. As the horrible scent of death filled her nostrils, Violet walked by many crushed and mangled bodies. She felt ill as tears rolled down her face.

So many killed. This is not fair. This should not have happened. This is just evil. There should be more shelters.

Suddenly she stopped. Violet rushed over to a small stack of debris because she felt sick. While she lost her lunch, she heard Cinder say,

"I'm sorry, Violet. I wish I could have prepared you for what we were about to see."

Violet wiped her mouth with a tissue from her purse. Sadly, she always carried tissues in case she had to clean blood from her nose from when the Lepels hit her.

"It's ok," she said as she threw the tissue on the ground.

Violet took a breath, before saying, "When an unspeakable act of this magnitude is committed, I don't think there is any way to spare a person from such horror. I also don't think I should be spared this reality. I didn't know any of these poor souls, but what happened to them should be remembered."

As they continued their journey, Cinder suggested that she try to not look at all of the dead. Instead, Violet forced herself to look at every corpse she could see. She wanted to sear every victim into her mind. That way, no matter how much time passed, she would never forget their fate at the hands of a monster. Not just the Hell Bishop, but government officials for not protecting all citizens- rich, poor, and in between. Selfish political figures had done this by not building more shelters and choosing instead to build those stupid, ineffective walls. Not to mention the fact that the shelter could have held many more people. Closing it to protect the governor was equal in her mind to murder.

When they got to the car, all the windows were shattered. The tires were busted, and there were several large dints throughout the body of the car. This lead Cinder, like others around them, to use several spells to fix the damage. Once the car was fixed, they got inside. Cinder gave Violet a stick of gum to chew while they waited for traffic to start moving.

According to a recording on a loudspeaker, emergency teams would be able to have the roads clear very soon. If Violet had not seen Tawanda's family use construction magic several times, she would not believe the roads could be cleared so quickly.

As thirty minutes went by, Violet and Cinder sat in silence. Eventually traffic started to move. Violet looked at all the destruction as they drove. For some reason it made her think about the pole Cinder had kicked, which made her remember how Cassandra had made similar moves. Part of her felt as if she was getting too personal, but she had to know why he was able to do what he did.

She said, "Umm… forgive me if I am being too personal, but how were you able to leap in the air earlier? It looked like what Cassandra did."

Cinder was focusing on the road as he said, "That isn't a personal question. I used a type of wind magic when I did all that jumping. It was also how I pushed that pole out of the way. It's not an easy spell to cast. If I didn't train to participate in charity and other fun runs, there's no way I could have cast that spell, which means that I would never have gotten us to the shelter in time."

Violet said, "Wow, you are involved with a lot of stuff."

Cinder continued, "You could say that. But I could live without participating in the runs. I only got involved in them because I lost a bet to Arkell. Then I made the mistake of placing first in the darn thing. After that I always let myself get pressured into participating in another one. But I'm not going to complain because all that running helped me gain a grasp of wind magic. Mine is nowhere near as powerful as Cassandra's; however, it comes in handy. Hmm… we are moving faster than I thought. We might see the corpse before they clean it up."

Violet responded, "That's right. So, the Hell Bishop attacked Buckhead, then ran to the Old Fourth Ward before circling back to Midtown."

Cinder said, "I think that is what the news said. We're getting close."

As the car got closer to where the monster's corpse was, to Violet's surprise, she felt oddly calm. She was surprised that she was not scared to be within eye shot of a demon, especially since as she recalled only a few hours ago she was completely terrified. Part of her thought that her calm feelings were from the monster being dead.

While pondering her feelings, she heard Cinder say, "We will be in the spot with the Hell Bishop's corpse in a minute. If seeing it makes you uncomfortable, just close your eyes. I will let you know when we are past it."

Violet felt the blood rush through her cheeks. *He is so considerate. I know I'm not scared. There is just something about the way he shows concern for me. It makes me feel special. Dammit, he's married. Stop letting yourself get flustered every time he is nice to you.*

In a nervous tone, she said, "It's ok. A part of me wants to see it." As they neared the corpse, Violet felt a strange sensation. She told herself that there was more to it than her crush on Cinder or the thrill of seeing her first dead demon.

"Are you sure?"

Violet assured Cinder, "Yes, I know it's dead, but I want to look that murderer in the eyes if possible."

Cinder replied, "Alright."

The car reached the section of the city where the battle with the monster occurred. Cinder slowed the car down a little bit so they could get a better look at the monster. There was a massive thick blue plastic covering the lower half of the monster's body. Meanwhile, red blood seemed to be slowly seeping out of the monster's neck.

The beast's eyes were still open as its head stood perfectly upright despite the large slash in its neck. As for the cannister that was on the demon's back, it was nowhere to be seen.

As Violet gazed at the beast she said, "Wow, I thought when we got here, I would freak seeing that thing in person."

Cinder said, "You are probably less bothered by it since it's dead."

Violet responded, "I guess you're right. What happened to that canister thing it was holding? I don't see it anywhere."

"From what I know about that thing, Cassandra most likely used her magic to melt it."

"Why would she do that?"

"The canister was dangerous. That Hell Bishop may have not gotten a chance to use the canister to open a void, but if that thing was left on the ground for a day, then a larger demon void would open anyway."

"Then I am really glad she destroyed that thing."

Cinder shared, "You know, one time when I had to go to Idaho, the town I was in got attacked by one nasty monster. That thing was so huge it almost blocked out the sun, at least from where I was standing."

"That must have been scary."

"It was very nerve-racking. But thankfully an Eden Witch who was in the area killed the thing. Unfortunately, I was unable to get her name."

"They seem to be on the beat if they show up that quickly."

"Not really. Like anyone else, teleporting long distances is not a very good idea for them. Most of the time they arrive after a void has been opened. The only reason why you don't hear about a massive slaughter every time that happens is because of the demon handlers."

Violet acknowledged, "I think I have heard a little about them. Aren't they like mercenary soldiers who hunt devils?"

"Yes, the government pays them to keep the monsters under control, should the defense force fail, and an Eden Witch is not close."

As they started to get away from where the monster was, Violet could see Cassandra talking to an officer. As the officer spoke, Cassandra rubbed the back of her neck before taking a breath. She was no longer holding her handguns, which made Violet wonder what happened to the guns since Cassandra didn't have them holstered. She couldn't see the sword Cassandra had earlier either.

Violet thought, *I know I saw it. But I still have a hard time accepting she took down that monster by herself.*

Just then Cassandra looked in Violet's direction. Violet's body felt completely frozen as Cassandra looked at her. She could feel her heart start to slowly beat faster and faster as she found herself unable to get herself to break away from Cassandra's gaze.

Why am I still looking at her? I, I need to stop staring. It's rude. But I can't. Why can't I turn away?

Cinder said, "Are you alright?"

This made Violet jump. As her racing heartbeat steadied, she replied, "I'm fine, just caught up in my own thoughts."

Cinder remarked, "Can't blame you, after everything that has happened."

Violet thought *that was strange. I was staring at her as if I knew her. I've never met her before. But I can't shake this strange feeling, like there is something about her I should know. What am I thinking? I'm probably overthinking the situation.*

She said, "Yeah, the mid-afternoon monster attack was more than a bit much."

Cinder sympathized, "That devil attacking is part of what I mean. I'm mostly talking about you having to deal with all those nightmare dates, combined with what happened on your birthday. Not to mention, I bet you are still trending on the internet. I must admit, Violet, you are really tough. There is no way I could have gone through all of that and still be standing tall like you."

Violet tried not to smile as she said, "It's not that big of a deal."

"You may see it that way, but I can tell you right now the hurdles I've seen you climb over in just a few days, definitely were not easy."

"Thanks, I guess. Umm…so Arkell mentioned how you had a famous partner when you started your restaurant."

She thought she heard Cinder swear under his breath, which made her feel as if she had said something wrong.

Cinder said, "Sorry if I seemed a little disgruntled. I told Arkell multiple times not to tell anyone about that. My former partner wanted to maintain a low profile."

"Sorry for bringing it up."

"You don't need to apologize. Let's change the subject. Did you see the bat Rose had?"

"Yes, I'm surprised you let her in with that thing."

Cinder said, "I didn't, and according to my hostess' statement, plus security camera footage, she checked Rose for any weapons. So, I'm at a real loss as to whatever spell Rose used to sneak that in. Although the more perplexing question to me is why she came to the restaurant armed with a bat in the first place."

"Wait a second, if you didn't know she had a bat, why did you expect her to be able to bash up Mira's car?"

"Donny wanted Rose to beat up Mira's car with a weapon so that Mira wouldn't be able to prove Rose was responsible, because Rose would never be dumb enough to bash up the car with eyewitnesses present. So, Mira's only evidence would be the security footage. Of which I told you, I won't give her, just because I don't like her, and she has no recourse to make me turn it over."

Violet wondered aloud, "Is it for the same reason my date from the other day cannot come after you?"

Cinder told her, "For the most part. Anyway, the other reason Donny would want Rose to use a weapon is so that there would be no magical signature to be traced back to Rose. Even though I won't help Mira, I don't give a crap about Rose getting caught. I even told Rose that Mira was ecstatic about having just purchased a new car because Rose has been purposely looking to mess up anything Mira likes; for whatever insane reason Rose has conjured up in her mind."

Violet realized earlier that Cinder must not know what Mira did to Rose and Donny. She decided she didn't have the right to tell him.

She said, "Interesting. I never knew that the magic signature could be tracked."

Cinder explained, "That is probably because it's not a thing for anyone outside the elf race. The elf community has the magic signatures of an elf registered when they're born. So, it's easy to track any elf who steps out of line. The rest of the magical community doesn't do the same. Mostly, because the elf registry can and has been abused for personal gain."

"Why do elves have to register their magic signature?"

"Elves tend to live in their own closed off communities. They have very strict rules for life in their communities. Some of those rules involve volunteering for the registry, not eating meat, limitations on non-elf guests, et cetera.

Mira has some sway with the elf council that runs Rose's community. This was why Donny would be scared of Rose getting caught if she used magic for violence. Despite what he wanted, he most likely also knew he could not mess up Mira's car without Roses's help. At least that's what I am assuming."

They chatted about the events at the restaurant. Thanks to all the destruction, it was twilight by the time they reached Violet's neighborhood. As they drove by, Violet was shocked to see how many homes had been destroyed. She worried if her home and her friends' homes were still standing. Even worse, each time she saw an ambulance drive by, she worried how many people had died and did she know any of them.

Cinder asked, "Are you alright?"

"Yeah, it's just with all of this destruction I'm worried that a lot of people died. I'm also afraid that some of them may be my friends."

Cinder sympathized, "So am I. It's never pleasant when one of those monsters attack. The only thing that is certain now is that both the governor and the president's approval ratings will go down."

"Probably", Violet said, "but I don't want to think about politics right now."

Cinder informed, "You should. Because if the status quo stays the same, then stuff like this will keep happening."

They reached the gate leading to her house. In front of the gate were Akeem and June standing next to a blue Lexus.

Cinder parked the car. June and Akeem both quickly hugged Violet when she got out of the car. They were holding her so tight she thought they were going to crush her. When they let her go, they both started to thank Cinder. Violet also thanked Cinder for all his help, to which he told her it was no problem. As they moved out of the way so he could leave, part of Violet wanted him to stay. She immediately scolded herself for that feeling.

As he started to drive off, Violet told herself to take a final look at him because after today she was not going to let herself see Cinder again. Violet knew the romantic feelings growing inside her were not that strong. But she didn't wish to give them a chance to grow because she didn't want to turn into a homewrecker.

Once Cinder's car was gone, June quickly muttered a spell. This spell turned Violet's clothes back to the yellow outfit. She quickly looked over Violet's attire before saying, "Good."

Akeem asked, "You didn't get hurt when that thing attacked, did you?"

"No, Cinder made sure of that."

"Really? In that case, this family is going to be doing a lot of business with his restaurant."

June said, "We can ask more questions in just a second. Et nusolvo vas."

Violet started to feel as if a small weight was being lifted off her body.

June said, "There, the curse I put on you should be gone now. Sorry I had to do that to you, but it was the only way to fool my sister."

Violet smiled at her aunt as she said, "I'm not mad about it anymore. You were only trying to help."

Akeem said, "With the mess that monster made, I forgot you went on another date. How did it go?"

"It was kind of fun being set up with someone who wanted things not to work out either."

June said, "I'm glad you had fun, and lunch."

"Yeah, Cinder's food is really good."

Akeem suggested they all get in the car so they could drive to the house.

Once they were in the car, Violet told them how Cinder got her to the shelter. Both her aunt and uncle looked like they were going to faint for a second. Then June changed subjects and started to tell Violet about their experience.

June said, "The whole house was shocked when the ground violently shook. Thankfully everyone was alright. The attack destroyed the property's security system. I don't know what everyone else was thinking, but when the shaking stopped, I was confused as to what was going on until I heard that thing roar.

When that happened, I told everyone to head for the shelter. We all went except for Drusilla and her staff, who refused the offer of shelter. After I was sure that the family and the staff were inside, I closed the shelter. Then I had a talk with your uncle about how your granddaddy built the shelter. Later, I reopened the shelter, letting several of our friends and neighbors in while Meg tried to call you."

"Sorry I didn't pick up."

"Don't worry. You were trying to get out of harm's way."

Akeem said, "Speaking of that, Violet, turn off your phone volume and hide it and your credit card."

Violet replied, "You're right. I should do that now. Speaking of Aunt Drusilla, why did she and her staff not want to go to the shelter?"

Akeem said, "I'm not sure, but Meg thinks it is because she probably believed that we wouldn't let them in if they came. Which isn't ridiculous considering we wouldn't have let them in. Also, your grandma is fine. She somehow slept through the whole thing. But we are going to move her into the house for a while. None of us are ok with her being alone during another monster attack. Your friends and their families are fine too. They went home when the attack was over."

June said, "Honey, we need to fill Violet in really quick. We'll be at the house soon."

"Oh, you're right."

Violet asked, "What happened?"

June replied, "Nothing. I just need to explain what the plan for your date was. I knew that Donny Person would have no real interest in you. His ex-wife and his agent were at your birthday last night."

Surprised Violet said, "They were what? Why were they there?"

June explained, "His ex was there to spy on his agent, who was at the party via Drusilla's request. I discovered too late that Drusilla had made a deal with the club owner. So, that is how she was able to sneak in and why that Mira woman was on the guest list. As for Donny's ex, I have no idea how she got in.

She approached me after you left with Drusilla, and she offered me a way to help you with your date. For part of her plan, she tried to give me some old T-shirt from an old tour Donny did. Apparently, every time a tour ends, he ditches his shirt design. This is only a huge deal because he makes a huge fuss over it. So, his fans make a fuss over it."

Violet interjected, "I get what you're saying, Auntie. Donny also made it pretty clear that his fans would be bothered by him going out with someone wearing his old look."

June continued, "I'm glad you get that part. Anyway, Williams told me the shirt she gave me smelled funny. I suspect it smelled like lamosvagen. That's a very popular meat substitute among elves, but it stinks. So, I enchanted Meg's old outfit from one of his tours. I turned it into a yellow dress so Drusilla and her people would not figure out my plan. Oh, also, I sold all your clothes."

"What?"

"Violet, per my agreement with my sister, I get to buy you new clothes three times a year."

"I know, actually now that you say that, why does Aunt Drusilla always want to pretend that she is the one buying me clothes?"

"Don't worry about that. Anyway, I decided for the plan to work I needed to exercise this right early."

"Wouldn't Aunt Drusilla be suspicious?"

June cynically announced, "Sweetie, Drusilla and Ollivander are not the wisest of people most of the time. That's the main reason why we have been able to sneak you things. Since I needed you to wear a specific outfit on your date, I ordered your new clothes this morning. Last night, after you fell asleep, I snuck into your room and used a packing spell on your clothes and bags, having them transferred to the storage room."

"Auntie, are my things still here? Zhang Li's grandma made me a care package."

"So that's where you got that from. Its cover disappeared when I was transferring your things. The staff found it when they were doing a final check on your old things. The bulk of your new things have already arrived. Williams supervised the refilling of your closet, but I would not be surprised if that attack messed everything up. Janet was under orders to make that care package look like a Birkin bag. I also had her add a kitchen feature to your island so that you will be able to warm up the food we sneak you."

Akeem said, "We are going to start giving you care packages in tins like the one Zhang Li's grandma made. Later, I will teach you a spell that will keep your closet from smelling like food."

Violet, in an unsure tone, said, "I know you feel Aunt Drusilla isn't smart, but won't she, her husband, or Ollivander notice the spell on my closet island or on that metal container when he checks my closet?"

June said, "Normally, yes. Where we always failed to pull the wool over his eyes in the past, TJ found a new person who is good at a few not so legal spells. That will mask the magic we use in your closet, part of which is blocking the spy equipment. From now on we do not have to break the spy equipment. Whoever is watching will see what we want them to see. Understand that we aren't allowed to know the person responsible for casting the spell's real name. Just know we should call him Jack. He is pretending to be a butler, but do not talk to him too much."

Violet asked, "Have you guys hired someone like that before?"

Akeem answered, "We have been hiring people who perform illegal spells for years. We have used these spells in the past sometimes to help with your situation, other times to help us with certain business matters."

Violet felt Uncle's words hit her in the face. She wondered how ignorant she truly was about what goes on in her home.

June said, "Anyway, your dear Aunt Drusilla has some kind of association with Mira. I don't fully understand what this Mira person's intentions are, but I do know Drusilla snuck her into your birthday party so that Mira could decide whether she wanted you to marry Donny."

Violet said, "That's just crazy."

June continued, "I agree. Donny's ex, what was her name?"

"Rose."

June wondered, "How did you know that?"

"I met her at the restaurant."

June verbalized, "I should not be surprised by that. So, she hatched the events that happened to you at the restaurant. Rose apparently didn't tell Donny about it. She just set things in motion for him to fall for her plot. She made some kind of plan for Donny to take her phone. Then she made sure some investor saw that video of you that is trending. I did not get all the details, but I took the deal. It felt like the best way to kill your forced dates."

"Well, her plan worked. But why did Aunt Drusilla need to rip my dress?"

"She didn't," Akeem said as he parked the car. It was then Violet realized they were in the garage.

He continued, "Drusilla ripped your dress because you were happy."

Violet groaned while saying, "I can believe that."

When they got out of the car they headed towards the elevator. After getting to their floor and stepping out, Violet saw the damage to the house caused by the Hell Bishop.

Paintings were hanging askew on the walls. Some had fallen to the floor. Broken glass and other shattered decorations were everywhere. A few of the walls were cracked. The staff were running around trying to fix the mess, except for the Lepels' employees who were standing around complaining.

Violet, her aunt, and uncle headed for the kitchen. According to June, it was the only room that had been completely reorganized. At first, Violet felt nervous about going into the kitchen without permission. She reminded herself she had gone in there that morning without permission. Then she reminded herself that she needed to stop following the Lepels' rules.

When they reached the lower level of the house, the floors were covered with glass. They found Drusilla pacing in the foyer with her arms tightly folded.

Drusilla snapped, "What are you two doing with Violet?"

June grumbled, "We picked her up at the front gate, remember? A friend of Arkell called. He said he would drop her off for two hundred dollars. Your husband made Arkell abandon her at that restaurant."

In an exasperated voice, Drusilla said, "I know, June. You don't need to give me the details."

June said in a nasty tone of voice, "Then why did you fucking ask the question if you don't want the damn answer? Now, on to business, you know what happened with Violet's date. Sucks to lose, doesn't it? "

Drusilla glared at her sister. In a harsh tone, she said, "Shut the hell up, June."

311

"No, bitch, you have had too much say in what goes on in my house. This ends now."

Drusilla snapped, "It's my house, too!"

Akeem responded, "Ha, no it's not. Your mother gave the house to May and June because Mathew wanted to build his own house on that plot of land he found. Meanwhile Ap...Ouch!"

Akeem started to rub his head in pain. At the same time, June seemed to be a little unsteady. Before Violet could react, June suddenly seemed to lose her balance. Thankfully, a still clearly in pain Akeem, quickly caught her. As he helped her steady herself, June began massaging her forehead.

Violet thought *something strange was going on. This is the third or fourth time either Aunt June, Aunt May, and now Uncle Akeem had a sudden weird headache.*

In a condescending tone, Drusilla said, "What were you saying? I, I didn't catch that."

The others ignored Drusilla. As they made their way to the kitchen, Drusilla followed them, stomping her feet.

When they entered the kitchen, May, Meg, and TJ were sitting at the table. June sat down at the table as she massaged her forehead. Violet, seeing her aunt and uncle in pain, offered to get them some painkillers. She went to the cabinets to retrieve a couple of drinking glasses and filled them with water from the refrigerator. Her Aunt June told her that she would find aspirin in the top drawer next to the refrigerator. After delivering the water and medication, Akeem quickly took his pills and sat the glass down, while June swallowed her pills and drank some of the water slowly.

After a few minutes, Meg asked, "Are you guys feeling alright?"

June said, "Something is a little bit off with me. For some reason when your uncle was about to name someone, I think was it a cousin? Umm, umm what is the, OUCH! Damn, why does my head keep hurting?"

Akeem said, "I was talking about the apartments May and I think Ap...OUCH, SHIT!"

He then paused for a minute like he forgot something. Then he said, "Anyway, I was talking about May's apartment."

May asked, "What about the apartment?"

Violet thought *apartment nothing, he was about to say something important. What are the odds that they both would get a migraine out of nowhere at the same time? The same thing happened yesterday at Aunt June's office. And when I asked Auntie May questions in the aquarium, she got a headache as well. Something very fucked up is happening, and I need to know what it is.*

Before Violet could bring up the subject, Drusilla who was glaring, snapped, "You may have won our wager, but that doesn't mean I'm loosening Violet's leash. I'll just have to hire a matchmaker. Then I can have her married in a week."

Violet wanted to cuss her aunt. However, she knew better and held her tongue.

Violet thought, *what the fuck is wrong with this woman? She is obsessed with me getting married, for what she says is my own good. After everything I learned in just the last few days, I know that's crap. I have to find out her real motive.*

June looked at Drusilla and asked, "What the fuck is wrong with you? This obsession with marrying Violet off needs to end. She needs to go to college. One day she will meet a nice man and get married when she is good and damn well ready."

Drusilla laughed as she said, "You're joking, right? Violet doesn't have the wherewithal to pick a good spouse or to even take care of herself."

Just then TJ said, "Drusilla, you're full of it."

TJ was standing next to the kitchen island. He continued, "For whatever your reason, you feel a sick need to punish Violet for existing. I don't know what kind of tiff you had with your brother, but the crazy needs to stop."

In a harsh tone, Drusilla said, "Shut up, TJ. You like to act like you know everything when you don't know shit."

Meg snapped, "Don't talk to him that way!"

Drusilla folded her arms as she said, "Ha, I can do whatever I want. Have you forgotten what will happen if you don't let me have my way?"

Violet said, "Aunt Drusilla, you need to stop acting like having a single threat means you have strong leverage over the family."

"Violet, what kind of stupid shit are you talking about now?"

Violet, in an angry tone explained, "You're simple-minded. The only reason you agreed to let me stay here was because you and your husband have nowhere else to go. The second I get married or get shipped off to the facility, you two will be kicked out of this house."

Drusilla snapped, "You're full of shit."

Violet declared, "Don't try to act tough to hide the truth. I'm not a little girl anymore." Violet felt confident as she continued to say, "After the hell you put me through, sending me to the facility isn't going to make a difference in my life. Also, it doesn't matter which asshole you pick. As I told that bitch Mira earlier today, it is my call who I marry. You never had a real say in who it is."

"Excuse me?"

Violet proclaimed, "Face it, your only leverage over the family is threatening to send me to a mental facility. That place may house some very dangerous people, but if you send me there, I promise they'll fear me more than anyone they've ever met. Not only that, any bastard you pick for me to wed will quickly be made to regret ever meeting me. The only thing you'll get after everything is said and done is thrown off of this property. Well, that and a major lawsuit, considering last night's party isn't the first agreement you violated. I doubt the statute of limitations is up for all the other contracts you broke with your sisters and brothers-in-law."

Drusilla looked at Violet as if at a loss for words. Meanwhile, the rest of Violet's family didn't know whether to be happy or worried. As for Violet, she felt strong. She realized that for the third time she had taken down one of her tormenters. At that moment she knew how much power she had.

Just then Arkell walked in with a depressed look on his face. In a somber tone, he said, "Mr. Lepel is waiting for all of you in the foyer."

Violet wondered what was going on as they all headed towards the entrance. When they arrived, they saw Victor standing in the middle of the room with his usual scowl look on his face.

He glared at Drusilla as he said, "Stupid bitch. Your failure at coupling Violet with that rock star has made me do something I didn't want to do."

He turned his attention to Violet. He said, "Attempt to make yourself presentable. I have made a deal with my business partner for you to marry his son. His family will be coming to dinner tonight to go over wedding arrangements."

June said, "Hell no. A demon just attacked the damn city. It's not a good time for a dinner party or bullshit engagements."

May said, "She is right. You guys lost the agreement anyway."

Victor laughed as he said, "Stupid bitch. From what my dumbass wife said, the agreement only bars us from sending Violet on more arranged dates. It said nothing about just immediately marrying her off."

Violet was frozen in shock as TJ, Meg, Akeem, May, and June started to yell at Victor. Some of the staff ran in to see what all of the noise was about. Suddenly, Victor screamed for everyone to silence themselves.

As for Violet, she felt her temperature rise. As she stood thinking, *they hadn't won. I won't let them win.*

She shouted, "Just send me to fucking Greenages. I'm better off there than dealing with your bullshit."

In a worried voice, May said, "Violet, don't be rash."

"No, Auntie. If I go, then all of this will end. The Lepels won't be in your lives anymore. Even if I must live with killers, at least I will know that the family is not being constantly tormented by these people."

Akeem said, "No, Violet. Under no circumstances are you ever going to live in that horrible place."

Violet replied, "Uncle, I know how you feel, but you guys have been fighting for me for years. The only reason the Lepels keep winning is because of what the court said. But if I go to Greenages, then they lose that bargaining chip. So, that is what I am going to do."

Drusilla laughed as she said, "You will never actually willingly go. You're just saying that to act tough."

Violet glared at Drusilla. She said, "Call the facility now. I'm going to say my goodbyes."

Victor frowned as he said, "Such a shame. Don't waste time packing. A uniform will be provided for you when you get there."

In an eerie calm voice, Violet said, "Fine."

TJ quickly said, "Wait, you don't have to do that."

Violet exhaled as she replied, "Yes, I do."

TJ, trying to find a silver lining, stated, "No, you don't. This guy they want to hook you up with might not be so bad."

"TJ, let's not play this game."

"I'm not playing. All I am saying is you should at least meet the dude. Give him a once over before you agree to ship yourself off to an insane asylum."

Violet looked at her family. She could tell they were terrified of what she would say. Deciding it would be nice to at least stay one last night at home, she decided she would at least agree to what TJ suggested.

Chapter 19
Puzzle Pieces

Violet was pacing back and forth in her room. She had changed into a green lace evening dress. A gold necklace hung around her neck while a pair of gold diamond-studded earrings hung from her ears. She couldn't stop thinking about everything she had discovered over the past few days. Each time she reflected on the things she had learned, Violet felt she was trying to put together a puzzle. The only problem was she didn't have all the pieces. In a fit of frustration, she stomped her foot and declared to herself that her brain was about to explode, and she marched out of her bedroom.

When she entered the hallway, she decided to go to the aquarium. When proceeding down the hall, Harold shouted for her to stop. Violet halted before folding her arms. Harold marched up to her. He pointed in the direction of her room and shouted, "WHAT IS WRONG WITH YOU?! GET YOUR ASS BACK TO YOU ROOM NOW UNTIL YOU'RE TOLD OTHERWISE!"

Violet laughed, and then she slapped Harold so hard he staggered for a moment. When he regained his footing, she pointed her finger directly in his face.

She snapped, "Listen, you fucking turd. Your bitch-ass is just a very unwanted pest that I can't wait to throw in the street. So, if you know what's good for you, you'll stay the fuck out of my way."

Harold's brows furrowed as he raised his claws to slash Violet. Before he could strike, Violet waved her wrist as she said, "Cere orum."

Harold screamed as he was suddenly dragged down the hallway. Eventually, he slammed into the wall, causing a large painting to fall. Violet noticed it was one of Drusilla's favorite paintings. It smacked him in the head hard, knocking him out. Meanwhile, a still smiling Violet, headed for the aquarium. She thought about the painting that fell and how much Drusilla loved it. Knowing it just busted over Harold's head brought her a great deal of joy.

Violet sat on the bench in the corner of the aquarium. Her mind was still racing trying to understand why the judge had ruled in favor of the Lepels all those years ago. She had heard more than once how unusual it was for custody of a child to be given to strangers, especially in this case where her father had left specific instructions that her Aunt June and Uncle Akeem were to be given custody of her. What were the Lepels up to? What plan were they discussing in the dining room? Why were they so determined to marry her off? Why, as Arkell had explained to her, did the governor and other important officials care what happened to her? She didn't even know these people. Who was this mysterious aunt? Most importantly, why did the members of her family always get migraine headaches whenever she asked about this aunt or anything about the past? They even seem to forget what we were discussing in the first place. Violet didn't remember any of them having migraine headaches in the past. Why now were they suddenly all plagued by the same condition? Violet was also perplexed by the weird statement from Drusilla about her father choosing her mother instead of her. That is just messed up.

Violet realized that she had too many questions that she had no way of answering alone. However, the people who could answer them seemed somehow incapable of doing so. She looked up, and her attention was immediately drawn to the grimoire. She decided that it would be wise to look through the spells. Maybe there was one there that would help fix the headaches.

She walked up to the book and performed the motions to remove the glass case. Violet felt weaker than she had the first time. Quickly, she opened the book and began looking through the spells. With each page she turned, she felt more and more drained. Eventually, she was forced to accept that trying to use the grimoire without training was foolish. She should have listened to her Aunt May and not messed with the book by herself.

Before closing the book, she noticed a spell called reflector. It was made to deflect spells while they're being cast. But the most interesting thing about the spell was that unlike most powerful spells, this spell only consisted of a single word, "Relut." Despite her desire to keep looking at the spell, she felt as if she was about to fall asleep. Quickly, she closed the book, and then she performed the motions to reseal it in the glass case. Not wanting to sleep in the aquarium, Violet walked out of the room.

Violet left the aquarium and started to walk down the hallway. After taking only a few steps, she realized that she was far more tired than she thought. Not believing that she could make it back to her room, Violet decided to head into her old room.

When she opened the door, she was greeted by an unfamiliar sight. The pink room full of toys and games had been replaced with a room with a much more modern look. The floors were covered with white carpet, while the walls were painted baby blue. There was a canopy bed near the left wall and a couple of cherry wood nightstands on each side of the bed.

The front wall had windows with an amazing view of the lake, and a large TV hung on the right wall.

Violet walked over to the bed and lay down. She thought about how much she liked the changes that had been made to the room. She had been given this room after her parents died. It had been chosen because it was next to Meg's room. Violet remembered being plagued by nightmares after her parents' murder. She would wake up screaming hysterically every night. Although her aunt and uncle tried, it was only Meg who could calm her.

A part of Violet even felt like being really daring and moving back to the family wing. Violet knew that after their marriage, Meg and TJ occupied a much larger room in a different hall in the house. Her aunt and uncle's room was farther down the hall. So, if she did reclaim her old room, she would have privacy. She looked around; this room was twice the size of her current bedroom. She felt happy thinking of a future where she had some control of her life. However, she knew that her guardians would cause more problems for her aunt and uncle if she moved back to her old room. As that sad thought crept into her mind, tiredness completely overwhelmed her, and she drifted off to sleep.

Violet found herself standing in the middle of a dark snowy forest. She was shivering because all she had on was a white shirt and long, tight brown pants that had holes in the legs. Even worse, her shoes were not helping the situation because the black boots were old and worn.

She thought, *I should be there soon. Damn Oliver, he's going to pay for..."*

Just then she heard the echoed sound of a child crying.

She cried out, "Where are you?"

A little boy's voice echoed, "Go away."

"But you can't stay out here."

"Go away. I have to die."

"What, don't say things like that."

"Everyone hates me."

"Not true."

"Yes, it is. Mommy and Daddy don't want me. They told me I should go die."

Violet's heart leaped as her anger rose. As far as she was concerned, anyone who would say that to their child had no right to be a parent.

She shouted, "Listen, I don't know who you are, but I know your parents are stupid for saying that."

"They're right."

"No, they're not. They are just stupid."

"My daddy is the mayor of Vermatho. He's gotta be smart."

Violet thought, *his father is the jackass I was on my way to cuss out. OK Oliver, I hope you said your prayers. As soon as I'm sure your kid is safe, I'm going to kick your ass.*

She shouted, "Your daddy may be mayor, but he is a fool. If he wasn't, he would not try to throw you away."

"Really?"

Violet was able to tell that the child was behind a nearby tree. She looked behind the tree and saw a shivering elf child. He was curled up and crying into his arms. His skin was brown with a head full of curly blue hair. The child was wearing a red coat and black pants with no shoes."

She smiled as she said, "I mean every word I said. Let me build us a little fire so we can get warm. Then we can head to Vermatho and grab some hot cider. I bet that sounds…"

Violet leaped up in the bed. She felt her heart beating in her chest very fast, while she heard Arkell apologize for waking her. As she started to calm down, she tried to remember the strange dream she had.

It felt so real.

She looked at Arkell while saying, "Did something happen?"

"No, the Lepels are looking for you. They are insisting that the man who they picked for you is on the way. I found you in here a while ago, but I left to let you get some more sleep. I'm only waking you now because I can't stall anymore."

"I guess I better head downstairs."

"Before you do, can you wait a minute? There is something I need to talk to you about."

"Sure, what is it?"

"There is something off about your family, and I'm not talking about the Lepels."

Chapter 20
Headaches

"Arkell, what are you talking about?" Violet asked.

He responded, "Lately, they all seem to develop sharp pains in their heads whenever they are about to say something important."

Violet was happy to hear that someone else noticed the same behavior that she had seen. She then said, "I've noticed that happening recently, too."

Arkell continued, "Just a little while ago I was talking to your cousin. She was wearing a necklace that she said was a gift. I asked her who gave it to her, and she told me it was from her aunt. However, when she tried to name this aunt, her head started to hurt. As soon as the pain started, she forgot what we were talking about. But she was aware she forgot something important."

Violet thought aloud, "I wonder if she was talking about the aunt my Aunt Drusilla mentioned."

Arkell questioned, "Excuse me?"

Violet thought, *I can't figure this out alone. I guess I should trust him if I want answers.*

She explained, "Aunt Drusilla mentioned that I had another aunt when I was eavesdropping on her."

"Interesting. Have you mentioned this to anyone?"

"I told Meg and Aunt June about it. When I did, Aunt June got a horrible headache. And she was not the only one. Aunt May and Uncle Akeem also got head pains when they were about to answer my question. I felt like you said, that they were about to say something important."

"Hmmm… this more than likely plays into something I saw earlier."

"What happened?"

"I did more than pick up Victor when he demanded I leave you to pick him up."

"What happened?"

"When I arrived, he was with a man by the name of Lincoln Banner. He is the father of the man you're now engaged to."

Violet sighed, "Great, what's my soon to be father-in-law like?"

"I see him as motivation for me to do my job. To answer your question, he is your standard asshole."

Violet said, "That bad?"

Arkell continued, "The man was gloating about how dumb his wife is for practicing Islam. He also went on a tirade about how no matter how many times he hit her, she would proudly proclaim that she was never going to abandon her faith. As far as he was concerned, people belonging to any religion are stupid. He was also complaining about how she needed to give him control of her accounts. In his opinion, no woman should be in charge of the money. The man is a sexist prick."

In a sarcastic tone, Violet said, "He sounds like fun to be around."

Arkell smiled and replied, "Yeah, he's loads of fun. Anyway, your uncle and this Lincoln person had me drive to a strange address. During the entire drive, Lincoln continued with this sexist and anti-religion rant, which was hypocritical in his case."

"Why?"

"Because he blabbed about how The Way of the New Dawn is the only true religion. Victor told him to shut up about it, and then he checked to see if I was paying attention. Thankfully, he is easy to trick. All I had to do was pretend to be oblivious to what was going on, and he believed me without a second thought."

"What is The Way of the New Dawn?"

Arkell continued, "Some kind of cult. I'm not too clear on what their belief system is; however, I do know they are plotting something very bad. I also think they are the ones who killed your parents."

Violet felt her eyes begin to well up. She tried to hold her tears back, but they still fell down her face like a river. Arkell quickly patted her shoulder, and then he went into the bathroom and grabbed a washcloth to dry her face. She thanked him. After she calmed down, Arkell continued his story.

Arkell continued, "They had me drop them off at what looked like an old government building. Victor told me to wait in the car for them. When they went inside, I followed them. Once they were inside, I saw them go into a room with a strange woman."

Violet questioned, "Strange how?"

"She was naked and covered head to toe in tattoos."

Violet wondered, "So do you believe that this Way of the New Dawn is a strange sex cult?"

"Thankfully, from what I have discovered, the answer to your question is no. Anyway, I spied on them. Victor was telling the woman that his lower staff still knew nothing. So, he and Ollivander would have no problem handling things when it was time."

A little fear in her voice, Violet asked, "Time for what?"

Arkell shared, "Sorry, I was not able to find out what that meant as for the lower staff not having a clue. I suspect he was talking about Harold and Kinya. Those two are just a couple of assholes looking for a big payday. This is probably stupid on their part because whatever this nefarious plot is, I have a feeling the cult will use them. How, I don't know, but I already think those two are not going to like it.

I should include myself as well. The Lepels think I am a greedy money-grabbing ass. Naturally, they think they can use me like Harold and Kinya. I'm hoping that their ignorance of my true intentions may play in our favor."

Violet put her thoughts into words and said, "Ok, so maybe I can piece together one part of the puzzle. Could it be that the governor and several other important people belong to this cult? But what do my parents have to do with anything and why would they kill them? I also know that my custody case without fail was always overseen by the same judge, which means that he is likely a member of this same cult."

Arkell said, "This cult must have a lot of reach. Victor was even saying at this point everything should fall into place before it was too late. And then Lincoln stated that it was a shame one of their own had to be directly involved."

Violet asked, "What can that mean?"

Arkell explained, "I didn't understand what he meant at first either. But after I thought about it, I think they were referring to your intended. This apparent loss of one of their own pissed off the woman. She told Victor after all they did to get the Evergreens out of the way, that Victor and Drusilla messed up hooking you up using the arranged dates. Now, they need you to get married in two months. Otherwise, you're going to become self-aware. When that happens, they'll have to do something drastic to achieve their goal."

Violet nervously asked, "Wait, what do they mean by I become self-aware?"

Arkell continued relating his information and answered, "I have a theory, but let me tell you more about what happened. The woman told Victor that she regrets every day that she allowed you to be handed over to him. He told her to stop complaining about it because if he and Drusilla hadn't become your guardians then their plan would have failed long ago. Then she changed the subject and declared that your wedding must take place next month."

A perplexed Violet questioned, "What is so damn important about me getting married?"

"Apparently their plan will not work unless you do."

Violet said, "Now I have even more questions than I did before. If Victor and Drusilla subscribe to this cult, why did they let the rest of the family take me to church every Sunday? From what you have told me about Lincoln's behavior, this cult seems to have a problem with other beliefs."

Arkell told her, "I wish I could answer that. However, I feel I have started to put together a few of the pieces of what is going on."

Violets heart leaped with anticipation. Quickly she said, "Really?"

"I suspect you and your family are under a very powerful memory curse."

"What?"

Arkell began to explain, "Violet, your family is rich as hell. There is no way they should have not been able to have your custody case overturned. Hell, I had a feeling that shortly after the Lepels got custody, that they would have had them killed."

"No, they wouldn't."

"Your Aunt June told me that if that first date I took you on worked out, then I was to shoot your date in the head."

A shocked Violet attempted to defend her aunt and replied, "Shit, you must have misunderstood. I'm sure she was just joking."

To make her face reality, Arkell stated, "Violet, she's not playing around. That is also what I meant by making you an accessory. I'm only willing to tell you now because I realize you need to know that information. But even if that wasn't the case, the sudden memory loss is a red flag. I suspect a very powerful memory curse has been placed on you and your family. Whoever did it must be a pro because I couldn't even sense it."

Violet wondered, "Are you sure it's a curse?"

Arkell said, "Your situation is too strange for it not to be a curse. Show me your right hand."

"Why?"

"It's the only way to be sure."

Violet handed him her right hand, and he stared at her palm for a moment. Then he whispered a spell that Violet couldn't understand.

Suddenly, a glowing red mark in the shape of an octagon appeared on her palm.

She screeched, "What the fuck is that?"

Arkell, in a soft voice said, "A very powerful curse. Dammit, I have to talk to my father."

"What does this have to do with your dad?"

"I'll explain in a sec."

He muttered another spell, and the glowing symbol disappeared. Arkell took a breath before sitting down in a blue armchair that was near the window.

As soon as he was seated, he said, "This is going to be complicated."

"Is it going to be hard to remove the curse?"

Arkell said, "Not hard, but time-consuming. The only way to remove that curse is with a Sandsheen potion. It takes three weeks to make, and my father is the only one who has the recipe. He hates my ass, so I'm going to have to steal it from him."

With sympathy in her voice, Violet asked, "Why does he hate you?"

Arkell said, "He and my mother just don't like me. No matter how hard I tried to prove myself, it was never good enough. Eventually, they threw me out. I begged them for another chance, but they just laughed at me. My so-called parents told me I would be better off dead."

Violet felt a sudden urge to remember her dream. But she found herself unable to. This made her feel as if she was forgetting something important. She tried harder to remember, but her head started to hurt.

Noticing she was in pain, Arkell realized that the curse was active. He told her to stop trying to remember. Otherwise, her head pain would only get worse until it was unbearable.

She said, "Dammit, I can't take this crap."

Arkell explained to Violet, "I understand your frustration. But you're not going to be able to remember anything until after you drink the potion. I will talk with you and your family about this problem tomorrow. Right now, you should get going before the Lepels try and find you."

Violet agreed before heading downstairs.

Chapter 21
Happy Family???

The staff had finished most of the repairs to the house, making it look much more presentable to have guests over. Meanwhile, Violet and the other members of the family, except for May, Victor, and Drusilla, were sitting in the living room.

The walls of the room were a soft baby blue. The floors were made out of oak wood, the same as the rest of the house, with a large blue oriental rug covering the area where Violet and the family sat. In the center of the space was a glass coffee table. A ceramic vase filled with yellow daylilies sat in the center of the table. Three white couches with blue decorative pillows were positioned in a semicircle around the coffee table.

Meg, who was wearing a black cocktail dress, sat between Violet and TJ. TJ wore a dark blue suit. Sitting on the couch across from Violet was Anas, who was wearing a black suit and tie. Next to Anas was Akeem, who was dressed in a red suit with a black tie. June sat next to her husband, and unlike everyone else, June was wearing a very old, faded orange T-shirt and a pair of raggedy blue jeans. To top off her outfit, she wore a pair of very old, dirty white tennis shoes. She had both of her arms and legs crossed, and she had an angry look on her face. Her eyes looked cold and were filled with hate- something that Violet had never seen displayed in her aunt before.

When Violet joined the family in the living room, Akeem, Anas, TJ, and May all had terrible headaches. May's head hurt so badly that she excused herself and went upstairs to lay down. Slowly, everyone else recovered.

TJ said, "What is going on? I've never had constant severe headaches in my life. Now, suddenly almost every hour my head is hurting."

Everyone in the room agreed that something suspicious was happening. Why were they all getting headaches at the same time? Despite her family's suspicions, Violet decided to remain quiet about the truth. The Lepels were going to walk in at any moment, and it wasn't worth risking them finding out she knew about the cult. So, she decided to talk with everyone in the morning.

She wondered if the man she was to marry is a member of the cult Arkell told her about. Why did they see it as a bad thing for him to be directly involved? This made her wonder more about the Lepels.

They were a part of a cult, a cult whom she suspected messed with the memories of herself and her family. A cult whose members murdered her parents, and in so doing denied her the life that she should have had. She thought with anger about Drusilla, who always took the time to scream at Violet, accusing her of killing her brother. All the while Drusilla may have been the real murderer, or at least knew who was responsible for his murder.

Suddenly, she remembered Drusilla's strange accusation that her father chose her mother over Drusilla. She refused to believe her father was involved in an incestuous relationship with his sister. But she couldn't deny what Drusilla said. She was reminded of the stipulation in her father's will stating that Violet was to be kept away from the Lepels. She wondered if Drusilla wanted to have that kind of relationship with her father, but her father rejected the idea.

333

The more she pondered the situation, the more she cringed. Meg noticed the look on Violet's face and asked what was wrong.

Violet said, "I'm fine. I just remembered something gross."

Meg asked, "What happened?"

"I don't want to say anything. If I do, then it's not going leave my mind."

June rang for a servant as she muttered about wanting bourbon.

Akeem looked at his wife and said, "I get your frustration, but I don't think you should be drinking right now."

June took a breath before responding, "My bitch sister wants to marry my niece off to a man I suspect is a lazy trust fund baby who probably doesn't understand any form of decency. He will most likely burn through her inheritance and drag our family name through the mud. So, I think a drink is more than necessary right now."

Agreeing with his wife, Akeem said, "My love, you're right. I should get a drink, too."

One of the Wilds' maids, a short mousy woman with large brown eyes and dressed in a green maid's uniform with a white apron, entered the room. The maid's long curly auburn hair was tied back in a tight ponytail. Her honey brown skin was blemish-free, and her eyelids were painted with a soft blue eyeshadow. Her lips were covered in ruby red lipstick.

June looked at the maid and asked, "Bridget, will you please bring my husband and me a shot of bourbon?"

Bridget said, "Right away, Ma'am. But before I go, may I ask a question?"

June replied, "Of course."

Bridget continued, "I know none of your staff is allowed on the Lepels' wing of the house, but since Miss Evergreen is being forced to marry… I didn't mean to say that."

June commented, "Yes, you did, and it is all right."

Bridget questioned, "Since she must get married, are we allowed to assist her now instead of that Kinya woman? After all, the whole point of keeping us away was to keep us from sneaking her food. My goodness, now that I said it out loud, the whole thing sounds even more insane."

June responded, "Don't worry. Everyone except my crazy sister and her husband feel that way. As for your question, none of the staff is allowed in the Lepels' wing of the mansion. At least not until I throw the Lepels and their staff out of the house."

Bridget smiled as she said, "Really? When will they be leaving?"

June announced, "As soon as Violet is married."

Bridget's smile disappeared faster than it was created as she said, "Oh. I will go and get those drinks."

After she left TJ said, "We might get lucky, and he turns out to be a nice guy."

June laughed before saying, "TJ, I respect your optimism. But, wake up and smell the coffee. My sister and that husband of hers are completely out of their minds. The demons are more likely to try and befriend humanity than those two hook Violet up with a somewhat decent man."

Anas said, "I wish your analogy was not so accurate. Speaking of which, why did you beg Violet to meet this young man?"

TJ answered, "I'm just trying to stall until we can figure out a way to get out of this."

Violet said, "I don't think there is a way out of this mess other than letting them send me to that place."

June replied, "Don't think that way. If we can succeed at making sure those arranged dates of yours failed, then we can get rid of your intended."

Akeem said, "Speaking of him, how much longer do we have to wait for him and his family to arrive?"

June responded, "My bitch sister refuses to tell me the exact time the bastard and his shit family are arriving, so we can't even guess how long we have to wait."

Meg groaned in frustration before saying, "Mama, are you trying to tell us that these people are going to make us wait all night?"

June said, "Probably."

Anas responded, "I hope they are not that rude. I don't want to wait all night."

TJ said, "Uncle, if they take too long, then why don't you just go up and rest. I know reporting on the attack took a lot out of you. We can always call you with the details."

Anas said, "As nice as that idea is, I can't do that. Your Aunt May is upset about a groom being selected. Remember when she went to lay down? Well, she told me I'm not allowed in the room until I can give her a thorough report about Violet's intended. I want to get a look at this Kwasea who thinks he's good enough for my niece."

Meg asked, "Uncle, what does Kwasea mean again?"

Anas answered, "It means…"

Just then the door opened and Drusilla walked into the room. She was wearing a gold evening gown.

She shot an angry look at June and shouted, "June, what the hell are you wearing?"

June looked at her sister with a cold gaze. She said, "What I'm wearing is whatever the damn hell I want to wear."

Drusilla stomped her foot before screaming, "Dammit, June, you need to change this instant!"

June rolled her eyes as she said, "No, bitch."

Drusilla announced in an arrogant tone, "Honestly, June, this young man is going to elevate Violet's station in life. I thought you of all people would want the best for her."

"Bitch please, I don't know why you're trying to force our niece to marry some asshole."

Drusilla started to comment on what her sister said until she noticed Anas sitting on the couch. In a cold tone, she asked, "And who the hell are you?"

In an annoyed voice, Anas replied, "I'm your brother-in-law. I married your younger sister May years ago. Also, we have met over a hundred times."

Drusilla rolled her eyes as she said, "I have no time for this. Lincoln and his family will be here in a few minutes, and I need to make sure that sorry cook is not messing up dinner."

Bridget returned with the drinks. After giving June and Akeem their drinks, she excused herself.

Akeem started to sip his drink while his wife swallowed it all in one gulp. This made Akeem frown as he gave June a critical look.

June responded by saying, "Babe, don't be that way. I need to be a little tipsy to not murder Violet's intended."

Anas said, "I won't complain this time. After the demon attack and now this madness, it has been a difficult day."

Meg said, "Speaking of the Hell Bishop, Violet, I can't get over how close you were to that thing."

Violet said, "To be honest, I think the only reason I was able to handle the situation was because of Cinder."

TJ asked, "Who is Cinder?"

Violet answered, "The chef who supplied the food for my party. He owns a restaurant called Taste of Magic."

TJ asked, "Oh, wait, why was he with you when that monster attacked?"

Violet explained what happened with Arkell.

TJ said, "Ok, in that case, I am glad he was with you. With these monster attacks getting worse, part of me wants us to move. But there is no place that is truly safe from those things."

Meg said, "I know it's not wise, but let's try not to think about it, only because of the problem we are dealing with right now.

Just then Victor rushed in and said, "Violet, the Banner family is here. Make yourself presentable."

He noticed how June was dressed and screamed, "Dammit, you knew this was important to Violet's future! Get out, you selfish bitch!"

Akeem stood up as he said, "What the fuck did you just say to my wife?"

June quickly asked him not to get upset, which made Akeem grudgingly sit back down. Victor started to demand June leave again; however, at that very moment Ollivander walked in. He announced that their guest had arrived. The Banners then entered the room.

The first to enter was a tall man. He had deep rich dark brown skin. He was wearing a dark green suit with brown leather shoes. The moment Violet saw the man, she quickly turned away. She found the gaze of his serious brown eyes unsettling.

As soon as Victor introduced the man as Lincoln, a woman walked into the room. Lincoln introduced the woman as his wife Jemila. She was wearing a pink hijab and a very plain pink dress with plain flat pink slippers on her feet. Though her face was dry, her big brown eyes looked tearful. She had smooth brown skin, a tiny nose, and dry cracked lips.

As Lincoln sat down on the couch, instead of taking a seat, Jemila stood next to him.

Jemila was followed into the room by a young woman who appeared to be three years younger than Violet. Jemila said that the girl was her daughter Malika. Like her mother, she had smooth brown skin and sad-looking brown eyes. Unlike her mother, her lips were moist and smooth, and she had a large flat nose.

Malika was wearing an orange hijab and a plain brown dress with a pair of beige slippers on her feet. Like her mother, she didn't take a seat and instead choose to stand in the right corner of the room.

The next person to walk into the room was a young man Jemila introduced as her son Chaquille. Chaquille looked a bit younger than his sister. He had deep brown skin with angry brown eyes. He had a large flat nose and a small scar under his right eye. His head was home to a lot of wild thick curly hair, while his face housed a thin mustache.

He was followed by an older gentleman Jemila introduced as her father-in-law Darius. Just like Chaquille and Malika, he had a large flat nose. His brown skin was wrinkly while his hair was short, curly, and gray. Darius was hunched over and used a cane to balance himself as he walked.

Darius was wearing a gray suit and tie and brown leather shoes. His brown eyes looked very angry. Akeem offered him his seat; however, Darius declined the offer. Then he and Chaquille walked over to the right corner of the room where Malika was standing.

Victor looked at Lincoln and asked, "Where is the groom to be?"

Lincoln replied, "He is on his way. You know how young men like to dilly dally whenever they need to be on time."

Victor replied, "Understandable. I was the same way when I got engaged."

Violet noted that Jemila would occasionally look in the direction of the door.

She thought, *his wife seems to want to bolt out of here. After what Akeem told me, I wonder if this cult did something to her. There is still a lot I don't know.*

June said, "I bet Jemila was pretty mad at you for acting that way."

Jemila started to respond, but Lincoln quickly put up his hand as if to signal for her to be quiet. In response, she frowned and folded her arms.

Violet noted to herself, *he's an asshole.*

Lincoln said, "I was married once before. At the time, my first wife knew her place. She was never bothered by having to wait on me. But Jemila and I fell in love at first sight. We got married the same day we met, three months ago. Our children are having a little trouble adjusting to the new blended family unit, but with a little more time, they will adjust."

Jemila scoffed, which made Lincoln shoot her a sharp look.

Violet's thoughts raced by what he just said. *Did his first wife leave him? He said he and Jemila got married the day they met. I wonder if he manipulated her into marring him. I'm still not sure if it is safe to talk to Jemila. I need to find a way to figure out if I'm right about her.*

Drusilla said, "Isn't that just sweet. Victor and I were in a similar situation when we married."

June laughed as she said, "If you call a false pregnancy scare fun."

Drusilla, smiling said, "My sister has a strange sense of humor. June, do not make up things like that. It's not funny."

June expounded, "Sis, the only thing funny was mama threatening to shoot Victor in the balls with her rifle if he didn't marry you right away. But I think the real fun didn't start until the two of you were married, and you found out you were never pregnant."

Victor quickly said, "Anyway, how quickly do you feel we can get the two lovebirds married."

Lincoln said, "Hmm, good question. I originally wanted to have them tie the knot before the week is out, but my wife wants us to have a big wedding at the mosque. Also, since we recognize this will be a mixed-faith marriage, she thought it would be nice to have a second wedding at your church the same day."

Violet thought, *that sounds extravagant and tedious. She may be on my side and is attempting to stall.*

Lincoln continued, "My boy also desires to push back the wedding a little bit. He wants to get to know Violet a little better."

Chaquille, while standing in the corner, voiced, "Actually, before tying the knot, my stepbrother just wants to do some blow while enjoying the company of two or maybe three hookers. A note to the bride to be- my stepbrother likes group sex. I'm sure, Miss Violet, that he will make your life hell as soon as you marry him. Thankfully, he is easily bored after a week, so he'll probably disappear maybe for a month or a year. Don't worry, though. Eventually my stepfather will find him in some prostitute's bed, high on crack, and drag him back home to you.

Lincoln snapped, "Chaquille, I have had enough of these lies. Young man, when we get home, you and I are going to have a talk."

Chaquille persisted, "Lies indeed. Why don't you talk with your son about not hiding his drugs in my room? Even better, why don't you get him to stop stacking my sister?"

Malika lowered her head and began twiddling her thumbs as her brother spoke.

Darius said, "Chaquille, hold your tongue."

Darius turned his attention to Violet and her family saying, "Please forgive my grandson's behavior. My daughter-in-law's remarriage has been a difficult adjustment for my grandchildren. Unfortunately, acting out is one of the results."

Victor said, "I understand. Change can be hard on young people."

Just then Hattie May walked in and announced that dinner was ready. As everyone rose to go to the dining room, Violet couldn't shake the feeling that these were the strangest people that she had ever met. Not only that, but she had a foreboding sense of danger.

Chapter 22
The Final Breaking Point

As Violet took a seat next to Meg, she noticed Jemila sitting between her children, while Darius sat next to Lincoln. This seating arrangement seemed odd to her. Before, Darius seemed to want to be as far as he could from Lincoln. Now he was sitting next to him.

Akeem looked at Lincoln as he said, "Lincoln, I just realized I haven't asked you your son's name."

"Oh, I'm so sorry, I assumed the Lepels told you. My boy's name is Damion."

Akeem sighed and muttered something under his breath that Violet couldn't hear.

Hattie May uttered a simple teleportation spell. Dinner plates appeared before them. Each plate held one whole roasted Red Snapper lying on a bed of saffron rice and green beans as a side dish. Two smaller plates appeared, one containing a small avocado salad and the other a dinner roll. Filled water goblets came next.

Violet doubted that in front of the Banners her guardians would not allow her to eat. Her mind suddenly thought about the cult. It then dawned on her that maybe keeping her in constant hunger was part of their plot. She couldn't think of why they would need to do that. But she instinctively knew whatever the reason was, she wouldn't like it. Violet suspected that Lincoln and his son were the only Banners in the cult. Maybe the rest of that family were just victims of it.

She decided the best way to test her theory would be to eat. Anyone who reacted negatively to her eating was part of the cult. Anyone who didn't care if she ate wasn't part of the cult. Violet didn't feel it was the best experiment, but she was hungry, and after the day she had, she was not going to deny herself the opportunity to enjoy the lovely looking meal that lay before her. With that thought in mind, she laid her napkin in her lap and reached for her dinner fork.

Almost immediately, Drusilla said, "Silly girl, you know that you have had more than enough food for today. Put that fork down."

Violet looked at her aunt with a defiant gaze. She then gripped her fork tighter in her hand.

In a stern voice, Drusilla said, "Young lady, put that fork down this instant."

Violet took satisfaction in her aunt's irritation. As she felt her lips form into a smile, she picked up some of her fish with her fork.

Both Victor and Drusilla snapped at Violet not to eat her fish. To which Violet responded by taking a bite of fish. Drusilla jumped up and shouted, "WHAT THE HELL IS WRONG WITH YOU?!"

The room fell silent as Violet defiantly slowly chewed her fish. When she swallowed it, she looked at Drusilla, still smiling.

In a very calm voice Violet said, "Dear auntie, what is the matter? I am just eating my dinner like a proper lady."

Both Akeem and June seemed to be trying not to laugh. Anas, Meg, and TJ didn't bother to try to hold back their smiles. Hatti May, who was standing in the right corner of the room, had a look of pure victory on her face.

As Drusilla angrily retook her seat, Victor shot an angry look at Violet. She could tell he wanted to hit her; however, she knew with their guests and the rest of her family present, there was no way either of her guardians would hurt her. Violet felt her smile widen as she started to eat a little more of her fish. It was in that moment she realized how much in just the last two days her guardians' power over her had weakened.

Jemila said, "Umm, shouldn't the two of you be excited she is eating?"

Lincoln replied, "What on earth are you talking about?"

Jemila continued, "I was not going to say anything, but Miss Evergreen is a little too skinny. You can't expect her to be able to carry children, or even have the strength to take care of them."

Lincoln corrected his wife and said, "Stop being stupid. If anything, the girl is far too fat. I admit it is a bit of a worry for me knowing how popular Damion is with the media. I was only willing to accept her as a bride for my son because Drusilla promised she would make the girl lose weight."

Both Jemila and Darius looked shocked for a split second, while Chacuille muttered something about not being surprised. Malika just looked down at her plate as she ate her dinner.

Drusilla said, "I plan to keep that promise. Also, per our agreement, I will send her to the doctor for tests next week."

Violet thought, *what the hell would I need to be tested for?*

Suddenly, she remembered the conversation she had overheard the other morning. She had a sudden realization. *They want to find a more powerful spell to make me obey.*

Akeem asked, "What does Damion do for a living?"

Lincoln smiled as he answered, "He is going through a transitional phase right now."

Anas asked, "What does that mean?"

Lincoln answered, "Well, he was not too happy at his previous job, so he is taking a break to figure out what he wants to do."

Chaquille said, "Basically he is going from the guy who never shows up to work at the illustrious fast-food burger place. Now he's the guy who sleeps half the day and parties at clubs all night."

Lincoln chimed in, "Chaquille, for the last time. Do not talk about your brother that way."

Chaquille answered firmly, "He is not my brother!"

Jemila signaled to her son to calm down, to which Chaquille responded by saying that he needed to get some air. As he got up, Malika announced she needed some air, too. Then she rushed out of the room as if she were being chased by wild dogs, passing her bother on the way out the door.

Oh, my goodness. She ran out of here like she was on fire. I think I am right about Jemila. I need to find a way to speak to her alone. Other than Lincoln and the son I have not met, I'm more confident the rest of this family is not involved in the cult.

Lincoln said, "Please forgive my daughter's behavior. She is very shy, and being around so many new faces can be overwhelming for her."

Victor said, "I understand."

Just then Harold entered the room. He announced that Damion had arrived. As he walked out of the room, Damion walked in.

The very second Violet saw him, her heart jumped. She immediately recognized him as the man Arkell almost hit with his car just two days ago. He was even wearing the same clothing he had on the first time she saw him, which made her wonder if he had even bathed since that night.

Damion also seemed a lot older than Violet originally thought. His eyes looked a little bloodshot as he looked at everyone. This gave Violet the feeling Chaquille was not lying about the drugs. Damion's gaze zeroed in on Meg, and Meg responded by giving him a look of pure disgust.

Damion pointed at Meg and turned to look at his father and said, "You seriously expect me to marry that?"

Meg groaned as TJ snapped, "Don't talk about my wife that way, you dipshit."

Damion glared at TJ as he said, "What did you just say, motherfucker?"

The room began to fill with an angry tension until Lincoln made things more awkward when he let out a laugh.

Everyone stared at him as he said, "That's not your bride to be. She's too old."

He then pointed toward Violet, and at that moment Violet's body tensed.

He said, "This is the woman I chose for you."

347

Damion frowned as he said, "Why did you pick her?"

Lincoln in a calm tone said, "Now, son, calm down. This marriage will bring a lot of money for you. Then you won't be dependent on your new mother and me to help you. It's a chance for you to get a fresh start."

Violet thought she couldn't be surprised anymore, but Lincoln's words both surprised and angered her. As she said to herself, *he wants his son to have my inheritance, but Arkell told me the cult was involving one of their own, which I thought meant a member of the cult was my intended. There is always the possibility that Damion has no idea what is going on. I can't know that for sure. Also, what Lincoln said might be a cover. That doesn't exactly mean they are not after my inheritance.*

Damion replied, "Whatever."

Damion then proceeded to sit down in the empty chair next to Violet. The second he got closer to her, Violet had to force herself not to cover her nose. Damion reeked of body odor, cigarette smoke, and alcohol.

Victor smiled as he said, "Good. Now that Damion is here, we can get his input on the wedding details."

Anas said, "Hold on a second, Victor."

Anas looked at Damion with a serious gaze before asking, "Quick question, Damion, how old are you?"

Damion replied, "I just turned thirty-eight five months ago. Why?"

Violet's heart leaped. Meanwhile, the rest of the family except her guardians all said, "Thirty-eight," in unison.

In a tense voice, Meg said, "Umm… Lincoln, don't you feel Violet is a little young for your son?"

Lincoln replied, "Nonsense. She is at the right age to have his children. If she loses all that fat, there should be no problem."

Drusilla said, "Exactly. Now, we need to have the wedding as soon as possible. Lincoln, how do you feel about…"

Akeem said, "Excuse me, Drusilla, but there is a huge problem. There is no way in hell I am about to let my niece marry a thirty-eight-year-old deadbeat."

Anas said, "I agree. There is no way I will ever allow someone like your son to marry my niece. He will just try to spend all of Violet's inheritance and leave her with nothing."

Lincoln snapped, "My son is not a deadbeat."

Damion replied, "Dad, calm down. I see where these people are coming from. I admit that I have not been the most focused person in my adult life. I spent so much time partying that I flunked out of school, and I have never been able to hold down a job. But since I have been going through this transitional phase, I have realized that it is time for me to man up and start being more responsible. That is why taking a leadership position at the Evergreen hospital will help."

Both June and TJ groaned, while Akeem asked, "Do you have a medical degree?"

Damion answered, "No."

"Do you have a business administration degree?"

Damion responded, "No."

Akeem continued, "Do you have a degree or any field experience in anything to do with medicine or business?"

Damion answered, "No, but I did volunteer for a few minutes at a vet's office back when I was a kid. That is pretty much the same thing."

Anas voiced, "Young man, were you born dumb, or did someone slap you with a stupid stick?"

At that moment the room exploded with shouting. Akeem, TJ, and Anas were arguing with Victor, Damion, and Lincoln. Meanwhile, Jemila was attempting to stop June from attacking Drusilla.

Darius, on the other hand, sat calmly in his chair as he tasted his fish. After swallowing his first bite, he smiled for a moment. Then he turned and looked at Hattie. She was wide-eyed and frowning, while her eyes darted around watching the unfolding chaos in the room.

Darius, acknowledging Hattie May, said, "This fish is delicious. You did an amazing job cooking it."

Without turning her head to acknowledge Darius, Hattie said, "Umm… yeah thanks."

Darius went back to eating his food while Violet could not begin to understand how he could be so calm while almost everyone was shouting and screaming at one another.

As Violet saw Jemila somehow succeed in talking June out of strangling Drusilla, she thought, *this is my fault. I should have just let Aunt Drusilla send me to the facility.*

She felt as if she could no longer stay in the room, so she jumped up and rushed out of the room. The moment Violet was in the hallway she felt a little better. Thinking like Damion's step-siblings, she realized that she, too needed some air. So, Violet headed for the veranda.

As she walked down the hall, she remembered she was no longer allowed in the back yard. Why, she had no idea. It was just another of the stupid rules her guardians enforced to make her life hell. But in that moment, she could care less about those two people and their stupid rules. After all, she was nineteen, and as June and Akeem always told her, this is her home. The Lepels were just unwanted guests.

When she reached the glass French doors leading outside, Violet found herself unable to walk outside. She stared at the softly light veranda while thinking, *this is too much. That guy they chose is a complete bastard. All that about his drug use, not to mention the fact that she had seen him looking and acting like a bum on the street. Dammit, I know this is all a part of a wicked game. I just wish I knew what the scheme is.*

She took a breath before making her way outside. As the cool air of the night washed over her, making her feel more at ease, Violet stared at the garden lights reflecting on the distant lake.

While watching the lights dancing across the dark lake waters, she heard a voice say, "Well, that dinner went to shit quick."

Violet turned around and saw Damion standing behind her. She frowned as she replied, "You probably should have realized taking care of animals is not the same as hospital management."

Damion remarked, "You're right about that. To be honest, I was nervous about meeting you and your family, at least the members of your family who are not the Lepels. I already know I'm their favorite person. They want this wedding to happen more than I do because of the big payout."

Violet questioned, "Excuse me?"

Damion said, "Listen, I'm not going to pretend that this marriage isn't about getting ahold of your inheritance. Thanks to my dad, I need the money."

Violet asked, "Why? Your family isn't rich?"

"No, my stepmother is rich. That's why my dad married that silly widow after his company went belly up."

Violet said, "So, you're trying to marry me because she won't let you have any more of her money."

Damion spoke frankly, "No, that bitch's late husband must have feared that she would marry some smooth-talking fortune hunter. He stipulated in his will that if she should remarry, and by some chance die, his fortune and his company's ownership would go to his father. Not only that, if his father is no longer alive at the time of death of his widow, everything goes to his children. That bitch also has my dad on a small allowance, which he has to split with me so that I can have some cash. So, my dad and I are in hot water should anything happen to her. That's why I've got to get hitched."

Violet suggested, "Wow, question- why don't you try not leeching off of people."

Damion quipped, "Bold words from a trust fund baby."

"If I was a normal trust fund baby, then you would have a point."

He rolled his eyes while saying, "Whatever. Since we have to get married, we might as well start talking about wedding stuff."

Violet said firmly, "We don't have to get married."

Damion laughed and said, "Stop being stupid."

Violet responded, "You're the dumb one. Getting married is something that two people have to agree to, and I'm not agreeing to this arrangement."

"Bullshit. You have to marry me."

Violet contradicted him and said, "No, I don't. I feel pretty dumb for even allowing things to get this far before realizing this. But after tonight, I never have to see you again."

Damion announced, "Stop playing games. You know if you don't go through with this marriage, then you will get sent to the Greenages facility. That place is for the worst serial killers, domestic terrorists, and other nut jobs. So, don't pretend you don't know that the place is old, filthy, and underfunded. Greenages also has a rep for people being held there mysteriously dying."

Violet spoke frankly to Damion, "You don't need to tell me that. My guardians remind me of that almost every day. Hell, the rest of my family is in constant fear of me going to that place. My aunt and uncle pretty much let my guardians have them run their house to keep me from being sent there. But I don't give a flying shit anymore."

A disbelieving Damion said, "Yeah right."

In a calm voice, Violet stated, "I'll give you the benefit of the doubt only because you don't know me. But I meant what I said. So, let's let everyone know I'm taking a trip to the nuthouse. I'm better off living with a bunch of dangerous killers than marrying you."

Before Violet could react, Damion's fist made contact with her face. This caused her to fly backward and roll down the stairs of the veranda, before landing hard on the grass.

As Violet touched her bruised cheek, Damion screamed, "I have heard enough shit out of you!"

He took a breath before saying, "Tomorrow you are going to go with my stepmom to meet the wedding planner. My dad pulled a lot of strings to get some super exclusive wedding planner, so be grateful. After you guys do that…"

Violet was not paying attention to what Damion was saying. She slowly forced herself to get up. Once on her feet, she walked back towards the veranda. With each step she thought, *I'm not doing this anymore. I'm not doing this anymore. I'm not doing this anymore.*

While Damion continued to talk, Violet looked at the glass cat sitting on one of the white wicker side tables.

Without a second thought, she quickly grabbed it and threw it at Damion's head. Sadly, he ducked just before the cat could hit him. He then glared at Violet while he marched towards her.

Violet was backing up as she screamed, "Stay away from me!"

Damion yelled, "Shut up, bitch. You're about to learn a lesson."

As he swung his fist to hit her, she yelled for help. At that moment, there was a bright flash of green light. When the light touched Damion, an invisible force grabbed him. Violet watched in shock as Damion was pulled into the air. Fortunately, Damion was not high off the ground. Yet, unfortunately, Violet had no idea how to get him down.

She stood in shock, mostly out of surprise that she had the power to pull someone into the air; however, her shock quickly disappeared when she realized the limiter was not burning her arm. She wondered if she had somehow deactivated it.

Damion shouted for help. Violet had been levitated herself by Arkell and more often when her guardians wanted to torment her. So, she knew how nightmarish it was. But this bastard had hit her hard in the face and had knocked her down the concrete of the veranda, so she had no sympathy for him. He tried to hurt her again just because she had no interest in him as a life partner, not to mention he was trying to take her inheritance.

As Violet debated with herself exactly how to handle the situation, the patio door flung open, and her family and the Banners rushed outside.

They were then followed by Ollivander, Harold, Williams, Janet, and Hattie May.

Lincoln stared at his son in horror while everyone else was trying to make sense of what was going on.

Drusilla said, "Impossible. The limiter should have prevented this."

Victor grabbed Violet's arm, squeezing it very tightly. Violet tried to free her arm, to which Victor responded by squeezing harder.

Violet cried, "Uncle, you are hurting me."

Victor snapped, "No I am not, you stupid crybaby. More importantly, I am your father, and you will…"

Anas jumped in and separated Victor from Violet. He glared at Victor while saying, "What's wrong with you? She's a young woman. You shouldn't grab her like that."

Victor shouted, "Shut up, Anas. How else was I supposed to check to find out what has happened to her magic limiter?"

June said, "Simple. You just look to see if the damn mark is glowing. You don't need to practically rip her arm off."

Victor replied, "I was doing no such thing. I was just checking to see what is wrong with the limiter. We may have to call an ambulance."

Williams asked, "Mr. Lepel, why would we need to call an ambulance? Mr. Banner seems to be fine. We just need to get him down."

Ollivander snapped, "He wants the ambulance for Violet. If the limiter spell is broken, then we are all in danger."

Jemila said, "Well, it has been a pleasure meeting you all, but we will be leaving. Kids, get your things. Papa Darrius, do you have your cane?"

Drusilla said, "Calm down, Jemila. Everything is fine. We will get your son down in just a second. Then, we can go back to planning the wedding."

Jemila rolled her eyes as she said, "That fool is no child of mine. I never wanted this wedding. If anything, I am a contentious objector to it. I believe that people should marry for love, not to grab the bride's fortune."

Lincoln shouted, "Have you idiots forgotten that my son is stuck in the air?"

Jemila replied, "Good, let him stay there. I'm going home."

Lincoln snapped, "What the hell did you say to me?"

Jemila snapped back at her husband, "You heard me."

Lincoln rushed over to his wife with his palm raised, ready to slap her. When his hand flew, the others didn't react in time, except for Darrius, who hit Lincoln hard in the chest with his cane. The impact pushed Lincoln backward, causing him to almost lose his balance.

Violet thought, *like father like son. Thank goodness the old man stopped him.*

When Lincoln regained his footing, he put a hand on his chest as he looked at Darrius. He said, "She is not married to your son anymore. Why waste your time defending her?"

Darrius looked at Lincoln with a serious gaze. The look that Darrius gave Lincoln made Violet realize that Darrius was not someone to be messed with. This brought her a strange comfort.

Darrius said, "My son may be gone, but Jemila is still my daughter-in-law. More importantly, she is the mother of my grandchildren. Even if she was not, I would not have let you hit her. No real man lays hands on a woman. My family has done our part in playing whatever this sick game you and your son are playing here tonight. We are leaving. You and your boy can find your own way home. Or maybe better yet, find a new home."

Lincoln looked at Jemila. She said nothing and turned and walked away with her family following close behind.

Janet escorted them to their car. Meanwhile, Damion yelled, "What the fuck is wrong with all of you?"

This interruption made Violet jump because she had somehow forgotten about the floating man. Williams walked over to Damion and looked at him for a moment. He then snapped his fingers, and there was a quick flash of white light.

Suddenly, a screaming Damion started to spin around very fast in midair. Then, without notice, he suddenly stopped. He looked sick. As his father shouted at Williams, Damion was suddenly launched into the lake.

Lincoln, Drusilla, and Victor ran towards the lake. They were worried that Damion was too dizzy to swim and could drown.

Violet chose to remain on the veranda because she didn't care if Damion did drown. From where she was standing, she could see Lincoln dive into the lake to rescue his son. She imagined it would be a little too petty to judge Lincoln for doing what he did. At the same time, she somehow knew that Damion was still a child-man because his father was always rescuing him.

Just then she heard Ollivander yelling at Williams for sending Damion flying into the lake.

In response, Williams smiled as he said, "It's not like any of you tried to get him down, which is quite odd."

Ollivander snapped, "What are you babbling about?"

Williams responded, "I am not good with levitation spells, which means that, sadly, my method of getting that poor shit down was

357

admittedly not the best. All of you can think of how to levitate Miss Evergreen to torment her, but not one of you could think of a way to get your golden boy down."

They heard Drusilla in the distance as she shouted, "Thank goodness!"

Violet turned in her aunt's direction and saw Damion being pulled out of the lake by his father. She then heard her Uncle Akeem say, "Dammit, he survived."

June said, "I'm not surprised."

She then looked at her husband and whispered something Violet could not hear. June turned her attention to Violet. She could tell her aunt wanted to see if the limiter spell was still active.

Violet decided that she might as well let her aunt look at her arm. As June examined Violet's arm she said, "That's interesting."

Victor asked, "What's interesting?"

Violet jumped, not realizing her uncle had walked up to them.

June replied, "The limiter spell is still active."

In shock, Victor said, "But it did not stop Violet from hurting Damion."

June replied, "Technically, she didn't hurt him. Really, despite him floating for a bit, he was in no real danger."

Victor snapped, "Liar, she put him in harm's way! Violet, I insist you go and apologize to Damion. Honestly, I don't know what possessed me not to give you that order sooner."

Violet folded her arms as she said, "No."

Victor's brows furrowed while saying, "What did you just say to me?"

Violet spoke with authority and said, "I said no, Uncle. And I am not taking any more orders- not from you, my aunt, or anyone else."

Victor in a cold tone replied, "You are going to regret talking to me that way, you little bitch. I'm going to teach you a lesson."

Victor raised his hand, aimed it at Violet, and started to perform a spell. The words he spoke were in a language unfamiliar to Violet. She didn't know why, but she could tell that should he finish the spell something very bad would happen. However, something in her was different. Where she had once felt fear, she only felt anger and determination now. Violet quickly raised one of her fingers and calmly said, "Relut." Suddenly, Victor was shrouded in a strange pink mist.

He shouted, "NO, NOT ME!"

A minute later, she, her family, and everyone else looked at the scene in shock. Victor was being slashed left and right by some invisible force. He screamed and begged for the pain to stop. The mist finally disappeared, and Victor fell to the ground bleeding.

Violet put her hand over her mouth. She knew Victor wanted to hurt her, but she never imagined he would do something that terrible. The next sound anyone heard was Drusilla's screaming as she rushed to her husband. The rest of her staff followed, except for Ollivander who was calling for paramedics.

Drusilla glared at Violet. She shouted, "Monster, first you killed my brother, and now you are trying to kill my husband!"

Before Violet could respond, June put her hand on Violet's shoulder. She whispered for her to come inside. They needed to talk about what just happened. The both of them started to head inside when Drusilla shouted for them to wait.

Drusilla snapped, "June, where the hell are you going? My husband needs help."

June shrugged as she said, "Why the hell would I ever try to save him?"

Violet walked inside the house. She smiled as she thought about how the tables had turned. For most of her life, the Lepels and this cult had controlled everything she did. But now the ball was in her court, and she was going to make sure whatever they were plotting would fail.

To Be Continued

In

Violet Evergreen

In

The Rebel Spirit

If you enjoyed this story, then you may want to pick up a copy of my book *Curse of the Frog Prince Part 1*. Available now on Amazon. Also check me out on Social Media.

Facebook: @mcButterfly777

Twitter: @MadamCrystalBu2

Instagram: mcbutterfly777

YouTube: Madam Crystal Butterfly

www.ingramcontent.com/pod-product-compliance
Lightning Source LLC
Chambersburg PA
CBHW071207250626
47159CB00001B/241